SEEKING

BY THE SAME AUTHOR

CONTOUR
Hardback ISBN - 978-1906221-447
Paperback ISBN - 978-1906221-430

APPLE GIRL
Hardback ISBN - 978-1905886-715
Paperback ISBN - 978-1905886-623

TWELVE GIRLS
Hardback ISBN - 978-1906510-381
Paperback ISBN - 978-1906510-947

TRIG POINT
Hardback ISBN - 978-1848761-254
Paperback ISBN - 978-1848761-216

WINDBLOW
978-1848762-428

BENCHMARK
978-1848765-283

JON BEATTIEY

SEEKING

For Lynn

Jon Beattiey x

Matador
9 Priory Business Park
Kibworth Beauchamp
Leicester LE8 0RX, UK
Tel: (+44) 116 279 2299
Fax: (+44) 116 279 2277
Email: books@troubador.co.uk
Web: www.troubador.co.uk/matador

This is a work of fiction. Characters, companies and locations are either the product of the
author's imagination or, in the case of locations, if real, used fictitiously without any
intent to describe their actual environment.

ISBN: 978 1848767 447

British Library Cataloguing in Publication Data.
A catalogue record for this book is available from the British Library.

Typeset in 11pt Book Antiqua by Troubador Publishing Ltd, Leicester, UK
Printed and bound in the UK by TJ International, Padstow, Cornwall

Matador is an imprint of Troubador Publishing Ltd

For Annabelle and all those who seek inspiration from words, poetry and music.

᪥

Think you mid all this mighty sum
Of things for ever speaking
That nothing of itself will come
But we must still be seeking?

Wordsworth: Expostulation and Reply

$\mathcal{O}ne$

Overture … the beginning

I can remember when our spirits collided.

She wouldn't know, not unless my thin interpretation of our mental powers indicated a major misunderstanding; but I'd love to think of it as an unconscious subliminal connection too powerful to ignore. Not even a suggestion, not a whisper of acknowledgement unless a brief turn of her head was one such, but the steady walk continued along the cracked and uneven grey paving, a happy, chattering teenager alive in her trio of contemporaries, alert only to the trivia of the end of a school day.

How did those leylines of human connection link, at such a time, in the unremarkable side streets of a dowdy market town clenched in the dour grey paucity of a late September afternoon? She walked away, out of sight around the corner of a Georgian stone house, elected by our unknown mutual fate, the chosen one of a group who'd scatter into characteristic social oblivion.

The one. Determined by casuality, a whim. The One, after:

As one aspect of many facets of survival in an uncertain ratio of expense over income, I dabbled in antiques and housed in this backwater lay a heterogeneous collection. The car I managed to park along the wall, wriggled into too short a space thus the angle untidy, but needs must, given there was nowhere else. The entrance was unwelcoming, the light levels low, the enthusiasm often diminished with no resurrection from a surly welcome and I pitched into an untidy space. The walk round amongst the dust, peering into smultzy corners, lifting uncertain prospects, checking chips and provenance in the same hand, sneering at overly optimistic pricing, working steadily through the debris. Nary another being in sight with whom to commiserate or communicate either, merely the one lost soul seeking treasure in a morass of tedium.

Earlier on that day I had struggled to garner any enthusiasm for the miscellany of life that came my way; neither from the auction, the subsequent indeterminate luncheon with Briony or the three hours I did as part-time book seller in the admittedly up-market second hand class establishment under the half-timbered house by the river. A last mug of dusty tea and two digestive biscuits shared with Samuel, he who owned the vast stock of everything from Chaucer through Coleridge to Chesterton; then on to this, the last chore of the day.

But it wasn't to be another crossed-off wasted hour, not on this day. At the back of a deep shelf, lying where maybe I had looked before, yet maybe I hadn't, was a bowl, a fine edged gem of a bowl, where the glazing had been the work of an artist. Not any artist either. A delicate hand was now required, and a little more light. I lifted it with two hands, cradled, felt the powder sharpness of the metallic glaze; the shock of this uniquely hand-thrown item ran up arms to a brain suddenly aware. One piece of luck has to be given to every person at one time in his or her life, but twice? For at that precise time the destined second wonderful part of the day's luck was yet to walk away up the pavement beyond where the car's irregular parking caused me to check if traffic would emerge from that lane. And that was when I saw her. The One.

2

I'd exchanged a couple of grubby brown notes for the precious parcel now in the anonymous plastic bag gripped with a tensioned hand. I also exchanged a few words with the dour woman behind the dusty paper laden counter for politeness's sake and to disguise my excitement, then to emerge into the residual damp of that dull day, aware yet not aware of the luck. I was not to know how the sheer chance purchase of this hand-thrown totally unique charger – you know what a charger is, a dish thrown in an open way that works wonderfully well as a fruit bowl – would become synonymous with an unresolved link between two souls.

Even from a hundred yards or so, etched into my mind were details. She was fairly tall, the long uniform navy skirt swaying with an easy grace; the bag, satchel, whatever, also swinging in a casual hand. Shoulder length hair in untidy curls brushing a short coat collar over the navy sweater with its vee of red, a proud shape to her belying whatever teen years she'd experienced – after all, a sixth former couldn't be more than eighteen, surely?

At the car door I must have stood, fixated on this vision until she was out of sight. Ten seconds? A minute? Two? And did she glance back? Briefly – and that to me was the surety, for she'd had no call to. Our spirits had called, collided, and I knew we'd meet again.

The short drive home was accomplished in a routine blur of unconsciousness to the end-of-terrace pad. The car jammed near to the fence – the only way I could keep it close to home – the parcel carefully placed on the tired grass before I locked the worn-out old Morris Traveller's door. Then the opening of a creaky gate, the Yale key in the latch, the knee to open a jammed rain swollen door, the collection of the parcel, and the door slammed hard to shut behind me. Home.

Laugh if you wish. Home is where you make it, and a guy two years out of a two-one degree in English can't be too much of a chooser. No, I wasn't fully employed, no, I hadn't got flush parents, yes, I was a free spirit, yes, I was – am – an eternal optimist. And a firm believer in coincidences, luck, divine intervention and a number of other ethereal religions. Well, you know what I mean.

The parcel laid on the bargain shop settee, (pay for it next year, maybe), the kettle on, the telly on, the shoes off, the coat off, the curtains drawn – yes, good curtains, I made them myself – and the surge of pleasure as I remembered, lurking in the bread bin, were teacakes I could toast.

The smell of toasted teacakes is high on the pheromonal list. Unwrapping newly bought bargains is pretty high on another list. To collapse onto a half decent sofa to eat buttered teacakes, drink a decent cup of tea and gaze at a wonderful piece of individually crafted studio pottery fresh out of tatty newspaper wrapping also ranks fairly high. I'd placed it, with two-handed great care, onto the sideboard. Nineteen pounds I'd paid. The single pound note change I left in the bowl, an unconscious action of profound significance. Twenty quid. Not bad for something worth, at a conservative estimate – albeit mine – two thousand at auction. And an image of a girl, ephemeral spirit though she may be if dry reality was the truth of the day.

The television was talking to itself. Normal, that was. Another round of teacakes was also normal, along with another half mug of tea. Gazing at the charger wasn't normal; neither was seeing the said ephemeral vision appearing against the light stone coloured wall like a genie out of a bottle. A vision of a girl spirited out of a Lucy Rie charger, so that's what I'd call her – Lucy.

So after that afternoon or evening, so after that miraculous day, life took on a different dimension. You have to understand, I was never one for the girls at Uni. Most of the ones I'd ever thought worth cultivating were way out of reach and somehow it never bothered me. Too involved in doing what you're supposed to do, I think, like studying and researching, browsing through interminable numbers of books in the college library. Don't get me wrong, I enjoyed myself, socialised, went to the pubs, did the May Ball thing, the odd bit of punting down to Brooke's garden (*Stands the church clock etcetera…*), never worried that some contemporaries spent more time in cahoots with the opposite sex than studying. But then, I got a decent degree, a memory for poetry and a lot of satisfaction from the tutor's comments. The fact I didn't take a relationship – consummated or no – away with me from Cambridge meant nothing. But after this afternoon's Experience I almost felt I was committed to sharing my life. Foolish? Yeah, very.

So, now what? Another stint in the bookshop tomorrow morning. Maybe another lunchtime shared with Briony. An afternoon shifting furniture with the old guy in the second-hand shop at the top end of town; he was a decent old stick with a dry sense of humour and I enjoyed his company. Go to bed, Jones. And don't dream.

⤚

Lucy – and that was truly she, for Jones's coincidental choice of name was a twist of fate – has had a good day. The term started well, a decent crowd, the prospect of the opening in the prestigious hotel chain confirmed in the morning's post, the subsequent interview with the Head of Sixth to explain, with the anticipated dismay that she'd not take up the potential offer of a University place – understandable, given she'd collect good grades at the end of the year. Then finally she'd been the recipient of the polite smile and the resignation, the acknowledgement of what must be a *fait accompli,* for that morning after the post had come she'd scribbled a quick acceptance reply to the Hotel trainees' manager in her best handwriting, kissed her mum, hugged her dad, snatched up her bag and fled. And now, at the end of the day, she'd walked down the lane away from the school with her mates to experience, suddenly, the weirdest feeling out. A fizzy feeling between her shoulder blades, an odd light-headedness, that tingling sensation when something nice has happened. Not comprehending, wondering what on earth had occurred, she'd given an instinctive glance behind her and something told her, a weirdly discovered realisation, that she was destined to share her joy of life with another person, unknown but there, definitely there.

Was that person standing by a car door, staring at her, the one? She walked on, feeling the pull of unseen forces elasticate, thin out and twist in the air to not quite virtual nothingness, but still stretching out; a mind's immense power to create an attachment. Even in her most innocent thoughts there'd be a connection unforgotten. Whatever had stirred these weird, weird feelings wouldn't go away. Ever. Sometime, someplace, the light would go on, the connection would re-establish and the threads would strengthen. She knew with complete certainty they would. Destiny would decide, as it had in the past, and because it was the day she'd had the letter and accepted, it was a lucky day.

Her friends giggled and jostled, she laughed in her turn at the silly comments, tried hard not to show any change. Sheena ran off at the corner, down to the fish and chip shop where she did an hour or so's serving before going home. Marie's house was at the next crossroads; Julie kept her company until she too turned off towards the detached pad her parents rented up the hill. Lucy had to finish her walk home alone, an extra half mile. Home to the routines, the couple of hours or so on the piano, her attempt at an essay, supper, then to bed, for tomorrow was another day.

≪

Jones had been happy as a loner, ever since he could remember. Not that it had affected his scholastic career. The old fashioned, traditional grammar school, pleasantly situated on the rising edge of the small market town, suited his temperament very well, the class size not too large, the teaching staff mostly well placed and believed in what they did, vocationally turning out 'good citizens' with a modicum of knowledge above the norm. Of course, ideally, they wanted their product to go on to higher education for that was what was expected, but if a boy wanted to go into commerce, or engineering or farming, and it was what he was evidently good at, then so be it. To have a happy and rewarding school experience was what counted. And Jones thrived on the approach. In his day, the school was single sex. The Girls' School down the lanes was foreign territory; its population deemed equally foreign and woe betide any boy seen consorting with an inhabitant of that forbidden land. So he grew up devoid of the explosive mix that occasioned so many disasters in the secondary modern co-educational school the other side of town. No incautious fumbling in cinema back seats, no wandering upstairs in a carelessly parented girl's house, though he did go to the youth club and swung the girls around when they had country dancing on the menu. He'd kissed a few. Nice, but not *that* nice. Some of them had sweaty armpits.

His parents ran a traditional tobacconist's, as old fashioned as the rest of the town, and did well enough, but that put him in the 'middle class' bracket so his socialising didn't include the country pursuit set – you know, huntin', shootin', fishing, but perhaps the time would come …

Streamed into the art side after the second year, the subjects offered heightened his interest. History, geography, English, of course, both language and literature. With difficulty, Latin. Art, well, sort of, though he appreciated the bearded art master's bohemian approach and the genuine attempt to provide not just rudiments of drawing and painting but also the explanations of what the old artists had attempted to portray. The rest of the timetabled things he tolerated. R.E. Maths. P.E. Swimming in the summer, though the old outdoor pool was way past its prime. One thing he was good at, oddly, was cross-country running. Sufficiently so to give him a modicum of street cred amongst his peers and prevent overmuch attempt at bullying one designated as a 'swot'.

Thus he spent five years in the conventional forms before rising to the dizzy heights of the sixth form and a recognition that, surprisingly in the minds of some, he *was* University material. Once thus determined, the school did its best and he achieved two A's, a B and another 'O' level pass in 'Use of English' to add to the earlier collection of seven. Maybe it was a fluke, maybe it was his demeanour, maybe it was a touch of the 'old boy network', whatever, he got a place at Cambridge and away he went. In those days, the system paid most of the fees and the accommodation, especially when the undergraduate came from a 'humble home', so it wasn't a drain on scant domestic resources. He supplemented his allowance by dabbling in antiques and working in one of the town's many bookshops, plus a few hours a week teaching remedial English to some of the dimmer pupils from the school next to his digs, an odd perk that came his way after a chance meeting in the aforesaid bookshop with one of the school's teachers. The parents paid fairly well of course; it wasn't in the school's gift.

At the end of the three years, he was not only rather well read but could turn his hand to many another skill. And easygoing, with no intense desire to disturb the equanimity of any State system unlike some of his peers; equally he had no strongly held views about an ongoing career. He might have welcomed a chance to stay at

Cambridge, but the examination results only gave him a good Second, so that was ruled out.

He responded to an advert in the T.L.S. "A part-time position in a significantly well-known second-hand bookshop in Stamford", equidistant betwixt University and home. Another chance remark led him to consider the offer of a house for a cheap rent in return for merely occupying the place whilst the owners were abroad; so that's where he went, job in the bag. Sheer coincidence, fortune, luck, the gods' hidden agenda, call it what you will, but that's what happened. Jonesmanship.

Two

Fugue ... Succession

Lucy is an only child. Her parents come from the upper middle class of the day, her mother is an accomplished pianist and her father a chartered accountant. She has never known another house, growing up in a cosy world, received a decent primary education at a private school just down the road and has so many local friends that her early birthday parties were like an extension of a school day only lots more fun. Mother used to play the piano for the 'ring-a-ring of roses' and other boisterous games while father was a dab hand at finger puppets – and dishing out the blancmange and jelly. Going on to the High School was considered automatic, with no long bus rides or anything tedious like that.

She is a fair scholar, paying exactly the right amount of attention during lessons and gets just the right level of marks to keep the school reports up to scratch without being regarded as a swot by her friends, thereby avoiding having her long hair pulled or being the recipient of ink-laden pellets from elastic band equipped miscreants.

A lively girl, she excels at gymnastics, has become a brilliant pianist, is more than a passing fair artist, loves her Austen, her Brontë and her poetry and is an excellent cook. Her soufflés and sponges are the envy of even the Domestic Science teacher. Collecting nine 'O' levels has made her the envy of a few of her year, but the long summer holidays have intervened and by the time she returns to the first year Sixth none of her remaining contemporaries offer acrimonious remarks about her talent. She matures considerably in that first-year sixth, puts on a few more inches in all the requisite directions, moves the School's Annual Concert audience to tears with her rendering of a Chopin Mazurka, and becomes a starred pupil in the 'A' level mocks and is in the definite running for Head Girl. Then she gets to talk to the assistant manager in the local big Hotel and thereupon knows exactly what she wants to do.

Her mother is bitterly disappointed. 'Not take up your music, Lucy? When you're so, so, talented?'

'I can still play, mums. That'll never leave me,' she replies and looks to her father.

With his background, he can see the advantages of a management career, even in an hotel. 'You could do a lot worse, Lucy. And with your social skills you should do well in that environment, even if you're not too keen on figures. You've got a good brain in that pretty head of yours, even though I say it. We've got a talented daughter, my dear,' he says to his wife during the discussion, 'so don't let's stifle her ambitions. She'll do well in whatever she does.'

He goes with her to the interview, sits at the back of the room and listens to her answers, to her little dissertation on 'why I want to join the Company' and is chest tighteningly proud of her. And is not at all surprised when she gets the letter of acceptance, nor surprised that the place they offer is in town. Well, not only is it a 'proper' hotel but with a splendid reputation and she'll not have to leave home. That is the best bit – and his little telephone conversation with the Manager, who he knows quite well, has obviously done the trick. He'll not tell Lucy, of course.

৵

She knows she is pretty. Her lustrous deep brown hair with the tints of auburn, the dark eyes and the high cheek bones. The way the boys' heads turn when she goes shopping on Saturdays and the one or two snide comments from her contemporaries, especially the ones who have stupid crushes on some young men and bring both their exploits and dismay back to school with them. She tries hard not to capitalise on her attributes, but it isn't easy. When she'd particularly wanted to spend more time in the Library after school, a privilege only granted to the rare few, she'd posed the question to the young male English teacher in charge. As she'd seen his eyes drop when she'd unselfconsciously lifted her chest, it sort of dawned on her that a little harmless exploitation to achieve an end was fun.

Now in her room and getting ready for bed her mind is still running through that weird experience she'd had, coming home. She isn't uncomfortable with it, quite the reverse; it is giving her a nice warm glow. A feeling as though she'd done someone a favour, or given them a longed-for gift, or played a decent piece of music to an appreciative audience. And all she'd done was walk home along the lane and coincidentally seen someone leaning up against a car a hundred yards away. But that was precisely when she'd felt the pull, the leap of affinity, something magnetic. Was it from the person, a young male? He couldn't have seen that she was pretty, not from that distance, and anyway, it had been getting on towards dusk. She'd been with Marie, Sheena and Julie. Perhaps it had been them? But no, not really, else she wouldn't have felt it, that pull.

If, as the way her thoughts are running, it is a precursor to another chance opportunity, a future meeting, then so be it. There isn't any feeling of fear, merely one of curiosity mixed with anticipation.

She slides under the bedcovers, stretches out, flexes her toes, considers reading for a while, instead, switches out the light and closes her eyes. As she's already said, "Tomorrow is another day".

I'm Jones. I lie in bed, awake but reluctant to tell myself so. The sky isn't doing me any favours; the dull grey overcast no encouragement to leap out of bed. So I simply lay here, letting a restless mind churn through the usual things. Like, why am I here, why hadn't I got a decent job with a decently large salary, why am I so satisfied with being a idler – or what amounts to one? If I'd got expensive tastes, worked up a desire for a long holiday in the sun, decided to change the old Morris Traveller for a new Wolsey or Sunbeam, hadn't got an absentee landlord who was using me for an excuse not to pay extravagant buildings insurance then yes, I'd have to go for a teaching job fulltime. I wouldn't mind, actually, but this mooching about was a lot simpler and easier with no homework to mark.

Lunch with Briony to look forward to; she's fun, in a highbrow, bluestocking sort of way. An elegant lady with a penchant for acting like mother or elder sister, a substantial investment income, no current husband (she'd seen one off only six months ago – '*such a boring man, no concept of what makes us real women tick*') and I feel sure she's got an ulterior motive. While she pays the lunch bills I don't mind; probably the simple reason is she feels conversation with an intelligent (yes, intelligent, that's me) ex-Cambridge student is worth the few quid at Hannah's. (That's the current name for the bistro place, by the way). So long as she doesn't see me purely as bed-fodder – not that she wouldn't improve that side of my deficient education, I feel sure, and I'm *almost* tempted – though once one starts going to bed with a woman like Briony, there's no knowing where it might end.

So I'll get up. An hour until Samuel expects me. Breakfast as normal – tea, toast with an abundance of homemade marmalade. (Another thing to learn about me is that I'm very domesticated; I can cook, make the aforesaid marmalade, sew – I mentioned the curtains, didn't I – wash clothes (essential) and I even tried knitting too. Hah!)

The corded trousers will have to do another day. But a clean shirt – I can't abide the smell of sweaty clothes – and so it's a decent wash, an athletic rub and scrub. Works well, gets the old circulation going a treat.

⊷

Jones likes walking. He leaves the car outside the house most days, and strides athletically around. He meets and greets several of his local acquaintances on the way down the hill and across the river towards the church. The bookshop is buried in a series of low ceilinged, dingy, ancient rooms, redolent of old paper, parchment, dust; an antiquarian's delight – or dilemma, dependant on a browser's mission. If you want a pristine copy of this year's Booker prize winner, do not call here. All you'll get is a little black irritating hopper (flea to the uninitiated) in your ear. Samuel doesn't care for most modern publishers, (an exception may be Faber and Faber, thanks to T.S.Eliot), nor for many of their readers. *'Commercial crap,'* he says, often and with considerable emphasis. Mention some so-called best selling authors, household names to many, and he'll ask *'who? Never heard of 'em'*. Such is Samuel's world. Oh, and never, ever, call him Sam – or Sammy.

Today is to be another eventful day.

I like Samuel. He's stooped, as is essential in his premises, built circa Elizabeth One. He's also white haired, smoothed back onto yellowed collars; wears a burgundy (I think) corduroy jacket over dull green (I think) trousers with turn-ups. I do not know how old he is, and, I suspect, neither does he. He lives, (dare I add 'I think') above the shop, in a two-roomed assemblage of furniture as antique as the building, but I do have to say, keeps himself and his Eliot cat very well fed and watered. He also knows his wines. The one time I was granted access to his chambers, I got the impression that he knew how to look after himself better than would a wife. Just as well.

Anyway, today, there was more of a gleam in his eye than usual. He told me to sit down – a rare occurrence – and as there is only one chair, a very well creased red leather broad armchair with buttoned edges, I sit. The feeling is one of inferiority. He is standing, towering, I am trapped and very low. The chair's legs are only three inches high.

'Jones,' he is saying, 'I have a proposition for you. You understand me. I would not have tolerated your continued presence otherwise. You have an eye for the finer things in life. Alas, I am fully cognisant my years are not in my favour.' The gleam is more; it is an intense stare. Is basilisk the word? 'So do me the extreme honour of accepting a half share less a pound in the business – stock and goodwill only, you understand – and work full time. There. What say you?'

I had to swallow. A half share? Work full time? This was his life, this shop. To be offered half of his life? (Less the pound, of course, the controlling interest. No flies on Samuel.) From my disadvantaged position, all I could see were dull green moleskin trousers and a frayed leather belt over a Viyella shirt. He always wore a checked Viyella shirt. (Didn't I say? Sorry.)

'Can I think about it?'

The inevitable response, I suppose, unless you were a desperate shelf-positioned maiden pushing thirty-five when you'd have shouted 'Yes! Yes! Yes! But wasn't I in similar straits? Considering, only earlier this morning, in fact not an hour or two since, the offer to prostitute myself in the teaching profession in order to ensure a continued supply of more adequate funds? Full time would double the (small) regular income, he said, but would it also mean less freedom?

The vision of trousers moved. He leant back onto the Greek Philosophy shelf, the one propped against the outer left wall so it wouldn't fall over.

'Think about it?' he was saying. 'Think about it? There's nothing to think about. An offer of becoming a business partner in the best antiquarian bookshop this side of Tower Bridge and you want to *think about it!* Rubbish, man. Accept or I withdraw my offer. I'll count to ten. One, two, three … '

So I accepted.

At a smidgeon before one o'clock, I left the shop – my shop, I said to myself – and walked the quarter mile up into the old town centre for my lunch date. Hannah's was *the* place to eat at lunchtime, with its solid light-oak tables, its well cushioned chairs with rounded backs, the light and airy atmosphere of fractionally off-white walls and modernistic paintings (Samuel would never eat there). The waitresses were always smart in their frilly white blouses, little black skirts, barelegged, with Dutch style shoes and ankle socks. Cute, I thought. The menu cards were always clean, too.

Briony sat in the corner, our accepted table position. I walked across, dodging the shopping bags left alongside pushed-out chairs, and smiled at her. A nice woman to smile at, Briony. Always impeccable, near platinum white-gold hair pinned up with a decorative comb, a crisp cream blouse that gave credence to the contours below, emphasised by the jewelled dark red stone dangling in a secretive valley, small jacket over, tight tweed skirt in a lightweight grey. Class, pure class, the diamond ring still in place.

I risked it. 'Still married, I see, Briony.'

Her eyes narrowed down but the smile was still there and she tapped the finger on the table. 'Waiting for a new one. Any chance?'

One of these days, when I am feeling totally reckless and in the need of a pick-me-up, I might, just might, see what is on offer. After all, we'd known each other for some time and comfortable with it. A bonus from a concert I'd gone to, when we'd shared a space at the interval drinks counter and got talking.

Today I ignored her leading question. I had news to impart.

'Samuel has made me an offer.'

She laughed. Briony's laugh was a lovely musical chime of a laugh. Like a schoolgirl's, I thought, and instantly my spine tingled, *Lucy!* I didn't ignore the twist of a reminder; I merely let it slide to the back, like a joker card in a poker game.

'Better than mine?'

I shook my head. 'Briony, my love, one of these days we'll play a risky game, but Samuel's offer is money. And security, I guess. He wants me to stay in the business. Take a partnership.'

'Lord help us!' I could see she was genuinely amazed. 'Old books! You'll suffocate!'

Her reaction, I suppose, wasn't unremarkable. Whereas she, I know, is a cultured woman, intelligent, appreciates fine things and so on, to believe that a life around all the civilized expression of years of learning and literacy leads to suffocation is incorrect. Anyway, she's already offered me the glimpse of an opportunity for light relief; her neat grey skirt is too short and I have an instinct for artistic curves. The waitress girl was poised, biro in hand. Poised, absolutely.

The salad of the day was chorizo and avocado. Apple juice, the proper crushed version. Then a chocolate muffin and decent coffee. Briony always copied my choice. Wicked lady. We parted with a kiss.

'Bye, Jones,' she said, catching my eyes. 'Same time tomorrow?' Perhaps it was then that she knew I was hooked, the rebound from my vision.

I'd already explained to Samuel about my promise to help Chas with his furniture and not to expect me back. Not a lot he could do – even if he wanted. A promise was a promise.

Chas's place is a shambles. Second hand furniture reeks of sadness, desperation, loss. It affects all those who work around it, making them equally desperately sad; Chas is no exception, with a face like a dejected dachshund sausage dog.

Shifting a massive mahogany wardrobe first, we followed that with two settees onto the first floor. A pile of kitchen chairs from the top floor (five flights of stairs, why he didn't suffer from a bad back I'll never know) to the 'loading bay', a glorified name for a space at the back of the corrugated tin shed next to the clattering doors. Then two tables, a corner cupboard and an art deco style sideboard (plastic laminated, don't get excited).

Tea is always on offer and strangely the mugs and the teapot were always pristine. Perhaps, I thought, uncharitably and rather worryingly, he doused them in bleach. This is when I get the usual sob story, the wife who left him, the business partner who ran off with the spare cash (and I always wondered over the 'spare' cachet) and the business rates. Well, we all have business rates, said I, as one who had suddenly and unexpectedly entered the 'I pay business rates' club.

'I'm working full time with Samuel as of Monday,' I told him. 'So if you need a hand it'll have to be evenings or Sundays.'

'S okay,' he muttered with no change in facial expression. 'But ain't you got a girl to shift about of an evening?'

The vision appeared, holistic, ethereal. A metallic glazed Lucy Rie, a charm of a charger, sitting on my sideboard; wherein lay the single pound note to remind me. Of the One. Lucy, in a swirling skirt, as seen in a distantly vague dimension and truly remembered. Oh lor.

'I'd best be off, Chas. Give me a bell when you next need some muscle, at Samuel's.'

He grunted, gave no parting smile, and I went home to my charger and its resident genie.

Burghley Park

Three

Fugue 2… Subject

My new position with Samuel and his – our – bookshop worked well. Before we knew where we were, Christmas was upon us with all the attendant aggravation. You'd think customers would have some idea of which book to buy when seeking presents, but, oh no, they browse and browse then shuffle up to the desk and ask silly questions. The commonest one suggests that we know – have read – the contents of every single book on the shelves. 'You know the one I mean. Written by – oh what's his name – the chap who also wrote something about flowers …' Or trees, or monkeys, or about Roman temples or Judaism – any subject under the sun and they always thought we'd know. Flattering, I suppose, but totally unrealistic. However, we got by, with a complex mix of guesswork, sublime intuition or a reasonable view of what we could get away with and what they could afford. Samuel never complained about my wildest forays into client intellectualism, in fact he had started paying me monthly and more than I could have realistically assumed I was worth. All good stuff. And in case you've wondered, the Lucy Rie charger was still sitting on my sideboard, along with its resident pound note. I loved it, stroked it, and every time the jazz of tiny tingles in my spine recalled the fleeting glimpse of a slender female figure who I'd not seen nor sought since that evening last September three months since. We'd meet again. I know we will. Sometime.

I don't like winter days. Too cold, too dark, far too miserable. Why couldn't I have had a yen to visit Portugal, or Tenerife, or Morocco? Somewhere warm. Samuel had a healthy respect for the stock – books don't like being damp and when it's cold you have to reduce the temperature to lower humidity. Daft, but it's true. Unless we could install a proper conservation grade heating control system, we just had to shiver and trust customers were already wrapped up warm when they jangled the bell-dressed door. I wore a thick knitted woollen sweater most of the time, over a thermo-something vest. Samuel appeared oblivious in the constant comfort of his burgundy jacket. The only sop to a lower temperature was a very Sloanish silk scarf in a violently Paisley patterned yellow. Of such sartorial gentlemanly attire one couldn't be overly critical – he'd been about too long.

Briony and I now have an "understanding", that discreet euphemism for a relationship beyond the 'bedroom door'. Maybe our regular lunches, which now, probably as a result of a mutual consideration of budgetary concern, are limited to once a week – normally on a Friday – brought us to that cruciality. I can't bring myself to provide chapter and verse, because she does mean a lot to me and I won't divulge, suffice to report she was brilliant as a mentor in matters sexual and I seem able to satisfy both of us. Brilliant, did I say? Gorgeous actually. Naked, she is gorgeous. Between … the ways in which we … no, I said I wouldn't. Use your imagination and take it to bed with you.

She bought me a new sweater for Christmas, probably as a consequence of finding the one I usually wore had developed a hole at the left elbow from leaning on the bookshop desk. I bought her a far too expensive bottle of the perfume she wore. The present exchange took place at her detached house on the northern outskirts of the town on the evening after the Christmas Eve lunch. I stayed the night, as was now of weekend normality.

She wore the perfume. I wore the sweater. We had an entertaining evening – night, and from what I can remember, our activities carried on into the early hours. Christmas Day. Lovely, relaxing, indulgent and very very decadent. We drank coffee laced with brandy. We ate mince pies also laced with brandy. Pulled the odd cracker or two. Wore silly hats and not a lot else. Eventually we went back to bed.

On Boxing Day, we went for a long walk around the park. There is only one proper park. It surrounds the lovely Elizabethan house on the outskirts of the town; grand old lime trees covered in mistletoe stand sentinel amongst rolling pasture with the fallow deer roaming around as they have for generations. Perfectly attuned to my mood, Briony kept quiet. We held hands, swung them, I kicked at decaying autumn leaves and she nestled into my side.

'Jones,' she broke the silence. 'Do you actually love me?'

Isn't that a rhetorical question? After all, we'd done everything most couples – especially married couples – did. Ate decent well-prepared food – we took turns at cooking – listened to music, read, occasionally (very occasionally) watched telly, undressed (usually each other), slept, washed (showered, actually), dressed, parted, met for lunch, argued in a very civilised way from time to time, kissed to make up. Kissed. I swung her round and captured the wonderful softness of her lips, her mouth, under a tree with its mistletoe. I was getting good at this romantic stuff.

'Love you,' I said, automatically. Ah yes, what every chivalrous male says to the woman he's satisfactorily bedded. She picked up my hand again and found my eyes.

'Then marry me.'

'*Marry you?*' A proposal? Lordy!

'Uh huh. Come and live with me. Full time.'

'Briony!' *She didn't mean it, did she? Carried away by the magic of the moment and a surfeit of sex?*

We walked on, lost in our own entanglements. She still nestled into my side, the sophisticated, elegant, expensive lady ten to fifteen years my senior, my arm round her shoulders. I should be proud of her, the lovely woman that she is. I should also be grateful she had taken me 'under her wing', though I'd been under other places as well. A meal ticket; a stimulating, intellectually demanding companion, an extremely athletic and demanding sleeping partner, a distraction. Marry her?

When we got back to her house, the Edwardian villa many another would envy, the December day slipping imperceptibly into dark and the cold bringing moisture to the air and mist to our breath, she paused me at the door.

'Jones,' she said, 'you're being rather slow. Can't you make up your mind? What did old Samuel do to make you give *him* an answer?'

I laughed. 'He said he'd count to ten. Then withdraw the offer.'

She turned, unlocked the door and drew me inside, shut the door behind us. 'One,' she said, removing her scarf. 'Two,' and laughed as her coat came off. 'Three,' and her sweater followed. Temptress. 'Four,' and the skirt fell on the floor. 'Five,' and she reached for me – you get the idea?

Later: 'Marry me?'

I stared at the ceiling, at the gold edged crystal glass of the triple chandelier, from the advantageous position alongside a warm, living, loving naked woman. So easy to say yes, except the role reversal was demeaning. Why hadn't I taken the lead, wooed and won her from the conventional masculine position of strength? Then she would have given me the traditional 'hard to get' reply, something along the lines of 'give me more time' or 'I'll think about it', neither of which I could use. Not me. I rolled over and buried my face in the depth of the pristine white feather-down pillow. A rustle and a movement by my side and fingers massaging gently down my spine, inching down, another movement ...

'Call me,' she said the following morning, standing on the doorstep in her wrap-round fluffy cotton dressing gown, 'when you've come to your senses, you silly boy.' No acrimony in her voice, though perhaps a tinge of sadness. Maybe she did love me.

I entered the cold unwelcoming depths of my terraced home, sniffed at stale air, drew curtains back, let some light, mid-morning dim light, into the place. In the front room, Christmas hadn't happened.

Briony had stolen my Christmas. I slumped down onto the bargain basement settee; sagged into unpaid-for cushions. On the sideboard, the Lucy Rie charger stood and that, I knew, was why I hadn't answered Briony's question. Lucy, a puzzlingly ethereal fleeting female magnet. A magnetic force I couldn't pretend to understand, a force that had spanned a hundred yards of dismal back road and gripped my perception of what mysteries existed between two human brains to create an indivisible link I couldn't comprehend. I wondered if she did – even if the link had been equally apparent to her?

Back to Briony. What was she to me? Stimulating, in every which way. Comforting, in so far she provided shelter, warmth, food and conversation. A source of advice, guidance and support. If I rejected her offer, an unsought, surprising and extremely flattering offer besides being staggeringly generous, would we remain friends, very good friends or revert to a mere cool acquaintanceship? Would she be hurt – something I'd most certainly wish to avoid – and would I mourn the loss?

For lunch that day I reverted to simplistic comfort food. Baked beans and cheese on toast. Another facet of living part-time in an Edwardian villa was the cultivation of gourmet tastes. Briony didn't believe in baked beans, on toast or not. Come to think about it, her toast was a carefully precise performance with only the best Seville (W.I. homemade) marmalade to accompany the Lazy Sunday brand of Taylor's coffee. Me, in terrace pad mode, I made the most of my own marmalade on the cheapest sliced and a spoonful of instant granules in the Denby mug. Well, at least the mug was quality. I loved it because it had been a constant companion throughout the whole of my Cambridge career. I'd bought it from Robert Sayles as a birthday present to myself on the first occasion of a tutorial 'A' plus. Having survived the rigours of undergraduate life and being dropped more than a few times, it had done well to come thru' the years unscathed. I spring-cleaned it every so often when the inside's patina would brew coffee without granules.

Baked beans and cheese. I momentarily wondered what my virtual Lucy ate for lunch – if a virtual girl ate anything.

That afternoon I walked down to the shop and let myself in. We weren't due to re-open after the Christmas break until the Monday after the New Year. Samuel wouldn't mind, he was probably snoring his head off at his sister's in Grantham. And if you wondered about the cat – a Persian Blue, plus pedigree – well, he took it with him in a wicker basket, if only to annoy the aforesaid sister. Pampered pussy. Talking of which … I reached for the shop phone.

'Briony? Jones. Did I say thank you for a wonderful time? … ' Did she know what I was going to say? 'Let's keep us on a level footing, shall we? At least we know what we like. Shouldn't want us to muck things up. We can always count to ten.'

She chuckled down the phone after the thoughtful pause, as I rather thought she would. 'Okay. Okay, Jones. Forgive me if I was too face-on for you, but I don't want to lose you. Ever. But anytime...'

I put the ebonite handset back on its antediluvian rest. It had to match the surroundings. That done, I could breathe easy once more and I guess my mythical Lucy would too. Status quo.

∽

Jones spends the rest of the afternoon browsing. Something in his mind repeatedly nags him about extra sensory perception. He looks up a definition that leads him on to clairvoyance, telepathy and precognition. There is a suggestion that information about an object (was Lucy an 'object' in this context?) can be gained by means other than those presently recognised – understood – by the physical sciences. Has he suddenly acquired this faculty? If so, what information can he gain about a distantly seen young lady, other than this ever-present notion that he is destined to have more to do with her at some indeterminate point in the future. Is it clairvoyance, and if so, why just her and why not other things? He hadn't had any pre-knowledge that Samuel was going to make the substantial offer of a position. He may have had an inkling that he would end up in Briony's bed before over long but that wasn't clairvoyance, it was just so bloody obvious, though the other very serious proposition from her came as a surprise. Nothing had prepared him for an offer of marriage, largely because in his book, women didn't generally propose to men, except on leap year days, of course, but it wasn't February, it was a damn chilly December. He'd not known he'd be given the opportunity to live in a nice small terrace pad at peppercorn rent. Or that he'd find a Lucy Rie charger stuffed amongst junk on a dimly lit back shelf in a grubby antique shop. Or that he'd actually notice a certain young woman in the lane, but he had, and the sight of her slim figure or more so her *presence* had triggered the most surprising and powerful feeling which came and went like some errant toothache. Except that it isn't a pain, it is a mind-tingling delight. There wasn't much else he can read into the future.

Which sets him on to wondering about his ambitions. What did he wish to do with his life? Follow Samuel into a perpetual attachment to old books? Climb onto indubitably more moralistically higher ground and revert to Plan B, take on a teaching post? Go on a year-long expedition into hitherto undiscovered parts of South America to come back to an FRGS and a substantial cheque from some publisher for the rights to the subsequent book? Try to persuade Cambridge to take him on as a Research Scholar that might ultimately lead to a Fellowship? Or marry Briony and become her lap dog – and is that a better definition than toy-boy, the latest description for an athletic guy in both conversation and connubiality?

Problem. Rolling a naked Briony around the marvellous king-size bed is becoming a powerful drug and one that can become addictive. And she is rather splendidly generous in every which way. Marrying her will give instant financial stability and something of a substantial social position – though undoubtedly there are those who'd sneer. The jealous ones, that is. He still can't believe where he is with her; surely some other guys are out there, sniffing after her delights despite her intellectual superiority. A divorcee with money, a decent figure, still the right side of forty? Gawn, how come she'd taken up with him, a near penniless guy who works out of a second-hand bookshop?

He closes the encyclopaedia. Without looking for more esoteric tomes, he isn't getting anywhere. This unsought link-up with a total stranger, and a girl to boot, is the weirder side of weird. Has she been equally clairvoyant or perceptive, or whatever the paranormal types call it? And if so, is she deliberating over the same feelings, or has she dismissed them, to shrug and get on with her quest for good grades? No telling.

The shop is shut up, and he retreats back to his terrace dwelling. No, he isn't going up to see his paramour. He'll let her perspire – sorry, glow. That's what women do. Men perspire, or is it sweat?

෨

And Lucy (the real one)? She is five foot eight (one and three-quarter metres if you prefer metric), tucks in at fifty-five kilos (a smidgeon over eight and a half stone if you prefer English), and she loves her music.

A diligent girl, she puts in at least two hours piano practice per day, polishing her nicest pieces with an aim to achieve perfection by the end of the month. Her mentor and sharpest critic is mother Elizabeth, she who had performed at the Wigmore Hall in her later youth and is determined her daughter ought to follow suit. One big problem. Lucy's ambition lies in management, to run an hotel where guests will never wish to leave. So why music? Because it is her relaxation, her outlet for the artistic side and because it presents another personal challenge.

'Mother,' she says, after another drawn-out discussion roaming around such regular subjects as school, a degree course, the hotel management trainee scheme and becoming a professional pianist, 'I *know* what I want to do and what I believe I'm going to achieve. And I shall *always* play the piano, even after I've got the job of running the George. Believe me.'

Her mother sighs. This daughter of hers. Such a pretty girl. Dark eyed, glossy rich chestnut hair, a natural bloom on those cheeks, not an ounce of surplus fat – or muscle – anywhere, she occasionally feels jealous, given her own figure and skin tone has begun the decline into middle-aged mediocrity. But another topic has to be aired and now is about right, as her daughter's attitude appears calm and conciliatory.

'You're eighteen next month, Lucy. Do we need to widen our discussions to more, um, *basic* matters? You've never talked about any boy friends. No,' she adds quickly, seeing her girl's eyebrows rise, 'this isn't necessarily lecture time. But you will always be up-front with us, won't you? Please?'

Lucy knows exactly what her mother will have on her agenda. All decent mothers need to bring matters biological to the forefront at some time, before ignorant experimentation leads to a discreet appointment at the newly established abortion clinic. She mentally shudders. Not for her, no way. She has seen what had happened to Phyllis, a silly sex-mad girl with a low IQ.

'Sure, mother. I haven't come across any male worthy of *our* attention, not yet. But I *know* there's someone out there for me. I can feel a,' and she doesn't quite know how to phrase this odd feeling of hers, 'strange attachment to someone I've not met, physically, that is.'

Her mother's look. A wondering, half-concerned, half-condescending glance. 'That's a strange concept,' she says dismissively, thinking her daughter is growing-up a little too rapidly, 'not venturing into the paranormal, are you, my girl?'

Lucy's shoulders go up and down in an elegant shrug. 'Be pleased, mother. I don't believe I'll step out of line whilst my virtual attraction is around.'

Later in the week, Lucy's mother comes up with a suggestion. There is a concert planned for early March in aid of the latest disaster fund or some such worthy cause. She has been asked to play but decides not to. The organiser's evident disappointment puts an idea in her head and she explains. He looks both ponderous (heavy jowled, red faced) and dubious.

'Are you sure?' he asks, 'because we want this to be a top-notch affair.'

This far too-pointed criticism puts Lucy's mother's back up. Her daughter has a wonderful feel for the music that rivals her own. She puts the man in his place and stalks off. Now Lucy is going to be committed whether she likes it or not.

'You need to be seen, Lucy dear. Hiding in that drab school uniform all the while will not show your talents to advantage. I want you to perform in my stead at the Barn Hill concert at the end of March. Well within your competence. And I'll make sure the right people are there. Do you good.'

So Lucy practices her speciality, another Chopin piece she presented at the school. 'Will it matter if they've already heard me play it before?' she asks, but her mother thinks not. Another Prelude is also mastered, just to be on the safe side.

Her father – with an eye for these things, takes her shopping with her mother's approval. He'll spend the right sort of money, Elizabeth knows, and she trusts his judgement. He has often chosen her outfits in the past, so the dress Lucy comes home with is stunning. A full skirted – she has to sit well on the piano stool – and beautifully cut pale grey silky thing with diamante trim, short sleeves and not too low a front, though low enough, and a smart little lacy black bolero top. Her mother is impressed.

'If you don't get some boy or other trailing after you I'd be very surprised,' she says, wishing she were as near twenty as Lucy is. 'I love that misty look, makes you appear ethereal, like some goddess.'

'Which I am, of course,' Lucy replies with a wistful smile and wonders if she is really doing the right thing.

The concert day looms. The tension mounts. Lucy plays through her repertoire again and again. She catches her father whistling the Chopin theme as he polishes the car one Saturday afternoon. She grins at him.

'Dear dad – if I catch a cold or something, will you whistle the piece in my stead?'

He straightens up, gives the Singer's bonnet a last quick swipe with the duster and grins back at her.

'Lucy, my darling daughter, the audience would soon boo me off the stage. Whereas you'll be pressed for an encore. I can see you doing evening recitals in that hotel of yours.'

'It's not my hotel, yet, dad. Though I shall be working on it.'

'That I will believe.' He puts the duster down and opens his arms. Lucy willingly moves forward to be enfolded in a masculine hug. 'At least you've got another string to your bow, so to speak, if it goes pear-shaped.'

She laughs at him, aware of his choice of phrase. 'Hah hah. The *keys* to my success, eh dad?'

'Yeah. Let's go and make tea. This time next week …'

And next week comes, all too soon. Strangely, she feels only a few faint butterflies as she does a final run-through in the afternoon. Her mother listens with as critical an ear as any.

'The last *rallentando*, Lucy. Perhaps a smidgeon too *lentamente*? Chopin, dear. Not Schubert. Otherwise, enchanting. You'll be a hit, I know you will. Now, a bath and a half hour rest, I think, don't you?'

Lucy agrees. Then she'll have a light omelette and a mug of precious Lady Grey tea before allowing her mother to dress her hair. She'll change up at the concert premises, even though it has barely adequate facilities.

The building is a buzz of conversation. For an event like this, with decent publicity and a justly deserving charity, there are a substantial number of the good, the godly and the generous visible. Not to be seen would incur some small derogatory comment in the higher social echelons of the town. Lucy's parents have a pair of decent seats a few rows back from the front. The local Youth Orchestra is assembled, the incredibly talented String Quartet will also perform, and there are two soloists. Lucy has the second to last slot in the first half.

'Good,' says her mother, scrutinising the programme. 'The audience will be well settled and not getting fidgety. And she'll be talked over during the interval.'

Her husband nods. 'Can't wait,' he says. 'I love my daughter.'

Lucy's mother leans over and presses a kiss on his cheek. 'I know you do. So do I. She's special.'

The leader of the Youth Orchestra enters: the audience clap politely. The guest conductor walks briskly across and steps up onto the small podium. He turns towards the assemblage and delivers a well rehearsed spiel about the need for generous support, etcetera etcetera. He is to be the presenter for all items on the programme. Another polite clap, he turns again towards the players, raises his baton. Away we go, into a brisk Viennese waltz to get the right mood going.

Towards the back, under the gallery, sits Briony with Jones. He is a tinge apprehensive; actually this is the first time he has formally accompanied Briony to an event as up-market as this. Okay, they met here, ages ago, but that was then, and this is now. She's been very proprietorial, greeting her friends and including him in all the social chitchat. Her friends, in the main, are very well aware of his involvement with her and so he has been subjected to a variety of glances. Slight amusement from her fellow members of the Athletic Club and her tennis playing set. Eyebrows raised by those who knew Briony's former husband, now well away from her social circle. A definite air of envy from the dishy dark-haired slim too-young-to-be-a-widow woman in a very expensive dress. She hasn't managed to persuade anyone to escort her, so Briony has taken pity on her.

'You don't mind Daphne joining us?' she'd asked as they'd met her in the foyer and she slips him a ten pound note to pay for interval drinks. He's glad he decided to wear the only decent suit he possesses, which compliments Briony's dark burgundy evening gown in some shiny material. He thinks it is taffeta but can't be sure. Daphne's frock hasn't any straps. Jones ponders over how well it stays up, given Daphne's chest is the size it is. He casts a wary sideways glance, but everything is still in place. Daphne catches his eye and lowers her eyelashes. He offers Briony a smile instead. She takes his hand as the conductor's baton goes up and the concert begins.

The String Quartet moves the audience into raptures. The tenor soloist is on top form. The Youth Orchestra show their enthusiasm. The conductor/presenter is well briefed. The audience is alert. They've reached the crucial moment for Lucy.

'It is my great pleasure to introduce the delightful daughter of the pianist we all know and love; her talent has been successfully extended towards the next generation. This is Lucy's debut – I know she will enchant us. Please welcome ... '

And Lucy steps forward, does her walk across to the Steinway especially hired-in, gives the little bow her mother made her practice, sits, manages her frock beautifully, waits for a brief moment as the clapping dies away, places fingers on the keys, closes her eyes momentarily, and plays.

She feels it, those chill shivers running up and down her spine. A presence. *There is someone out there.* No matter, the music has her in its grasp and she can do no other but extend her spirit into her fingers, fluid, flexed and phenomenal. The notes melt into ecstasy. Chopin, at his best. Her mother is shedding tears and Lucy doesn't know, but what she does know is she has achieved a goal. Reached a pinnacle. And within a fragment of mind's dimension, another tenuous link, a microfilament of mental cognisance, is woven betwixt her and another soul, no not *another* soul but *the* soul. The one with whom the tie of thought has been forged. Not of any wish of her eyes, or ears, but of her mind. And she does not know who.

Jones feels her strength. The amazing girl on the piano stool in a swirl of grey with glistening shining pearl drops of diamante who has captured his virtual soul. He is drawn towards her but cannot move. The girl of the evening pavement, of the shadows by the school, of the time he acquired a Rie charger and has experienced its power ever since. His mind is shrinking, pulling, as if it wishes to take wing and fly towards her, but it is captive in his brain and his brain is within his body and his body is restrained between the two beautiful women either side of him. They who have physical power between them, the power of their breasts, their thighs, their shining looks and their captivating actions. He is lost and needs to seek The One but cannot.

Lucy stands and takes her applause. She does another small curtsey, with her hand poised at her cleavage, just as her mother insisted. She is perspiring and feels the trickle of sweat run between her breasts, tickling her, and she still has to smile, drop another curtsey as the applause goes on and a few folk out there get to their feet. Including her parents; she can just make them out. Then more get to their feet. This is silly, she thinks. I'm merely a local school girl who is wearing a better dress and whose mum has shown her how to play a piano. Nothing all that special, is it?

The conductor steps forward, takes her elbow, whispers in her ear. '*Encore,*' he is saying. She nods. She has practiced a short *Polonaise.* She sits, the noise abates. A zing of thought hits her. *Lovely*, it is saying. *You … Are … Lovely.* Bent over the keys, fingers cascading in the run of the notes, the flush in her cheeks cannot be seen.

The George Hotel

Four

Fugue 3... Episode

It is summer. The daily exodus of High School pupils over the ancient pavements around the stone buildings, which have housed these pupils successfully for their year's tuition, ends. The throng, dissipated into all the crevices of their family's lives, await results in disparate ways. Some go abroad. Some take up small jobs. Some leavers not going to university put in countless hours at extending their techniques in commerce, artistry, sport, or horse riding, or fortunately in a very few cases, sex.

Jones has already extended his technique. Briony lends him to Daphne, or, more correctly, has engineered matters so adroitly that he has no option but to service her unspoken requirement with discretion, concern and understanding. He cannot work out why this Briony allowed, unless it is a subtle way of getting her own back after his side-step of a marriage proposal. Now he is shattered and it is past time for him to go back to his work-a-day position in the bookshop. His current bodily position is horizontal, and he cannot alter it because she will not move. Well, she does move, but the significance of her movement is finalised with a thrown back head and a fascinating noise, a cross between an animal yelp and a cry. Jones is too gentlemanly to expand on his own feelings.

Pheromonally, she is very different so he can leave her with equanimity.

He enters the bookshop within the half hour, quietly, absorbing the familiar smell and the comforting feel. Daphne's small two bed apartment in the newly erected block of town houses by the river is clean, antiseptic, a mirror of her body. She leaves no scent on him, nothing in his mind, no reminiscence to enjoy. A woman with a woman's body but not one to satisfy the soul. There is a consistent blank space in his mind that neither Briony nor Daphne can fill. A black void with golden edges, as though it is the container for a present yet to be bought or given.

Samuel casts a raised left eyebrow expression in his direction, the one Jones knows well. He also knows Samuel knows and condones this *ménage a trois* because Daphne is a distant relative of an acquaintance of his and is aware of her need for some comfort to assuage the loss of a husband. Samuel has spoken, in paraphrase fashion, of the matter, so Jones has no concerns over how his ability to fulfil another human's need for aspects of physical satisfaction within the vague and broadly undefined bracket of 'love' will affect his employment position. His own personal doubts about how it affects his empty mental box is another matter. So …

❧

I wish I didn't feel so embarrassed. This occasional foray into less familiar places certainly provides interesting relief from the more accustomed gymnastics but none the less, as I am seen as Briony's man, to climb out of another's bed and appear completely unabashed does smack of, say, ungentlemanly conduct. *Not done, old chap. Stick to the one filly, eh?'*

Who said that? No one in my hearing, but nevertheless, it echoes in my brain every time I wander into my favourite watering hole,

31

the up-hill rival to the George Hotel. This is Briony-free territory, largely because her ex. appears in here from time to time. I have no worries. I can always swear complete innocence over the intimate details of her – Briony's – *chambre,* largely because I now also have details of Daphne's own on tap, if it comes to entering into that level of dubious conversation. Unlikely though. Ex of Briony is a golfing man and has his own circle of idiot friends with a strange language of their own. *Birdies,* indeed. My birdies come equipped with their own personal approach to 'holes in one'.

I hope I don't shock you.

High summer brings its own problems, usually in the form of excessive quantities of tourists and foreign ones at that. I mean, Stamford is a very nice town, don't get me wrong, but apart from some genteel strolling around streets more familiar to those who watch period drama on their telly screens, there's not a lot else. Apart from the Big House, that is. There I spend delightful hours, soaking up the aged ambience, reliving the grander moments of the past, browsing through the library, wandering from room to room in the spirit of the Burghley family's Elizabethan forbears. The house staff know me well, as I know them, and I receive an approach.

Jones, she asks (she is the House Manageress or whatever the Trustees call her), 'I'm short on guides after next weekend. So, I wonder …'

I didn't, not for a moment. She isn't unlike Briony in the best possible way, and as I know the history of the place backwards of course I accept. So here I am, loitering with intent, about to embark on the first guided tour. But what of the bookshop, I hear you ask? Well, it's a Sunday, and as Samuel can't (thankfully, he says) go to his sister's and as I am entitled to some time off (during the working day that is – Briony doesn't care for me taking time off from her appointed schedule unless I'm on Daphne duty – which is no more than once a fortnight), it fits in well.

The guided tour is a roaring success. I make friends with them all. My mentor is pleased. I am pleased. I even get a free tea.

So this turns into a regular event and widens my experience. No, not that way, certainly *not* that way. Having a frolic with a punter would be very *infra dig*. These are not Elizabethan times and I am not at Court. Anyway, one and a spare is enough for any man.

Then, towards the end of the summer, on one Sunday unknowingly to become another special day, I am going back to the car park in the Kennel Yard after my morning stint. My faithful Morris Traveller awaits. I get in, start her up, and drive slowly out of the staff area. Before I get very far, over towards the Porter's Lodge a small group of people catch my eye. Nothing unusual in that, I hear you say, but then there is that *zing* in my head and a fine gossamer silken micropore thread of commonality – I've felt this before – becomes a reality, for I will recognise that girl anywhere. Lucy, for heaven's sake, last seen in gorgeous grey and heard producing the most exquisite sounds from a Steinway. It is The One, within vision. We are two hundred yards – metres if you like – apart, but she turns her head and looks straight across. *Zing!*

Then she is walking away with her friends as if nothing untoward has occurred. But we both know it has, I'm sure of it. I drive home, park the Morris up against the fence, open the door, close it behind me, enter the kitchen, put the kettle on, return to the sitting room and gaze at the Lucy Rie charger. I reach into the bowl, lift the pound note, smooth it between my fingers like a fine piece of silk and let it drift back down. Lucy is captive, in my bowl, but I cannot seek her, nor reach out for her.

∽

It is the last day of freedom for Lucy. Tomorrow she must report to the Hotel Manager. Her job description:- Hotel Management Trainee. Her duties: – initially she has to get to know and understand the significance of the role of every one of the two hundred people employed within the Hotel – as outlined in pages and pages of job specifications. Her head reels, her mind spins. But this is what she has said she will do.

Her parents have friends staying. She knows them, of course, and is polite, enjoys the conversation and the adulation. Everyone she knows has heard about the concert performance. She is embarrassed over the constant requests for appearances at this event, that concert, and the necessity to refuse each one, politely. She is also bemused by the school's reaction. The Head had sent for her and tried, in vain, to get her to change her mind and apply for a place at the Royal College of Music. For as she explained, she has already accepted a Traineeship with the Hotel Group and isn't about to switch horses.

Now she has another set of people to convince that she knows what she is doing. Myra, her mother's particular contemporary from years ago, is explaining the joy one gets from being a Concert pianist on tour. Lucy listens, but is unimpressed. She can play the piano at any time to sooth her own soul. She doesn't need to be paid for the privilege, nor does she wish to be beholden to another's idea of what to play, or when. As far as she is concerned, the Barn Hill concert was a one off, though there was one specific aspect that she is keeping very much to herself. That same weird knowledge of a connection with someone else, someone who must have been in the hall that night. The tenuosity of the feeling isn't at all frightening, indeed, it remains reassuring. The strength of the link has been inspirational, like a current flow over invisible wires that had energised her playing that night, so much so she couldn't believe she'd played like she had. And those words that came into her head, repeated, repeated, *you are lovely, you are lovely.*

After lunch, they will go and show her parent's friends the Hall. It is what they do, *de rigueur.* They take their friend's car, park and walk towards the entrance. Lucy is content, well fed from lunch, happy with her mother's especial friend's comments about her playing, happy that she will be at the start of her career on the following day. She walks towards the door and is hit, as though struck by a brief electric charge from a lightening strike or a foolish touch of bare wires.

A *zing.* She recognises the feeling immediately, and is at once briefly alarmed and then unexpectedly, pleasantly surprised. Mother has explained to her the feeling a girl is meant to have on those *special* occasions. Orgasmic. Is it like an *orgasm?* Never having – knowingly – encouraged her body to produce this symptom of emotion, she doesn't know, but what she is feeling is *special.* She looks around, sees nothing unusual, though there is an old car about to leave the staff car-park. Hasn't she seen it before somewhere? The feeling ebbs away and they enter the building. This is weird, sweet and lovely but weird.

The following morning she leaves home, dressed in her new two-piece costume in muted colours, with low-heeled sensible shoes and a very small amount of make-up. Her father kisses her; her mother embraces her. She takes twelve minutes to walk to the Hotel. The Manager welcomes her in his office. She notices his inspection, from shoes to hair; he does not intimidate her, nor does he seek to be overtly friendly. He takes her on a tour around and introduces her to each of the department heads; the head chef, the restaurant manager, the housekeeper, the concierge. He shows her a desk in the corner of the administration office that she can call her own, and gives her a document wallet with a dozen sheets of paper of photocopied instructions.

She is on her own. No longer a schoolgirl, but a young lady on the threshold of another phase of her life. Her training is about to begin. The memories of her virtual contact with an ethereal being yesterday – whoever, whatever, have been filed away. Today is today.

The days shorten, the evenings became velvet grey and a slight mist comes off the river to hang above the water meadows. Jones is jaded. The jazz of the summer days with Briony begins to pall, though their mutual ardour does not diminish. She is, after all, an intelligent woman and has a penchant for inventiveness. And it is not because he lacks either the energy or the will to parry her thrusts, nor she his, but it is the same house, the same room (well, rooms; as said, she is inventive) and he is beginning to feel that the horizons are closing in. Daphne has had her fill and there is another dog sniffing at her heels. He has not experienced any further revelations from virtual Lucy, despite the occasional dalliance with the pound note that lives in his Rie charger. Neither, and this surprises him, has he had any further inclination to trawl the antique world since last September – a year ago – but then, the bookshop is now his business, not his pastime. Samuel continues to educate and tolerate. The cat – did we say its name? No? A Persian Blue must have a suitable name. How about Nebuchadnezzar? Or *Chad* for short. (That's pronounced cad, like cat) well, whatever, it continues to alternately annoy and amuse Jones.

He also alternates between singular weekday domesticity in his terrace pad and the Edwardian Saturday thru' Sunday comfort and style of pad Briony. Pad Briony has its merits, sure, but when it comes to mental serenity, the pad terrace wins. It is a Friday evening. The mist has risen, the street has a Victorian feel which, had there been a gas mantled street lamp, would be pure Dickens. He unlocks the door, pushes the door mat straight with a foot, stoops to collect the single piece of mail (guess what, a bill from the power company) and wanders into the kitchen. What to cook? It is a Friday evening – and though he does not have a fixation about Fridays – if he had been with the other half, she would have prepared a fillet of sole with dainty chips and *petite pois*, to be served with a chilled Chablis. Always on the button with her wines. The fridge yields precious little inspiration. The new deli will be thronged with weekend shoppers and the cheapy Supermarket is anathema now he's been living *á deux* for so long. He pulls a face and makes a decision.

The George's rival establishment is surprisingly full to bursting; he spies Ex Briony through the lounge bar window and abruptly changes his mind. To struggle against such rabble tonight is not an enjoyable prospect. So the George it will have to be and hang the expense. Fleetingly, he thinks of giving Briony a ring and inviting her out to supper, or rather, in her company, to dinner. But then it would mean eventually escorting her back to her home and her bed and he is not in the mood. Down the hill a-way he goes, a little further from home.

The George exudes quality. Warmth, comfort, understated elegance. The dark grey suited lady with bobbed hair greets him. Dinner, yes, certainly, have you a reservation? No? and a marvellous gesture with her immaculate eyebrows suggests that it should have been nice but doesn't matter, they will squeeze him in somewhere. She passes him on to the *Maitre'D* and he is found an armchair not too far away from the blazing log fire in the lounge, given a huge menu and is asked if he would like a drink.

This is going to cost him money. The experience will be worth it, he decides, and his mind suggests a gin and bitter lemon. A young lad in waistcoat and bow tie is summoned, the order given and the *Maitre'D* glides away. Waiting, he surveys the area. Two business men avidly discuss a prospective deal, their papers sharing the table space with two glasses of red wine. A young couple hold hands in the dim corner. The group of five must be celebrating an event with hilarity and an overflow of assorted glasses. The restaurant beyond the trim plants – real – is subtly lit and about half full. No blaring musak. No loud voices. His drink arrives, on a tray, placed on a coaster, a square of paper serviette folded diagonally left alongside. Two thin slices of lemon, a few ice shapes, a decent sized glass.

Jones metamorphoses into an aristocrat. He leans back into the red moquette arm chair, sips his drink – not too much lemon – and pretends he is very familiar with his surroundings. The menu delivers and he mentally blesses Briony's good taste that gives him the edge. He chooses, beckons, the waiter take his order and moves away. Ten minutes and an empty *apéritif* glass later, his table is ready. There is one thing wrong. He is alone, and alone in being alone. That is unsatisfying. He works his way through the steak, cooked to unbelievable perfection, wonders about the artichokes, but is well fed. Offered the dessert menu, he chooses a lemon soufflé. Coffee, yes, and the very acceptable conventional mint is crisp and nutty. The experience has absorbed his evening to the full and, even after scrutinising the bill, he decides it was worth the exercise. Like travelling first class Pullman when second class still gets you there, but the feeling … ah, like Briony versus a.n.other. Silk versus cheap much washed cotton with weak elastic …

As he crosses the deep pile carpet towards the doorway he gets a strange sensation, a small tug at the back of his neck, akin to a twisted nerve, as though he'd raised an arm too suddenly or lifted a heavy pile of books sideways. He winces, raises a hand to rub the affected part. As he does so, in the corner of his eye, he sees the slim figure of a girl as she moves from the reception desk into the office behind. Instantly, instinctively, he knows. He stops, frozen, because his eyes cannot leave the space. She will reappear, and she will see him, and their eyes will meet and their thoughts will collide and she will know as he will know but they cannot acknowledge the meeting. He is captive in a warp and weft of his own manufacture and neither is she free to greet her destiny, not quite yet.

∝

I could not understand why, thinks Lucy. The same effect as I'd felt in the concert, making those small hairs on my forearms prickle and stand on end. Moving from the reception desk into the back office at a specific moment, not chosen, not planned, a mere matter of routine that required a check on the system, and as I walked away from the desk, a guest came out of the dining room to leave the hotel. The figure seemed comfortably familiar yet I'd not seen his face. I did my check and left the office to return to the desk (it was my night for reception duty). The guest was standing still, looking at me, and I could feel the tingles on my scalp, the shiver run down my spine as our eyes met. A moment when, as the saying is, time stood still. Then as his expression softened as if in sorrow, he walked through the doorway out into the dark.

I should kick myself, thinks Jones. A perfect opportunity to offer a greeting, a chance to break the spell, and I walked away from it. Why? Because I didn't know the girl and lone males do not make overtures towards pretty girls in hotel foyers unless they wish to appear predatory. Because I was taken off guard. Because I had an overwhelming feeling she didn't want contact at this time. Because – forgive me – I am Briony's man and hence no longer technically a virgin. This image of perfection had an aura about her that surely would demand purity, unsullied by such as I. So I walked away.

Back in my own home, I feel instinctively obliged to reach for the pound note and rub it through my fingers, to give warmth and take sense before carefully putting it back in the centre of the charger once more. Lucy. Lucy, the One. Our eyes had exchanged a look. The threads of awareness pulled briefly tight. Oh yes, the threads that tied me to her, virtual or real, would never break.

Lucy: I didn't feel at all concerned. It wasn't as though I'd been stalked, or accosted; no, nothing like that. Instead, a knowing, a realisation that perhaps something tied that young man to my ghost, my virtual being. Did he feel the same about me? As I twisted a pen in my fingers, staring at the old oil painting hanging on the staircase wall opposite the desk, I felt a warmth, as though I had a cosy woollen shawl placed around my shoulders; a comforting, pleasant warmth. Then it faded and I went to make myself a drink. Another hour before I could go off duty, return to the small room I was allowed to use whilst on evening shift. The hotel was very good that way. I didn't need to walk deserted streets at two in the morning.

Jones: So now I know where she works. Nice, that. Gives me a proprietorial feeling.

Five

Rallentando ... Slowing Down

Christmas looms. It is also anniversary time. Jones has been with Briony over a year, and Samuel's business partner for about the same period; now Cad the cat ignores him. The Lucy Rie charger with its single pound note has been on the terrace pad's sideboard for something like fifteen months, and the bargain sofa is finally paid for.

He bumps into Daphne in the pedestrianised main shopping area, outside the old theatre. She smiles sweetly at him and they stand close together. She slips an arm around and he feels uncomfortable; it's not as though he doesn't like her, but there's an unconscious need to maintain his independence. There's a look from those mysterious steel grey eyes in which he reads desire. What happened to the other new man in her life? She explains and he begins to feel sorry for her. He shakes his head, wondering how any man could walk away from this undemanding and appealing lady, then realises he is doing just that. Perhaps once more for old time's sake? He accepts her invitation to a supper sometime, offers a quick peck on her cheek and they separate. He'll call her, maybe.

It is Friday lunchtime; he was on his way to Hannah's, which is busy. Hannah's is opposite the large church of St Mary's that broods over this corner of the town. Occasionally he will slip inside and absorb the quiet and the timelessness that gives him a sense of peace and belonging, a contrast to the superficial attachments his spirit tolerates and even enjoys in a masochistic way.

At Hannah's, Briony is there, at 'their' corner table, in a lemon yellow cashmere jumper under an expensive brown leather jacket. The contemporary skirt is unusually short; he moves the chair to sit down and briefly glimpses a mounded triangle of white as, he believes, she purposefully adjusts her legs. She asks him where he has been and he tells her. Her eyes narrow and her lips purse into a straight line. It is obvious she isn't happy, and expects him to cancel the arrangement. Jones's newly acquired feeling for independence surfaces and a picture of the Rie charger focuses in. Briony, he says, suddenly reckless, I don't have to answer to you who I see and who I don't.

There is a silence, interrupted by the waitress. Briony orders a steak sandwich and a side salad. He decides on a small ploughmans. She recrosses her legs again, slowly, as if to remind – or tantalise – him, but her revealed underwear no longer tempts him in the same fashion as it would have done a year ago. She changes the subject, reminding him of the next Concert. The meals come, and they eat. He is still very aware of her and feels uncomfortable.

'I'll expect you for dinner tomorrow?' Her tone of voice suggests the question is rhetorical, for that has been their arrangement for months. Saturday night in, a sleepover, a lazy Sunday breakfast. Her proposition of nearly a year ago has never been mentioned again, presumably sublimated by his weekly presence. She stands and tugs her skirt down. Jones maintains his direction of gaze and she smoothes her thighs once more. She pays the bill, as normal, and they leave the bistro. As they part, they hold hands briefly and kiss, as normal, but Jones feels the tug of other unseen forces. This relationship is losing its power over him as different threads have imperceptibly begun to strengthen. He walks back to the shop for the last few hours of the day. Over a year ago, he had visited the old antique place and fallen for a sublime piece of a potter's – Lucy Rie's – art, and simultaneously seen a girl and fallen ... no, that would be too direct a word, too positive, and there was nothing mathematically positive in this connection. The connection has a tenuous feel to it, a subliminal effect, a nebulous dimension and yet, a strange dichotomy, also powerful. He'd felt this pull every time he'd seen her, now, what, three times?

⤜

Lucy is summoned by the Manager. As she makes her way through to his office, she has a flurry of thoughts.

I've been here three months, and I know I'm due for an appraisal. Now I've been round every department, he'll want me to say which one I prefer. He'll also cast an eye on my appearance, he's so very fussy over how his staff are presented it's as well I've had my hair cut and shaped. And mother checked my hemline this morning, thank goodness.

She knocks on his door. The 'Come in!' echoes.

The Manager is always very courteous, never presumes on their acquaintanceship and she appreciates his professionalism. She sits in front of the desk at his request, hands folded in her lap, her neat dark grey skirt smoothed down over her knees. Her feet are together; her low-heeled black shoes are well polished. Her tights are straight and have no runs. Her blouse is buttoned properly, freshly washed and her single thin sliver of a silver necklace has no worrying pendant. The jacket sits well over her shape.

He is equally well dressed, dark suit, white shirt, dark blue tie. He offers her a rare smile, pitches his hands and fingers as if in prayer. 'Lucy,' he says, informally, for mostly he calls her by her surname, 'I am pleased with your progress. The staff like you and the guests seem to appreciate the way you respond to their requests.'

She waits.

'We'd like you to take on a more responsible position, to see how you shape up.'

Her heart leaps. About to say 'thankyou,' she stays silent as the Manager goes on. He explains he cannot promote her within this Hotel for he has no vacancies, but he's discovered that a small independent hotel towards Oakham is looking for a deputy Assistant

42

Reception Manager to cover maternity leave. Would she consider taking this on for perhaps six months? She would be able to live in. And she would have a small increase in pay, plus a responsibility allowance. He would keep her on their books here, so take this as though she was on loan?

All this, after barely four months? Lucy is dumbstruck The Manager smiles. 'I think they have a very nice piano in the resident's lounge,' he adds, 'which I understand can be played for the guest's benefit from time to time.'

This she cannot believe. 'When do I start?' she asks, her voice carefully moderated to mask her enthusiasm.

'Perhaps a week next Monday?' the Manager suggests. 'I have to let them know – and obviously they would like to see you first.' He pitches his hands once more and offers her another smile. 'I shall be sad to see you leave us, Lucy, especially with Christmas coming. But of course you'll be able to return, though who knows when. I would personally like to think it will be before too long.'

She knows, or believes she does. There is ambition lurking within her soul, and though she does not wish him ill, she sees herself behind that desk. She stands and returns the warmth of his smile before she turns and leaves the office. A temporary Assistant Manager's position! Her father will be bucked. Her mother won't be as pleased, with her daughter living away from home. Lucy grimaces. She is sure she will receive another '*now you're growing up, perhaps I'd better explain a few more things …*' and then comes a strange thought. She'll be leaving the town where there is a connection. A strange, abstract, intriguing connection. She has an odd twinge of regret and wonders if the gossamer thread of this connection will stretch the eight miles or so and stay in place, or whether it will snap and she'll lose the tie which, she knows, has unconsciously kept her in control of her emotions, her *feminity* as her mother will no doubt call it when that conversation takes place. As take place it will. She walks back to the reception desk to resume her day, mind awhirl.

Later, she experiences a feeling of serenity, an almost religious peace. Has her shadow come near, she asks herself? She glances through the wide glass paned door, towards the deep navy blue of the street's dusk beyond. Has he passed by? With a small stab of unease, she questions her mind's suggestion that she positively needs to see this person in whom such power rests. The power to keep her on an even keel. The power to draw her thoughts into channels she never knew existed. It may be – dangerous?

And the largest query, is it a sexual attraction? Since she'd left school, or since that autumnal evening when the phenomena first appeared, she'd felt no pressure to clinically consider her move through puberty, or the end of her adolescence. Leaving school to assume her role in the world had been natural, a graceful transition. So unlike that of her peers – conversations she'd had with Marie and Julie at different times told her they'd both suffered from some rash probationary experimentation in relationships. For the absence of any urges in that direction, she owed her shadow grateful thanks, unaware of what chaos exists in his life at this specific time, or her part in that confusion.

I still have this uneasy feeling. It came on during the afternoon yesterday and I put it down to the way Briony and I parted after lunch. The persistent aggravation stayed throughout the evening so not even the telly's delights – what delights, do I hear you ask? – could abolish the ache. I slept badly, with wisps of an unconnected dream, an odd experience as mostly when I dream, it's pretty dramatic stuff and wakes me. This didn't, to leave me this morning with a sick empty-headed feeling. The day in the shop wasn't good either. Samuel snarled at me, Cad the cat scratched me – unusually – when I attempted to tickle its ears, and I gave the wrong change to one of our most regular customers. Not good at all. I was glad to get home to my tea and crumpets, but even they didn't eradicate this disquiet. She – Briony – will be expecting me, this night, to do my duty, to perform, to satisfy her demands – well, you know what I mean – and I do not feel up to it. A certain limpness or apathy that may not be eliminated even by a steak *au poivre* with mushrooms, baby onions, roast potatoes with a crispness only Briony can produce, and another bottle of *that* red wine. A fiver a pop, that wine, and it's good, damn good. This thought does actually make me feel better – I'm hungry after a typical Saturday no-proper-lunch day. I grin. Briony, dear woman, you're going to have exert all your feminine wiles tonight if we're going to get anywhere at all.

I luxuriate in a shower, a rare occurrence given how basic an arrangement of pipes pushed onto taps can be. (You'll remember I usually have a strip wash in front of the basin, athletically, and it's cheaper) I dress informally, as ever, but put on an old Cambridge college rugger shirt, (it is clean and not at all ragged). It is to remind her – and me – of where I came from. And, for once, I take the car for moral support. Usually I walk, not only for the exercise but also to ensure there's no give-away sitting on her driveway overnight. Maybe everyone knows, but it's what we do, act discreet, even after a year.

She is surprised. 'Why the old banger?' she asks, opening the door wide as I step across the threshold and take her in my arms, pushing the door to with a deft rearward push of a foot. 'I thought …' is all she manages before her lips are sealed.

We emigrate to the lounge in an ungainly and still attached manner and collapse onto the ever-so-soft large settee. Despite my earlier concerns, the essential component rises to the occasion and she whimpers at the appropriate moment. Back to normality then?

An hour later, we eat, and it's well up to standard. The food, I mean; but I suppose it's all other things as well. After the second glass of wine, I become reckless and start to explain I've got these feelings … *Lucy, my love, please help, this is me.*

Her eyes grow large. She thinks – or so I think she thinks – that I'm going to agree to matrimony now we've reached a one-year's anniversary. Not so.

Inexplicable feelings, as though I've seen a ghost, deep inside. There's a tug, a pull, an intangible concern. And the vision reappears … that's what it was! My wistful dream was of her, The One, seen and not seen.

I get up, walk around the room. 'Briony,' I say, 'I don't know how to explain this, but I've seen this other girl …,' and I can see her face muscles tighten … 'who I don't know but I do, if you see what I mean.'

Now she's not a happy lady. I stop and lean against the doorjamb. 'I've not even spoken to her. I don't know who she is, other than she works at the George.'

'Huh, a child,' Briony says, shrugging her shoulders. 'Jones, you're not making sense.' She gets up and comes across to me, her head on one side and her hands reaching for mine. 'Let's go to bed.'

It is getting on for eleven, so hers is a reasonable suggestion, seeing as I haven't a clue what else to say. My virtual companion will, to preserve her virtue, have to turn a blind eye to the next hour or so. And if she wants to communicate, I hope she's got a better idea than wispy dreams.

෧

Some time after midnight, with a sleepily purring Briony beside him, Jones experiences the tug again; as though someone has slipped inside his skull and wants to get out. *Stupid explanation, but what else?* He eases away from her, lies on his back, hands behind his head, and contemplates the ceiling, vaguely discernible from a combination of streetlights and the moon. Why this stupid hallucinogenic nonsense? She's only a girl who's crossed his path a few times, and as he told Briony, he's not even spoken to her, *but he can't get her out of his head.* She's there now, tapping away at him and he can feel her concern. She's going away. She may not see him again. She says he is the only one to make sure she stays in control of who she is, what she is, where she is going. Please, *please, please don't forget me … .*

In the morning, when he wakes up, he cannot recall any of the worries or the odd thoughts of the previous night because he ultimately slept very well and arises with a smile and another cuddle for the lovely bundle of fun alongside. She's happy again, and again …

෧

Lucy is happy too. It is Sunday. Her father is taking her to see the manager of this hotel where she's going to do a *real* job. It is three weeks before Christmas and the day is cold and chilling but she doesn't care. She'll be answering the phones and talking to potential guests; she'll be meeting the new guests as they arrive and dealing with all their queries. She'll be the face the guests remember and the person in whom they'll confide. The thought that she may also be directly in line of fire for disgruntled customers to snipe at doesn't enter her head.

The hotel is an old stone building which may have been a large farmhouse years ago. Lovely old barns nicely converted into simple bedrooms, a pleasant garden she can imagine as a gorgeous place in which to sit during the summer, three pleasant dining rooms, a cosy lounge with a proper log fire and yes, a piano. Not the grand she'd had in her mind, but a piano none the less. The Manager's name is Sam, which is what she is to call him, so he said as he guides her and her father around. Lucy sees her father frown; he prefers good old-fashioned polite correctness.

She talks of being both happy and sad. Happy in the prospects of the new job and the compactness of the buildings, far different from the rambling ancient warren of corridors and staircases of the George; sad she'll be leaving all the friends she'd made. And unsure – though this she does not communicate to her father – about leaving her virtual friend too, despite the fact that she'd sent him – and how school girlish was that – telepathic messages to try and explain. Sometimes she felt a contact; sometimes she felt a solid rebuff, an unyielding black rubber like mass against which her little arrows of thought bounced. But if these actions kept her in control, then it couldn't be anything other but good. Strangely childish maybe, but in another odd way also extremely adult.

She smiles, a trifle wistfully, and tells her father she loves him. Her father takes it all in, studying her earnest face across the pristine white damask. There's something else in his daughter's mind too, for he can read her well. He asks, but she shakes her pretty head and makes her hair bounce and he thinks he's the luckiest father out to have such a unique daughter.

Jones has gone home in his car. It is Sunday and his day for doing not a lot. Briony attempted to keep him, to persuade him to go with her to some literary luncheon party *-it's your thing, isn't it, and we'd be ever so welcome* – but somehow it didn't fill him with the delight she obviously sought. So a disappointed and ever so slightly cross woman shut the door behind him with more force than was necessary. Now he is cogitating on their future as he strips off and has yet another shower under the crude arrangement of rubber pipes and a hook on the bathroom wall above the bath. He can still sense her scent as he scrubs. It is mid-morning. He'd had a decent breakfast; he'll give her that, so lunch is not high on his agenda. Towelled down, he collapses on his bed to catch five minutes.

She is a strange girl, his Lucy Rie virtuality She's tried to project her thoughts his way, he's sure of it, but they aren't connecting. Maybe it's because of Briony. He could never marry her – Briony, that is. He shouldn't be carrying on with her either, not in the way he is. For one thing, it's making him feel used, for another it has risks despite precautions – hers – and he has no intention of being lured into a marriage with a scheming potentially pregnant woman, even if she could conceive whilst approaching thirty-five. So ...

He wakes up with a much clearer head and far less muscularly stressed. He rolls off the bed, puts on a warm shirt and familiar cords, finds another old sweater and goes out to the car. A run out into the country, maybe a pint or two in a quiet pub. It might do him good. He's no idea of precisely which direction to take but has no worries. He has a good sense of direction to aid his return.

The old Morris will welcome a decent run out. It's been ages since he went for a spin merely for the hell of it, and though it is a jolly cold day, it is clear, and dry, and he might not get another chance for a while if the winter sets in.

Out of town, past old Chas's place – it's been some time since he'd heard from him and idly wonders if he is still in business. The doors are shut and the blinds down. Maybe he'll call in after shop hours one day soon and see what's up with the old codger. Coming to the road fork he hesitates. Right goes north, left westwards – and where the sun was edging three hours down towards the horizon. Maybe he should have started earlier. Will he make a pub before they shut? It is Sunday after all. Left then.

No other traffic. Quiet roads. Something he likes. After twenty minutes he sees an old stone farmhouse style complex on his right. There's a signboard on the neat lawn edge. An hotel – a small one, a gravelled car park beyond a layout of shrubs. That'll do. He pulls in and parks up alongside a shiny dark green Singer, a car he'd love to own. And senses something, a prickling sensation in the back of his neck, down between his shoulder blades. He shivers as he climbs out of the Morris. What is it? A winter chill or a premonition?

He glances at his watch. Half past one. Maybe a sandwich to go with a decent pint – there may even be someone he can talk to. Perhaps – more than perhaps – there'll be a log fire to sit by. An inner smile as he thinks about Briony with her educated and gossipy but critical luncheon group and is glad he's not involved. The bar must be round the corner. As he pushes open the door to see the polished wood counter and the gleaming racks of bottles at the end of the room, he senses he's being watched. He turns his head towards what must be the dining area. And is shocked into a state of confusion, for *she's there*. The One. Sitting with an older man, perhaps her father, and she looks up. Their eyes meet, clash, then she turns her head away and says something to her companion. He's smiling at her, they are getting up, she is smoothing out her skirt, brushing her hair back, and Jones feels something of a power catch at his soul. The intensity of her presence radiates out, as though the waves of her being rise in a swell towards him, a virtual force that can take away his self-possession; that could knock him off his feet.

They pass within two yards of him, he catches her smile despite that he is transfixed and cannot say a single word or move a muscle to respond. Then she is gone and he hears a car crunch gravel as it departs. A dark green Singer moves across his confused vision and leaves him bereft.

Now Lucy is in a trance. Her father glances at her once the Singer is in top gear and travelling smoothly back towards the town. There is no other traffic within view. She says nothing, stares at the vista of the open road. 'What's the matter, Lucy?' he says, 'you look as though you've either seen a ghost or you're deep in thought? Isn't this the job you wanted?'

She blinks, gives a small shake of her head; offers him a lovely smile. 'Both, I think. Did you notice him?' she asks diffidently, unsure whether to absorb her father into her mystery world.

'Who? The young man by the bar in the lounge?' There was no one else he could think of who might have attracted his daughter's attention and ponders over this extended reaction.

She nods, now even more unsure about the way this conversation might go, and wishing she had kept him, this realisation of her private dimension, secret in her thoughts, her warm and possessive thoughts.

Her father is more perceptive than she gives credit, for she did not mention the position on offer for which she had come, but the young man. The one with a casual attitude to dress who had correctly, in his brief proximity, offered no more of an acknowledgement of their presence than was socially acceptable, a small smile, a slight nod; he had pleasant features, intelligent eyes. Polished shoes and a clean appearance despite his dress. What young girl would not have measured his potential? His Lucy certainly has done. His Lucy is into her twentieth year. His Lucy is, in his view, an extremely personable and pretty young lady. What young male would not have considered her attributes? He does however privately acknowledge that his own streak of paternal guardianship also contains a vein of jealousy.

Lucy is surprised by his chuckle and her smooth forehead wrinkles, not unsurprisingly nor unprettily. 'Father?' her voice comes over with a questioning tone.

He grins at her. 'You are of an age when any personable young man might deserve your attention, my young lady daughter. Please remember whose daughter you are, and I consider you as a very precious person who must take extreme care over the choice of suitable male companions.' They are approaching the outskirts of the town and he has to concentrate. 'Please talk to me or your mother if you have any, ahem, *inclinations.'*

'Oh yes I will, father, I will, ' and she lapses into a comfortable silence, able now to wrap up her thoughts and knowledge of this meeting – *this ordained meeting* – into another small cosy package in her brain and keep it safe.

∽

I get my pint and a very decent ham and pickle sandwich. I need this pint. Ensconced in a comfortably firm leather armchair within sight of where my vision and her father had obviously had lunch, I bring my thoughts under control. Why had she been here, why had I chosen to stop here; why, again, have I come under the same powerful spell that leaves me mentally stranded without a sane explanation? Have I given an impression, any impression, to either her or her father, which may have left a dent in their minds? And do I care? Another pint, I think, while I consider.

⋙

Briony is experiencing a plethora of mixed emotions. She has just put the phone down on two – no, three, decisions. It is now time for a revitalising cup of tea and a slice of Battenberg. She loves Battenberg, unsure whether it is the cross-matched colours or the almond marzipan that attracts her, but she buys at least one a week from the only decent confectioners in town. Jones even laughs over her addiction, preferring his choice of her own home-baked fruit loaf. He say the pink and yellow is far too *frou-frou* for him, reminding him of little girls' frilly dresses. What does he know about such things? She has never worn a *frilly* petticoat, let alone a pink – or yellow – one.

The tea will be nicely brewed by now. She carries the tray through from the kitchen to the lounge and puts it down on the small Queen Anne table, the one with the slender legs. Her bone china teacup reflects her style, plain but with a decorated edge, a fine gold rim. Wedgwood, of course. The teapot, sugar bowl and cream jug are from the same pattern. Her two slices of cake are on a seven inch plate; she uses a small silver teaspoon and stirs one small spoonful of sugar into the clear amber of her Earl Grey and then adds a touch of milk. Jones prefers Assam, which is not unsurprising after years at University (though college tea parties can be fairly serious occasions, she seems to remember from her days at Girton).

Sitting on the small two-seater settee, she pulls elegant legs up under her and contemplates the wintry monochrome garden seen through the conservatory and its array of over-wintering shrubs. She has had some good times here and sighs at the thought. Ever a pragmatic lady, she has finally reached the point of action although very aware it will leave certain parts of her far less satisfied. Jones has been good to her and she will miss all of that. She will try to persuade him to keep in touch, to keep her informed of his progress and his future plans. He will have an interesting life, of that she is sure.

The cake disintegrates after her first bite and sheds a cascade of large pink and yellow crumbs down her pale lemon cashmere and onto the folds of the Harris Tweed brown check skirt. Delicately picking up each morsel and transferring it back to her mouth is an act of controlled precision that has no impact on her patience.

Will he call this evening? She wills him to come; a strong mentally induced telepathic urge to come and offer her comfort – and solace. Then she will tell him.

Six

Interlude ... Between

I am shocked. Or still in a state of disbelief, to be more accurate. It is Monday morning and I am still far too attached to this dilemma. You will, of course, have guessed that I spent Saturday night and all day Sunday with her because I had this psychological feeling I ought to, and I'm becoming rather susceptible to cerebral urges. I eventually tore myself away from her comforting wrap-around needfulness early this morning while it was still very dark and very, very cold. The contrast is just too awful a state and I am tempted to succumb. She wants me to succumb, that I know. I want me to succumb too as I peel off a cold-dampened sweater and click the switch down on the one-bar electric fire, but there are other forces at work telling me not to give way. However, this dual standard life ain't doing my Jones one bit of good. This alternation between hedonistic bliss and monastic sparsity might be akin to jumping into a snow edged Scandinavian ice pool after two hours in a sauna – not that I've ever experienced such an activity, it's only something I've read about.

Perhaps I should ask her to beat me about the back and buttocks with birch twigs in the garden after half-an-hour in her shower. Would it encourage an elevation or a diminution of an essential part? Damn. The thought is providing far too much stimulus.

The phone begins to ring. I look at the clock; it's a smidgeon after eight. It can only be Briony, looking for answers.

But it isn't. It's Samuel. A croaky, hoarse voiced Samuel. This is *not* good.

'I'm ill, boy,' he says. 'Get yourself up here,' and rings off.

Boy? He's never called me 'boy' before. With all other thoughts now sublimated, I struggle into my work-a-day cords – aping Samuel's dress code but in a different flavour – and don the Briony sweater previously worn to remind me of her constantly – or her constancy – during the day. I forget to switch the heater off (which means at least I come back to a warm room later) and head off down the hill towards the shop, swathed in scarf, duffle jacket and the peaked cord cap *she* insisted I wore.

He's right. He *is* ill. Last seen on Friday afternoon, he'd have manned the fort on Saturday but as we shut on Sundays in winter with far too spartan a customer flow to warrant any opening, he manages to tell me he stayed in bed all day with Cad the cat to keep him warm. (Do not try to visualise) He croaks, he shivers, he looks grey and won't eat his Shredded Wheat. I send him back to his second floor eyrie and telephone his sister Doreen, something he will *not* be happy about, but needs must.

❧

The next episode isn't something I enjoy writing about, but essential for continuity. I'll be brief. Doreen came that Monday afternoon and phoned the doctor. The doctor came at six o'clock and sent for an ambulance. The ambulance came and took him to the Hospital on the eastern edge of the town and during the night he took a turn for the worse and died in the early hours of the following morning. Pneumonia, you know, the old man's friend. Huh, some friend. Seems he'd had a 'shadow on the lung' for ages – well, I know he coughed a bit but ...

Doreen doesn't actually blame me openly, but it is obvious what she has on her mind. I can't tell you what's on my mind. The funeral is to take place in the middle of next week, just before Christmas. Some Christmas.

᷍

Lucy sees the report in the local paper and comments to her mother over the breakfast table. She is taking two days holiday before she starts in the new job. 'The old man who owns that wonderful old bookshop by the bridge? It seems he's died. What'll happen to it? Be a shame if it closes.'

Her mother is immersed in a copy of 'The Musician' magazine. 'Eh, what? Oh, yes. Old Samuel. But he's got a nice young assistant in there. Good looking young man. Very pleasant, found me a copy of a poetry book I'd wanted for ages. Now what are you going to do today, Lucy? Want to come shopping with me?'

Something she's never really enjoyed, as most of the shopping expeditions in the past have been for uniform and other school things, but this may be as good an opportunity as any to spend some of her salary on proper clothes. She really must get a Christmas present for her father too; her mother's was easy – another Garden Token, boring, but from past experience, appreciated. She agrees and a while later they walk into town, arm in arm.

᷍

Jones is living on automatic pilot and is very down. Somehow the cold and miserable weather suits his mood and he does not notice. Briony has tried to talk to him on the phone, but he cannot summon sufficient – any – enthusiasm for her wiles. He's all fucked out, he tells himself, crudely, and that evening resorts to propping up the bar at the Bull and Swan. Not a good idea as he only spends money and gains a headache.

He opens the shop the following mid-morning, promises himself to close again at three. A procession of regulars pop in with lugubrious faces and hollow voices to utter words of sadness, which do him no good at all. He begins to feel ill himself. Doreen

55

has decided to temporarily move into Samuel's quarters in order to 'keep an eye on things' and the cat is evicted. Jones has to rescue it from the street, very tentatively, but no, Cad, with an instinct that rivals Jones's own links with telepathic females, begins to purr.

Stroking pussies to create a purring sensation are not entirely unknown in Jones's immediate past and the phenomena results in him taking Cad home with him. Doreen yells at him as he leaves the shop. Something about 'on your head' he thinks she's said but her voice is so high pitched it is drowned out by noise from a passing truck.

The day after he goes in that little bit earlier. Doreen has gone out – she won't have anything to do with the books so he's quite safe on that score. By an hour before midday he has regained some of his bounce as he manages to sell a rare copy of Charles Darwin's Evolution. Samuel would have been proud of him; he tells himself, so makes a decent cup of coffee as a reward. He is sitting in the old chair, sipping coffee and contemplating fate when his rare instinct gives him a nudge. He carefully puts the coffee mug down on the floor and stands up just as the door opens with its accustomed double mechanical 'ping' from the spring-loaded bell and two women walk in. With the brighter light of the street behind, it is never normally possible to see faces with clarity until actually into the depths, but this is not normality.

Lucy and her mother have come to pay their respects.

He is talking to her. The One. Lucy, the One. And they behave perfectly, as two people should, even if their eyes are cognisant of who is within vision and their subliminal minds are telling them their souls are intertwined. Lucy's mother has introduced her daughter to the nice man who managed to obtain her book for her and offers their condolences. Jones has acknowledged her politely and exchanges his very first words with his reverie. So now they are on a social footing and need not be shy of each other's power to attract. She can say to him 'Didn't I see you at the Barnsdale Lodge Hotel the other day?' and he can nod and smile and say 'Yes, weren't you with your father?' so now she can turn to her mother and explain to her, 'We've sort of met before,' and be accurate but not so accurate, for they have been aware of themselves several times before but did not know *how* aware.

Their conversation expands and lengthens. Lucy's mother has all the naturally inherent protective instincts allied to her maternity. She also has another instinct and calls upon it. 'Lucy,' she says, holding her gaze on Jones, 'Shall we invite this nice young man to tea? Perhaps he'd like to hear you play.'

Jones's mind wakes up. And Lucy's mind is saying 'yes'; he can sense the vibrations let alone read nice thoughts into her coy smile. So miraculously it is arranged and they leave; Jones waits for them to move out of earshot before he vents his understandably boyish enthusiasm in strange whoops of immature joy. The gloom occasioned by Briony's revelations has vanished; only after the boiling up emotions fall back to a gentle simmer does the prospect of his future bring down the clouds once more.

Doreen returns. The clouds are on her face. Jones folds his arms and leans back on the more substantial end of the historical section shelves. She squares up to him and his judgement of her mood is accurate. Thunderclouds are fact. She has been to the solicitor and been read the Will. The solicitor's exposition has apparently been clarity itself. She inherits the property. She does not inherit the business, which leases the premises from the owner. Samuel, and the solicitor's words were translated to him via Doreen, had 'nouse', by which she meant (and said in a disparaging voice) that he was a 'clever dick'. There was a clause that denied the owner the right to impose rent increases above inflation and the determination of the tenancy could only be occasioned by a grant of planning permission to develop the site. And as the premises were 'listed', fat chance.

'So who picks up Samuel's share of the business?' Jones asks, having fully expected Doreen to admit it would be hers. Not so. She spits the words at him, a syllable at a spit. 'You,' spit, 'do,' spit. Then she turns her back on him and goes. He hears footsteps clumping up the stairs, listens for the thunder roll of the door slam and is not disappointed.

'Ah,' he says, out loud. 'Samuel, dear man. I'll miss you, I really will. *Requiescat in pace.*'

And what on earth am I going to do now? I never set out to become a bookseller, let alone own the ruddy place. Doreen ain't going to take this lying down, I know. Will she attempt to live here, out of sheer spite? Probably not. She may even decide to let me rent the upstairs from her – or let it to someone I'll hate to have above me. I'd best get home. There's a generous cat to feed.

❦

The specified date and time for his visit to Lucy's for tea is today, at four thirty. No one is going to begrudge him the early closing for most locals are aware of the circumstances and it is not the season nor the weather for idle inquisitive tourists. Doreen comes and goes, coming empty handed and going with a clumpy heavy bag in each hand. Jones idly wonders what on earth Samuel managed to stash up in his loft that Doreen needs to take away, but his depth of curiosity does not extend to actually asking a question. It is not his business. Trade is poor, as is expected and allowed for at this time of year. So he closes and locks the shop access to the street – Doreen has her own key but there is a rear doorway she can use more discreetly. He walks back to his terrace pad, watching the lights come on as dusk deepens into a chill December night and in crossing the river bridge sees the mist rising and flowing over the silent dank meadows.

Cad the cat miaows and rubs up against trouser legs, as though he has always been best friends with him. How fickle can one cat be? The Rie charger sits there, remaining in pride of place with the currency note still present. Jones lifts it out, smoothes it between his palms to warm it, touches it to his lips. 'Lucy,' he says aloud. 'Lucy, Lucy, Lucy.' And neither Daphne nor Briony enter his thoughts, for *she* is filling his mind with her smile and her lithe shape and her bouncing hair and the slender fingers that can tease magic out of ivory piano keys.

He risks the Heath Robinson shower. Then dresses carefully in his comfortable cords and the cream Viyella shirt, no tie, but a decent

58

vee-neck pullover under the tweed jacket. His shoes are always polished, a trait inherited from his father who once was in the Army. He looks at the reflection in the mirror with its small corner crack, pats his hair flat over his right ear, grins and looks for his mac. It may not get wet but it will surely come colder and there is no telling how late he'll be.

It is a fifteen minute walk. Though he had no idea where his vision lived before now, he does recognise the address. As he walks his mind is floating; there is no anchor for his thoughts because the actions of meeting this young potent lady are as tenuous and potentially imagined now as they were over the year ago. To have their minds forge the lasting link, for it to survive his descent into and ascent from carnality, surely is an indication of the power within. Has he sought this being? Has he demanded her allegiance? Has she clung to him for herself or for what they are? His footsteps echo on hard paving in empty streets. The mist has thickened to bring down the visible distances to less than three lamp-posts length. He feels the fine damp drift across his cheeks. It will be dark within the hour.

At the entrance to the paved driveway he pauses. The house is large but not forbidding. The lights are on below the porch and above the door; there is a step onto the encaustic tiled area before the panelled and studded oak door and he recognises the replication of Lutyens style. The bell push is white in its polished brass circle. Footsteps.

Lucy is not nervous, nor apprehensive. In her position at the Hotel she has been exposed to many different and strange people and their eccentricities for four months and has become an able adult in her specific world. And Jones, yes, she now knows his name, has been – virtually – with her for an awful lot longer. She can connect him with the shadow at the end of the school lane, with the thought projection in the concert hall, with the presence as a dinner guest in the George, during the visit to Burghley with their family friends and last week, at her new Hotel. Each time a little closer, each time a tug, a pull and a link. Closer and closer, and with her mother they unknowingly enter his world, the world of the bookshop, to move into conversation and a clash – no, not a clash, a connection – of eyes, that most direct link from the world to the brain. And her brain is humming. She is washed, dressed and inspected. Her mother is fussing. Her father, home early by request, is faintly amused. It is a quarter past four. The kettle is on the stove, the cups laid out, the sandwiches and the cakes arranged on the two-tier cake stand and all is ready.

'Mother,' asks Lucy, 'what ever made you suggest inviting your 'nice young man' to tea?'

'Lucy,' her mother replies with eyebrows slightly raised and a vaguely supercilious tone, 'don't you *want* to meet a nice young man? Your father and I would very much like you to. Provided he is suitable, of course,' she adds.

'And *he* is?' She feels a giggle emerging and suppresses it. Her mother won't know anything about the feelings she's had for over a year for *'this nice young man'*, ever since that afternoon, walking back from school. And that had been so *weird*, because she'd kept her friends back for half an hour later than usual while she searched for – and found – a stray book. The book was beside her bed even now. *'Tales from the Paranormal'*. Weird – 'cos otherwise maybe it wouldn't have happened.

Her father adds his comment. 'If your mother chose to put on this spread, Lucy, then he must be. And working in a bookshop, well, what better? Especially if he stands a chance of inheriting some goodwill from dear old Samuel's sad demise.' Now he is poking fun at them both, which she can see from the smile on his face.

'*Dad!*' she exclaims, as they hear footsteps on the path and the peel of the bell.

Jones sees. Sees his *alter ego*. Sees in the figure of this elegant and smiling young lady someone with whom he feels sublimely comfortable, as though she is a beloved sister, someone with whom he has grown up and adored since time began. There is no need of a voiced greeting – she is holding the door open and he steps inside. Through the unfathomable iris pools of brown he can reach into her soul, and she into his. She closes the door behind them; she takes his hand and leads him onward, along the click clack of the tiled hall and into the softness and welcoming depths of the sitting room, the front parlour of ten decades ago.

He sees Lucy's mother in a crinoline, hair bunched up high, strings of pearls at her pale neck, gloved hand held out for him to take, bow over and offer dry lips. He sees her father, cut away jacket with tails, smooth trousered to spats over high gloss shoes, stiff pointed collar, a silk neck tie. He sees an aspidistra, ornaments on every surface, the dark gloss grand piano, pictures on red damask walls and thick hanging drapes over windows with coloured art deco lights.

Then Lucy's mother speaks and the imagery of the world whirls away into pale grey-blue walls, deep cream carpet, luxuriously cushioned settees and she is wearing a dress, beautiful grey wool to her ankles, a gold chain around the pale neck. The piano is still there.

'You're very kind,' he hears himself say, with her daughter standing close behind him; he can feel her warmth though she is more than a foot away.

A handshake, a firm handshake, from her father. 'You were at the Barnsdale,' he is told. 'Well, it is nice to see you on home ground. I believe you worked for Samuel. Very sad, very sad.' Jones feels the scrutiny, a dissection of his demeanour. 'Been there long?'

Polite exchange of pleasantries sets them into easier interaction; he is asked to sit and chooses the settee. Lucy sits alongside and the material of her dress's skirt falls softly against his leg. 'I'll fetch the tea,' her mother says; her father follows her out of the room, which leaves them alone.

Lucy giggles. Their faces turn towards each other, he takes her hand, pliant and gentle, brings it to his lips. 'Lucy,' he says in familiar fashion, 'how is this?'

She shakes her head. 'I don't know. But I knew this would happen. For ages.'

Their eyes lock together again, as fingers have, intertwined, now she has his captive, resting on her thigh. They both know. There is a rattle of teacups, the door is opened, a trolley is pushed into the room. Lucy does not withdraw her hand but he feels so obliged, for convention's sake.

Her mother is bright, her conversation well chosen, arrowed at his past, Lucy's future; her father's is mellowed and subtle, prising carefully at the intricate detail. The sandwiches are excellent. The tea is also excellent and he says so.

Lucy's mother smiles, a face so beautiful with the dimpled cheeks. He sees Lucy ten, twenty years older in time and is enheartened. 'A blend,' she explains, 'we have it made up for us. Such a nice town for provisions, don't you think? Do you cook?'

He has already explained how he lives on his own, has always looked after himself, experienced after years in college, and so is this is not a rhetorical question? But he expands on his prowess, carefully in order not to appear boastful.

'Ah,' says Lucy's father, 'then you have an advantage. I'm hopeless in the kitchen. Let the women do their job, I say. Have a cake,' and he lifts the two-tiered stand to move it closer.

'Try the lemon cup cake,' suggests Lucy, reaching past him and helping herself to an almond slice. Her forearm has a delicate sheen of fine golden-brown hair and he notices two little brown spots – fairy foot-steps as his mother used to call them. Charming.

Conversation falters. Jones wonders whether he should politely suggest he ought to go, though is very reluctant to do so. Lucy has him in her thrall; he would wish to shrink her, wrap her up, put her in his pocket and take her home, to let her sit on the mantlepiece with her hands under her bottom, to smile and swing her legs. She wouldn't look right if he placed her in the Rie charger. Dreams.

'Right.' He jumps at the word; Lucy's mother puts her cup down, the fluted Spode cup with the fleur-de-lys pattern in gold. 'It's time for Lucy to show off,' she says, moving over to the baby grand and lifting the lid with a practiced and accomplished action.

Lucy obeys her mother's command, rises, the fabric of her dress falls into place. She looks back at him with a smile. 'You've heard me before, I think,' the nearest to an acknowledgment; an acceptance of his telepathically expressed feelings on her performance at the Barn Hill concert. He nods and nestles into the cushions as Lucy settles onto the piano stool. Her father also leans back on his chair and crosses his legs. Lucy's mother is standing alongside her daughter, ready to turn the pages of the music Lucy now places on the rest.

The first notes drop like fine dew onto early morning grass, to produce the goose-pimpled frisson of sheer magic. He cannot close his eyes but he would if *she* wasn't playing. Music has that effect on him; why he goes to concerts, how he had met … and the vision of a perfect naked woman's body hovered. Another dimension of the past.

So exquisite. 'What do you think? Poulenc. He's so different.' His eyes snap open. So he did close them? She's turned on her stool; holds his look. 'Mother thinks I should turn professional. Follow in her footsteps. Shall I play something else?' and she flips over the sheets on the rest. 'How about this?'

Again the music cascades, trills and dances, draws out his emotions and he finds his eyes moistening. This girl is so infinitely precious in all the ways which match his best instincts, she is – has always been – the missing fragment of his being. Until that day he was not complete. Now, he is. Like the vessel on the potter's wheel, spun, drawn up, moulded, fined to an edge; she has cut him from his base and lifted him with tender and gentle hands and placed him on the kiln bed to be fired and irrevocably changed to contain her soul, her being, her life. Lucy.

There is silence after the last chord, the last note. The echoes drift.

'Bravo!' Her father breaks, shatters, the silence. Her mother frowns, then smiles. 'Well?' she asks, as Lucy replaces the sheet music back into order, spins round and sits there, hands beneath her. It is as though she expects him to clap.

Jones marshals his thoughts. 'I'm honoured,' he says, and wonders how to express himself without seeming patronising. 'Wish I could play like that,' is all he manages.

'Do you play at all?'

He shakes his head. 'Once, when I was maybe twelve, thirteen. Never stuck at it, I'm afraid. I love going to concerts though. Especially piano. You were very good, Lucy, that evening at Barn Hill. But tonight, so beautiful. I think your mother's right. Shame not to share your talent.'

Lucy's mother beams at him. 'Well said! I wish I could persuade her. And to think she'll bury herself in some stuffy hotel!'

The girl rises, her expression non-committal. 'I like working in a hotel. I meet all sorts of interesting people and I get paid regularly.'

Jones senses the conversation may become contentious. It is time he went, however reluctantly. 'I must go. This has been a true pleasure, Mrs ...' and he hesitates. He does not yet know their surname. Lucy's mother does not respond to the hint.

'If you're sure. It has been our pleasure too. Perhaps you'll come again when Lucy has learnt another piece, then you can offer us your thoughts?'

'That would be a real privilege. You've very kind.'

'Not at all,' says Lucy's father, and gets to his feet. 'We don't have much opportunity to entertain intelligent young people like yourself,' as his grin lessens any chance of a stiff reply. 'Shall I show you out?'

Lucy shook her head. 'No, father, I'll go.' She leads the way, closing the sitting room door behind them. '*Parents!*' she hisses. 'So stuffy,' and treats him to a full blown grin. 'Mother can be a bit like that, and father, well, he's one of the old school. Glad you came in a jacket even if you didn't wear a tie.' She opens the inner of the two porch doors. She is close, very close, and her eyes are dancing. 'Glad you came? Hope you appreciated Poulenc. He can be a little clunky at times. I've just added him to the repertoire.'

For two pins he'd catch her round the waist and kiss her. Would she accept his salutation or back away? 'Of course I'm glad I came.' They stand eighteen inches apart, conscious of the power that holds them together yet apart. Magnetic forces.

'Then give me a kiss.' She holds her head up and closes her eyes. He obeys, not holding her as he would wish to, though in closing her pursed lips with his, the shock of her mouth against his fuses them together.

Abruptly she steps back. 'Now go, Jones. Keep me close.'

The front door closes behind him and the houses vanishes into the black darkness of the December night. Lucy is to be kept close. Always. It is what they both want.

... I will not let thee go...

St. Martins

Seven

Diminuendo ... Diminishing

Reality comes hard. Jones is held in a dichotomy. For over a year he has been a consensual occupant of a sensual woman's bed for an average of a night every week, but now Briony is leaving, at least for a while and he'll miss her. He has also provided another lady with a missing part of her required experiences for a short period. Poor Daphne, he feels sorry for her. But now he is deeply and irreversibly committed to another person, a female with an entirely different claim on his affections, who would, he feels sure, laugh at his misdemeanours at the same time as she would chastise him for being easily led astray. If he tells her, that is. The threads that bind them together would be tried and tested if he did, though they would not break.

He goes home. And the hole in his soul hasn't grown any larger; in fact it has shrunk. In prospect, he can face tomorrow with equanimity.

And tomorrow? The departure of two of his immediate circle, to whom he owes much; from the one came an expansion of his social horizons, from the other an unsought hence entirely unexpected immense boost to his fortunes.

Lucy continues to hold him in her thraldom and for that he must be ever grateful towards an inanimate object, the charger, a beautiful conception from the loving hands of a potter, once malleable clay, now vitrified into immortality. Unless ... the thought of any disaster, any breakage – indeed, that would truly herald an endless suspended sentence. Only the permanent and irrevocable possession in full reality of its conceived virtual occupant could ever replace the charger should the worst come to pass.

⤺

I can't believe it. Coincidentally, and after so long, a woman decides to walk into the shop and offer condolences, together with her daughter, and her daughter is The One, my virtual reality, oh, my Lucy. The zing of her presence. Yet we manage to behave ordinarily, without the flicker of a muscle, she and I. She and I. How the spirit lifts in the pronunciation of the togetherness! If Samuel had not succumbed from whatever infection in his lung had multiplied to irrecoverable proportions, perhaps Elizabeth would not have called that day. It is a way forward, for we may now acknowledge each other's being.

⤺

Doreen has taken charge. I am not to open the shop this day – as if I would – and we are to be at the Church by a quarter to eleven. She will follow the coffin, I am to be in the first pew with a seat reserved. From this you will have gathered there are no other family members expected – and as Samuel never spoke of matters *familias* I bow to her knowledge about these formalities.

I dress with care. My suit will do; Doreen has provided me with a black tie that I strongly suspect is – was – Samuel's. I have no qualms over its use, *au contraire* I feel a sense of correctness about the matter.

As Samuel was a respected gentleman, albeit a lazy church-goer, he is accorded the bells, one chime for each year. I cannot say I counted them, though Doreen may well have done so. Before the last vibration has died away, I am in my appointed place in St.Martin's. The church is cold, the day is cold, the light is cold and my spirit flags. The pews are randomly filled; the old gentleman did have many acquaintances even if he did not rate them as worthy of full friendship. He was a very particular person. I shiver, and look round to see if the ritual is near commencement. And instantly the grey dullness of the occasion lifts, for there, not many pews away, on the end closest to the aisle, she is. Immediately we link thoughts. Soul seeking soul.

Samuel is brought, words are said, hymns are sung, a eulogy expatiated. He is subsequentially taken away and we mourn his departure. I walk up the aisle and Lucy slips alongside, casually to take my hand as though we are brother and sister. Her parents do not move for the moment that allows us to join souls. 'Jones,' she whispers, 'we've not to lose touch,' but her fingers drift as we reach the door and go out into the cool day.

I watch her in conversation with others, obtain a smile from her mother so as to acknowledge my position as a 'social acquaintance' but I cannot, at this time, expect more. As she gathers her daughter and her husband to her and they start to walk away down the neat paved path, Lucy turns her head to catch my stare and once more that *zing*, as another golden thread is woven into the strands to hold us.

Briony might have been there, but no elegant lady in a dark grey suit emerges from the congregation of mourners. No, she will be waiting alone for her personal mourner. I walk, walk alone through sombre streets, with no awareness of passers by, of unheard traffic, of shop windows that silently shout 'it's Christmas, buy, buy, buy.' My steps are slow, the unhurried gait of one who wishes to go nowhere fast. The world is spinning its change around me; only I am still, yet moving. Moving towards another demise. The permanent one, now concluded with the exit of a coffin from the church, was not of my arrangement. This other, I strongly suspect, is of my causation. 'Marry me,' she had asked, not a year ago. I had not agreed, for we are different people who, ironically, needed each other because we *are* different. Since then our constant socialising, our conversations and almost contractual copulation kept us together; we cherished our orgasmic feelings as seriously as our social stimulation but the soul had finally said 'no', and now she is going.

'I have to spin my web elsewhere, Jones,' she'd said a few days ago, 'as I can see you and I rely on too mundane a connection to survive. You need other stimulation – I know,' and a finger came up to stop my retort, 'you're seeking someone else,' and quoted Brooke at me, ' *"And I shall find some girl perhaps, and a better one than you, with eyes as wise, but kindlier, and lips as soft but true."'* She paused briefly, to finish with a tear in her eye and a catch in her voice, *'"And I daresay she will do",'* adding longingly, 'but you were right to hold me the way you did.'

So I held her once more. And we also made love once more, although 'love' in this context is the oft quoted euphemism for gaining an ecstatic genital feeling through erotic and frictional stimulation. Very scientific a description, she commented as I delivered both the verbal definition and one infinitely – intimately – more physical, and she laughed. A woman who laughs as you reach profundity could run the risk of all manner of responsive emotions. Some could lead to violence, even to a killing. Some self-seekers would merely grunt, content in their own private achievement. Others, especially if erroneously committed to long-term association and support (i.e. a disorganised marriage) might seek subtle revenge on any level. The thinking and loving ones would laugh with her, as I did, for I knew this woman inside out. She came without histrionics.

'Jones,' she'd asked as I, moments later, wilted away, 'will you find another woman?'

"And I shall find some girl perhaps and a better one than you ..." I reminded her, so she chuckled, maybe a tinge wistfully.

I'd eased apart, put my hands behind my head and considered the chandelier, so well studied now I could have drawn the thing from memory. Should I explain? Having formerly intimated there was another girl in my head and been laughed at – *a schoolgirl*, she'd once said, scathingly – the reservations were strongly against opening this increasingly sensitive aspect of my soul towards any potential further ridicule. Lucy demanded only the highest approbation.

'Maybe,' my only comment.

Which had all been days ago, now I am walking towards the finality of that relationship. Briony is going. The house I know so well will be let to someone else – she'd offered it to me, in a jokey sort of way, knowing full well her letting agent would demand far more than I could ever pay – even if I'd wanted to move away from the terrace pad.

She is going abroad, away from the town, the country, and me. Have we reached the end of the road? I'm not sure. This last year, I know I've changed. A year ago, – more, – I was carefree, living on my wits, confident, happy in my youthful enthusiasms. Then I collided with the Lucy and, as I argue with myself, turning the corner into this desirable part of the town, she may have been the catalyst that precipitated my move into Briony's arms, just as if I'd recognised I needed that something extra to fit onto my character. Like sex, I wryly thought. There'd been plenty of that, and some of my less studious contemporaries at Cambridge couldn't possibly have dreamt how much, when all they'd had was the odd – and occasional – casual screw at a weekend. And now? Why, seeking Lucy, not for sex, but infinitely more, indefinably more – and exactly for what I know not, though I sought the answer.

Briony's house stands at the end of the avenue. The avenue, tree lined and a pleasant green tunnel in summer, now gives the impression of being under guardianship by spectral ghostly creatures, gaunt grey shadowed skeletons of sycamore – a stupid tree to plant in the suburbs. The gate stands vacantly open, unusually, as if she'd gone. The pathway, familiar, a walkway towards wicked carnality, leads me to a symbolic doorway, symbolic as the portal to a young man's loss of his virginity. Now I was a slightly older young man, wiser and maybe sadder, as they say. I knock, out of politeness, before trying the handle. Has she gone already? But no, the handle turns, I walk in.

'Briony?' I call. An echo, then a distant '*I'm up here-err!*'

Upstairs. Dangerous, but I tread the oft-trod path to her bedroom. She's still packing, the second suitcase. She looks up.

'Won't be a moment,' she says, folding up the light blue dress and laying it on the top. It is the one she wore when I first saw her and the picture comes flashing back to destroy all firm resolutions. She means a lot to me, this woman, as a woman. I step towards her, hold out my arms and she welcomes my embrace. We kiss. My arm is round her back and I can feel her bra strap below the lacy blouse. The kiss deepens, her arm goes around my neck and we're back into the risk business again. And why shouldn't we be? This hasn't been a *brief encounter*, it's lasted a whole year, and in that year, other ties have been woven. She now knows that, I certainly do. And Lucy – she will also know, in fullness of time, and I trust will allow me this last indiscretion.

I could give you chapter and verse. I can, you know. Every single last movement, every action, each tiny detail towards the frenetic chaos and torn cotton. Cotton, not silk, though with a delicate lace edging in scalloped form and a soft pattern of interwoven pink flowers; the design etched into memory as intimately as they were discarded. Then naked, that's how I will always remember her, naked. A dear, dear woman – lady – to whom I owe a great deal, and this is our finale, the last curtain call on what turned out to be the last performance. The Show has closed. It has to be. For now she is moving on, and I seek another world.

⁓

It's early evening now. She'll be on her way south, heading towards Heathrow. I'm sitting on the settee at home, nursing a familiar mug of coffee and letting thoughts flow. The charger sits on the sideboard, accusingly. The scrumpled-up ball of torn cotton with its lace trim and musky scent I had tossed alongside, as a memento, a trophy, an ephemeral keepsake. Some of my more rabid contemporaries hung similar on their college room walls as if they were dead birds on a gamekeeper's gibbet, except the birds who wore them (*briefly* – ha ha) were still very much alive. Pink, white, plain M & S grey, narrow scraps of red, black – yuugh, purest blue, French, torn, cotton, silk … like carving notches on a Hall or Manor bed head, itemising the maids who ran the risk of summary dismissal if they … though Briony wouldn't. We were intelligent enough to avoid repercussions. And now she was beyond reach.

" … *For you and I are past our dancing days* …" End of the chapter, Jones.

Louth Parish Church

Eight

Variations ... Changes

I wake up with a headache. It's the day before Christmas Eve and the last shopping day before Christmas. I must do my duty and open the shop, if only to mark the passing of Samuel. He, to whom I owe much, will be the ghost, the Christmas Spirit. I hope I don't hear rattling chains. Mrs (or more accurately, Miss, as she remains, not unsurprisingly, a spinster) Doreen will be upstairs and, hopefully, be preparing to go back to Grantham for solitary festivities. Then I can lock the place up, retreat back here and mourn the connubial absence of Briony. She'll be in New York by now, I guess.

I breakfast on two Weetabix, a slice of indifferent toast and a mug – the comfortable old Denby one – of coffee. Then I walk down the hill.

❦

Jones has an appalling day. The shop is colder than normal, or so it seems. He has a few customers, none of whom spends meaningful money. He also deals with a number of sombrely faced sympathisers. Doreen bustles down mid morning with her heavy shopping bags, actually wishes him a 'Happy Christmas', more likely in cynicism than joy, announces she'll be 'back in the New Year', and goes. His desolate spirit yearns for Briony, her warmth and feistiness. At four o'clock he checks all the shutters, the windows, the rear door, and locks up. Then, on the point of setting back home, has a thought, unlocks, goes back to the desk, writes out a card, places it in the window of the door and re-locks.

The shop frontage looks forlorn, desolate and un-loved, but then, it has lost its spirit. The card reads, "Closed until further notice".

On the following morning, Christmas Eve, Jones flings his things into the back of the Traveller, checks around the rooms, has a sudden thought and scrabbles around in the cupboard under the stairs for some paper wrapping and a box. He wraps up the Lucy Rie charger, the pound note still inside and, with considerable and gentle care, places it in the box, adding, with a wry smile, Briony's intimate parting gift for extra packing. He places the box on the car's floor by the passenger seat, returns and locks the door of the terrace pad. Then drives away. Oh, yes. The cat? Did a runner the night before last. Must have sensed the vibes; very intuitive, that cat. Maybe it'll come back. Maybe not. Let's hope it doesn't get run over.

Lucy's father takes time away from his office to drive his daughter out to the new position as Acting Reception Manageress at the hotel eight miles out of town. He will miss having her at home, as will his wife Elizabeth, who tearfully bade her girl 'goodbye' on the doorstep. This is the first time ever she'll be away from home on her own other than occasional nights in at the George, which didn't count.

'I'll be fine, mum,' Lucy says, trying not to suffer watery eyes in sympathy, 'and you can always come for lunch tomorrow …'

Which must have struck a chord. Before going home, with Sam the manager standing smilingly by, he gets her to book both he and

Lucy's mother in for Christmas Lunch. Then he shakes Sam's hand, gives Lucy a cheek and cheek kiss, and leaves.

'Your father is a gentleman,' says Sam, 'he's obviously very proud of you, justifiably. Now, let me show you your room. It's across the yard.' He picks up her bulging case and leads the way. The 'yard' is actually the enclosed garden area, a sort of cloister intersected by stone-flagged paths. Her allocated room is on the top floor, overlooking the fields, quite small, single bedded, but nicely decorated.

Lucy is impressed. 'This, just for me? Don't you let all the rooms up here?'

Sam grins at her. 'Not at this time of year, Lucy. Not too much call for singles. No, you're welcome. So long as you don't expect chambermaid service. It's a make your own bed and do your own cleaning arrangement, I'm afraid. Now, settle yourself in, come down for early lunch and we'll go through the routines.' At the door, he turns back to her with an added comment, 'very glad to have you here, Lucy. The George probably don't realise what they've given up. So long as you live up to your reputation. See you later.' He closes the door behind him; she's on her own.

She collapses onto the bed, kicks off her shoes, stretches out. '*So long!*' and she giggles. '*Wonder what the George said about me. Given up? They haven't given me up, just lent me out. I hope. But it feels friendly here and Sam seems like a nice man. Hope the others are the same.*'

By the end of the day, she's comfortable in what she has to do. After tea Sam tells her to get a book to read whilst she's on evening duty behind the reception desk. 'Then you can go off duty at eight,' he says, 'I'll be around for awhile after that. I don't expect anyone will turn up late this evening. Not on Christmas Eve.' He grins at her. He's got a nice, uncomplicated grin. 'Will Santa pay you a visit tonight, d'you think? Or doesn't he know where you are?'

She grins back at him. 'Shall I hang up my stocking, then?'

'You never know your luck, lass.' He moves away and she looks after him, thoughtfully. She hopes he is all he seems and doesn't hide potential problems.

The evening passes uneventfully. She enjoys nice conversation with some of the guests who are mostly elderly, genteel folk, escaping from frenetic young families. The conservatory dining area is dressed with holly and silvery shapes, lit by orange globes on the walls and the sparkling white fairy lights scattered amongst the overhead tracery. Outside, the garden area is also discreetly lit, contrasting with the stone buildings and the depths of deep blue sky. It has a magical feel, absorbed by the guests, some who are happy to talk with her, to express their delight at the celebratory atmosphere and the wonderful evening meal they'd had.

'You must really love working here,' says one old lady, relaxed into her armchair.

Her husband nods. 'We always come here at Christmas. Takes us away from all the fuss and bother back home. Not that we don't love our family, but ...'

Lucy has to smile. She can understand, even though she's not ever experienced a mad Christmas. 'I hope you continue to enjoy your stay.'

'Oh, we will. Are you still on duty, my dear? It must be strange, having to work on a holiday. Hope they pay you well.'

She checks the time. It is a quarter past eight. She shakes her head. 'Technically, no, but as I'm resident, it doesn't make much difference.' Then she gives away the secret. 'This is my first day here. I've come to stand in for the lady who's gone to have a baby. Margaret.'

'Oh, *my dear girl! Christmas!*. Where were you before? Do sit down and talk to us, if you're allowed.'

Lucy sits. It's nice to feel wanted. She explains where she's been these last four months, what made her choose to enter the hotel trade, something of her background. The old couple seem genuinely interested, the old lady's eyes twinkle and the gentleman's age-lined face is warm and friendly. She relaxes even more and hopes Sam won't think it wrong.

'Have you a nice young man in the background, dear? Someone who puts a sparkle in your eye?' as indeed the old lady's eyes sparkle at the thought of young love.

Lucy shakes her head. 'Not really. I'm not 'going out' with anyone.' She wonders how – whether – she could possibly explain her weird attachment to Jones when they've not exchanged more than a couple of hour's social chat, and that at home. She thinks of him, wonders where he is, whether he'll miss her, when they will next meet. Oh, yes, they *will* meet again. She knows it as a fact. Until then, she's her own girl.

'That's a shame, deary. Or are you merely putting us in our place? We don't wish to pry, do we, Hubert?'

Hubert – what a lovely old-fashioned name, Lucy thinks, – shakes his head and offers an excuse for their interest. 'It's only because our only daughter left it till very late to find a husband, d'you see. Now she can't have children. It's our son who's given us the grandchildren.' He shifts in his chair. 'We married early. That's best,' and his gnarled and liver spotted hand goes across to rest on the veined parchment of his wife's.

Lucy is touched. 'I'm not quite twenty,' she says.

'Exactly my age when Hubert proposed.' and the old lady's voice is proud.

She takes heart. 'Actually I've sort of found a, well, possibly you'd call him a kindred spirit. And more of a spirit, p'raps,' said with a slight smile. She goes on to explain how this inner girl of hers reacts to this person's presence, hoping it doesn't sound as weird to them as it does to her, though ironically, talking to these two dear old souls is helping to clarify things in her mind.

And as she talks, little waves, vibrations, cross between her shoulder blades and ripple into her arms, down her spine. *Jones, where are you? Come close. Don't forget me.*

'Ah,' says the old lady. 'Then you mustn't let him go. A meeting of two spirits can be a very special thing. Seek him out, young lady; I'm sorry we don't know your name.'

'Lucy,' she replies, 'and you are?'

'Anna,' the old lady responds, 'and you know my husband's Hubert. Tell her, dear, how we met.'

Hubert pitches his fingers, rests his nose on them, and his eyes go dreamy. 'You know the lines from the song, "*You may see a stranger, across a crowded room*"? Well, I was at a conference thing. This is a good few years ago, mind,' and Lucy has to smile at them both, 'and when I walked into the hall, I had this sixth sense. Later, at the lunch table, I managed to come close to this lady. Got a feel about her. We looked at each other, d'you see, and started chatting. I took her out to dinner that night ...'

'And I married him,' Anna interrupts. 'There was never anyone else. And here we are, pushing eighty and still in love.' Their eyes meet.

'Oh, how lovely.' Lucy feels honoured, impressed, even humbled; how different from some other stories she'd heard. Her mum would have liked to listen to Hubert's explanation. Now she feels slightly embarrassed and rises from her chair.

'Thank you for talking to me. I'd better just check everything's all right on the desk. Please excuse me.'

'Certainly, my dear. Perhaps we'll see you tomorrow.'

She nods. 'Goodnight,' and moves away.

Old lady Anna watches the lithe figure go gracefully across the room, skirt swaying, hair shimmering in the festive lights, and sighs. Hubert tightens his clasp on her hand. 'That's you, m'dear, at twenty. Still the same lass, y'know.'

A tear squeezes from under a thin wrinkled eyelid. 'She may be a very lucky young girl, that Lucy. Shall we go up?'

∾

Jones makes good time. There isn't much traffic on the A15, but then it is Christmas Eve. It takes him about two hours, without pushing the old girl much above fifty. He is tempted to stop off in Lincoln, but at the last moment, changes his mind, turns right and drops down off the Lincolnshire Heights to cross the fens on the long straight road to Bardney. The vast open skies stretch above the wide horizon, the thin clouds give the day a dullened edge. The Traveller's steady engine note lulls his mind, deadens the empty feeling in his head. His life on four wheels, all he has in the world packed in a bag. And a box. His *other being*. He thinks about her. Wonders where she is, what she is doing, whether she'll miss him, when they will meet again. Oh, yes, they *will* meet again. He knows it as a fact. Until then, he's his own man. Not Briony's, not any more.

He enjoys the last dozen miles or so, winding across the Wolds, seeking the first glimpse of the delicate point of the church spire above the trees, St.James Parish Church, the highest spire in the country. Where he was marched in crocodile form from the Grammar School to Ascension Day services, where his father does verger duty, where his parents were married, twenty-five years ago. A landmark.

76

There! He starts to whistle, something from one of the shows, *South Pacific*. Soon be back. Christmas at home.

He parks, for the moment, alongside the shop. The door opens against the bell spring, just like the Stamford bookshop and his heart lurches. He's going to miss Samuel, dear old man. Inside, the redolence of tobacco and old mahogany fixtures assails his senses. All the curious old advertising placards. The glass case with the expensive cigars. Shelves stacked with the brightly coloured cigarette boxes. And he'd never, not for one single second, ever been tempted. Like his father, strangely, who sells tobacco but never smokes. At least that helps to maintain profitability. And he thought of a bookshop, how one could read the stock but still sell it … 'Dad!'

'Son! You didn't say …' The two men, father and son, clap arms around each other.

'Last minute. It's okay isn't it? Mum won't mind?'

'She'll be delighted. Stunned maybe, but still delighted. Just as well we've a big turkey. You're staying?'

Until when, you mean, and he grins. 'Until whenever. Tell you later. Can I put the Morris round the back?'

'Of course. The old girl still running well?'

Jones nods. Old girl! Dad's previous car, a hand-me-down. A gift. An appreciated gift. He and dad, friends.

His mother, large, full of warmth and happiness, has the kettle on in a trice. 'Oh, Al, so glad you're home for Christmas. You didn't say,' she says, echoing her husband.

'No, mum, sorry, last minute thing. Don't mind?'

She plonks a mug in front of him, together with a large buttered scone, fresh out of the oven. 'Here, that'll keep the wolf from the door. You hungry?'

He grins. 'Mum! Can't wait for Christmas dinner.' Inwardly, he grimaces at the family name. Al, short for Alphonse. *Now you know why he's called Jones.* His college chums never knew about Al and neither will anyone else if he can help it. Not even Lucy, and he feels the pull from her; from wherever she is, he knows she's there. *Don't let me go.* Briony's image is fading.

∽

Christmas Day, and she stirs. Questions where she is, why the bed is so small. Why the light is different. Her eyes widen as reality brings her to full awareness. Because it's not her own bed, nor the one at the George, because the window overlooks open country, not streets, because she's at Barnsdale. And it's Christmas! She remembers Sam the manager's comment about Santa and is half inclined to crane her neck to look at the foot of the bed where her dress is still lying from last night's sleepy shedding of clothes – just in case, before realising she locked the door anyway.

The surprise had been the late night party, when most guests had vanished to their quarters and Sam had done the rounds of the entire staff, pulling them into the small cosy dining room, the one with all the pictures next to the kitchen. He'd opened a bottle or two, given them crackers to pull and hot mince pies, handed out little presents. 'Happy Christmas!' No stuffy formality, just plain good fun, and she thrilled to the thought she'd been taken as one of the team, even to having her own present – the red and gold silk scarf. It had been well after midnight when she'd crept in, hence the disparate spread of clothes around. Normally she folded them up carefully, ready for the next day. She peers at the bedside clock. Nearly nine o'clock. If she wants any breakfast, she'd best get a move on. Back on duty at ten, yes, even on Christmas day, though no one was booking out. Parents coming to lunch. How strange that will be!

She has a shower. Lovely, having an en-suite bathroom. Dresses carefully. No uniform dress, just *'be modest and neat'*, Sam had said. Her George Hotel grey costume skirt would be all right, he'd added, but wear a different jacket or even a sweater. She chooses the dark green lightweight cotton twill dress instead, the one with edged revers she'd made at school, but recognises she may have to spend some of her next wages on something else.

As she opens the door to go down for breakfast, a Christmassy bag slips off the outside handle onto the floor. She picks it up. A label says *'a present from Santa'* in familiar handwriting. Inside, a white lacy blouse, all wrapped up in tissue. And an envelope. It's a Christmas card, from her parents. Oh *dad!* He'd obviously left it with Sam, with instructions. Typical! But very nice and really lovely, a lovely thought. She goes back into the room, lays it on the bed. She'll put it on before lunch so she's wearing it when they come.

⤚

Jones wakes up in an unfamiliar yet familiar room. Where he'd slept everyday since whenever, until he went to Cambridge. Years ago. Well, four or five years ago. It is Christmas Day. Last year – and it is a jerk at his emotions – he spent the holiday with Briony, merely a phone call to his parents to wish them a 'Happy Christmas' before he and she had eaten breakfast together. The walk in Burghley Park. The offer she'd made which he had spurned. Now she's gone out of his life and this is the result. He stares at the ceiling. No chandelier. No Briony.

He rolls over and buries his head in plain cotton-covered pillows. Worn cotton pillows. A powerful negative reminder of what could have been. Silence, not a sound, a cloying, drowning silence.

I'm stupid. I've left the shop, left the terrace pad, left a few friends, left Lucy. Abandoned them and run off home to mum. Not thinking, just did it. So okay, what next? Do I stick with it all, wait and see what happens? Do I jack it all in and follow Plan B? Or Plan C? One thing's for sure, something's got to happen. I can't just drift, can I? Briony, dear lady, why did you have to decide to leave?

… Because of me? …

That's Lucy's voice – in my head. What's she doing in my brain? So can I connect with her, wherever she is?

He tries to imagine her, bring her virtuality to mental reality, and cannot. There's a block.

⤚

It's getting close to lunchtime. The tables are being laid and because nothing else seems to be happening, she lends Beth a hand. Beth is a raven-haired, olive complexioned tall girl with a pleasant smile and very dextrous. From Beth she learns how Sam likes his tables set out,

79

how the napkins are folded, which glasses are used for water. She is given the boxes of crackers – one cracker for each place setting – and alternates them, red and green. 'Well done,' Sam says, coming to inspect. 'What I like to see. Versatility. But you won't neglect the desk, will you, Lucy?'

'No, sir,' she says, 'and thank you for acting as Santa.'

He laughs. 'That was a simple pleasure,' he replies, 'and do call me Sam outside the guests' hearing.' Then he adds, almost as an afterthought, 'you play the piano, don't you? Well, have a go after three when Rhona takes over. Background music for teatime? If you'd like to, that is. No pressure.' He doesn't look for an answer, but strides off to check the kitchen.

The Christmas lunch goes well. Lucy's parents are impressed and say so. She has an opportunity to sit with them for a brief period while coffee is served in the lounge and before she needs to see to the day's departing guests. Not everyone will stay over through to Boxing Day; it's the Christmas lunch most of them have come for, staying overnight is the optional bonus, part of the package.

The upright Kemble piano stands angled into the corner. Lucy's mother comments, nodding her head in that direction. 'Have you had the chance to play, Lucy?'

'Later this afternoon, mum,' and she checks her watch. 'In another hour. I'm off at three and Sam, the manager, has said I can entertain the teatime guests. Will you stay?'

'That'll be nice, dear. Shame they haven't a grand.' She gets up, crosses over, lifts the lid and tries a couple of chords. 'Hmmm. Not bad. At least it's in tune. You have some of your music here?'

Lucy guesses it is a rhetorical question, so simply nods. 'I have to go back on the desk for a while. Just enjoy the fire.' Indeed, the log fire is crackling away nicely, the lounge quite comfortably warm and at least three guests are sleeping off their lunch.

Elizabeth picks up a magazine. 'Don't you fall asleep, dear,' she says, passing her husband another copy of 'Country Life'.

Just after three, Lucy returns with a handful of music. She has changed into the only decent dress for formal wear she has with her, for naturally the smart concert dress is still hanging in its covers in the wardrobe back at home. She's in the burgundy one bought for the end-of-school prom a year ago and is surprised that she can still do up the zip, though the bodice feels tight. The skirt's full enough and not too short. She also has the correct shoes, right for the pedals.

She acknowledges her mother's smile; her father, with legs uncrossed, exerts a measured pull to sit up straighter than the easy-lounge position adopted when relaxing. She sits, adjusts the stool, opens the lid again and settles her music onto the rest. A few of the dozen or so guests still in the lounge – most awaiting their tea, it has to be said – take notice. One gentleman puts down his paper, leans back into his chair and folds his arms, intelligently aware of her intentions.

The Chopin *Nocturne*, the piece she begins with, is familiar, one she knows well. She is aware the sound isn't quite the same – resonance is diminished, the action choppier, and therefore adjusts her fingering accordingly. *'That's better,'* her ears tell her and she gains confidence. A quick glance across towards her mother catches a slight nod. Her father has his eyes closed, a good sign. Lucy cannot see the gentleman who is tapping his fingers and falling into the rhythm with a gentle head movement, the one who sat up straight, but her mother has abruptly noticed. Doesn't she recognise this man from her past life? Lucy sees the vague frown on her mother's face and wonders. Is she still at the right pace? Another twenty bars and she's done. It wasn't too bad. She bows her head, waits.

The small audience is now fully cognisant they have a virtuoso pianist within the room and the clapping brings Lucy to her feet. 'Bravo,' says the man Lucy's mother now is certain sure she knows. Heavens! With a pointed movement of her head she signals to Lucy that she should continue, hoping that it will be another challenging piece.

Her daughter mind-reads, shifts the music around and takes the plunge. A piano excerpt from Bach's Brandenburg Concerto No 5; pity she doesn't have the string section handy! She hasn't fully memorised the piece yet, and, slightly ruffled at having to turn over the pages, catches a wrong note but presses on. Quietly, without causing a stir, the man Elizabeth is now positive comes from the London music scene rises, moves to Lucy's side just in time to reach and turn the next page for her, exactly right. She's naturally surprised but accepts his presence. A few notes are not quite perfect but she's happy with the cadence. No-one has noticed the audience has been swollen by Sam, the waiting staff and one or two more standing just inside the far door.

On the last note, held and left to diminish into silence, she's a happy girl. Another glance at her mother; Lordy, is she wiping an eye? Lucy rises, faces the majority in the room and gives an elegant curtsey, just for fun. To the man who turned the pages she acknowledges his help with a bow of her head. Has she overdone this piano accompaniment bit – Sam is coming over?

'Ladies and gentlemen,' he says, standing next to her. 'May I present Lucy Salter, who only yesterday joined the staff of this hotel. I suggested she might like to entertain you during afternoon tea, but I had no idea quite how well she plays.' He turns to her, 'thank you, Lucy. Now, perhaps you'd like to place your orders?' and signals to the waiting staff.

He takes her by the elbow and shepherds her across towards her parents as the lounge resumes its normal function.

'Mr and Mrs Salter, you have a very, very accomplished daughter,' he says quietly, 'and she's totally in the wrong place. I think her talents would be far better deployed in the concert hall than merely booking guests into an hotel – not that I am in any way suggesting I want rid of her, far from it, but to play like that? And on the old Joanna! Now, please do order what you will from our teatime menu – and it will be at my pleasure, no,' as Lucy's father starts to protest, 'the least I could do. Lucy,' he adds, 'don't forget you're back on duty in the morning, the early shift. Until then, you're free to do what you like. And thank you again, that was wonderful.' He walks away.

I don't believe this. First full day here and the manager wants me to go? I don't just want to play a piano, I want to have responsibility, take decisions, make lots of guests pleased with their stay at my hotel. Okay, it wasn't too bad, but I made a few mistakes and the piano is rather crummy, so it's no big deal, is it? And mum will have another go at me, I can see it happening! And, oh, the man who knew when to turn the pages, he's looking at me! Coming over ...

'Good afternoon. My apologies if I intrude – you *are* Elizabeth Salter? My card.' and he hands over a crisp pasteboard card in pale ivory. 'Basil Fortescue, as I believe you now remember, Mrs Salter,' said with a smile and faint trace of irony. Lucy's mother reads it, hands it on to her husband. 'No, please don't get up,' he says as Elizabeth starts to rise out of her chair. He turns to Lucy. 'Miss Salter, you have turned my stay here from a mere casual break in the country to an occasion of tremendous delight, and potentially, of great significance. May I?' and he takes a chair from the nearby empty table and places it where he can address them all. 'May I call you Elizabeth – as I once used to, all those years ago?'

Lucy watches her mother simper, incredulous. Basil Fortescue? He whose name appears in the Sunday Times? And seen on the promotional adverts for concerts at all sorts of super venues? And he's been her page-turner? Golly gosh!

He's talking to her. 'Lucy!' Her mother brings her daughter back to earth. 'Mr Fortescue's talking to you!'

'Oh, sorry. Sorry, I …'

'Dear lady, I quite understand. Now may I ask who taught you to play, your mother? Because I would not be at all surprised; you have the same feeling for the composer. Your mother was extremely sympathetic to original scores. An appreciation sadly lacking in many, I fear. You're going to go to the R.C.M.?'

'I er, well, no-ooo, I'm …' Completely off balance, she turns to her father.

He rescues her. 'Mr Fortescue, my daughter's convinced she wants to run a hotel. She's here as a trainee, as the Manager explained?'

'Oh dear me. Is that really the case, young lady?'

Lucy nods.

'Hmmph. Wasted, wasted. I'd like to hear you play on a proper instrument. Come to London next week,' and as Lucy begins to protest he raises a hand. 'Won't hear of any excuses. You're not to deny your talent, my girl – isn't that the case, Elizabeth?'

Lucy's mother faintly agrees. Basil, her old impresario from over two decades ago, is talking about her daughter as though she was the same prize-winning concert pianist as she had been. And after all the discussions they'd had, she and Lucy and the school's headmistress and Myra, all to no avail – but here *he* was, wanting to sweep her away from all this hotel nonsense? *Now* will Lucy see sense?

I can't bear it. Oh, mums, mums, what ever do I do now?

Her father stands up. 'Lucy, dear. Mr Fortescue's been extremely kind to you – to us – and maybe, just maybe, he has a point. I understand, I really do, and I'd like to make a suggestion. You carry on here as if nothing has happened for the next few days, then you and I will go to London as he suggests and we'll discuss what happens after that. There's no decision to be made here and now and it will give you time to think.' He looks down at his wife. 'Elizabeth, my dear, it's time we went home and let our daughter resume her duties. Thank you very much indeed, Mr Fortescue, for recognising Lucy's talent and offering her an opportunity to discover where it may lead her. It has been an eventful Christmas Day, I think. And I for one have very much enjoyed it. My dear,' and he offers Elizabeth his hand to help her rise.

Mr Fortescue accedes that he will not yet progress matters further and also makes his apologies. 'I have to get back to London this evening, sadly, but I will be in touch. Lucy, my dear, keep on practicing. You do, don't you?'

'When I can,' she replies, 'but it isn't easy, with my work and things.'

'You must. There were a few little errors, you know. I can tell. But your playing moved me. Yes, moved me,' and he pats her shoulder. 'I look forward to our next meeting,' and he leaves them alone.

Her parents leave soon after and she goes back to her room. There she sits on the bed and stares silently at her image in the dressing table mirror. The world has become, in the space of half a day, a wild and confused place. She enjoyed playing, especially the challenge of the lesser-known piece, the adulation from the guests and the respect of the man who must have been so much part of her mother's world ages ago. She did not expect to be confronted with the threat of deciding whether she should go along with what has been said.

There is recourse but one fraught with impossibilities. Will he? Respond to her thoughts, her rising ache? Or is she so absolutely, totally, naïve to even give a second's consideration to such a fanciful idea, to contemplate asking a near-virtual person for advice telepathically, for that is what her mind is discussing. The query goes back and forth.

She pictures him, deep in her mind's eye, a shadowy, once mysterious figure from her school days when first she experienced the shiver of intrigue. The intrigue complicated by their recurrent collisions of presence, at the George, at the concert, at Burghley Hall. The mystery lessened later on, after her mother's surprise tea party invitation. Afterwards her bold action invited his kiss, a seal on their involuntary coming together in such a coincidental way. *'Keep me close'*, she'd said. So. She goes to the window, gazes into the purpling dark, across the unseen fields, the depths of open country, the miles, the aeons of time and concentrates.

… I will not let thee go…

≫

Jones, away in the Lincolnshire Wolds, miles away from Stamford, is not presently thinking of Lucy. His day oscillates between food, conversation and unrevealed reminiscences brought back into play from last year's debauchery. By four o'clock, all have had their fill and the evening drags.

'I'm going for a walk,' he says and pulls himself out of the sagging cushions of the old brown settee. His mother nods sleepily, his father is gently snoring and they won't worry. The evening is cold, fortunately dry and with only wisps of cloud above, clearing skies will pull the temperature further down to below freezing. In the hallway, he wraps a scarf twice round, buttons on the thick coat over last year's Briony sweater – where is she now? He sallies forth.

It is a brisk ten to fifteen minute hike along Eastgate, across the deserted main road, over the cobbles by the church, its massive near three hundred foot spire scratching at the sky, and along Westgate past the Girls' School's boarding house, so evocative of early days. Through the tired timber gate the meadows stretch mysteriously away into the depths of the night. A moment's pause, looking up at myriad stars and the faint luminosity of a crescent half moon beyond the northern treeline and a sudden shiver; another swallows the silence. He walks on, instinct guiding footsteps.

There's a light in the windows of the Mill House. A solitary surprised dog's single bark instantly shut off. His shoes crunch on loose gravel, he moves onto the higher path. This is familiar territory, albeit from years ago. With additional care, conscious that tree roots across the path may cause him to trip, and with eyes now accustomed to low light levels, he walks on, only a brief thought of concern on whether he would meet any other nocturnal ambler.

At the fork he takes the lower path to descend into the valley below, the moon's rise briefly catches the silver sheen of the river. An eerie place to be, especially this night of any. Few would venture thus.

He stumbles, catches at the fence, recovers, decides the foolishness has had its day and crosses the upper bank of unmown grass towards the little stone memorial, in order to cross the river there and return on the valley bottom path. His footsteps thud echoingly on the timber of the bridge; he stops, puts two hands out and leans on the rail, catching the dancing reflection of the moon in the gentle flow of the waters below. Silence drops in, icy; a thin layer of chill silence apart from the ever-rippling river.

Suddenly, without warning or thought, comes an image. Not the sensual warmth and heart pulsing woman of his past year, she who stole last year's Christmas from him, but the persuasive image of a slim, dark haired girl who drew magic from a keyboard, who caused his soul to leap, to reach out in essential need for togetherness. *Seen across a silent street. Seen across a hallway, a courtyard, a concert hall, a hand held across an aisle. Across the miles.* Lucy then. Must be. No one else – certainly not Daphne.

Lucy, how can she stay so tenaciously in my mind?

I should have left her back in Stamford. Left the charger on the sideboard. She doesn't need me. She's to be cherished for what she is – pure, chaste, a figurine in porcelain. Not by one who's given away his chastity to a siren of a woman in lust.

...Oh no, No! I'm not a porcelain doll. I am a lonely girl who has a growing ache for something she doesn't understand, something so powerful it is reaching out to you across the stars and I need your strength for the next step towards what we will be. Trust me – keep me close. Please, please, please...

A single call of a tawny owl. *Whu-hooo.* Jones starts, turns, looks up at the treeline, the darker naked branches against a dark sky. *Whu-ooo-oo.* Imaginary, or weirdly odd? A girl's voice in his head? Too much ruddy alcohol!

Voices in my head? I ...

The impact is nearly too great. She's there, her figure in the trees. He looks away, down at the river. A vision of her face is shaking in the water, just as she stood, eyes closed, waiting for his salutation, his kiss. He remembers that kiss. Across the loom of the lower mown grass, dim in the nightglow, along the path, another vision of a figure, swaying skirt, school bag at her side. Stripped away, another picture appears, of the girl in a beautiful grey dress accompanied by the rippling sound of her music.

He shakes his head, rubs his eyes, wonders what he's eaten, walks off the bridge, along the path, fast, faster, striding out, to get away, away, to get home, to curl up, to remember and forget how beautiful a woman's body can be, moulded into his after they've been close, close, close ...

At the last gate he turns and looks back at the deserted, empty, fraught blackness of the valley.

Help me! I must decide! Her voice. Low, urgent, *hers*!

In his head the refrain: *Keep me close. You are lovely – you are lovely. Keep me close.*

So at last, he succumbs.

I love your music, my Lucy – though I bought you in a virtual way, you are your own girl, yet you have captured my mind with the music of your being. Your music has enraptured my soul. There. Are you a contented girl now?

How utterly ridiculous was that? Now he strides out at a steady pace, which takes him home in twenty minutes. His parents have gone to bed, so he makes little noise, undressing, falling into the over-soft single bed and not bothering to read his usual chapter before sleep.

From out of the purpling dark, across the unseen fields, the depths of open country, the miles, the aeons of time, Lucy hears a voice, or thinks she does.

I love your music, my Lucy – though I bought you in a virtual way, you are your own girl, yet you have captured my soul with the music of your being. Your music has captured my soul. There. Are you a contented girl now?

She takes one almighty deep breath, sighs, undresses carefully, slips into her cosy bed and curls up. *Mother, dear mum, I promise I'll try.* And goes to sleep, relaxed and settled in the decision she's had taken for her, for oh, those wonderful thoughts; and yes, now she's a contented girl.

$\mathcal{N}ine$

Intermezzo … In the Middle

To be honest, I have no idea what came over me last night. Waking up in the old familiar room, at first thought I believed I should have been up ages ago to get ready for school. Stupid. That was years ago. Been to Uni since, had a job, and … *realisation.*

Living in that woman's pocket, working for poor old Samuel, generally acting like some dumb numskull. Doreen, Samuel's sister, she'll be livid, having no one looking after the shop. Did I leave the heating on in the terrace pad? Gawd, I must have knocked a few back yesterday. Didn't I go out last night?

What the heck am I going to do next? I don't want to run the bookshop any more, not that one, anyway. Too many memories. Some bad, a few good. Not under Doreen's roof. No way. Jones, old son, you'll have to take hold of yourself.

I get up. Dress in old gear. Give my mum a 'good morning' kiss. Dad's doing a preliminary stocktake, end of the year job. I give him a hand. Quite like old times. We get on fine, he and I. Especially since Cambridge. Mid morning, we retreat to the kitchen for a decent mug of coffee and some left-over mince pies. A flashback. Mince pies equals Briony, last Christmas, she who went round the kitchen starkers. At least I wore the long sweater.

'Dad,' I say, 'D'you think I should keep on with the bookshop?'

'Why not,' he comes back at me with, 'as your boss guy's kicked it, so you do as you please. Do a good day's work, it's all yours. Act rubbish, get rubbish. Not my scene, but then I didn't get to go to Cambridge.'

'Samuel kept the shop for ages. That's all he ever did. I don't want to flipping die in that old place from book dust inspired pneumonia.'

Dad gives me a funny look. 'Reckon? Book dust? Never thought. Hmmm, might as well take up smoking if you want your lungs to kill you.'

As I've said, dad never touches tobacco. Sells it, yes, uses it, no. More sense. P'raps I am too close to the mark on the book dust theory. Theory, mind you, nothing proven.

'There's a shop going in town if you could afford it,' dad adds. 'Old Yeates is packing up. Retiring. You could live at home. Suit your old mum, that would. And it isn't all old books, neither. Some decent stuff, I reckon. Just a thought. Now, shall us finish this lot afore dinner?'

He had me thinking. A *proper* bookshop? I knew the one, top of the Market Place, bow fronted window, four storeys, got character to it, same as Samuel's, 'cept you didn't need to keep your head bent to avoid clouting the beams. Wonder what he wants for the place – and would I sell Samuel's business for enough? That would put Doreen in a spin.

I stayed at home until after the New Year. No point in being enthusiastic over a business one intends to get shot of – the placard on the shop door window, *Closed until Further Notice* would suffice. And Doreen didn't know where I was, she could bang on the terrace pad's door for ages or until the neighbours shouted at her – so I was safe. One tiny niggle though, right at the very back of my mind, concerning that Christmas night's walk through the Hills. Didn't I have a curious conversation with my conceptual girl friend – the one whose virtual namesake lives in the Lucy Rie charger in the form of a much fondled pound note? Whatever it was, she hasn't troubled me since. And as for the other woman, Briony, I think I'm getting over her. No more dreams. Sad in a way, living the monastic life. I'm sure someone else will turn up eventually.

❧

Jones goes back to Stamford, leaving his Rie charger at home to ensure he'll fulfil his mission. He's put an advert in the T.L.S, the London Times and the trade magazine Samuel subscribed to at enormous expense. (Nearly a tenner a quarter for a mere thirty pages a week – daylight robbery. Still, limited circulation equals captive audience) Doreen is hopping mad. The locals find out and some say *'don't blame you'*, others moan away, one or two nosey parkers act clever and suggest they want to buy the place merely to discover what it's worth.

He manages to maintain a reasonable weekly turnover, shows a few prospective people over the place. The accounts are dollied up by an old accountant friend of Samuel's and don't look at all bad. The stock is still reasonable too, as Jones manages to buy the entire contents of a decent library from an historic house sale just over the county boundary.

Eventually, up comes a middle aged semi-retired college lecturer from Oxford. 'Just what I've been looking for,' he says, and being short, rotund and with a white goatee beard, is exactly the right character part. Jones places him somewhere in Dickens's pages. A few weeks later the sale reaches completion. Freedom.

❧

Our Lucy has left the hotel. On Boxing Day morning she had a lengthy chat with Sam, a friendly, intelligent conversation. Then he offered her the use of the telephone and left her in his office on her own to talk to her parents. Her mother, Lucy sensed, had tears in her eyes. Her father, with abundant common sense and a complete realist, concurred with her decision and knew he would have to make her peace with the George's management. If Mr Fortescue's concept bore fruit, that is.

The following week he and his beloved daughter catch the train to London. The day punishes them both. Lucy plays, and plays, has discussions with different groups of people, with Mr Fortescue and with the Principle of the College. Late in the afternoon, the consequences are declared. If funding can be found, she may enrol as a mature student and start within weeks, at the beginning of the next term. She is told that her continued place depends on her progress, that her acceptance is out of the norm and she must not only appreciate the special circumstances but to endeavour not to play on them. There is a small, shared smile at the pun. It is of little help hearing a less expensive and more secure option vanished once she'd left school and chosen another avenue.

It is also a perplexing time. Lucy maintains a diplomatic silence as her father discusses all the financing options with the administrative office. They do not reach any definite conclusions though her father doesn't appear to be concerned. She feels slightly sick and asks for a glass of water. Now he is anxious, for it is unlike his daughter to behave in this way. 'Shall we go home?' he suggests.

'Yes please. It's been rather a strain. Worse than a busy day on the desk,' and she offers a faint smile. 'I'll be fine.'

In the train they sit opposite, across a table. It's a fast train, and smooth. Lucy feels as though she wants to close her eyes and let go – to relax and empty her mind. Her father seems to have already started a doze, so she follows her inclinations. Immediately, questions begin to flit through her head. Have I done the right thing? Will I regret leaving the Barnsdale where they are so nice? If it goes wrong, will they take me back? Do I really want to live in London? Where is the money going to come from? Father? Her own savings do not amount to much, she realises – and how will she live? Perhaps she'll do some concert work if the College will allow. The constant noise of wheels on track ultimately lulls her so efficiently that finally she falls asleep.

A dream? If so, a happy one, with an audience on its feet and the clapping going on and on, her hand held up by the conductor – ultimately allowed to leave the stage with an armful of flowers. This must be where she is going to make her name. Someone is holding her arm, whispering, *Lucy, Lucy* … She wakes. It's her father. 'Our stop,' he's saying. She rubs her eyes, sits up and looks at her watch. 'How are you feeling now?' she's asked. After the sleep – and the nice dream – she feels a lot better. They climb off the train, walk out into the wintry evening, reach the car and drive home. It's been an awfully long day.

Her mother is waiting, anxious, wishing she could have gone as well but believes it would have been seen as too pushy. She greets her daughter on the doorstep, holds her tight, hugs. 'How do you feel, Lucy, dear? Do you think … '

Her father interrupts. 'Elizabeth my dear, please let us take a breather and get our coats off. Is there a cup of tea?' He is smiling, aware of the pressure, aware too, that the first hurdle is behind them.

How to pay for her tuition and her board becomes the vexing question. There is no other decision to discuss; it is evident from the light in her eyes, her skipping steps and the immediate difficulty in prising her away from the piano stool that she's happy with her choice. After the weekend at home, she is to return to the hotel with her news. She promised.

Her father drives her, as before, but waits in the car for the reaction. She is gone nearly twenty minutes and as he gets out to walk across to find her, she erupts from the reception doorway and hurls herself towards him.

'Hey, steady on! Tell me, why you're looking so pleased?'

She can hardly draw breath. 'Remember Christmas Day? The old couple – who I chatted to? Anna and Hubert Schweitzer? Told me how they first met.' She has to stop and wipe her eyes. 'Lovely people. Well, Sam told them about me and how I might possibly follow my music. They said to get in touch with them – they've gone home now – because they hinted, so Sam says, they'd like to help. He thinks they …' She stops. 'Sorry, dad. You won't want them to pay for me, will you?'

He eases her away, pulls out a handkerchief to dab her tears. 'You'll have to talk to them. Then we'll decide, depending on their inclinations. Churlish to ignore a kind thought, you realise?'

She nods. 'Please come and say 'hello' to Sam. He's been awfully good about this.'

They return to the reception; Sam takes them through to his office. Settling into his large round-armed chair, he repeats his earlier conversation for the benefit of her father, 'Lucy, once I'd heard you play there was no other option in my mind. I know, because I go to concerts when I can. I didn't realise it was you who'd played so magically at Barn Hill last year. At the Charity Concert – where you wore a grey dress with sparkly trim?'

She nods. 'I know I played well that night,' and the vibes came flooding back. *Jones and his 'You-are-lovely'.* She must thank him.

'So the impromptu concert here was putting the pieces together. I think the fates conspired, Lucy. You mightn't have had the same chance to play at the George, certainly not in front of your friend Mr Fortescue – nor to meet with the Schweitzer's – so it all falls into place. You're a lucky – and talented – young lady. The worst part is losing the nicest new member of staff and my resident pianist. I'll ask you to come back and play for us again, some day. Will you do that?'

She nods through another flow of tears. Of course she will. And she'll bring Jones. It'll be a while, but it will happen. She knows it will.

Sam – so understanding, so big hearted, a true believer in people, he'd been her trigger point, the decisive factor that produced this amazing turn-around in her life. Him and Jones, of course. But thinking back, it is her mother, coercive and persistent all through her cognitive years, who had brought her to this level. How stubborn she'd been – believing she only had the one role in life, yet now, with a situation forced – no, not forced, but one developed from a different set of circumstances – she could see her world from another perspective. So her mind runs as her father takes her home. Away from Sam, the lovely little room he'd let her have, the hotel, the people she'd met who worked there – like Beth – and her idea of a career. They draw up in front of her house. Her father turns towards her.

'Lucy, darling daughter,' and he has his hands folded in his lap,

'I believe you'll come to see this turning point as a truly momentous one, not to be regretted. Yes, I think you'd have done well with managing a hotel, but you'll do well in anything if it's right for you. You're my daughter. And I'm very, very proud of you, and I love you … '

Lucy hears the break in his voice, sees moistening eyes and is overcome. She cries, she can't help it, and screws her hands in her skirt to try and stop herself. Then he pats her knee and offers her his handkerchief again. Ultimately they grin at each other.

'Best go in. Your mother will want to know how you got on. And we've got to get in touch with your friends, the Schweitzer's. If they want to help, it's because they need to. Never disparage another's offer of help, Lucy. A giver may have an equal necessity. Okay?'

They go indoors, Lucy's father goes into his den, her mother embraces her daughter, holds her tight. Elizabeth knows the strain imposed on Lucy will take time to wear away, but her music will sooth her. As an artist paints or an author or composer writes from inspiration, so too a musician truly needs inspiration to play, to gain an experience they can share with their viewer, reader, or listener. This Elizabeth knows well. Lucy will need to build on whatever inspiration has brought her thus far. She asks how the conversation went at the hotel. Lucy explains.

'Mum,' she says, 'Sam – the manager – was at the Barn Hill concert. He first heard me there and remembered my dress. That's when he thought I was good. Not just at the hotel, but he linked with my playing the same piece.' A pause. Should she? 'That evening, in the audience, someone reached my mind, mum. Told me how lovely my playing was. It helped.' *Inspired me, made me feel so … wanted?*

'We all need encouragement, Lucy, dear. A true musician cannot play mechanically and give a listener the right feel.' To humour her girl, Elizabeth asks the question but already believes she knows the answer. 'Do you know who that someone was? Not your Sam?'

'No, mother, not Sam. But I'm sure I know who. The young man from the bookshop you took a liking to and invited for tea; did you feel sorry for him or was it something else?' She needed to know. Her mother wasn't in the habit of inviting stray young men for tea so perhaps there is something else – and if so, what?

Elizabeth is caught. Her assumption is correct. Her instinct guided her well. But where does she go from here? She cannot be seen not to understand, though she is perplexed. That young man, reaching into her daughter's mind? How could that be? But then, she'd invited him to their home on a whim.

'I, er, I liked him, Lucy, and he'd been very good, getting me the book I wanted, so it … well, seemed a nice thing to do. And you do need to meet a few more people your own age,' she finished, with a more commonsense reason.

'Nothing else?'

Elizabeth shakes her head. Lucy has her own thoughts but decides to let the query rest. She goes up to her room, sits on the edge of her bed and ponders. Mother's answers didn't fool her. That invite came out of the blue … *out of the blue! That weird thing again! It's all adding up. The constant thought, it's all* meant *to happen! Everything! Ever since that day when she was coming home from school.*

Encouraged, she changes into a less dressy frock and returns downstairs. Her mother has gone into the kitchen. Lucy's steps take her towards the piano. She sits, closes her eyes and concentrates. *Jones.* Nothing. She tries to imagine him and where he is. Nothing. *Jones!* Nothing, not a glimmer or sparkle anywhere in her head. *Has he deserted her, now that she's committed to her music?* She fingers the keys, idly, wondering what she should play. The notes follow each other, the chords lead on, her hands take on an aspect of her brain, she plays from her mind, her spirit flowing into her arms and the quiver of some impossible to describe feeling runs through every nerve. *Orgasmic,* this must be the definition. It is *her* piece, the one she knows so well, played that evening, played at the hotel, played for the assessors in London, and now, again, for her and for her *alter ego.*

And at that absolute moment, back it comes, the voice in her head. *You are lovely … You have captured my soul with the music of your being* …and she plays on, enraptured. She does not notice, but her mother comes to the open door, to listen and watch her daughter play with head bowed, eyes closed, arms rippling and fingers dancing. Her father also comes and puts his arm around his wife as they stand and wonder and hear their daughter's expressed perfection in music as she seeks to offer her soul in ecstasy to the spirit who brought her to this belief in her being.

∽

And what of Jones? At this absolutely precise moment? He is walking through a redolence of rooms in an old building just on the edge of the town centre. An *ambiance,* no less, in which he discovers himself perfectly at home, at ease. This place saw him as a scarcely-out-of-short-trousers lad seeking to drown in books, a place of refuge from the mundane and for the misunderstood. It also saw him as an earnest seeker of specific knowledge, browsing through book after book, becoming not a nuisance as someone less understanding may have thus have him labelled, but as an interest for the now elderly man who wishes to step aside.

The situation had been outlined, discussed and elaborated upon over mugs of tea in the owner's own den upstairs on the fourth floor. He had listened, encouraged. Jones was still seen, from his lofty heights of many years, as a callow youth. Inexperienced and immature as defined – inexperienced in that he had less than a decade's absorption of what makes a decent seller of books, immature in that he had run from a situation which would have been the envy of many another.

'Why run?' he had asked of Jones on a previous day.

'Run?' Jones had queried, 'I didn't run – did I?' and the question had him probing the *raison d'etre* of his actions. Maybe the old man was right?

'The opportunity to carry on such a specifically decent business in Stamford – no sane person would have jettisoned the option. No, there must be some other reason. Tell, for it will help clear your head,' he was told.

So Jones had to perforce explain, from the emotive aspect (Samuel's constant ghostly presence), to the emotional one (Briony's departure), the relationship one (Daphne and Doreen) and the incomprehensibly mystifying one (Lucy).

'Ah. Your Samuel's overriding presence I understand, as I do that of an overbearing or a clinging female, but I am not qualified to comprehend how the departure of a woman friend can urge you to such an action.' (Yeates was unmarried, akin to Samuel, and Jones wondered whether there was a sinister aspect to bookselling he hadn't yet disinterred) 'Neither do I quite see the point regarding your virtual friend (as Jones had so explained her involvement). 'If she's in your head one moment and not the next, surely this can happen anywhere, here, there or wherever.'

They'd parted soon after their conversation and now Jones is back, having yet another browse and reliving the past. He takes a book off the shelf, idly flips pages, replaces it and selects another, absorbing – or trying to – the philosophy behind Yeates's choice of stock. He lifts another and it is a biography of a composer. *Zing!* and Lucy is there, in his head. He can hear her playing, poised over the keys in the sublime picture of a grey dress.

… You have captured my soul with the music of your being …
Such profound thoughts.

… This will not do. I cannot allow myself to despoil your bright and beautiful being. You don't need me, you have your music. That is all you need. Live your life, Lucy, as I will lead mine. Maybe we'll meet again. If the fates conspire, dictate. I'll keep you safe. I promised.

Jones shakes his head, replaces the book. What on earth is he doing, messing about with a girl in his head? He goes to find Yeates, immersed in some more obscure reasoning behind today's Times newspaper. 'Can we do a deal?' he asks, as Yeates looks up and grins at him over a much-folded paper.

Royal College of Music

Ten

Allargando ... Enlarging

Lucy steps off the pavement, her music case swung jauntily in one hand, her little umbrella clasped firmly in the other, thrilled with her end-of-year assessment. She's on her way home. She isn't looking behind her, only towards the lovely concept of a nearby lime tree's Spring-inspired tremendous surge of green, lime green leaves, and a dream of what's in store.

The taxi swerves, its driver's hand hard on the horn, and though the three-quarter ton block of a black cab doesn't actually hit her directly, the effect is to spin her round and throw her back onto the kerb, front first. The sprawling catastrophe of a girl lies still, hands outstretched, a leather case protecting one from the harsh abrasion of concrete, the grip on a rolled-up brolly preventing her other fingers from harm. So a pianist's assets are saved. But her leg is badly jarred and an ankle is twisted. She is shocked, hurt and rather frightened, unaware of the extent of damage done. Good Samaritans surround her; the taxi has vanished into Kensington traffic anonymity. She is helped in her struggle to stand, though only by leaning heavily on a burly male can she do so.

'Here, laas, gie us that case,' he says, and she relinquishes her grip. 'Now, cans't walk?'

'Best see if ought's broke,' says a different voice, whilst a woman in an old green serge coat picks up the brolly.

'You a student, then?' asks another. Lucy's head is throbbing, but she cannot determine why. With the one free hand she points back at the College.

Between the assemblage of concerned helpers, she limps up the steps under the canopy and is escorted through the heavy wood and glass paned doors and into the lobby. Here the college staff take over and thank the passers-by for their aid. The burly man stays a few minutes longer, ensuring she knows she has both case and brolly. 'Ee laas, thou camest ah right purler. Next time, tek a guid look 'ahind 'ee,' and with that near incomprehensible smidgeon of dialectal advice, he goes.

Sat into a reception comfy chair, she experiences the fuss and concern of Sally the receptionist, from one of the passing tutors from the percussion section she only vaguely knows, and from her friend Beatrice who was five minutes behind her in tutorial. They mull over options and suggest a visit to the nearby hospital. Lucy is not impressed, she has no experience of hospitals and no wish to learn. 'If I wash it clean and perhaps a bandage?' she offers, relieved there's nothing broken but only bruised. Her ankle's pain may take a while to go; however, once back home it'll be tolerable, or so she hopes.

Beatrice is a brick. Travels the Underground in company, sees her to Kings Cross, persuades the station staff to allow her past the barrier to 'see her friend into the train', checks she's still able to move her leg once she's installed in her carriage, that the ankle swelling isn't too great and promises to telephone Lucy's parents. 'Thanks,' Lucy offers with a partial smile, thinking it's a good job she doesn't have to change trains and it's only an hour and a bit's time of a journey.

'Sure you're okay?'

'I'm fine, well, sort of. See you next term. Have a good holiday. Oh, and regards to your parents, Bee. Thanks again.' Lucy lets herself sag into the cushion, grateful the compartment's empty. 'Best go, Bee, unless you want to get caught on the train.'

Another woman enters the compartment, glances at her, puts a bag on the rack, takes out a magazine – Good Housekeeping – and ignores her. Two minutes, and the whistle blows.

It's not the train she wanted to catch, but a slower one and therefore not crowded. No one else enters the compartment and after ten minutes of train noise Lucy finds her eyes closing. A hectic morning, an adrenaline rush receiving the assessment comments and the shock of the accident (silly girl, she reminds herself) all together too much. She isn't asleep, just dozing, letting a brain slow down from all this banging-about it's had.

A year. Well, no, about seven months. Feels like a year. Gosh. So much's happened. And now I've a whole two months break. Sort of. Still got to practise, though. Three local recitals mother's organised – trust her! And I'll go back to Barnsdale, as I promised. Her mind jerks. *I said I'd take my near-virtual friend …* she's been so pre-occupied *… so long ago now since I connected with him. I really must try and find him. I really must …* and the reverie deepens into sleep.

The train pulls into its first stop. The loss of movement and reduction in noise wakens her to a minor state of alarm – but no, this isn't her destination. The woman opposite who's not said a word, stands, turns round, takes her case off the rack and goes. Lucy's alone. Her leg is throbbing. Another half hour.

Hope father's meeting me. Said he would. What will he think about me having an accident? Mother'll be panicking. Bet she's cooked a nice meal, despite the fright she's had.

This journey she's done so often now. Up to London on Monday, back on Friday. In digs for four nights. She's lost a lot of her immaturity, even given she'd been in the hotel trade for what, five months? Does she miss it? Yes and no; misses the people contact, the buzz, the nice glow she got when guests thanked her for doing something well. Doesn't miss long unsocial hours, snatched meals, constant attention to trivial detail. Misses Jones, now she's thought about him. Wonders where he is, what he's doing. Shame he sold the bookshop. Mum likes the new owner though, says he reminds her of Mr Pickwick.

We're here. Glad I'm not carting my luggage about. Hope father's on the platform.

Lucy can't run to meet him, but he's hurrying towards her, looks her up and down, takes the music case. She holds onto her brolly but she still manages to give him a hug. 'Thanks, dad,' she says, 'sorry I missed my proper train. I guess Bee's phone message upset things rather. How's mother?'

Her father shakes his head. 'Concerned,' he says. 'Can you walk?'

'Slowly. I jarred my left leg and twisted my right ankle, though it's okay at the moment. Good job I didn't hurt my hands. All my fault, mind on other things,' and this was the best bit. 'I've been told I can study with …,' mentioning a name father wouldn't know but mother jolly well would. 'only it's in Paris. The *Conservatoire*, you know. Sometime next year, a short-term exchange thing. Shows I'm well thought of.'

They walk slowly down the platform; her father has an arm round her waist as a support. 'Well *done*,' he says. ' Trust my daughter to do things right.' His arm squeezes her tighter, just for a second. He'd drop a kiss on her cheek, but there's some funny looks coming in their direction; him a middle-aged man with his arm round a very pretty girl …

Her mother's waiting, takes both hands to hold her daughter as she's scanned up and down. Lucy laughs, 'Mum, really – I'm not that bad. Nothing a few days taking it easy won't sort. Bruised leg,' and she pulls a hand free, lifts a skirt hem to reveal a red abrasion on her lower thigh and a bruise beginning to colour on her leg muscle. 'That and a ricked ankle.'

Her father's standing by. ' Tell your mother the other news. Take her mind off your war wounds.'

'What news is that, Lucy?'

'I'm going to the *Conservatoire* in Paris. With … '

And, as predicted, the name *was* known. 'Oh my goodness! Lucy, you lucky girl! He's *the* interpreter of Chopin, everyone knows that.'

'I don't,' says her husband, dryly, 'but if it will help …'

'Oh, it will, dad, it will. He's got all the contacts. I shan't want for engagements, not after that.'

'So I'll lose my daughter into the rarefied world of the concert round.'

Lucy risks standing on tiptoe like a ballet dancer to offer him a pecked kiss on his cheek. 'I'll always be your daughter, dad.'

'Happier as a piano player than playing manager in some hotel?'

She nods. 'Now, yes I am,' and remembers to whom she owes so much. 'Mother – do you know what happened to the young man we had to tea that day, ages ago? The one who ran the bookshop?'

Elizabeth lifts a quizzical eyebrow and Lucy's father gives a slight cough. 'I'll be in my den,' he says, retreating from girly talk.

'My dear, I believe he went away. The lovely old man who now runs the shop may know, if you really want to find out.' She eyes her daughter carefully. 'Does he mean anything to you after all this time? I mean, you've not said anything about boyfriends.'

'Later, mother. I'd like to have a bath, change, perhaps we'll have tea. Then I can be me.'

'Very well dear.' Elizabeth is starting to accept her daughter, her nineteen and a half year old daughter, is understandably showing very adult tendencies and womanly ones at that.

Lucy goes upstairs and lets the bath water run while she slips out of London clothes, grimacing at a frayed skirt. The bruises look worse. *Silly girl,* she mutters under her breath again and pads nakedly across the landing, back to an excessively full bathtub.

Elizabeth waits until she hears the bathroom door close, then moves into the hall to the phone. She has to thumb through the directory first; it isn't every day she talks to the bookshop. '*Ah – there it is, now what was his name? Timothy, Terence? No, definitely Timothy. Lovely fellow, so intelligent, dry sense of humour.*' She is talking quietly to herself as the phone is ringing out.

'Timothy? Good afternoon. This is Mrs Salter of Greenhouse Lane. I wonder, do you happen to know where your predecessor went? We'd like to get in touch.' Explanations were not to be given unless absolutely essential. He wouldn't understand.

Mr Pickwick – she'd always think of him as such and would have to be careful about the epithet in public – did his characteristic *hmmpph hmmpph* noise before a pause. She can sense his thought processes, like *should I tell her* and *where did I put his address?* 'Ah hmmm,' she hears amidst a rustle of papers. 'Somewhere up in Lincolnshire.'

She frowns. '*This* is Lincolnshire.'

'Ah hmmm. So it is, so it is, always think of it as Rutland, d'you know. Louth. Yes, Louth. Mind you, what the young man's doing now is anyone's guess. Said he was fed up of old bookshops. Did me a favour, d'know.' Another silence; she wonders if he'd say anything else meaningful, but, no, it was merely a 'hope you're keeping well, Mrs Salter,' and that was that.

Louth – as in Lincolnshire, not the county of the same name in Ireland. That was all. Lucy will not be satisfied with merely a town's name. It may not be a huge place, but still large enough, and into which he'd easily disappear. Her peculiar instinct for these things surfaces and she enters her husband's sanctum. His den, as he calls it, where he takes refuge.

'Adrian. Can we take a couple of days away?'

He looks up from totalling a lengthy column of figures, with an anticipated frown.

'I know. Sorry. Should have waited until teatime, but this is important.'

He leans back in the captain's chair, his pride and joy. 'How important, Elizabeth?' He never calls her Liz, or Betty, for which she is eternally grateful and another reason to love him.

'For Lucy's sake?'

The frown goes, replaced with a grin. 'The darling daughter. So why away?'

'I'd like us to spend a weekend in Louth.'

'Louth?' He is surprised. 'Why there, for heaven's sake?'

'It's got a very nice parish Church.'

He grins again. 'And?'

'I think Lucy'd like to find her secretive admirer. The young man we had for tea ages ago. After Samuel's death.'

'He's there?'

'So Mr Pickwick thinks.'

'Mr Pickwick? Who on earth is he?'

Elizabeth laughs. 'The bookshop?' then hears the bathwater go. 'If we can find Lucy's friend it'll please her no end. Keep it as a surprise?'

'All right, my love,' and yes, he would like to do something for his daughter before she grows too adult and thus away from him.

❧

Jones has had a busy six months or so. Yeates – a very canny man – kept him on a string for at least three weeks before the sale finally went through and he became the proud owner of a proper bookshop. Proper in the sense he now primarily sold new titles as well as a few second hand instead of purely the latter as in Stamford. Made a refreshing change, for it has altered his perception of a customer base; no longer was he purely dealing with academics, collectors and seekers after bargains but with – and his parents laughed as he explained – real life people. Of course, it pretty well soaked up all his inherited equity – for though the business of the Stamford shop sold well and left him with substantial funds, Yeates had driven a hard bargain. Mind you, it did include the freehold of the premises, something he'd never have had from Doreen. She'd muttered and moaned at him for the few weeks it had taken to quit the place, but he managed it in the end.

Another down side was giving up his household freedom. Whereas before, in the terrace pad, he could please himself and everything done was his responsibility, now he had to live at home and obey mother's rules. He sold the settee and a few other oddments, left the curtains but carted the rest home with every trip he made. When he handed the keys back to the agent there was real regret on both sides, but it couldn't be helped.

He never went back up the hill on the north side of town to revisit old haunts. Haunts indeed; the earlier oft-seen mental picture of Briony in her various states of *dishabille* had done his state of *sang-froid* no good at all. Neither did he visit Hannah's – too expensive for him on his own, and rumour suggested it might founder. He'd had a couple of postcards from Briony, en route to her present abode somewhere on America's west coast. She'd kept them fairly low-key; the wonderment was that she'd sent any – given she'd run away from what had become a turbulent relationship. That last night – phew!

But Lucy, as a virtual image, she never left his side. True, he didn't talk to her often; what he did was total madness, smoothing out and talking to an old pound note that lived in the Rie charger, now in pride of place on the little desk in his bedroom. He wouldn't have entrusted its continued existence downstairs in the sitting room to his mother – she dusted far too vigorously. Occasionally he thought more of the girl, occasions that occurred at random, usually in the evenings, often on a Thursday night. He wasn't to know Thursday night was concert night at the College when students were routinely put on a stage to get real-time experience of the concert platform. When Lucy played, she thought of him; he in turn experienced thought waves of how much he missed her music.

∽

Jones: I actually love this place. It's become part of me, its Georgian bow window, its quirky doorway with the big step (keeps the push chairs out, for better or worse) its little rooms and the windy staircase. I love it. And. moreover, it's actually making money. Yeates said it would – the accounts showed he kept the place in the black most months – certainly I bank more than I'd expected. Maybe it was a new face, the curiosity factor, maybe because I am pleasant to my customers. Yeates, for all his bonhomie towards me, had a reputation for a blunt directness, like 'you've looked at it, now buy the bloody thing' or words to that effect as I understood from more than one regular browser.

One thing missing. You've guessed it? Well, I am a virile twenty four year old male, who's previously lapped at Venus's pool for many a month and now there's a part of me that is missing its regular exercise. Naughty, I know, but gazing at the Botticelli drawings in the 'Great Painters of the World' book amongst my stock doesn't quite compare with mental pictures of Briony in similar poses to Sandro's models.

Then one Saturday afternoon, late on, when I'm doing my weekly stock orders but finding it hard to concentrate, the bell tinkles. As was my wont, I down tools (pencil, scrappy pad, catalogues, sales list) and amble slowly down stairs to see who wants what late on this rather warm afternoon. Bookshops are not known for their busiest footfall on sunny Saturday afternoons at the backend of July. From top floor (office) to ground floor takes a minute or so and during my descent I get this odd feeling. I've had it before but not lately; the spine tingling, the heightened nerves, the idea of being on the threshold of a momentous happening.

I turn the corner of the stairs to where I can see into the ground floor, and there she is. The glossy rich dark chestnut hair, the slender figure, a lacey white blouse contrasting with lightly tanned arms, a swirly pale green skirt and the dark eyes with a mischievous glint staring up at me. The One, the one and only Lucy. Real life Lucy – and this I cannot believe. I stop exactly where I am and pull her into my soul, soak in her closeness, gather the totality of her being around me. We don't utter a word, for there is no need, not for this precious moment. The golden threads, so tenuous yet so strong, snap as tight as released elastic to bind virtual beings together, relief alloyed with apprehension.

Then the spell breaks and I take the last eight stair treads. Now her smile is coy, with the subtlety of an eighteenth century heiress or Jane Austen character, delightful dimples beginning to appear in the natural bloom of those cheeks. Her hands are clasped in front of her. I notice the ribbon in her hair, the simple silver chain with its small heart-shaped pendant, the wide leather belt with a tortoiseshell buckle, the plain white blunt-ended shoes with low heels.

'Do I come up to expectations, Jones?' Her amused voice, the ever-so slightly husky voice I'd ever remember; *keep me close,* the last words heard from another world. What can I say? Tongue-tied is the standard expression, the verbal equivalent of writer's block. Bereft of my customary bonhomie the silence is scary. Her very presence is un-nerving yet so natural, as if she belongs. We belong.

… You have captured my soul with the music of your being …

I take a step towards her and she holds out her hands.

'Surprised?' she asks as I clasp them together in my own. The warmth and our concurrent senses join.

'Surprised,' I say weakly, as our eyes link, brain to brain, mind to mind, soul to soul.

The stupidly simple question. 'How did you find me?' It wasn't as though I'd covered my tracks or anything, but merely because I could not believe we should meet in such direct circumstances. Or did I? Were the physical manifestations of our first intimation, the Rie charger and the pound note, now less than sufficient?

She relinquishes my hands and I feel bereft. 'Parents,' she says, tapping her nose. 'Detective work. My mother asked your successor in Samuel's old shop. And brought me up here as a surprise.'

'But ... '

'I know. He only said Louth. We walked around, I spotted the bookshop and *knew* I'd find you.' There isn't any trace of awkwardness in her voice, she's talking as though we are brother and sister. 'My parents are in the teashop down the street. I'd better let them know.' She turns towards the door.

'Lucy,' I say and she looks back at me. 'I ...,' and hesitate. What do I say to this girl who is part of me and yet isn't? '... I'd like to hear you tell me what you're doing, where you are. Can we share some time together?'

Her gaze is steady, forthright, and there is no hesitation. 'We're already shared our lives for a while, you and I, in a weird and wonderful way. But yes, I'd love to explain what I've achieved, because you're the one who's helped me.' Simple statement, so very adult, and I'm lost, enmeshed in this esoteric relationship that I doubt neither of us understands.

I watch her go, suddenly concerned for she moves awkwardly down the step. A girl like her surely would have skipped? The order list is abandoned; I check the windows, lift the takings bag from the till and lock the door behind me. The Bank is along the street, four doors down. It only takes a minute to lodge the stiff leather bag with its steel edges and funny little lock into the night safe. Then I retrace my steps past the shop and along to Joan's, the tea shop of which she spoke.

At a table towards the back, she is sitting facing the door, a parent on each side. All three stand and I feel dreadfully embarrassed. The last time I saw Lucy's parents – and her – I was a guest in their home.

Mr Salter offers me his hand. It's firm and dry. Mrs Salter takes her seat again, as does Lucy. Mr Salter gestures at the vacant chair.

'Please, do join us. I'm so glad Lucy found you,' and I see him look at her with an indulgent, fond parent expression.

Mrs Salter smiles at me. 'We thought we'd have a weekend away and as Lucy wondered what had become of you, we used the query as the basis for a small adventure. And here you are! Tell us how this all came about.'

Because I was fleeing Briony's memory? Because I couldn't stand Doreen? Because I kept on seeing Samuel's ghost? Or because I was frightened of the intensity of feelings I had every time Lucy came within a mile of me? Feelings that had every chance of drowning me in emotion and chaos even now?

'Would you like some tea?' Lucy's father waves at the waitress (young Clare, nice girl, comes and buys a new classic romance every month).

'Thank you, very kind,' I say, but aware the teashop likes to close at five and it is five minutes to. Perhaps Clare tells Joan who it's for, and she only takes a minute to bring another teacup and saucer and a fresh pot. She also brings a new plate of cakes and a lovely smile. Dear Clare. Take a couple of bob (ten new pence for the modern reader) off her next book purchase, I tell myself.

I explain how I went to school here, my parents still live in the patch and the bookshop just happened to come up for sale at the opportune time.

'But why leave Stamford? Such a nice place and Samuel's was *such* a lovely shop,' Mrs Salter persists.

I catch Lucy's eye. How can I say I was running away from the potential of damaging the fragile growth of a feeling for her? We both know – or at least I think I'm sure we both know – this spontaneous linkage is a powerful thing, so powerful it has the capability to destroy us both. Samuel, dear old man, I'm sorry, ... 'I couldn't cope with not seeing Samuel in the shop,' I say, putting on as mournful an expression as I can. True, to a point.

Her mother nods, an 'I understand' type of nod. Her father, with very much more of the prosaic accountant's view, adds, 'and probably not the most stable income?' Lucy stays quiet, not losing my gaze. She's a deep thinker, that one.

'I've done fairly well here,' I reply, with an honest view. The tea is welcome and Joan's cakes legendary. 'Would you like a private viewing?' Quite what produced that offer I'm not sure; the unreality of the whole saga is intimidating – the One and her parents, on the doorstep, totally out of the blue.

Mrs Salter – Elizabeth – likes the idea. Father goes along with it, Lucy merely smiles as though she knew I'd dish out the invitation. Father pays the bill, I thank him, we all get up and I follow them out of Joan's, giving young Clare a wave. Lucy's limping slightly. I catch up with her and politely pose the concerned query, 'Lucy, you're limping?'

'It's nothing, really. Had a brush with a London taxi because I wasn't thinking. Only a bruise and a sprained ankle.'

'Only!' I offer her a hand, which she accepts. Her parents are ahead and don't notice, at least I don't think they have. The contact jolts me again. It isn't difficult to remember the last tea party and her parting kiss. I think my head's beginning to spin.

The tour of inspection of my premises takes a good half-hour. Mrs Salter – *call me Elizabeth, please* – wants to buy a copy of Arthur Mee's Lincolnshire. Who am I to say no? I let her have it with a small discount, which makes her very happy. A small price to pay for keeping in her good books, if you'll excuse the pun. Lucy stays on the ground floor. 'Another day,' she says, excusing herself. Another day? There's a promise I will treasure. Then it's time to part. I see Elizabeth whispering in her husband's ear and pretend not to notice.

'Would you care to have lunch with us tomorrow?' he asks and behind him I see Lucy nod enthusiastically. 'We're staying at the Mason's Arms. 'Bout half twelve?'

'That is very kind of you,' I say, 'it will be a pleasure,' and suddenly I pluck up hidden courage. 'Would Lucy like to take a short walk through our local beauty spot before hand? If her bruises will allow? Say about ten – I can call for her?'

There's what can be described as a 'knowing look' between Lucy's parents and did the girl give a secret signal in the affirmative or what? Mr Salter looks at his daughter, eyebrows interrogatively raised.

'Yes,' she says, 'that would be lovely, provided it doesn't rain. I'm sure the exercise will do me good.'

I watch them walk away and wait. Yes, Lucy looks back. My heart goes ger-plunk ger-plunk. It never did that when I was with Briony, not even when we … well, you know what I mean.

Hubbard's Hills

Eleven

Affettuosa ... With Tenderness

It's Sunday. Day of rest and relaxation; well, for some. Jones is up early after a night of spinning dreams, a crazy whirl of mixed up emotions. He can't remember them all, though Lucy inevitably appeared in there somewhere, a misty figure floating through a vast concert hall with music cascading across a landscape of monochrome trees and water. *Keep me close,* she was saying, *keep me close.*

A vexatious Briony came into the hotchpotch somewhere. Probably jealous. She'd no reason to be. He hasn't any aspirations whatsoever to behave in the same way with Lucy. She is far and away too precious a being to tarnish.

His parents never ask questions; he's an adult living in their house as a stranger yet as a son, a lodger yet a welcome guest. He senses their continual pride and contentment. He leaves in good time to walk the half mile to the hotel, set into the Market Square as though the town grew up around it. Part of the scenery. The Market never changes either, the bustle of the commerciality of rural life only different in dress and merchandise from ages ago. Today it is quiet, as if the buildings looking down are holding their breath, poised to watch how another greeting will fare. Jones pauses at the doorway. He has rarely crossed this threshold; too young, too nervous, suspicious of how the establishment might swallow him up. That was before Cambridge, before Stamford. Before Lucy.

He knows she is there, waiting for him, their essential *personae* link simply and easily. Rising out of an armchair, just as he'd imagined. The same grace first experienced way back, the same aura. A simple dress, bare arms, legs, a ribbon in her hair. A smile as she steps towards him. Holds out her hands which he takes and feels the bond.

'You look nice.'

The dimples deepen. 'Thankyou,' she says. So simple.

Jones wants to kiss her, but what seems like a fragile thin glass of a mysterious sense of correctness between them prevents him. He is still seeking the answer to an inexplicable differential between his relationship with her and the other women. Two women of the past, hungry for part of him but not partaking of his soul. She has control of that.

He retains a clasp of one hand and watches carefully as she takes the steps onto the pavement. The sun's warmth greets them, released from the cool dim depths of the hotel's foyer. It is going to be a brilliant day.

They walk through the little passage, progress sedately across the road and towards the memorable stone mass of the Parish Church catching the sunlight and throwing sparkles of colour at them from ancient glass. She appears to have no trace of a limp today but he cannot help glancing down as they reach the cobbled lane. Her acceptance of his unexpressed concern comes with a turned head and another dimpled smile. This is unreal. Yesterday at this time she wasn't the pleasure of a close three-dimensional living warmth, merely a miniature perpetual presence living in the back corners of his mind. Today, she is the One, alongside him.

Six months or so ago, he'd trod this self-same route of a late evening, seeking refuge from cloying Christmas cheer, alone in thoughts and company, until …

113

'Lucy,' he says, suddenly, 'last Christmas, where were you?'

She thinks, very briefly. 'At Barnsdale. Why?'

'What happened?'

A chuckle. 'I played the piano at teatime. Life changing moment.'

'No more hotels?'

She swings their clasped hands. 'Nope,' and giggles. 'Unless I stay in one. At least I can see what's it like through knowledgeable eyes.'

'This one?' meaning the Mason's Arms.

'It's all right. Nothing like the Barnsdale.' She wrinkles a nose and sounds pensive. 'I've got to go back there and play for them again. As a sort of reward. I promised.'

'You happy with your progress?'

'Mmmm,' and her response implies 'not really, but I'm getting there'.

They reach the little wooden gate and she stares across the parkland. Small family groups are beginning to settle down to the serious occupation of Sunday picnics; a few are playing games. A couple of dogs are chasing around, another is being walked on a lead, correctly at the owner's heel. 'A lovely scene,' she comments and he nods.

'Boyhood haunts,' he says. 'Know this place inside out. It knows me, too.' He opens the gate for her and she eases past him. He catches a faint drift of a fresh, clear perfume, nothing akin to Briony's more rounded fulsome one. 'Lucy,' and she looks back at him. 'I've never forgotten the first time I saw you. Do you know when?'

The gate closed behind them, they join hands again and walk on. Her skirt brushes against his legs, sensed rather than felt. She belongs alongside. But hasn't responded to the question, as though it were rhetorical.

'Lucy?'

She turns her head towards him; he catches her eyes again. Once more they connect with a growing awareness of a power unknown. 'I'd just come out of school, and later than normal. Something held me back that day, I lost a book or something. After then, ever since then, we've...' and another intense smile '... been going out with each other,' she swings his hand, the mischievousness of her years bubbling forth, 'without actually getting too close. Weird, but good, don't you think?'

A very strange feeling. They walk on, along the road, cross the bridge, again he opens a gate for her, she's close, so close, and this time there's no hesitation. It is only the second time they've kissed; however the jolt passes through him like an electric shock. 'Don't,' she says, drawing away. Inside, she's confused, seeking a continuation but aware they are opening a new awareness between them, which has the spice of excitement and the flavour of danger.

He cannot say 'sorry' because he isn't. Instead, he picks up her hand once more and they walk on, conscious this delightful summer morning is akin to a simple golden present from heaven.

The little river narrows down, burbles along beside the path. They are approaching the footbridge, step onto it, pause and she looks into the water. This is where he'd leant over the handrail and listened to the self-same rippling stream late on a Christmas Day evening and heard her voice in his head, seen her as a ghostly vision…. what was it she'd said?

Listen to me, please. Please, I need your help. You said I was lovely, once. Didn't you mean it was how I stirred your soul with my music? My music is me. Isn't it? Don't you believe in me? In my music? Not me as a mere girl, surely. There's plenty of other women, aren't there? Should I drown myself in music, for you? Could you be my strength? I need your strength. Your help. Ple-eease …

They are close, leaning on the rail, and Jones can see … *the vision of her face shaking in the water, just as she stood, eyes closed, waiting for his salutation, his kiss.* 'Lucy?' and the image vanishes from the water as she looks at him directly. 'You left the hotel world behind that night, didn't you?'

She nods. 'Difficult decision.' She sees a bench across the grass. 'Let's go and sit over there. Rest my ankle.'

Immediately he is solicitous. 'Oh, I'm sorry. Have we walked too far?' They move off the bridge and aim for the seat tucked below the treeline. She stays quiet until they're seated, then reaches down to rub her ankle and unselfconsciously lifts her skirt hem to show the bruise marks on her thigh. 'Colourful, isn't it? Good job I didn't damage my hands at all,' and is about to pull the material back down, when Jones stays her hand.

He reaches out with fingers spread and gently, ever so gently, strokes those bruises as if to apply a healing touch. Then eases the skirt's fabric down to cover her legs once more. A perfectly natural thing to do, nothing more than a caring, natural action. She rests her hands in her lap. Other Sunday morning strollers pass by fifty yards away, the morning is warming up. They stay quiet, absorbing the peace and the togetherness.

'You made the decision for me.' Lucy's thought returns to that evening and the telepathic plea she'd made from her little hotel bedroom, not knowing where he was. A flash of inspiration and a specific recall of poetry. 'You know Browning?

He asks, 'which one?'

'Elizabeth,' she says and chuckles, hoping she'll get it correct.

'... *With stammering lips and insufficient sound // I strive and struggle to deliver it right // that music of my nature – With dream and thought ...* '

He takes a hand and smoothes her long fingers, her piano-playing fingers.

'Where were you?' she asks.

Jones smiles in the remembrance. 'Here. All on my own in the dark. Apart from a moon. I heard you, Lucy. I was standing on the bridge. Saw your reflection in the water. Your figure in the trees.'

... Across the loom of the mown grass, dim in the night glow, along the path, another vision of a figure, swaying skirt, school bag at her side. Another, the picture of a girl in beautiful dress and the rippling sound of her music ... .

'And I'm sure I heard you, too ...' her mind flicks back, remembers ...

... I love your music, my Lucy – though I bought you in a virtual way, you are your own girl. You have captured my soul with the music of your being. There. Are you a contented girl now?...

'So I chose the music career my mother wanted for me. What you wanted for me. Does it sound silly?'

He shakes his head. *Shelly.* Cambridge, wherefore art thou? And quotes:

'*"Music, when soft voices die, // Vibrates in the memory"-*'

Not after all that has happened, it cannot be silly...

116

"'and so thy thoughts, when thou art gone // Love itself shall slumber on" … '

There is something of a power in their less than co-incidental meetings, there must be. How else would he be able to behave, to act, in the way he does? This is a complete contrast to his association with Briony; eventually Lucy must know about the woman so he can let his conscience rest. But he must not damage her faith in him, not for a moment, not for a second.

'Do we matter, Lucy? You and I? Will we continue in this weird companionship of ours? Me, knowing when you need me, you hearing me, us feeling when we're close?' So now, while he has the courage … 'Did you know I've had a relationship with an older woman?'

She laughs. 'Jones, it can't have been like us. It couldn't be, so it doesn't matter. There's only ever going to be you in my inner girl, and I'd know if any other female gets close to your – your *soul*, I guess. You didn't think of me when you were with whoever she was – is – did you?'

'We – er – *slept* together, Lucy. But she's gone now. Gone to America. Said she couldn't compete.'

Lucy takes this in. *Slept?* She understands the euphemism and the implications. The conversations over coffee in College, let alone the comments from her erstwhile school friends have sufficiently widened her understanding of the ways of the world. She also understands – and appreciates – her mother's attempts to 'explain the facts of life'. Her mother may well be scandalised if she finds out that Jones has – isn't the word '*bedded*' – had a woman, and sever all the links which at the moment are working in their favour. Nothing in her mind, though, concerns her about Jones's revelations. After all, he's a male and everything she knows about him suggests his masculinity isn't in question. She is also comforted in the realisation she's not at risk from any unwanted actions whatsoever.

'But there's wisdom in women …'

She watches his smile at her quote. Yes, she knows her literature! She stands up. Strangely, her thigh muscles don't pull at her bruises quite the same. Was it his touch?

'We'd better retrace our steps if we aren't going to be late for lunch,' she says, and holds out her hands. He takes them, she pulls him up and this time easily offers her mouth for a simple forgiving kiss.

✄

The lunch goes well. I have the extra confidence in place following Lucy's matter-of-fact – and erudite – approach to my revelations about Briony. On the walk back we'd talked over the way I'd fallen into Briony's clutches and she'd said 'Poor old you' which was great. She'd said about her mother's attempts to 'improve' her social circle and how she'd told her not to worry because College life catered for that side of things and anyway, she'd added, 'I've got you,' which was an even nicer comment.

Her parents have been to the Parish Church service and Elizabeth says how much she's enjoyed the choir's rendering of a particular anthem. I talk about my ideas on improving the shop's stock, how I have linked up with a few contemporaries who are still around the town, about the Music Club that meets in my old school, and the thorny question about moving into a place of my own, out from under my parent's feet. Lucy doesn't add much to the conversation but I feel her eyes on me most of the time. As I've said before, she seems so much like a sister; we are so natural with each other it isn't true. Perhaps my Briony experience has stood me in good stead.

Then, over coffee, Lucy's mother drops the bombshell. I know Lucy and I will be apart for a while because nothing had suggested otherwise, but to go abroad? *Paris!* Out of the country! The iron clutch round my heart. Bloody stupid expression that, but so apt. A tightness in my chest because I am falling in love with the concept of the girl. Oh, I know we have been 'connected' in a peculiarly paranormal sort of way and we've exchanged three casual kisses (how can a kiss with this delightful young lady be 'casual'?) but the relationship is undoubtedly starting to deepen to a far greater extent – and we are both aware, not surprising since our minds link, erratically maybe, but whenever necessary, which is the important aspect.

So when lunch is over and their bags are stowed into the dark green Singer Gazelle, I manage a few tactfully arranged minutes on my own with the girl and hold her in my arms. Her head is on my

118

shoulder and I stroke that gorgeous head of hair and whisper '*I love you*' in her ear and she says '*I know,*' and twists up to kiss me and that was that. She'd gone.

… *And I shall find some other girl perhaps…* . Lucy, take care.

Schloss Mirabelle, Salzburg

$\mathcal{T}welve$

Andante ... Moving Along

Our summer turned to autumn, autumn into inevitable winter and Christmas repeated itself. I walked out into the grim chill of a snow flurried evening, a solitary and simply mad figure, hunched shoulders, hands in pockets, slouching along a muddy path towards a bridge over a silent black watered river, leant where we'd leant, felt her spirit, felt her absence, felt the love for my virtual girl echo in an empty mind and yearned for the bright days and the warmth of a cool held hand. *Love itself shall slumber on.*

I didn't actually see Lucy again, physically, for a year, a whole sorrowful soul of a year. She sent me a postcard of the Champs Elysée in early March when she went to France for her Master class month and stayed there for another three. The next postcard I had was from Salzburg where she'd gone to study under another famous exponent of Strauss. That trip brought us telepathically together – as I'll tell you later. Who funded her, where she stayed if she came back to

England inbetween times I never knew. What gave me comfort was the repeated message in my brain, *keep me close* – and the presumption that if anything happened to her, I'd know. Why we didn't write to each other didn't seem relevant. She was mine, I was hers; soul mates, end of story. Only it wasn't.

Remember we'd quoted poetry at each other (the problem with a decent literary education, you have to have a darned good memory), well, that line from Shelley kept reverberating,
… and so thy thoughts, when thou art gone // Love itself shall slumber on…

My thoughts often turned to music, the vibrations in my mind. It was her, her playing, I knew it could be no other.

The bookshop is doing well. Inspired buying, good customer relations, decent ambiance and a contract to supply my old school all play their part. Parents are proud of me, mother fusses, pa sings my praises in the Chamber of Commerce; I am their boy wonder. But I can't stay here indefinitely, can I? I have to move forward, maintain an impetus. Lucy's figure is a constant presence, in the shop, in the road, the tea shop, oh, everywhere. Not that I feel threatened, no, nothing like that. It's just that I feel the need to give ourselves adequate space and time. So I confine Lucy to the fortress of my mind and let the more worldly world take over for the time being.

You have to understand I am expected to show myself around, be part of the social whirl. And that includes escorting girls and therefore being, well, sort of lovey-dovey to maintain the correct appearances. I couldn't become a monk, not a twenty-five year old very eligible bachelor (decent prospects, clean and tidy, and evidently with an adequately masculine appearance and smiley face). So, yes, I take the nicer figured girls out every now and again to tea dances, the cinema, out to the coast, even up to Grimsby or over to Lincoln. They have their reward, I have mine whenever girl, opportunity and circumstance allow. (One especially, by the sea, hidden in the dunes on a beach towel, in the August sunshine and with sand in her knickers…) On a couple of occasions I have cause to think back to the College days and the trophy wall, but bear in mind the only sex souvenir I'd ever been given worth keeping is secreted in my chest of drawers. Briony's. I think of her too, occasionally. Had a Christmas card – didn't I say – from San Francisco of all places. Says she'd be back some time and hopes we'll meet up. Lucy, oh dear Lucy, please don't get upset. My love slumbers. Different from passion, at least of the physical variety.

Ultimately I make up my mind. I'll take someone on to run the shop in my absence, sometime after Whitsun, and comes the wry thought of putting an ad in the TLS where I'd first seen the Stamford job. Like I was a Samuel, *r.i.p.* Then I wonder about Doreen and Samuel's shadow fades away.

I advertise in the *Louth Leader* instead. The person I need has to live in the town. Twelve random people apply. Dad helps me sort the applications out. We select four for interview, to be held in the shop, top floor (the office room was *just* big enough). On the day, the one who's currently unemployed telephones to say he can't come because he's sick and I don't believe him. Down to three. The first interviewee turns out to be a devious refugee (thirty, heavily built, a smoker) from the butchery trade. Down to two. Next in line is a twenty-seven year old woman, fresh away from a divorce and having to find her own income. No children: in this case, a blessing. She is articulate, pleasant, and has a decent figure (not that it will influence the decision, of course …). The last candidate of the day is young Clare from Joan's teashop. I have a lot of time for her and the interview brings her out in a new light. So I give her the job. She knows me, I know her, but I'm not happy about stealing her from Joan. 'Don't worry,' Joan says when I apologise. 'I know she's really too good for my place – I was bound to lose her sooner or later. Anyway, I've got a replacement all lined up,' and explains. Which makes me feel a whole lot better, because the replacement turns out to be my original candidate number three, the divorcee.

Clare settles into her new role within days and I thank my lucky stars. After two weeks I give her a pay rise and a friendly platonic kiss. She blushes, very charmingly, and comes to work the following Monday in a different skirt and nicer top and with a modicum of make-up. Very pretty. The shop takings even go up. I can go on my adventures with a clear conscience.

The old Traveller is fine. Never misses a beat and as solid as they come. I pack my luggage in the back, sling mum's lunchbox on the passenger seat, shake hands with dad, get a sloppy kiss from mum and off I go. Quite like old times. Where? Anywhere and nowhere, as the saying goes. I need to refresh my mind, give life a chance.

∞

Lucy: It's been tremendous, really really tremendous. I learnt such an awful lot this last College year and the Paris thing has capped it. Mind you, very hard work, day after day, hour after hour, practice practice practice. Being told off *so* many times, but finally, he was pleased with me. I've hardly had time to think about anything else. Now he wants me to go to Salzburg. Salzburg! Heavens! Mum was ever so bucked when I told her. We had a *very* long chat on the phone the other night – poor old dad, having the bill for such a lengthy long-distance call. But it's going to be worth it in the long run. People are already talking about me. The late-comer girl who's had recommendations from such *eminent* pianists of their age. Me, up and coming, getting praise from them! And to think I might have been stuck in an hotel …

Then it hits her. Barnsdale, the Christmas before last. The choice, the decision, and her cry for help into the ether, searching for him … Jones, oh, my dearest friend, I've abandoned you! Since the weekend in Louth, I've hardly had a breath, but I'm still here. I know it's a long time, but you and I, we've been *so* busy. With you in my heart, I promise. *Keep me close!*

∞

She moves to Salzburg, into yet more lodgings, this time alone. Her introduction to her mentor goes well and once more she is plunged into a hectic round of playing, taking heed of all she's told, playing piece after piece, and finally, out of the blue, a challenge.

'I want you to play for my friends, my dear lady,' she is asked in

123

a lovely Austrian accent and she is honoured, perhaps bemused the better statement of condition. Of course she will, she agrees, having in her mind a select gathering of say, a dozen or so in the drawing room of a wonderful house. She has her concert dress with her, naturally, and takes it out of its tissue wrapping to try it on. Ages since the last event and once more her mind goes back to the first ever public performance. She pulls a face. Her playing is very much better now, though it was seen to be good at the time. And there she had moral support that she never will forget. Jones, her rock, her *raison d'etre*. Without those ties, she'd be meaningless and she's sure he will be cognisant of the situation.

The dress is a little tight on her, particularly on the hips and the bust. She carefully eases a seam, drawing on her school-instilled sewing skills, and tries once more. In the mirror she sees a stranger – an elegant woman with hair in ringlets, waved onto her neck, a creamy toned skin and a rising frontage – far too revealing for normal wear but seeing as it's for a *select* gathering, perhaps allowable. She tries a ribbon. And changes it for a bolder one. She twirls, thankful her ankle mended so well. And those bruises – ages ago now but they went, miraculously, after *that* weekend. Her *lovely* weekend, when they had exchanged poetic lines and – and their love. From a friend, a deeply thinking, ever faithful, always present friend. Her love always for him, always.

The evening of her 'coming out' as she calls it, has arrived. She will be collected from her lodgings at six. She is ready, dressed, a coat wrapped around, not because it is cold, but she needs to present a decorous appearance. She will change her shoes at the venue however, and add the ribbon. The cab is prompt and she is surprised to find she is to be accompanied – in effect, chaperoned. Conversation with her middle aged buxom chaperone is stilted – their respective national languages are not a strong point with either, so the destination and size of the event remain unclear.

It is only a short drive to the venue; the route takes them between substantial stone gate pillars, up the driveway towards the elegant mansion, the *Schloss Mirabelle* in the musical heart of the city. Other cars – and carriages – are parked, expensive, gleaming; those people she sees are extremely well dressed. Select gathering indeed, but this is Salzburg. Suddenly she is aware of the honour bestowed on her.

Welcomed at the door, escorted by her companion up the marble stairs to a small side room and there she meets her mentor and another aristocratic gentleman her host introduces, to her surprise, as a Count. She asks, how large a gathering?

'My dear Miss Lucy,' replies her mentor, 'the Count,' and he gives a small bow, 'has invited *all* his musical friends. So we are honoured with perhaps, eighty to a hundred of the most appreciative of his circle?' The Count nods politely and expresses his own appreciation of her acceptance of his invitation to play. 'So we will have an evening of pure pleasure,' he says, 'and with such a charming protégé of my great friend here. Do feel completely at home, my dear lady. I look forward to a *sublime* performance,' proffers another small bow and returns to his circle.

She's left with her chaperone to change her shoes, affix the ribbon and check her appearance in one of the wall mirrors. Not unlike parts of Burghley House, she thinks, and wonders how the concert room will affect her – she knows it is large, and the piano an historic masterpiece. She would have much preferred the opportunity to practice and to gain a feel of the instrument before hand; however, this is a test of her skill in adaptation let alone playing.

'How long?' she asks; the reply is ten fingers raised and indeed, a few minutes later the door opens. Escorted through and into the assembly, greeted, introduced; amazed at the elegance, the dresses, the décor, her head begins to spin. A far cry from Barn Hill where it all began. The white and gold eight-foot Bösendorfer is on a low small stage at the far end of an un-nerving, magnificently high ceilinged, gold and glittering marble hall. Finally she is there and the assemblage quieten down. The stool is fine, at exactly the right height, the correct distance from the keyboard.

The Count takes the stage for her introduction. There is quiet, other than a shuffling as the standing members of the audience move for a better view. She is announced, her first chosen item introduced. It is her moment.

First notes. She closes her eyes, seeks inspiration. She knows the piece backwards and the initial opening bars are slow, thoughtful, carefully moderated. But this is not her. Is it the occasion, or the ambiance? Is it because her mentor expects too much? Or something else? There is something missing – she can play, there's no doubt the music will be absolutely correct, note on note, however, the vital Lucy is not there. She knows her heart isn't in the music and her mentor will also know. She dare not look – but continues on, saddened but painfully accurate to the end. Twenty minutes of hell and precision.

The assemblage applaud, of course, enthusiastically in the main, and she acknowledges the applause, a curtsey, a walk away, the return, another curtsey, her hand across the yawning crevice betwixt her breasts. She retreats to cry, then to dry tears and wonder at how on this occasion of any, her opportunity to demonstrate a unique musical moment has eluded her and the essential magic just isn't there.

Her mentor arrives. He is kind but forthright. 'You play well, Miss Lucy, but *not* from the heart. Always, you must play *from the heart*. Remember who you play for; for your lover, your parents, for me; whoever, it has to be *from the heart. Always!'* She acknowledges his words with a tired small smile, accepting the truth. She has another half an hour before her next piece.

'Go into the other salon or into the garden,' he suggests, 'you will be safe, we will keep watch for you. Consider who you are, Miss Lucy. Who has brought you to this point, a turning point in your career? You can give much, much more if you find that *inspiration. Always, the inspiration.'*

The double doors to the long garden room are open from the salon below – the small orchestra is engaged in a Strauss waltz and no one has paid any attention to her as she has slipped away into the warm, moisture saturated air. A fragrance of flowers – a heavy scent not entirely unfamiliar but richer, a touch intoxicating. Another time and she'd have been happy to absorb sight of the luxurious growth of whatever plants were there, but this evening, no. A slow walk down the paving, careful not to tread in any puddles left from an earlier watering and splash her skirt. At the far end there is a bench, white, cast iron, a curved back, a cushioned seat, inviting. So she sits.

Around one hundred people – her mentor's and the Count's

friends, all of them influential to a degree, have all heard her debut – her Austrian debut – piece, played on the antique, beautifully crafted Bösendorfer, one she'd love to own. And she'd played mechanically, accurately but without the passion, the intoxication she should have been able to give. And why? Because her soul wasn't in tune with her body, or at the very least, her fingers. And the rationale? She'd played in concerts many times, occasionally brilliantly, mostly very well; at times – not often – like tonight, without expression beyond what the page inscription said. *Allegro, andante, adagio, lento.* More *lento* than anything else so far this evening. Why, oh why?

Her head cushioned in her hands, she thinks. Thinks through the journey she has taken from girlhood, learning the keys at her mother's knee when barely five, taking paid lessons before mother took over, and playing to the guests they'd had at home who listened, cajoled, encouraged. The School's own music teacher who pushed her through the grades. Mother again, and the launch into playing to an audience at Barn Hill. Nothing then until the Barnsdale incident and the upright, good though it was, hadn't been what she'd been used to, yet she played well enough to wet the appetite of Basil Fortescue and the Schweitzer's who'd funded the initial College fees, bless them, in memory of their family. She owes so much to them. Who else? Father, of course. The College tutors who believed in her. Jones ... and the pain shoots through her as though she'd been jolted by an electric shock. *Jones!* Her own beloved mysterious Jones, who'd believed in her, told her she was *lovely* at precisely the right moment though at the time she hadn't even met him face to face. The one person who'd been with her in mind ever since that evening ... never to leave her side; present in spirit, in thought and in *love.*

The disgrace, the sin, the worst thing she could ever do, is not to connect with his presence within her mind. *Forgotten him?* No, no no *no!* Not forgotten, merely – merely? – underestimated the power she has from his *being* within her, deep inside the vital strength of *her* being.

Getting up, standing straight, checking her tiny watch, she has barely ten minutes. The door to the garden is straight ahead. Soft grass, the scent of pine trees, the deep velvet indigo of the mountain-bounded sky pinpricked with stars, the sway in the trees the only sound. Jones, my love, where are you? Be with me, stay with me, *keep me close. Please, please* remember us on that Sunday morning?

"... With stammering lips and insufficient sound // I strive and struggle to deliver it right // that music of my nature – – With dream and thought ..."

She knows the words instinctively and quotes them out loud. *With dream and thought,* those words, so apt. *Jones! Hear me!* And holds her own inner self still, pulls all her nerves and muscle sinews tense within her and with all the power of her mind, sends the message out into space and time. *Keep me close!*

There. She can do no more, nothing more than pray. With two minutes to go, she walks carefully and slowly up the staircase, back to the marble hall. At the door she receives an assortment of acknowledgements, nods from the men, small inclinations from some of the ladies and an earnest quizzical expression on her mentor's face. She offers him a slow, diffident smile. Unless she is to be seen as vacuous, an empty-headed young girl with no more to her character than a memory for key strokes, she has to do better. And the only way is to regain her inspiration, and that from her *alter ego.* No other way.

Should she describe her state as trance-like? The stage is regained, her dress carefully adjusted over the stool; the Count – does she detect an edge to his voice that may be irritation or concern, she's not sure – announces her next piece, the Chopin *Nocturne.* At least it is a favourite and well received elsewhere. One more plea. Jones? Are you with me?

Then, as her fingers brush the notes, *he's there.* From deep in the labyrinth of her mind, the imagined phrase and the look in his eyes that special Sunday morning. *... You are lovely ... .* For him and for him alone, she plays. *Hear me, my darling friend, hear my music – it is for you.* Head bent to the keys, eyes closed momentarily, the marble hall has expanded, the walls vanish, the sky opens to her, the distance no barrier. It is for him.

The final note fades, quietly vanishing into the ether. Her soul, the soul of her music, expands in sheer amazing delight. This rapturous time, this performance has been her best ever. Lucy, my girl, you've cracked it. The knowledge hits her. She *has* to have Jones virtually by her side, always. Without his thoughts she cannot be herself. A phenomenal thought, mind-blowing. She smiles, a smile extending beyond the immediacy of her admiring audience. It has to be for her virtuosity and it will be for the two of them, they just *have* to be an inseparable pair. Not physically, though that would be nice, but in thought. Thoughts well over and beyond the wildest imagination of any plain person, for no one she knows could comprehend this link, not one.

It takes an age to quieten the gathering, to gather herself, to become free of clinging admiration. *I'm just a girl who can master the keyboard*, she hears herself explaining – but it is more than that. It is the way her soul pours into the music to take flight, to wing its way into the ears, the mind and the heart of her listeners. Emotion. Rapture. No adjective will encompass what the true musician can accomplish. Love, she knows, is what happens. Not *love,* as in textbook, but a blending, an amalgamation of twin beings. Jones and her.

As she is changing shoes again, preparatory to returning to her lodgings, running her philosophical meanderings back through her head, she reaches a strange state of humour. What if she has to explain the experience to someone, maybe an unfamiliar person, to endeavour to explain in a rational, scientific way? She couldn't, though the concept amuses her and she giggles, unable to control herself for she could be on the edge of hysteria. It has been all too much of an emotional strain and the potential disaster is only averted by the return of her mentor and the stiff faced chaperone.

'My dearest young lady,' her mentor says in the stilted and accented way he has, 'I am full of admiration, for your interpretation of the *Nocturne* was without doubt the finest rendering I have ever heard. You must know? That you placed heart and soul into the piece? The Count, he has no reservations, and I am honoured, honoured, to have assisted in your development. I can do no more. You have the world at your feet, *virtuoso* Salter. Indeed you have.'

Lucy is overcome and cannot reply. He too, must be affected, for there are glistening corners to his eyes. Tears, for her? One thing is left to do. 'A moment, please,' she manages, 'I'd like a few minutes alone, in the garden?'

Her mentor perhaps understands – but doesn't, for his concept is unaware of hers.

She escapes. Carriages and cars are disappearing down the drive, lanterns edge the trees, fairy-like highlights in a moonlit monochrome of the estate. This could be the time of Mozart with a little adjustment for modernity. Her footsteps are muffled in the soft grass, before her instinct guides her onto the paved area around the powering rearing Pegasus, the huge bronze wingéd horse. Water is still plashing quietly into the circular pool below, and she seats herself carefully on the pool's wide stone rim. She is finding the way to empower her thought waves and tightens her inner girl to concentrate. *'Thankyou, my soul's lover. Our magic has happened. Keep me close.'*

Two minutes, five, her bottom can feel the stone seat's chill percolating through her dress. Enough. Her route across the garden re-traced, she rejoins her chaperone; she is guided back to the Count to receive his effusive praise and thanks and then allowed to leave.

∽

And what of Jones? Where is he that Lucy can reach his thoughts? He has left his home town and his business to escape from the ever-present memories, brief though they may have been, of a weekend now nearly a year ago, when she was within his clasp, her soft hair on his shoulder, – w*eave, weave the sunlight in your hair* – her fragrance swirling about him, their thoughts so in tune. Why should he wish to abandon her – run away? Why hasn't he pursued her, bombarded her with letters, phone calls, taken time away to arrange to try and see her, in London, at her home, even to make foolish attempts at finding her in Paris or, subsequentially (as he discovered from another postcard to let him know what was happening), Salzburg?

One may well ask. Here he is, an educated, thinking, quasi-academic young man with a solid business beneath his belt (thanks to the late Samuel and his T. S. Eliot cat) and everything ahead of him, and yet he runs away from a mere slip of a girl? And after he's had considerable experience of amoral adventures with a nubile and avaricious lady of a similar academic disposition to his own? Tcha!

Then think on. Those very same sexual encounters may be the root cause, now one considers the situation more thoroughly. We are

130

already aware of his concerns before the final dalliance – if dalliance is the right description – immediately prior to Briony's departure. Lucy, as he'd mentally expressed his thoughts, should have kept her virtual eyes and ears closed for the duration of the conjoint exercise – for that's all it was, an exercise. As he'd expressed to the naked lady at the time, the refined definition of poetic romantic *love* didn't always correspond to one of mutual orgasmic relief.

So perhaps his conscience is troubling him? In the early days, when his and Lucy's shadows played tag with each other around the conurbations of Stamford, the spiritual aspects had lifted his mental energies, improved his outlook on life and encouraged the enthusiasm that, now it is considered, may well have inspired Samuel's bequest. Latterly the jump – figuratively and physically – into Briony's bed had undoubtedly altered his attitude. (We now also believe that ultimately befriending Nebuchadnezzar (Cad) the cat improved his inheritance potential).

If it is a conscience over Briony's bed – and recently the occasional semi-automatic meaningless foray into some local socialites' underwear for the sake of appearances – then we must believe Lucy *does* play her part in his life, though largely in the fourth dimension. He still has the ceramic visualisation of her initial acquisition with its symbolic pound note presently in pride of place at home, in his room. He can readily conjure up the close images of her soft voice, of her lively eyes, of her generous mouth and the subtlety and freshness of her scent, her sunlit hair, just as he can also hear her conjure the most magic of musical moods from the pianoforte, the *'klavier'*. She is *his* conscience, his other psyche. Over the months since last they had been two people together, he'd kept her image inviolate, a deity to be worshipped from afar. Hence the reluctance to pursue her physicality and so therefore he's seeking new ground for her sake. Her sake, not his.

So, like the day ages ago when he'd driven out of Stamford town, seeking something he knew not what, now he lets the Morris have its head, turning when the road direction seemed apt, driving towards aspects of the distance, hills, woodland, open country. No clear idea, go where the spirit wills.

Towards the middle of the afternoon, he's in Derbyshire. Coming via a convoluted route, he's enjoyed the leafy complexity of

Charnwood forest, worked his way northward and ambled up the old Carlisle route, the A6. It's getting on and he has to find a bed for the night. On an acute left-handed bend at the start of the Derwent valley he takes a right hander, peculiarly odd, given he has to stop for oncoming traffic. But it's what instinct tells him. The road narrows down and climbs. Two, three miles and into a miscellany of stone houses that huddle around a small market square. Roads go off at every tangent. He takes the straightest one – straight until it sheers left and he avoids the right angled bend. A sign. Crich Stand. Time to take a stand and he grins at his own pun. The Traveller feels over-warm, but then, she's had a lengthy day, unusually lengthy. The small car park is empty – unsurprising, given it's getting on, the sun has less than two hours left in the sky. Shan't have to wait too long before checking into a b & b or a pub, he realises, though is not fussed. If push comes to shove, he'll kip in the car, curled up. He's done it before, though some time back.

The silence comes down on him once the engine's off, apart from the tick ticking of cooling metal. He stretches, opens the door, stands up and stretches again. From here he can see for miles, miles and miles. The sturdy stone tower is a couple of hundred yards away, reminiscent of a lighthouse overlooking a waterless sea. It's a ten minute walk to the top of the path. He leans on a fence line and surveys the country below. From here he can see three sixty degrees. There's only birdlife to break the silence now, well, that and the lowing of some cattle from a farmstead a mile away. The sky is still clear, a few streaks of shadowy grey cloud to help catch the sun as it begins to colour up the western horizon. West isn't where Lucy is, she's over to the east. And a long way away.

It's a strange thing – having come away from where I last saw her, she's more in my mind than ever. Am I becoming paranoid about the girl? Why is she so very much in the forefront of things? Am I going mental – or is it a natural way with whom you're so in tune? She's so different from anyone else I've been with. Mainly Briony, I guess, but I know where that lady fits – body, body, mostly body, no proper mental connection of soul – though she tried, I'll give her that. Easy option, was I? Daphne, we know about her. Celice, Tricia, and Rosemarie the wicked seaside wench; all my lovely local girls and each one different in her own way, even Lila, the ex

Cambridge lass though she was rather hard going. But here, now, I'm alone with an idealistic dream.

He turns and faces east, resting his back and his elbows on the fence top rail. The sky is slowly and inexorably reddening behind him, reflections on the wisps of cloud still resting eastwards. The day was calming, ebbing away into the twilight and the dark.

Lucy, dear girl, where are you? Safe? Absorbed in your music?
This is daft! Plain lunacy! I'd better get down and find a bed. But I do hope she's all right. Perhaps I'll have a chat with her parents, if I can find a phone. I'm sure I've their number somewhere.

As a shift in the cloud allows a new aspect of light and colour, out of the sky he hears her. Echoes in his head. Slim echoes of lines of verse. Remember what she said: *keep me close,* then recited these lines – or part of them …
    … I strive and struggle to deliver it right, that music of my nature…
The echoes come across the miles, the pink tinged vastness of the empty sky. 'Lucy,' he concentrates,
    '… with dream and thought … you are lovely, remember?'
Will he ever be right for her? Has he always to seek her through the years, across the miles; is he doomed only to hear her voice and her music in his head? The shadows are growing, he's been there a good half hour or so. The clouds in front are a deeper blush of pink. Time to go. Her voice again.
    … Hear me, my darling friend, hear my music – it is for you …
The Barn Hill piece, the Chopin Nocturne he knows so well, runs through his head like a golden thread of delight.
    She is still his, to hold close, and now he can rest content.

Wigmore Hall

Thirteen

Agiatamente ... Freely

Three days. Jones is back in charge of both shop and his own soul. Clare has done well; he'll keep her on without any doubt whatsoever; having watched her hand-sell to a shop full of customers the day after his return from the sojourn in the wilderness he'd be daft to let her go. He waits until the end of the day, takes her up into the cocoon of the top floor office, sits her down and asks.

'Go?' she replies, her eyes opening wide and staring at him. 'Go?' she repeats, 'why ever would I want to go? Not unless you're unhappy with the way the shop is ... '

He shakes his head. 'Far from it, dear girl. I reckon I can take a holiday every other week the way the takings are up with you in charge; no, I want to ensure you're happy here.'

Oh my, he's seen that look in a girl's eyes before, sufficiently aware to be aware and inwardly concerned. However, the dice have been thrown whatever the outcome. Too late to back away, even if

134

he wanted to, which he doesn't. He likes the girl and she deserves encouragement.

'I'm very happy,' she says. 'Lots better than serving teas. Moreover, I get to read books for free,' then colours up. 'Hope that's all right.'

He laughs at her. 'I'd worry if you didn't take a lively interest in the stock. Maybe I'll quiz you every now and again to see what you know. There are those who assume you've read every book in the shop.'

She laughs in her turn. 'I know, I've had 'em. But it's amazing what you can get away with if you flannel, especially with a straight face.' A passing cloud of thought dims her smile. 'You're not going to ask me to leave now you've come back, are you?'

'No, my dear Clare, I'm not. In fact,' and he gets up from behind the desk and comes round to be nearer to her, 'I'm offering you a small increase in pay if you promise to stay,' and chuckles. 'Pardon the poor rhyme.' As she turns her snub-nosed face up to look at him, he can't help himself, bends down and offers a kiss, momentarily a full on, lip-to-lip kiss. 'S.w.a.l.k; ess double-you a loving kiss. That okay?' he asks, in retreat and wondering if he hasn't been dangerously overly familiar.

She's blushing again and looks down at her knees, delightfully peeping out from underneath a full chintzy thing with its mischievous lace edged underskirt. She's pretty, is my Clare, he thinks, and blesses his good fortune. Maybe she'll keep his mind off the duller, more basic views of his second self.

Two days later there's a postcard bearing an Austrian stamp from Salzburg in the shop's mail, a picture of the Schloss Mirabelle. On the reverse, in her neat writing, in triumph, *I knew you'd support me. Reached 'Virtuoso' level. Cannot bear absence. Meet me in London. I'll phone. Your Lucy.*

Is that odd sensation what is called a 'heart leap', or his pulse rate climbing? Sat behind the office desk, he fingers the card, turning it over and over. It has brought her into the top floor room as assuredly as if she was here in body rather than in spirit. He imagines her in the writing; he holds it the same way, collecting every nuance of the girl's being within him. Touched to his lips, a weirdly boyish gesture, the pressure of her mouth on his that Sunday is felt once more.

'Clare?' He calls down the stairs, looks to see her frizzy harvest-mouse hair jerk sideways and a smiley face grin up at him.

'Yep?'

Love the girl, the way she brightens the place up. 'May have to pop down to the Smoke sometime. Be okay on your own again?'

'Sure thing. And we need some more of these,' as she waves a copy of the latest fictional craze to sweep the pages of the women's magazines, 'this is the last one.'

The girl's a marvel. How many's that? Twenty in the last week? *Fiction has its place, Samuel,* he says quietly under his breath. Amazing what a little publicity will do to alter reading habits. Before the glossy women's' mags had picked the thing up, he'd never have sold a copy in six months – local fictional readers were *so* conservative. Once an author's name was bandied about in the media though, there was no stopping them, however good or bad the story and the writing. It was though a book took on a life of its own, becoming a social requisite, read or not. One of these days he'd write something himself. With a Cambridge degree and a c.v. to include his book shop experiences, some publisher would snap him up, especially if he committed 'My Experiences at – in – the Hands of a Professional Seducer' to print. Would Briony sue him for libel? Or, far more to the point, would Lucy disown him? He grins. Idiot ideas.

'Okay,' he says after this seconds long reverie, 'I'll add a few more to the order,' and returns to his eyrie.

Two days later, at four o'clock and moments after Clare has brought up his afternoon mug of tea and three chocolate digestives – another of her bonus points – the phone rings. He absently picks it up whilst scanning the month's takings, 'yes?'

'Jones,' and he doesn't have to be told who calls, the telepathy swings into place. 'It's Lucy,' though she knows she doesn't have to remind him who she is either. Neither does she have to explain what she needs, this is pre-ordained. 'Wigmore Hall, next Thursday afternoon. Three o'clock. I know it's short notice, but … '

No hesitation. 'I'll be there. Or better still, we meet before your concert. What are you playing?' It is as though they talk to each other every day, he and she. Like the brother and younger sister concept, the naturality to this conversation belies the potential significance.

'It's only a shorty. I'm having a go at Rachmaninoff's *Prelude*, There's three of us sharing the programme,' and he hears her chuckle. 'I think they're a bit scared, 'cos I'm new. It's Mr Fortescue's first presentation for me there, so I have to do it for free, other than expenses and maybe an honorarium. Mum will be there too. We're staying at ...'

'I'll find it. Lunch or high tea after?'

'Lunch would be lovely. Perhaps there'll be time to explore Regents Park.' Her voice goes wistful. 'A reprise of my Lincolnshire weekend?'

'Lucy love, for you, certainly. And you promised 'another time' when you were here, remember?'

'Not forgotten,' she replies. 'Find me a slot on a local concert programme.'

'I might just manage that,' and he thinks of the Music Club. Small, but select and in the setting of his old school Hall, what could be nicer. He'll have a word with the Secretary, another regular customer of his. 'I'll see what I can do, but a lot depends on what your agent charges. They're not awash with money here because the tickets aren't expensive. Any idea when?'

He hears a sigh down the phone. 'Not too sure. I'll have to see what Mr Fortescue says, but as it's for you ... '

'Angel,' he says and means it. 'Then I'll find you in the foyer or lounge or something, say elevenish?'

'Fantastic,' and her voice is as musical as her playing, charged with meaning and expression as with the parting phrase, their link, her signature, his constant wish. '*Keep me close.*' The purr of a disconnected line and he's back into reality. Lucy's image stays bright in his mind for a fair while until Clare's voice comes echoing up from below.

'Can I go? It's five o'clock?'

Really? Is it that time already? He glances over the paperwork on the desk in front of him. Nothing that won't wait until tomorrow. And he promised to take Celice out this evening, which recalled pledge brings a stab of irritation, for after Lucy's phone call can he really be the flirtatious male she will expect?

'Okay, Clare. I'll lock up. See you tomorrow.' A minute later the shop door goes and he's alone.

Two and a half hours later and fed, he is washed, spruced up, clad in clean flannels and shirt and en route for his assignation. Celice will be waiting for him on the corner by the Fish Shambles, the triangle of pavement where the fishmonger sets out his stall every market day. It is barely a two-minute walk from his parent's home above father's shop. He can easily visualize her, light brown hair curled on her shoulders, the perfectly proportioned neck, the busty front and the slight waist. She'll be wearing a floral floaty cotton skirt, with no stockings and flat shoes with barely an inch heel; she's that sort of girl. Intelligent, a good if simple conversationalist in the main, he hasn't regretted the cultivation of her acquaintanceship since their first meeting at the library and she's been his evening delight on a fair few occasions. Tonight, the cinema. Not the back row either, but somewhere on the side, tactfully away from where most sit.

She offers him a coy smile. Her knee high skirt is a red poppy design on a white and cream background, quite striking. Her blouse is a sort of organza with bouffant sleeves, a buttoned front with the top button undone. Close-up, the decorative edging to her bra is just visible. She takes his hand and they walk the barely five minute distance to the Playhouse.

Tonight's showing is going to be a laugh. 'Magnificent Men' – she is riveted and giggles foolishly at the antics of these pioneer aviators. Jones is grateful for the Cinema's choice that week. If it had been a romance, or worse, a gripping drama, she'd have been seeking to hang onto his hand, maybe even pull it over her knee. The couple of hours passes amiably without his need to disappoint her and they leave the cinema in good humour. It is just getting on for twilight and reasonably warm. She suggests a walk up towards St Mary's – not along the longer more open route around Westgate Fields. 'I have to be home by eleven,' she says, which suggests he keeps her company for merely another three quarters of an hour. Fair enough, he agrees for her sake and they stroll towards the grassed former graveyard, the central path a shortcut to the classier residential avenue. There is a convenient bench seat at the far end in the lea of a towering chestnut and she pulls him down.

The girl's warmth and rather brassy scent is easy to take as she snuggles close. He's been here before and falls easily into routine. She expects his customary investigative movements and doesn't demur. Their kisses are professional, the tension rises, the appropriate reactions lead him to offer a curved caress of definite desire; another few minutes will bring inescapable inevitability and now it is getting dark. Celice has experienced his ability and skill in these matters *pour la femme* on former occasions; she expects a reprise and isn't objecting. Ten minutes to reach her high point and he is rewarded by expressive girly noises. It will have to suffice – though her stimulation comes at some expense to his own. Never mind, she's a happy girl and he feels good about that, aware not every woman can respond as beautifully. His tutelage at Briony's hands has stood him in good stead, enabling a more than satisfactory conclusion to most evenings spent with any adventuresome and able *amour;* it all helps to maintain his sanity. Does he feel any consequential dilution of the tie betwixt him and Lucy? No, not really, for their relationship is on a totally different plane, ethereal and spiritualistic, not earthy and lustful.

Celice is acting like Samuel's cat after feeding, close and purring, her head across his chest. His arm around her shoulders tucks her in, her left breast is soft under his fingers. Her response is natural and womanly, as it should be. He has given her what she as a girl needed, as he has done successfully before and maybe will again without any risk to their level of friendship.

The other girls may seek similar reactions if and when he takes them out. Light-heartedly, it is what he does.

London in September. The train takes him to Peterborough and on to King's Cross. The Tube, rattley and congested thing that it is, annoys him, offends his aesthetic sensibilities. He would far rather walk to the Hotel where she will be but the distance is daunting, all the pavement bashing a smidgeon too much when he must stay in control, for Lucy will demand his support. It is becoming clear how much she has begun to depend on his willing maintenance of this element of her make-up, the weak spot. She cannot thrive without knowing he is there to care, to cherish, to keep close to her.

How strange it has become! On the one side of his personality he has all the natural desires for female company and its attendant possibilities, on the other a need to hold on to his perception of, not a goddess essentially, but a emblematic symbol of divine feminity. He is seeking perfection whilst aware of the dangers of destroying that which he seeks. A quandary he is wrestling with in his subconscious, clearly not sure of how this attachment will proceed. He must keep her close to his heart and mind, protect and strengthen her, and his attendance at the Wigmore Hall is in pursuance of this aim.

The hotel entrance is on a corner, overlooking the Park. It is a grand building and, to one more accustomed to rural establishments, even the Stamford George with its superb reputation, daunting. However, he is correctly attired in suit, tie and polished shoes so continues through the imposing doorway and into the depths of the foyer and its attendant plush décor.

He knows she is there, his feelings for her would not otherwise be uppermost in his mind. And she has seen him. Firstly, their eyes link. Then he clasps her outstretched hands, holds them. He doesn't attempt to kiss her, though perhaps they might have managed such a social greeting without embarrassment. It is still early days; he has only kissed her four times up to now.

'Come and meet my parents,' she says and with one hand still held, leads him across to the other side of the spacious area.

'Your father's here too?' he asks, already aware Lucy's mother will definitely be here.

'Oh yes. My debut at the Wigmore Hall? Of course he had to come,' and he heard her melodious small chuckle, 'Mother would not have forgiven him. And as he's not having to pay the Hotel bill …'

They are smiling at him, accepting the significance of his invitation, his presence. He loses Lucy's hand in order to shake her father's, briefly to hold her mother's as convention demands. Then they are sitting once more and a waiter issues menus. 'Drink?' asks Mr Salter, and Jones begs a gin and lemonade. Lucy stays with tomato juice, sensible girl.

Small talk over the early lunch picks up from their last meeting in Jones's home patch, travels over the place of literature in a small town, the way the season is moving into high summer and, infinitely more meaningfully, where Lucy might be heading in her climb to success. No mention is made of where next she may be asked to play.

Mrs Salter – Elizabeth – has travelled this route before, in her own right. She would like to see her daughter commissioned to undertake a piano concerto at the Proms, to play the Royal Festival Hall, to hear her on the Third programme. Lucy's face takes on a pinkish colouration for at heart she is an unassuming lady. Jones can feel her slight embarrassment.

'I'm sure she will become a sought-after person,' he states, 'but she is still young and without doubt will have great opportunities as time goes on. Better to improve her repertoire smoothly and slowly than rush to the highlights.' He knows he has said the right words as her expressive eyes lift to his once more. Her father appears to agree. They are becoming more at ease with him and Jones is pleased.

They take coffee in the lounge area, small white cups with gold edges and accompanying crinkled pieces of mint crystalled chocolate. He sits next to Lucy on the settee and senses her warmth though inches separate them. A single pleat of her skirt brushes his thigh. More conversation edges him towards the obvious follow-up query. 'Where will you be going next, Lucy?'

She plucks at the fabric of her skirt, not wanting to say. Mr Fortescue has ideas he only mentioned to her yesterday and these she has not broached to her parents let alone Jones. She is not sure that this is the moment. She has a recital to give first. 'Oh, I'm not sure. I did promise to play at your old school, remember.'

Jones nods, gravely. 'I have suggested it to the Music Club. They sounded keen enough, but it rather depends on your fee. I've given them Mr Fortescue's telephone number as you suggested. Apparently, there are still two slots in next season's program, after Christmas. Perhaps they'll phone in the next day or so.' He refuses more coffee but accepts another mint chocolate. A weakness, chocolate. He'd empty the dish, given the opportunity.

After that, according to Mrs Salter, it is time for Lucy to have a short rest before going onto the Hall for a rehearsal. They agree to meet there at two. She stands, as politely, so does he. Her mother

141

looks on, approvingly. 'Go along dear, we'll look after your Mr Jones for a while, then I'll come up and do your hair.'

She holds out both hands again and once more he clasps them together in his own. A unique thrill pulses through them both with the contact and hands squeeze imperceptibly. She will play brilliantly and he will listen to her music and know it is for him.

He watches her swing gracefully away across the room; she turns and raises a hand half way, offers a smile. There is a hollow feeling to the room when she has gone. He resumes his seat, for it would be churlish to depart at the same moment.

Elizabeth wastes no time. 'You like our daughter, don't you, Jones? She certainly seems to have taken to you.'

Mr Salter harrumphs gently. 'Perhaps that's a leading question, dear,' he says in mild reproof, 'maybe our friend doesn't wish to admit to his inclinations.'

Jones feels embarrassed. There's a question or two here. Is Lucy's mother asking in order to apply a maternal 'stop' message or to accelerate his interest? Is she wishing to establish or confirm whether he is aware of Lucy's disposition towards him? If she hadn't entered the Stamford shop that day, would he have appeared in her sights as a 'suitable suitor' – for he was under no misapprehension concerning her perceived role in Lucy's life. An eligible daughter, indubitably with considerable talent and hence a future, still requires a husband; it was *de rigueur* in society, at least in her concept of 'society'. She was the Mrs Bennett to Lucy's Lizzie. And Lucy was brought up to Louth for the weekend, which, come to think further, would *not* have occurred had he been dismissed as a mere *'chancer'*, so back to 'does he know how he stands' with the girl. Short answer, yes.

He has to be honest and forthright. He inclines his head, a sort of nod. 'I think Lucy is an incredible girl, and yes, I do admire her – who wouldn't?'

Mr Slater chuckles. 'Well said, my lad.'

There is a gap in conversation. Mrs Salter appears lost in thought. Jones grasps the nettle. 'We have an understanding,' he says, and Mrs Salter's eyes snap open.

'*An understanding?*' Tantamount to an engagement, yes, he knows that's how it will be construed and has to explain before this gets out of hand.

'She and I have always had this, call it a *rapport*, which I don't think either of us understands.' He knows it will appear weird, but now he is committed. 'A sort of telepathy. She knows when I'm around, when I'm thinking of her, and vice versa. I can't explain. It just happened. Suddenly, there she was, I was, and we've been conscious of each other ever since,' and this said, impossible to apply logical comprehension.

Elizabeth's mouth opened in a conventional jaw-drop before in a trice, she'd clamped it shut again. Then: 'so do you *love* her?'

Goodness, is this a question too far? Mr Salter shook his head, as though amazed at his wife's temerity.

Jones believes he ought to retreat before the conversation becomes too problematic. He will never deny the girl; however, this is neither time nor place to argue the definition of love. Briony and he had discussed the word in a completely different setting and circumstance; their *love* hadn't been anywhere near how he felt about Lucy. What went on between them was sublimely different and not for public – or parental – analysis.

He stands up. A brief answer and then he'll leave it to Lucy. 'Yes, Mrs Slater, I believe I love her for what she is,' to add two last words as he turns away, 'always will. Now, please excuse me.' He can feel two pairs of eyes on his back and the thought waves are close to tangible, like 'he'd better look after her,' which, in certain certainty, he will.

⇜

Lucy: *I am so so glad he's here. Having mum and dad about is fine, but not like my Jones. He and I. We're like twins. The brother I never had. So lovely, supportive, and he loves my music. It's all for him, really.*

Her dress shed, she is stretched out on the extravagant bedcovers in her room, gazing up at a wonderfully amazing ceiling, all swirly plasterwork with a gold and glass centre light, a sort of chandelier thing.

One thing about posh hotels, the interior décor is remarkable. Glad Mr Fortescue's paying the bill.

The room is pleasantly warm, not too hot, comforting in her chaotic state of semi-undress.

Is it air-conditioned? Wonder what they'll offer us as high tea after. I'll have an appetite by then.

She crosses her ankles, then uncrosses them, brings her knees up and her underskirt slips down her thighs. She links hands under her legs and rocks back and forth like a baby's cradle.

It's boring, this 'get a rest dear' thing. I'd far rather walk round the Park with Jones. Wonder what they're talking about. Me, probably.

She grins, kicks her legs out and uses the momentum to fling off the bed. Crossing to the window, she peers out. *There he is!* He is crossing the road, reaches the pavement and looks back. And up. She pushes the net curtain to one side and waves. *There, he's seen me!*

Their thought waves flow up and down, join, meld together, amplify, and strengthen. Lucy breathes in, holds her body erect, her chest up, feeling the chilly shivers run down the small of her back, along her fine golden-haired arms, the warmer glow between her thighs and on down her calves. Her hands are now against her unsupported breasts, touching the stiffened nipples and with a sudden shock, anticipates what it may be like if *he* was holding her. Their eyes are focused in, staring at each other. He is on the pavement edge, still, shoulders back, poised. One hand comes up like a salute, and then he turns and strides away. She is not disappointed, not in the least. She has this soft new sensation not experienced before and it is a very precious feeling. The telepathic threads thin down, gossamer thin, like a single silken spider's spun filament, so strong.

He'll be with her. *A lovely girl, my Lucy.* He'll keep her close.

Jones: *Phew! Lucy's mum certainly has her daughter's interests in the forefront of things! Wonder what she'll think? 'Course I love the girl, she's part of me, my life. Has been for ages. Why I broke up with Briony. Why I had to shift away from Stamford, well, that and Samuel's ghost, of course.*

He pushes through the hotel's doors, pauses to consider the use of the next hour.

It would have been good to stay with her. Couldn't really, not with the Salter's there. Bet she would have liked me to stay, too.

He watches the traffic, judges the moment, crosses the road, and on impulse, turns and looks back at the hotel. *She's up there.* There is a movement at one of the second floor windows, the white gauzy curtains shake, part. *There!* The same powerful prescience; this was due to happen. It's as though a beam of light, a searchlight, surrounds her. *She's waving!* He lifts a hand, waves back. Thought waves link. *Keep me close.* She's only in her slip or something, gossamer white, like an angel. He lifts a hand. *You are a lovely girl, my Lucy.* Then turns his back and walks on and into the Park.

∽

He sits alongside Elizabeth. Her husband is on the row end. They aren't too close to the front, but near enough, and on the left so her mother can see Lucy's hands. The Steinway piano is glossy, black, a powerful presence crouching on the platform. A challenging programme for these three Wigmore debutantes, Lucy and a fellow College student to be followed by a young Chinese lad over for the Piano Festival. The Hall is not full, these afternoon concerts are not always well attended unless a big name is doing a warm-up for a later event. Jones feels at ease. He had a pleasant half-hour stroll around the Park, exploring, though he will admit to a preference for the Hills back at home.

Lucy's parents, he senses, present an air of very slight detachment. Maybe his simplistic answer to her mother's '*do you love her*' question has put them on edge. Certainly unlikely they will discuss the matter further with him on this occasion and a good thing too. Allow matters to settle down – or develop, who knows. Neither they nor he are aware of the bombshell in store.

Lucy's performance is sandwiched before the Chinese youngster and after a tall, lanky blonde haired lass, whose style echoes her build, thin and watery. Elizabeth frowns intermittently and sighs. The audience's applause is polite but not extensive. Then it is her daughter's turn. Jones is aware of his neighbour edging forward on her seat, understands her anxiety though he is confident Lucy will deliver. They are as one, he and she.

And thus it is. Lucy's playing of the Rachmaninoff is not only flawless but produces a dreamlike quality which sends the audience into raptures. Jones can almost feel her heart beats, the intensity of the mind that drives them together. As she slides off the stool and stands proud, her search for recognition has achieved its aim. This is her moment – *their* moment. It takes ten minutes to get the audience back into order, to quieten the buzz of conversation for the last instrumentalist, for such has been the previous momentous performance. Elizabeth is constantly dabbing her eyes with a lace edged floral handkerchief, even her husband has discreetly to use a finger, diverting dampness from his eyes. Tears, him? Never. Jones; now all he wants to do is hold her, his soul mate, hold her, feel that heart beating against his own, sense the warmth and experience the reality of this unique person. Turn her from a virtual concept to a never-to-let-her go woman, to convince each other they can never part. *Love her?* Of course he does. She is the One.

At the small reception that follows, Basil Fortescue is in his element. His protégé has delivered and tomorrow the musical press will underline his success at discovering this remarkable new talent he has let loose on the world's stage. Lucy Salter, concert pianist, she who has a wonderful way of also presenting Chopin, such intense interpretation, such a dynamic range, and her Schubert, well …

Jones does not leave her side. Whenever they can, they hold hands. He held her as he promised himself he would and their socially correct embrace is to emphasise their bond. Mrs Salter has seen the answer to her query with her own eyes and has an additional new experience to add to the day. The first to see her daughter on the same stage where she made her debut all those years ago, the second, to accept Jones may be her girl's chosen escort in fullness of time. *C'est la vie.*

There's to be a toast. The champagne flutes are fizzing, Basil takes the floor.

'To Lucy!' His eyes search to find Elizabeth in the mêlée and he raises his glass in her direction. 'And to Lucy's mother, Elizabeth Salter, the finest pianist of her time! Her daughter has certainly demonstrated to whom she owes this incredible talent!'

Far too gushy, Jones thinks and squeezes Lucy's hand gently. Those fingers are precious.

'Now, I have some news to impart,' Basil is prattling on. 'I have secured an exchange contract for Lucy to go with Columbia Artists Management in New York. It's a wonderful opportunity. And to play at the Carnegie Hall – why, it will bring her talents to the world stage far sooner than merely playing the concert circuit in this country. So raise your glasses,' and he waves his around. 'To Lucy, and her New York debut!'

Fourteen

Capriccioso ... Capricious, Whimsical

Clare cannot understand why he's turned so morose. He goes to London for his girlfriend's concert and comes back like the proverbial wet week! He snaps at her when she asks if *'it had all gone alright,'* and whereas before she'd felt appreciated – to the point where she hadn't minded his occasional kiss or arm round her shoulders – now she could be a mere scruffy unshaven male with body odour for all the attention she receives. He doesn't cast a glance at her front or her skirt line, and it hurts.

She confides to her mother. 'Don't let it worry you,' comes the answer. 'That's men for you. He'll come round,' and her mother hopes she'll be proved right. Her Clare could do a lot worse; that book shop must be a little gold mine and the man seems a decent sort of chap. So ... 'Play your cards right, gal, and you never know, you could be in there.'

Clare isn't so sure. Jones doesn't seem the type to hook up with the likes of her, but glory knows, she wouldn't mind. (For the moment she isn't fully aware of his penchant for the not infrequent incursions into the emotions – and intimacies – of a number of other local girls, largely because they come from different social strata.) But then, if her mum says try, she'll try.

She spends some money on a visit to Emma's, the better hairdresser in town; on a handful of cosmetics from Boot's and finally plucks up courage for a foray into the inner depths of Eve & Ranshaws, the classy department store. Here she experiences the ever so slightly haughty demeanour of the elegant senior sales lady on women's fashions. She'd explain, but daren't. Instead she tries on loads of different things, evaluating the nuances of dismay or vague acceptance on the middle aged sales woman's face. She's good at interpretation, a gift used to advantage in hand-selling books – gained from an apprenticeship in pushing sticky and creamy cakes onto tea-time punters at Joan's. Sometimes she misses her job at Joan's, probably from the foregone opportunity of eating up the leftovers. At least she's slimmer now, which probably accounts for her ability to do up the zip on a lovely little frocky frock, size twelve.

'That's nice,' says her attendant sales woman instinctively, surprising them both. Clare daren't ask how much. 'Five guineas,' she's told. And gulps. Not much change from a week's wages. But it's sexy and lovely and she's got to try, so pays.

At home, her mum is demonstratively impressed. 'Clare, my lovely lass, that's a killer dress. And those knickers too, lordy! Love your hair do,' but frowns at the lipstick. 'Shade too red, love. Try this one,' and offers her own. 'Less tarty. I ain't having you cooling your heels on a street corner looking for …' stopping afore she reveals how much she knows about them girls that don't have any pride or underwear to speak of; mind you, them knickers her Clare's wearing, well now, in her day her own mum would have had kittens.

Clare goes to work on the following Monday in some trepidation. Her boss is already in his upstairs office, but on the phone. She tip-toes up, avoiding the stairs treads that creak, aware she's not only treading the stairs, but a fine line between curiosity and the sack.

'… I don't want you to go,' she hears him say. 'Lucy, dear Lucy, I

149

can't be with you, not over there.' There's a silence; she imagines the other person – Lucy – talking.

' … six months is a lifetime. You …'

Another silence.

' … I would, you know that, but I can't. Not abandon it. And there's Clare. She'd be devastated. Lucy, I don't know …'

Clare blushes. He's talking about *her!*

'… your parents, what do they say now? I know your mum thought it was a great opportunity, but now it's cut and dried …'

So that's what he's grumpy about! The girl friend's leaving him for somewhere. She could say *goody* but it wouldn't be nice. This Lucy must mean an awful lot to him. Then it clicks – she must be the same girl who had tea with her parents in the shop that day when Jones joined them late and she had to sweetheart Joan to allow her to provide another pot and a plate of cakes. And there'd been something so lovely about her, ethereal, sort of Greek classical, with smashing hair – no wonder he was nuts over her. She carefully retraces her steps back to the ground floor. Can she really exert her own feminine wiles, as her mum called them, on a guy who was so smitten with a lovely girl like what's-her-name, Lucy? Clare pulls a face. All that dosh, spent on a mantrap dress?

Five minutes later she hears him coming down the stairs. Well, she can't change her dress now.

'Morning, Clare,' he says, reaching the top of the last flight. Then he sees her. 'Wow!' He jumps the last three steps. 'You look fantastic! Give us a twirl?'

Her heart does a skip. No room, not to do a *proper* twirl. 'Hope I'm not too dressy.'

He shakes his head. 'I'll admit it's not what I'd expect on a Monday morning. However, seeing as what I'm a bit low, it's great to see you looking so lovely. I mean it, Clare. You look smashing.' And he does mean it, though these aren't the same waves he'd get from his Lucy in *her* dress.

They stand silent, looking at each other. He sees a lovely innocent nineteen-year-old girl with every attribute at peak of perfection, a gorgeous creature. She sees an intelligent and intriguing male with lots of charm. This Lucy girl must be nuts to leave him is the overriding thought in her brain, alongside the most oddest of other feelings, one of an almost motherly instinct. Not a passion as such, at least she can't think of it in those terms, but definitely something meaningful.

An early customer is on the doorstep, the door is pushed open and the bell does its ting-ting, announcing the end of the spellbound moment. He gives her a sort of beseeching look and returns upstairs as she switches on her 'can I help you' smile.

Later in the day he ventures out to seek further solace. He wanders into Joan's, ostensibly to gossip over Clare's performance though a quiet sit-down over a decent cup of tea and a sticky Chelsea bun will have a calming effect. Joan has become a true friend and sits down with him for a few minutes respite.

'So how's my ex-waitress doing?' Joan asks, reflectively stirring her cup though she doesn't take sugar.

Jones puts his cup down, it's rather too hot anyway. 'Fine,' he says, 'really come on well. Means I can get out and about; leaving her in charge is no worry.' He eyes the buns. Lovely load of currants. He hesitates. Will she mind passing an opinion? 'Clare's not got a boyfriend, has she?'

Joan gives him a sideways, old fashioned look. 'Not that I knows of. Why? Fancy her, do you?'

He shakes his head. 'Not like that. But she's come over all smart and dressy, new hair style, far more than a simple shop girl needs. I'm a bit worried. In case, well, you know ...'

Joan laughs. 'Egotist! You think she's after you!' She takes a good mouthful of her own tea. 'Worse could happen, my lad. She's a very decent girl, is our Clare. Has a hard-working mum, don't know much about her dad though, think he's gone awol. Doesn't mix with the riff raff. Bit young for you, I'd have thought.' She needlessly stirs the cup again and a quiet moment passes. Then: 'What about the lass who was up here with her folks, last year? Now she *was* something. Got an air about her, sort of secretive yet sexy. Intelligent too, I'd say. What about her? You two had something on between you.'

She's hit a raw spot and he can't help himself. 'Lucy. Yeah, we've got something between us you'd not believe even if I said. We – er – kind of mutually link without being physically together; I've known her for nigh on three years now. 'Cept she's going to the States for six months and I don't know if I can be as supportive. We try and talk to each other long distance, but it might be rather too far.'

Joan cannot comprehend, other than trunk calls cost money. 'There's phones over there.'

He has to grin. 'I know.' Joan won't understand about thought waves. He's not sure he understands either, but there's a distinct association. He and Lucy definitely connect. *Don't worry, she's saying, I'll be back soon.* His teacup is drained and there's only crumbs on the plate. He can't ask for another, because she's said it's on the house. 'I'd best get back and cash up.'

Joan stands, replaces the chairs and collects the dirties. 'Don't fret, lad. If she's worth it, she'll wait, and so must you if she means that much. Just don't mess with Clare.'

He nods. Good advice. 'Thanks, Joan. See you,' and he returns to the shop.

Clare is sitting by the till, reading, her feet up on another chair, the flouncy dress decorously draped over her knees. 'Oh, hi,' she says, setting her feet on the floor and tucking a bookmark into the novel. 'Enjoy your tea break?'

'Yes, thanks,' and immediately does what he knows he shouldn't. 'Care to come out tonight? I need solace and a shoulder to cry on. No preconceptions, mind.'

She stares at him. 'Me?' This she cannot believe. The dress must have worked.

'You. You're intelligent, pretty and probably understanding. Other girls only come out with me for ...' and he hesitates. What *do* they want when they accept a date? Celice *et al* have been happy with a flirtaceous probe into intimate places along established lines, never enter into conversation beyond the mundane nor utter promises they all know wouldn't be kept. Clare is different; far more of a Lucy than a Briony and it's a Lucy he needs. 'Please?'

'This isn't a try-on merely because I'm all dolled-up, is it?'

He sniffs. 'I wouldn't want to take you out if you were scruffy, Clare, that's true, but it's not a 'try-on' as you call it. And I'd have thought you realise I think more of you than that.' The nasty expression *'cheap lay'* comes to mind, but even Briony's lustful appetite would never fall into that category. 'There's a decent concert on in Lincoln. We could go there. If you're into classical, that is.'

Clare considers. True, it's not her scene but, with mixed emotions, she's prepared to give it a whirl. 'Okay then. When and where? And do I wear this dress or something less flirty?' Oh dear, she immediately thinks, why did I use the word flirty?

He's smiling at her in an annoyingly knowing way. 'Clare, love, you'll have to be a little less transparent. Now go home; I'll pick you up at six. No later. It'll take us the hour to get to Lincoln and parked. Go on, shoo.'

The Traveller is beginning to show its age, with rusty marks on the bottom of the doors, but underneath she's as stout as ever. The red leather seats are well crazed but comfortable. Clare swings herself in with an adroit dexterity, smoothes the dress skirt down and clasps her hands together between her knees. 'Right then,' she says, giving him a nice smile. 'Here I am, flirty dress and all. Will I do?'

'Of course,' aware of a scent not part of her shop dress-up package. 'That's a nice scent you're wearing. Your mum should be proud of you.'

'It's me mum's scent, actually,' she confesses, not really being a perfume lover, believing more in decent soap. 'You should be proud of me too. Stand-in girlfriend. I'll play the part. You don't drive too fast, do you?'

Jones laughs. 'In this old crate? No. And yes, I'm proud of you. In every which way.' He's tempted to lean over and give the girl an adulatory kiss but decides not to. The car in gear, they bump down the dead ended lane where she lives and out onto the main road. Not a lot of traffic about and the Traveller purrs along. Clare stays quiet.

The concert's in the Theatre Royal – other than the unprepossessing exterior, it's typical architecture of its period, raked plush velvet seats, gaudy deep red paint. It's comfortable though, somewhere to relax and forget the world outside. Unreserved seating, so he chooses a side row and allows her to make her own choice, end or middle. She goes to the end so he's no option but tuck her cosily in between him and the wall. At least no-one will need to squeeze past. The programme (price five shillings, expensive) allows her to see it's not all serious stuff, but actually a mixed bag, mainly local artists in an annual show-off. Orchestral, some solos, including a soprano, a quartet – Brahms, which he likes – and even a local girls' school choir. It's not going to be a packed house, that's for sure, but no matter, it makes a decent change and having Clare alongside even better. 'Last concert I went to was the Wigmore Hall. This is different,' Jones says. Conversation for the sake of it, or an opening gambit?

'She's a lovely girl, if she was the one with you last year in Joan's.'

He's startled. She can remember Lucy from all that time ago? 'Yes. And plays beautifully. The Wigmore's concerts are top of the range.' His deep breath-in sounds like a sigh and Clare feels for him. This Lucy, there really must be something special about her.

'So what's up with her? You said you wanted a shoulder to cry on,' and she wants to call him 'Jones' but it doesn't seem right. So far, she's got by without having to use the familiar because it sounds so odd, and 'Mr Jones' would be even worse.

The orchestra have assembled and the resultant tuning up is agonisingly loud so he can't elaborate. The concert gets under way and conversation stops.

Interval time. 'Come on, let's go grab a drink. What d'you think?' She doesn't seem unhappy so far.

'It's okay. Bit amateurish in places. I liked the soprano. She's got a decent voice.'

Jones is impressed, absolutely in agreement with his own thoughts. Well done, girl. They scramble along empty seats in their row and head for the bar. Over a glass of orange juice for her and a white wine – not a bad one, considering – for him, he reverts to her previous query. 'Lucy's been offered a few months contractual exchange with someone from the States. Means she goes to New York at the beginning of November. I don't want her to go, but there's not a lot either of us can do. She's under contract and truthfully, it's a great opportunity. But I'm scared for her.'

'Why?'

'Difficult to explain. She needs inspiration to play like the angel she is; when she's on her very ownsome, there's a problem. Don't get me wrong, she can play, but not with the depth of feeling which makes the world of difference. You can tell, you know, when someone's heart isn't in the music.'

'Like that quartet, you mean?'

He grins at her. 'Absolutely. Technically, not bad – but no soul. Lucy can be like that if ...' and this was the difficult bit, '... if I'm not around.'

Clare looks at him, then reaches out to take his hand from fidgeting with the wine glass's stem. 'She plays for you?'

He nods. 'We know each other's moods, you see. We've become linked, sort of telepathically. If I don't link up with her so she gets inspiration by playing for me, her playing's mechanical. Perfect, but soulless. If she goes to the States, I don't know if I can support her. It's a hell of a way.'

'So you reckon she won't play like she should 'cos you're not there?'

'Something like that. And if she doesn't come up to expectations, her reputation will suffer. Then she won't be like the girl I know. Her mother's a concert pianist, retired, and she knows what music is all about, but doesn't realise what Lucy and I manage between us. Make that music come *alive*.'

Clare is not at all sure about this, for it just sounds *so* egotistically weird. *Linking up with the girl telepathically?* She knows the word and something of what it's meant to mean, but this is the first she's heard of anyone believing in the idea. Jones isn't prone to fanciful thoughts, at least not in the day-to-day, and his friend Lucy also appears level-headed from what she can remember. She sips her orange juice and looks at him over the rim of her glass. 'If she means that much to you, or rather, what you mean to her, I can understand the inspiration thing, but surely, that'll be the case all the time, not just when you're thinking about her?'

He shrugs, then goes on to tell her the story of his trip to Derbyshire, the evening up at Crich Stand and how simultaneously Lucy had been subjected to a medieval sort of initiation test.

'Golly!' Clare's impressed. 'She had to perform in front of all them nobles and so on?'

'A Count, apparently, and all his cronies. She played the first piece in a trance, from what she said, then took a walk into the garden and I felt her searching for me. So I thought of her and what she means to me; she responded, played fantastically well and now she's going to New York.'

'She'll come back.'

'I know, but will she play well enough while she's over there? I don't like her taking the risk. If I could afford it, I'd go with her.'

'Jones,' and Clare doesn't care any more, 'all you have to do is keep her in your head. Have a picture of her on your desk. Surely, you've something of hers you can use to keep her in mind? And she's got to do the same. Have a picture of you on the music stand or tucked in her bra ...' She stops and blushes. 'Sorry.'

The bell for the second half is sounding. They get up, leaving glasses on the table and move back towards the auditorium. As they get jammed together in the crush of people in the passageway, she's very close. He puts an arm round her waist. 'Thanks,' he says in her ear, 'for listening and not laughing at me.'

She turns her head to look at him, only inches between them, slow moving down the corridor. 'She's a very, very lucky girl,' Clare says. Their eyes meet, hers a mysterious sea grey. 'Don't give up on her.' She leans upwards and kisses his cheek. 'Don't cheat on her either.' Then the moment passes and they're back in their seats.

✍

The evening becomes the first of many outings Jones has with Clare. Lucy has gone; he gets her expected postcard. She's not to know, but he cajoled Fortescue to let him have a publicity five by four photo of her, posed on a piano stool in front of the Wigmore's Steinway, her grey diamante dress artfully gracing the figure he knows so well. It's in a marquetry frame and right where she smiles at him across the book stacks, alongside a relocated particular piece of pottery we all know about. Clare approves. 'Has she one of you?' she asks, grinning, knowing he'll remember where she suggested it went.

He scowls at her in turn, then also grins. The two of them burst out laughing. Since that evening in Lincoln, they've become the best of friends and he's a different guy. She never presumes, he is always very polite towards her, but they are both aware how close they're getting. He lets her into the secret why he's called 'jones', he can see her cheeks quivering in an attempt to control her mirth – how his parents latched onto 'Alphonse' they've never explained. In another serious moment he tells her the story of the charger and how it – and its pound note, still there – kept him in touch with the mythical dream girl before he ever had a chance to speak to her. Clare's eyes had widened then, conscious of how privileged she was, him telling her intimate secrets like that.

Her mothering instincts extend. She tells him when his hair is untidy, straightens his tie for him, occasionally brushes his jacket. At least she doesn't have to worry over his shoes, they're always immaculate. He comes to depend on her and is worried stiff the day she phones in sick. When she returns the following day, he expresses his concern.

She bites her lip. How much does he know about these things? 'Jones,' she explains, 'I don't normally have a problem, but me tum was playing me up this month. Shouldn't have had curry at the same time.'

'Sorry?'

'Ah. Us girls, every month, you *know*, don't you?'

'Oh, *that*.' And, yes, recalls Briony's off days. Of course. 'Sorry,' he says again. 'You're alright today?'

She nods. 'Yep. Tough, that's me. Now, where do we put this lot?' The regular week's delivery of new stock. Business was good.

Later in the day he has a reflective moment. What can he do over Christmas that would be different? The last two have been spent with his parents, but living 'at home' is beginning to pall. The Christmas spent with his expert lady lover in Stamford is but a memory, though pleasant in retrospect. Recall the walk in Burghley Park and the marriage proposal? He could easily have said 'yes' to the woman subsequently and none of this would have happened. Lucy – lovely Lucy – would never have had his support, nor he her exquisite music. And since Clare's role in his world has increased, the urge to experiment with any other girl's emotions has diminished. Poor Celice – and Lila and Rosemarie, all cast aside. Tricia has pushed off to Italy. He needs to do something. An incredibly strange thought passes through his head to produce a rather wry smile and an apology, albeit an unspoken one, to his sacred objects, the photo and the earlier ceramic representation of his virtuality, his dream girl. What would his parents say? What would Lucy think?

Clare wouldn't agree anyway. To start with, her mother would probably play merry hell; secondly, his mum might throw him out permanently, though dad would merely grin. And how it would affect the boss to employee relationship, glory only knows.

'Clare!' He gives her a yell from the top of the stairs. 'Got a moment?'

She appears, munching a bun and holding a mug of tea. 'Here,' she says, holding out the mug. 'I'll just fetch mine.'

'And what about my bun, then?'

A head reappears from five steps down. 'It's coming, don't fret.'

She'll be fun. Loads and loads of fun.

As usual, she takes the books out of the angled chair in front of the desk and dumps them on the floor. (Samples from the publishing houses that sometimes get read, sometimes get given away, or sold, if they're not preview copies that say 'Not For Sale' prominently on the outside cover) Then she flops down and, with all the aplomb of a girl who knows she's well-thought of, lifts her feet up and tucks them on the other pile of books. They wobble, but stay put.

'Not the best sales day we've had,' she confides, 'but then, it's rather too wet. P'raps I should have had another day off, then you'd have been rushed off your feet.' Standing joke this; whenever she has her day off (yes, she is allowed one), the shop seems to get busier. They often argue over the possibilities that it's customers preferring Jones to serve (after all, the majority of readers are women) or a variation on the 'sod's law' theme.

She always makes a decent cup of tea. His germ of an idea begins to sprout roots.

'What are you doing for Christmas, Clare?'

She slurps, wipes her lips. No lipstick on today, she left in a rush this morning. 'Sorry. Not a lot, shouldn't think. Mum does a turkey and I don't much care for dried-up turkey. Why?'

'Come away with me. Staff outing. We'll have Christmas in a hotel, just the two of us.' He watches her face change, from puzzlement through incredulity to stern. 'Please?'

'What about Lucy? Are you abandoning her – or two-timing? She's listening,' and Clare nods at the photograph. Somewhere inside her there's a heart going thumpity thump – the maternal aspect partially to blame, with her girly hormones rudely stirred but it's the conscience that needs to be given a sedative.

'Lucy's in the States. And she and I are together on a totally different wavelength, so no, I'm not abandoning her nor, as you so colloquially put it, two-timing. I want company, Clare, because I've had dismal Christmases the last two years and a brilliant one before that I'd like to emulate, at least in some of its aspects. You and I get on well, you organise me and brew a decent cup of tea.'

'If we're in a hotel tea-making doesn't enter into it and you're easy to organise.'

'So it's a 'yes'?'

Her cheeks are tinged with pink and her mouth set in a determined line. 'Mum'll slay me,' but the grin was re-appearing. 'Why not? Provided you behave yourself.'

His turn to grin. 'Clare, dear, I wouldn't dream of doing otherwise. So *you* decide where, if you're that good at organising. I'll leave you to it. And thanks.'

Later on in the day, after she'd thought long and hard, decided she didn't want to go too far and then came up with a wicked idea. That'll teach him! Ten minutes or so on the phone when he was out of the shop and it was all sorted.

Lee Wood Hotel

Fifteen

Allegretto ... Pretty Lively

November drags. The weather encourages an early winter, snow flurries mess up the streets and Clare starts putting up Christmas decorations to add some cheer to the place. Jones begins to worry about the heating bill, though no way is he going down the Samuel route of extra clothes and be damned to the customers; he wants a cheerful atmosphere to boost sales.

He's asked her about the Christmas break; she replied 'all sorted' but wouldn't say more.

They go to the Parish Church Carol Concert and hold hands. He takes her back to her home and is invited in. Clare's mother is, as expected, a buxomly welcoming woman still with an absentee husband, something he'd sort of anticipated, because Clare never mentions a father. He's offered tea and mince-pies and accepts for politeness sake, though he'd rather have had coffee. Clare raises eyebrows when he says 'yes' to tea, but he shakes his head. She knows, clever girl. He doesn't stay more than an hour, though realises the mother thinks her daughter is home and dry. How Clare has got around the Christmas absence he daren't think, given she's not yet twenty-one, but decides not to ask.

Ten days to go. Business hots up; they are selling Christmas cards and wrapping paper too, a Clare concept that has turned out to be a winner. Snow flurries become the real thing and Jones spends a chilly half-hour each morning de-icing the entrance step and the immediate pavement. There's talk of the town becoming cut off by snow drifts across the Wolds roads. That would properly mess up the Christmas break idea.

Then it's the final trading day before the holiday and the weather has relented, even if it's a temporary respite. Hectic for the most part, last minute gifts chiefly bought by husbands, though a few wives dash in for the latest husband desired thrillers … The door bell pings for the last exiting customer and Clare spins the 'Open' sign round on its string. Closed. Jones empties the till, takes the money upstairs. Clare does some arbitrary tidying up, counts the left-over Christmas cards and pulls down the window blind. Five days holiday. She climbs the stairs, tired but happy. Tomorrow, an adventure and who knows what will happen.

'We've done well.' Jones leans back in his chair, hands behind his head, with a neat pile of notes on the desk. 'Two hundred plus, my girl.' He takes two five pound notes off the heap and holds them out. 'Christmas bonus. I'm very, very pleased for all you've done. Don't know how I'd have managed without you.' Hackneyed phrase, that, but what else to say?

She shakes her head. 'You don't need to. Working here and with a boss who shows his appreciation is reward enough. Let's spend it together.'

He's puzzled. 'How? What do you mean? I thought …'

She interrupts. 'If we're having these few days away, there's a bill to be paid. That's my bonus.' She reaches out and picks up Lucy's photo. 'She needs one too. Will you think about her, Jones, when you're with me?'

Silence. How will he be with Clare? The thought of Briony on the beautiful double bed below the chandelier sees her naked and in his arms. That's *not* what he's planned. Another picture, walking the parkland, kicking dried autumnal leaves, swinging a warm hand, now that *is* a possible. Looking at her across a white damask tablecloth, eyes sparkling in the candlelight is another. Listening to her reading her favourite poetry by a log fire. Watching her, just watching her … *weave, weave the sunlight in your hair.* Oh, Lucy, Lucy!

'I'll be your Lucy,' she's saying, bright girl. 'You can pretend. I don't mind. I know she's there, in your head, so I can be in your arms and you can imagine her, not me.'

Jones isn't aware it's Clare talking. His mind is away across the water, listening to the magical sound of a Bechstein in the Carnegie Hall and he hears her. *Keep me close. Any other girl …* in his arms, imagined.

Clare watches his eyes. They're unfocused, flicking; he's not with her, not in this room, but with the one who has him captive. Who is this girl that she has such power over him? 'Jones?'

'Eh? What, oh, sorry. Miles away.'

'So it seems.' She abandons any present chance of getting inside his head to find out what she can do to help. He's seeking another girl, not her, but nevertheless believes he needs *her*, because she is here and is as understanding as she can be, and Lucy is not.

In the morning, a crisp blue skied chill of a morning, he's at her door before nine. It's a Sunday, a Christmas Eve Sunday and the world has gone ultra quiet. She comes skipping out of the door and down the path to the little wicket gate, a duffle bag clutched in a gloved hand. She's wearing a red woollen Tammy hat with a scarf wrapped round her neck, loose ends swinging. Her coat echoes the duffle theme, camel coloured and with wooden toggles on leather straps. Dark green woollen tights under a tartan skirt. Her face is radiant, both in colour and smile. A truly wholesome, delightful picture.

'Clare, you're looking lovely.'

'Am I? Good-oh. Best go, before mother changes her mind.'

'She all right about this?'

'Uh huh. I won't tell you what advice she gave me.'

Jones laughs. 'I can imagine. So long as we maintain relations and have a good time, it'll be fine.'

She isn't sure about the 'relations' bit, but lets it go. 'Full tank?' she asks, to egg him on. He still doesn't know where they are heading, trusting her judgement.

'Yep. And a sandwich box and Thermos.'

She gurgles at him and has to say. 'We're only going into Derbyshire.'

'Derbyshire?' He's startled, thinking about his most recent foray there. 'Where?'

'Buxton?'

'Lord help us! Coldest place on the planet, this time of year. Oh well, your choice. Hope the hotel's got central heating or at least a roaring fire. And if it snows, we may be there some time. At least I put a shovel and a couple of old sacks in the back. Any good at pushing?'

She's settled snugly into the sagging leather. 'Nope. You can teach me to drive then you can push. Come on, else we won't be there before dark and I don't fancy sleeping in her, not even with you.'

He grins. A girl with a sensible attitude and very much as he'd hoped she'd be, not a clinging 'light my fire' type. He lets in the clutch and the old Traveller trundles off.

Clare's mother watches them go from the front room window, waves back as Clare waves her hand in farewell. *'Hope she doesn't get carried away,'* she murmurs as she thinks back to her own pre-marital excursions. Fun, but dodgy.

⤸

The roads aren't too bad. Snow is still piled up on the verges as they cross the Wolds but once they drop down off the Lincolnshire Heights and head across to the Trent valley, the snow disappears. They make good time, reach the A6 and head north. The road around Derby is almost empty, only a few other vehicles heading south. Once free of the built up area and into the Derwent valley, Clare sits up and takes more notice.

'Look at those cliffs! And these houses, all perched up the hill! Been here before, Jones?'

'A few months ago. When you looked after the shop for me.' *When Lucy was in Austria and called out for help.* 'We turn off here.' They run through Cromford and head up the Via Gellia. The trees are skeletonised, spooky in the blackness of the narrow valley. Clare shivers. 'Shouldn't like to be here on a dark night. Imagine a few witches flying about and all them bats.'

Jones keeps both hands on the wheel. He would like to pat her on the knees to reassure her, but daren't. It takes them fifteen minutes to drive out of the narrow valley and into the last of the wintry sunshine. The remaining journey up the road between Ashbourne and Buxton is accomplished in a steady silence, other than the reassuring rumble of the engine.

'Which hotel?'

She digs out the acknowledgment letter she's had and checks the address. 'Not far out of the town centre,' she says, 'On one of the crescents. Past the Opera House, second left at the junction. Faces a recreation ground.'

He follows some of the directions and some of his instinct, the little car climbs up the slope past the Spa buildings and there they are, home and dry.

'Well done,' he congratulates her and this time does pat her knee. It's a nice knee to pat.

At the reception desk, Clare shows the acknowledgment letter. Does he realise what she's done? Jones has not asked once, or even hinted he wished to know. He expects two singles though it was entirely her choice.

The reception clerk checks his diary. There appears to be some confusion in his mind and he looks at both Clare's letter and the book once more. 'I'm sorry,' he says in a stilted apologetic voice, 'we appear not to have the twin room reserved. We only have double rooms and one single left,' and his hesitation is forgivable. Clare's glance at Jones is curiously bland. Jones shrugs, not wishing to embarrass her, and she follows her inclination.

'A double it is then, please.'

Jones maintains an impassivity as he signs the register. Clare is equally moderate in her expression. One hurdle overcome, and so the porter carries the two bags up to the second floor, unlocks a door and places the bags inside.

'Hope you will be very comfortable, sir, madam. Dinner is at seven.' He hands them the key and walks away.

The two young people look at each other. He sees a vulnerable, yet confident twenty year old girl of whom he thinks the world and will not despoil, she sees a vulnerable and determined twenty five year old with whom she will endeavour to explore her latent sexuality, though she doubts she will ever take his soul away from another. They join hands, walk inside the double-bedded room and close the door behind them.

∽

Lucy: *I'm Stateside. Stateside! It's like a dream. The Royal College, then Paris, Salzburg, the Wigmore, and now, Carnegie. And all because mother taught me to play the piano!*

She's had the guided tour, been shown her room in one of the ever so tall hotel buildings, and one of the Institute's guardians will meet her shortly to take her down to dinner. Not quite best frock, but *'do dress well, please,'* the request. She's to meet some of the Directors, afterwards they'd like her to play a little taster for them. *'So they get an idea of what you can do,'* she was told.

The cross Atlantic flight over hadn't been too bad at all, only about half an hour of bumps and 'fasten safety belts'. Noisy, though. Every now and again she has to do the 'pinch herself' thing to believe it is actually her, a twenty year old ex Stamford High school girl, who is having this chance. Mr Fortescue has reassured her she's not the only one. Others have trod this same path, some didn't make the grade, others – and he named two whose reputations were now in the public domain – succeeded. 'You'll succeed, Lucy,' he'd said, shaking her hand at the airport terminal before she boarded the plane, 'because you have an inner spirit that must be unique. Provided you don't lose that spirit, you'll be fine. I'll pop across for the last concert.' Her mother and father had been there too, to see her off. Tears, of course, but nice ones. One person was missing, at least in body. Jones. Her spirit, her power, the essential part of her music. Every so often, she'd get a little buzz of thought and the feel of his arms around her, the excitement of his kiss. For him.

Dinner, in a grand restaurant. Best behaviour, trying not to be overly nervous. *I'm Lucy Salter, pianist. I make music for others to love. Jones, I love you for loving me and my – our – music. Keep me close, my dearest soul.* That way she manages to sparkle, as in the half hour recital she presents afterwards in the hotel's ball room to a very small and select audience. At the finish they all stand up and clap politely before one of the ladies in a posh velvet gown comes and takes her hand as the group fall silent.

'Fellow members of the Institute,' she is saying, 'I believe we have a young lady of incredible talent in our midst and I am so, so pleased the Carnegie will have one of its finest exchange performers for many years here for the season. Let us welcome her into our midst and provide her with all the warmth and support she deserves. Ladies and Gentlemen, Lucy Salter.'

More clapping, more conversation, she's nearly off her feet before being allowed to return to her room. The lady in the velvet gown sees her to the lift and hands her an envelope.

'Lucy dear, don't take offence. These are your instructions for tomorrow and a little something to help with any minor incidentals. Now, if you need anything, don't hesitate to call me. I'm Stephanie and I knew your mother when she was here. You're a very worthy successor to your mother's crown, my dear. This has been an excellent evening, but I know how draining it will have been. You've coped admirably. So good night, and I'll see you tomorrow.'

The lift door closes and she's being whisked up to the twentieth at high speed. She feels ever so slightly sick and hopes no-one will see her get to her room. Once inside the suite with a floor area as much as her parent's house back at home, she sits in one of the capacious grey velvet armchairs and opens the envelope. As promised, her call sheet for tomorrow, where she should be and at what time, how a car will call for her, what she should wear. And in a smaller, fat envelope, a wad of dollar bills. She cannot believe this. Counted and allowing that some are twenties, some tens, she makes it five hundred dollars. Five hundred! Incidentals! Incredible!

She carefully takes off her dress as preparation for bed and as she does so, believes she could buy another without worrying. This is New York, Lucy! Finally, in a silky nightdress, a last minute present from her parents, she is ensconced in an awfully wide, soft, ever so comfy bed and …

∽

The weeks go by. She has engagements, she has days sight-seeing, she has unbelievably mad days shopping for little things – or merely pretend shopping in some stores – and she practices hour upon hour for the big night. At night times she thinks of home, of her mother who'll be thinking of her, of the phone conversations they've had, and she thinks of her soul mate. She's sure he's thinking of her too, because at no time does she feel stressed or failing in her ability to pull the most magical of sounds out of the wonderful Bechstein. She must get everything absolutely right on her concert night. This is what it's been all about, and the posters scream her name. Her name! *Lucy Salter, ARCM.*

The concert is scheduled for Christmas Eve. It is to be a family concert and she will play three items. The Chopin Nocturne, for which her interpretation is famous, a Schubert Impromptu, and the latest addition to her repertoire, a Mozart Fantasia. Is she nervous? A little. Everyone should have some feeling of nerves, to keep the adrenaline topped up, to keep the body tuned into its peak. Stephanie has been truly wonderful, keeping her informed, taking her out on the sight-seeing visits and, only yesterday, shopping for another new dress, the important dress. There it is, lying on the settee, a wonderful creation in a dark green taffeta with a silvery purple sheen, wide short sleeves so as not to interfere with her arms, a semi-full skirt down to just above her ankles. It's a little low on the front but she's not worried. Her breasts aren't that full and a necklace is fine. A gift, said Stephanie, producing her store card at the crucial moment, for a beautiful English rose. She doesn't feel rose-like. More like *chrys an the mum* and she giggles. She takes her dress off, sits on the bed edge, swings round and stretches out, straightening her petticoat and easing her bra. Relaxed, she lets her muscles sag, pulls in her nerve endings like she's been accustomed to do when concentrating on thoughts and powers up her own private cross-Atlantic telepathic telephone. *Jones, where are you?*

Jones: *I can sense her mood, even from here. I know her. Every molecule, the minutiae of every sinew and nerve ending, every pulse of heartbeat, each and every rich brown strand of hair, the glow of toned skin, the shine in those eyes. Even the ravelled tangle of thoughts that make her so special as she is reaching out; mind to mate with mind. She has a challenge ahead, the uppermost thought, a challenge she will meet as she has my strength within her. I will hear the incredible sound she can produce, fingers flashing over keys, heart and soul and our minds together.*

Clare is with me. She is as near a physical embodiment of my alter ego as can be achieved, her closeness the best way of powering thoughts we can devise. I will not demean this gift of her companionship for it is what she alone decided and I cannot, will not, spurn or reject the ultimate gift a woman can bestow. We meld, she and I, and the projection of our twinned emotions must lift the essence of magic in mood towards perfection. Lucy will feel that power, come the moment.

Clare: He didn't object, neither did he appear surprised. It wasn't as though we were lusting after each other, not really. He'd asked, I'd said yes. He allowed me to organise it. What a risk! I could have arranged two single rooms, but somehow it wouldn't have worked. He'd have sulked; I'd be bored. The twin room seemed like the *meet me half way* ideal option. The hotel is to blame, I suppose. So we behaved, I think (not even having thought this through), like a boring old married couple. When it was time to go to bed – and we were both rather tired, either from stress or the day, I don't know which, he went to the bathroom and I slipped out of all my things, wriggled into the plainest of nightdresses I could find when I packed, and was all neatly tucked up when he came out. He turned the light out; next thing I knew it was nearly daylight.

So no, sorry if I disappoint you folks, we didn't. I wasn't surprised or disappointed and I'd determined I would let Jones decide. (Is it what's called 'making the first move?) I could tell his mind wasn't really on the opportunity presented. I mean, if he'd wanted to, I'd have let him. He did give me a simple cuddle, which was nice and I felt what a girl's supposed to feel, I think. Made me go rather, well, you know…

'Clare?' Now this is early morning and we're lying platonically, if a little embarrassed, side by side, gazing at the ceiling.

'Hmmm?' I look sideways at him then back to the ceiling.

'Do you know what Lucy's doing?'

'A concert in New York?' Why ask, for he's told me often enough. It's a fixation, poor man.

'Yes. A very important concert and it's taking place right now.'

'Now?' I have to humour him.

'Mmm. We're that much different in time, you see.'

I know what he's thinking. That Lucy needs him; it always seems to be the case. 'Don't you have to concentrate on helping her *inspiration?*'

'Uh huh. You're very understanding, Clare. You don't say I'm daft or anything.'

'Jones, I've been with you long enough to know what makes you tick.' My stare up at the plasterwork has made my neck ache. 'I've seen Lucy. I reckon it's you who makes *her* tick, and if that's so, you've been rather too good to me. If you've fallen in love with her, that is. I must be mad,' and I have to grin, 'being here as a celibate stand-in for your Christmas festive female. What she'd think about this idea I'm not sure. If it'd been the other way round I'd have got proper stroppy. Will you tell her?'

'What, that I've slept with a stray girl in my bed? Probably not, as I've slept with another woman where the euphemism is actually true. She …'

I have my hands behind my head and the blankets tucked decorously up to my chin. I turn from the boring ceiling to look at him again. I think he's gone red.

'Do I really want to know?' I ask, not sure if I like his 'stray girl' description, being the sweet little innocent that I am?

A noise that could be a chuckle emanates from Jones as he turns on his side and moves an arm across. I'm feeling very soft, comfortably warm, and rather too pliant.

Lucy is walking across the platform.

'How innocent?'

My emotions are now becoming dangerously unstable. I take his hand and move it to where I think it should be. Ought to be.

'Ah,' he says, and down below something interesting is happening.

I'm a silly, weak and rather too emotive a girl. I'm not a Lucy but it's Lucy he needs, and she needs him. So I've got to be his Lucy and I can't pretend it isn't what I want. Sort of.

∾

Lucy is sitting down at the keyboard. Now, she is saying, please, now, I need that urge, that super orgasmic flow within me, so I can expand on the immensity of our passion and bring the rapture to the ears, the minds, the souls of all within this huge hall. For me, for him …

᷍

Clare is in the bathroom, having a bath. It's nearly ten o'clock now. She stares down at the full length of her body, at the body of a woman. No longer a girl.

I'm all mixed up inside. There's two of me. Like a double image in an antique mirror, a disturbed image of nakedness under the scented swaying water. He took me for Lucy's sake. I know that's what it was all about. He probably didn't know what he said once underway … . He made love to Lucy, not me. He sought her and I found her, mainly for him but I can't pretend. I felt like the two of them together. Weird.

She's surprised at her feelings. All mixed up inside.

I don't suppose we'll ever be so close again, not unless something happens to Lucy and, no I wouldn't want her hurt. I'll always remember what we achieved between us, all three of us I mean. He wouldn't have … not with me – if this concert thing hadn't occurred. It was for her, I know it was.

Questions, very pertinent questions, she asks herself, with an ever so slight worry.

If anything happens, what on earth shall I do?

Jones: *Clare's been fantastic. I suppose there was a degree of inevitability about what happened. She won't believe me if I told her I didn't mean to. I'm not sure I believe it myself. Very demeaning for the girl, so I shan't have to say anything. Why did we …? Because it was for Lucy. She needed to have that power and how else could I have achieved it? Will she understand? Does she know how? It worked, I know it did, else Clare wouldn't have, well … oh glory be – Clare, my lovely Clare.*

She comes out of the bathroom swathed in a huge fluffy pink towel, hair all straggly. She looks as pink as the towel. I laugh at her, my lovely girl. My festive female, as she calls herself.

'Jones,' she says to me, rubbing her hair with a smaller towel. 'Don't think you have to say *anything. Anything!* Do you understand? What's happened, happened. I know. *I know!'*

She's fantastic. If she truly knows, then we're okay.

We have a very late breakfast. It's Christmas Day. The sun, a watery, insipid sort of sun, is trying hard to dispel the thin layer of cloud. I'm not sure I wouldn't have preferred an overnight snow fall to cover everything up with pristine white, to obliterate all the untidy mess of the night before. A clean slate. Clare has a glow about her I'd not seen before, what is it, an inner radiance? Other late breakfasters look at us with knowing smiles. Okay, so we're a honeymoon couple. Great.

'Darling,' I say across the toast crumbs and dirty coffee cups, 'what shall we do today?' and smile. She grins back at me with rather a coy look about her.

'Shall we go for a walk?'

Is this what honeymooners do? Or do they go back to bed? She knows, I know, that is not an option. Back in time to Briony land – yes, we did, then. But that was pure unadulterated sex for the orgasmic feelings we experienced. Perhaps not pure, and at the time, not adulterous. It would be now because I felt I'd committed my life to Lucy, and Clare, unwittingly, (or maybe not so unwittingly, for do I understand the girl's true feelings?) had become caught up in this shadowy world of ours of her own free will. There is one thing I must do, to be true to her – Clare – and myself.

'I want to make a 'phone call first.'

Clare's look. A steady, thinking, understanding look. 'All right darling. Don't be long. I'll be in the lounge.' She could have called me Jones, not darling. Is she being humorous or … and if so, do I care? I do, actually. I don't wish to hurt her and that's the stupid thing about all this. I'm using her, and I shouldn't.

∽

I fish the number out of my diary. It's nearly half eleven now. They could be out, of course, at a Christmas Day service. That would have been nice, to have gone to a service, heard the carols, made it feel much more like a proper Christmas Day. Then again, they might have stayed in to hear how she got on, which is what I'm hoping as the 'phone dials. The Hotel's public phone is rather too public, but what the heck.

'Salter,' and it's her father. 'Can I help you?' That's the professionalism.

'It's Jones; sorry to trouble you, but I wonder if you've heard how Lucy got on last night?'

'Jones! Well, Happy Christmas to you. You obviously know of her big event at the Carnegie?'

'Yes sir, I do. And a Happy Christmas to you and Mrs Salter.'

'I'll fetch my wife, Jones. She'll be the one to explain. Suffice to say we're very proud of our daughter. Hold the line.'

There's a moment's pause and some crackling in the earpiece, then I hear Lucy's mother pick up the handset. 'Good morning, Jones. So very kind of you to ring. You were thinking of her, weren't you?'

'Yes, Mrs Salter, I was.' *And how.* 'You've heard from her?'

'We understand she had a very successful evening. She wasn't able to say too much, because the line wasn't very good and of course, it's very expensive. Apparently Mr Fortescue, you know, her agent, will phone us from the States later. But, yes, she said she had a super time, the audience loved her. So all's well. Thank you so much for asking. Are you having a good Christmas?'

'Yes, thankyou. I'm (and I nearly said 'we're') up in Derbyshire. Cold, but dry at the moment. Do you know when she's coming home?'

'I believe Mr Fortescue will say. Call us again, say tomorrow. Have a lovely day.'

⊰

Jones goes back to find Clare, ensconced with a magazine in one of the deep moquette solid armchairs. The lounge is otherwise empty. 'Well?' she asks, looking up. 'How was it?' She's guessed, this remarkable young lady.

'A very successful evening, that's all Lucy's mother could say.

Her agent will ring them later, apparently he flew over just for the concert.'

'So we did all right for her.' Her voice sounds flat, her statement commonplace.

Clare, how can you be so mature and grown up and matter-of-fact over what happened between us? How can you possibly understand the ties between Lucy and me?

Jones is now torn between pleasure at Lucy's success and remorse at dragging Clare into an odd third party relationship. He sits alongside her. There are two thick chair arms between them.

'I'm sorry, Clare.'

She puts the magazine down on the low table in front of her. 'I'm not. You believed the strength of your thoughts would reach out and support Lucy. You used me like a medium. I knew the risks. If what happened helped, then it did.' She clasps her hands together in the well of her skirt and though it seems odd to say what's in her mind, she feels she has to. 'I enjoyed the experience. A girl has to go through the curtain some time.'

'Curtain?' Jones is surprised at her choice of words. Now he is feeling awkward. He took a very precious thing away from this very precious girl and she's calling it a 'curtain'?

'Draw the curtain back and you let in the light.' Her face revealed nothing.

There's a silence. Jones is thinking. Light? Perhaps it's not too much the moral degradation for her that it might seem to be in the cold clear light of this day, of all days. The Birth celebration, Christmas. What she wanted?

'Clare, my love. Tell me what you want me to do. Anything. Just say. I've messed up your life, haven't I?'

She shakes her head. 'No, I don't think so. Unless I fall pregnant.' There, she's admitted the action and the possibility. Until she actually said those words, it could have been merely a dream. Not now, it's real and it happened. 'Sorry,' and she adds, 'call it a *one-night stand*'. That's the expression, isn't it? Buy a girl a decent meal and a few drinks and she repays the debt on her back. Simple.' Then it hits her and she feels tears coming.

Jones leans across and picks up a hand. 'It's not like that. You know it's not.' He could say she had the choice; the place, the hotel, the room, and *she* chose to put herself in jeopardy, if that's what it is. 'Why, Clare?'

Wet eyes, and she takes her hand back to brush the tears away. 'I don't know,' and sniffs.

He's got this tense impossible to comprehend tightness in his gut, looking at her unsullied simplicity, the essence of all the girl means to him. Why he likens her to a Lucy, never as a Celice or a Briony, why he asked her to come away with him, so they could broaden their knowledge of each other, mostly because she'd grown on him, an unassuming yet essential part of his life. Does he love her too? She's real, this girl, and unforgivably, he's used her whereas Lucy has been a virtual person for so long, powerful, yes, but a mysterious if magnetic silhouette, a goddess to be held inviolate and revered.

Another silence. There's a very large question mark hanging over them now. What should he do? A return to the easy familiarity might be impossible. She must decide.

He reaches for her hand once more; unresisting, this she allows. The clock on the room's mantlepiece, a huge marble thing, ticks the seconds away. It would be nicer if they'd lit the fire. Perhaps they will after lunch. He's sitting on the edge of the seat, hunched towards her. He feels protective, concerned. Lines from Shelly flit through his head.

" *O Love! who bewailest // The frailty of all things here ... "*

But Clare is not frail, is she? Then there's another line, something about fountains and rivers, before:

"The winds of heaven mix for ever // with a sweet emotion // Nothing in the world is single; All things, by a law divine, // in one another's being mingle, Why not I with thine?"

From *Love's Philosophy*, from what he can remember. Oh, Lucy, Lucy, why did you have to do this to me?

'I'll get another job,' she says, looking down at the dull red swirly patterned carpet. 'It might be best.'

'No.' He's abruptly adamant. He does not want to lose her. 'Clare, love, it's my fault. I shouldn't have involved you.'

Her gaze returns to him, the sea-grey eyes. 'Then maybe your thought waves wouldn't have been as strong? And what about *my* feelings? Don't I count? Maybe *I* seduced *you.*'

The corners of her lips are turned up into the vestiges of a smile; as he watches, they quiver into suppressed laughter. 'You should see your face.'

Irony, acidic irony. So she *knew* she had the chance that he'd make love to her? Had she driven the event, not Lucy and his tramlined concept of paranormal power?

'You placed a lot of trust in me.'

'Maybe I thought you wouldn't want to do more than have me in your arms and pretend I was Lucy? You wouldn't have done it with Lucy. But you could with me.'

'Something like that.'

'Did you enjoy it? Did I?'

'Clare, you're not being fair.'

She tears her hand away and climbs out of the chair to march round the room.

'Jones, you asked me out for a couple of days away, and I thought you were making it quite clear you'd appreciate the option to sleep with me. Cleverly, you let me decide where and how, persuaded me it's all for dear Lucy; convinced yourself I wouldn't mind, now you're panicking in case I want to make it permanent and darling Lucy will have to look after herself. Aren't you?' Her breasts are heaving, her voice raised. '*I wanted* you *to decide!* Why do you think I dressed up, wore my hair differently? Showed my knees? Oh, for heaven's sake, Jones. I'm a girl who's stupidly fallen in love with you, a girl who has to live with a virtual Lucy just like you do. A shadow, that's all she is. I'm real. You know that, you've been inside me. Would you have done it with her? Bet you couldn't. She'd vanish, like the mists at dawn.'

'No she wouldn't. I've held her, Clare.'

'Bet you didn't suggest having it off with her.'

'Don't be coarse.'

Clare stops her parading about, holds onto the back of a chair with both hands and glares at him. 'Coarse? I'm not coarse. Merely practical. I'm here, she's not, I was in your bed last night, or more properly, you were in mine. Okay, so we didn't make it until dawn, when you cleverly suggested Lucy needed us to … oh, what the hell!'

'I'm sorry.'

'Sorry? What for? Shagging me or saying you never want to again?'

'For getting you worked up about all this. It's not like you.'

'What do you expect, Jones? First you say it's *my* choice, then it's Lucy's, now you're saying it's *all* a *big* mistake. Make up your mind.'

Jones sees Clare in a different light. From a shy and diffident girl she has now become confident and argumentative. Does he like her as much, or more? Does he want her in his bed again? Would he choose her in preference to Lucy if he had the choice, right now? More importantly, would Lucy now look to him as her lover? Clare is absolutely right, she's here and available, Lucy is not. There's a strange parallel with the Briony situation. *She* was available and proved it times without number, yet they walked away from each other without permanent regrets. Will Clare walk away from him, and if so, when? Now, or at some time in the future? Or will she cling tight and make any further link with Lucy impossible?

'I'm going to go for that walk. Are you coming with me or do I go by myself?' She's waiting for his reply, arms now relaxed by her side.

Jones doesn't answer, walks across the room towards her, puts a hand on each cheek and firmly kisses her unresisting mouth. 'You're a hard girl to please,' he says when he draws breath. 'Let's take that walk. Perhaps it'll clear our heads.'

Now she's grinning at him. 'Okay. Then we'll have our Christmas dinner and swop presents.'

Buxton – the Band Stand

Sixteen

Andamento ... Running

This was her moment. Initially, she could not hear the audience or see beyond the keys. The depth of sensuality between her and this magnificent instrument over which she experienced complete control had her gripped. A bond, an incomprehensible link forged over this past small span of time when music had flowed like wine, jewels over a ruby sea, poured out as a flood tide covers the sand with dancing wavelets from the immeasurable depths. As the last fading echoes vanished as a tide ebbs, so the silence had crept down, a blanket of softness before this shattering cacophony of clapping hands had fractured the mood. Had the chance been offered she would have immediately walked out into a place where her private delight in the consummation of this event could have been realised; to sit and relax, to let muscles release their tension, to appreciate the after-glow, to allow the intimacies of her inner woman restore her body to equanimity. For whatever magic their minds had conjured and conjoined had happened, it truly had.

We have expanded the immensity of our passion and brought rapture to the ears, the minds, the souls of all within this hall. For him, for me …

Whatever he'd done to reach her was immeasurably successful. It had been them, not her alone. She is only the instrument; her fingers, her hands, her arms controlled by a mind and a brain linked with another – his – to amplify one desire to another, of immense magnitude, a multiplication beyond her dreams.

And now it is over. The swell of sound triggers her response; the expected acceptance of the audience's expression of appreciation. She stands. The shoulders are back, the left foot is slightly in front of the right; the left hand lightly poised on the polished jet black edge of the keyboard. Then the right hand comes up to rest above her shadowed valley to hold her necklace's pendant as she bows, and again. The steady walk off the stage, the ten second pause, the nod from the steward, the walk back – all as expected, the routine. No, no encore. There is no need. The flowers – oh, the flowers. She can scarce hold them and is smothered in scent. Lilies, not her most favourite flower but, showy and expensive.

Awe, as expressed by the hall's steward's expressions, then congratulations from the rest of the evening's line-up, from the presenter; finally, there is Stephanie, her 'buddy'.

She is embraced, there are tears. Then champagne and … it is overpowering. Eventually Stephanie comes with her to the Hotel, sees her safe into her suite. 'Catch-up with you in the morning, babe,' she's told; finally she is alone.

There is a phone call to make. Her mother will be anxious. She does her filial duty, précised because she is tired. Basil, of course, rings from his hotel shortly afterwards. He is effusive, as always. She is earning money for him in company with raising his reputation. Is she a doll, to be fussed over, patted, have her hair stroked, her panties smoothed, her dress changed; to be put to bed, pretend fed, expected to give pleasure without compromise and without concern? She is abrupt, instructs him to direct his appreciative comments to her mother and puts down the receiver.

Now she is drained, undressing in slow and deliberate fashion, taking time to ensure the emerald green dress is perfectly hung on the fabric covered hanger. The bed-covers are precise and neatly turned back, her gifted long silk nightdress draped invitingly over the frilled pillow. The hotel staff are impeccable and diligent in their routines, but then, she is a Carnegie girl.

Once embraced in the bed's softness and the lights dimmed down, Lucy becomes her own girl once more; this allows her mind to skim back in gentle time lapse mode and reprise events. The necessary but boring features of the evening are consigned into mental oblivion, to leave only the golden glimpses of her performance. Her performance? *Their* performance. The inspiration borne on waves of knowledge of who they were, together; only *together* could this thing have happened. But the feelings had been different; deeper, more profound, stronger? An intensity in tune with the flow of the music, and, curiously, lifting in the same phrasing as the composer's intentions: her studies in Salzburg gave her that strength of knowledge. Tomorrow, once the morning's complications are sorted, she will talk with him.

࿏

Derbyshire in the middle of winter cannot always provide the weather commensurate with one's ideal scenario. A crisp frost jewelled picture of untrammelled beauty perhaps, as represented by countless Christmas cards – you know the sort of thing; postillions with horn, a coach and matched pair of horses, snow carpeted roads, bystanders with tricorne hats, adorable children attached to fur draped mothers, red-berried holly, the village church, stained glass windows lit by countless candles.

Sadly, no. Earlier snowfalls here as elsewhere in the country were dissipated to grey slush before a minimal rise in temperature. The day is overcast, though so far, dry. Clare and Jones set forth, booted and coated, to relieve the claustrophobic pressures of their day. Neither have knowledge of the town and hence no specific destination but downhill is easier. Ten minutes walk with silence between them, the only sound from occasional distant traffic and the trudge of boot on pavement, to reach the conglomeration of buildings that form the Opera House, the Octagon, the Spa, the Playhouse.

179

The Park lies beyond, the otherwise still and lifeless appearance broken only by a solitary dog walker. Clare shivers and draws her coat tighter.

'Depressing,' she says. 'Now where?'

Jones shrugs. 'Round the park?'

'Boring,' she replies. 'But better that than the High street and window gazing. Why did I suggest this place?'

'Pin in a map?'

'Something like that. Come on,' and she picks up his gloved hand and tugs him forward.

It takes around half an hour to complete the circuit. The little river has a few morose ducks on the water, otherwise there is little of inspiration. They come back to the bandstand, forlorn in its winter uselessness. Jones climbs up onto the platform and surveys the grey buildings across and below the parkland. Clare peers up at him.

'Shall I quote Shakespeare? You know, the 'Romeo, wherefore art thou' bit?'

He laughs down at her. 'Wrong way round, love. You'll have to swop places for that.'

'There's more.' She hesitates, he can almost hear her mind working, and then, with her earnest young face looking up at him, she recites, quite accurately: '*O gentle Romeo, if thou dost love, pronounce it faithfully: or if thou thinkest I am too quickly won, I'll frown and be perverse, and say thee nay, so thou wilt woo* ... How's that, Jones? Does it prove I'm literate? A good bookseller? Or am I better in bed?' and she looks away, turning her back.

He's holding onto the bandstand rail with both hands. 'Don't, Clare. Don't *ever* demean yourself.' He vaults over, grabs her and spins her round. 'You're the nicest girl ...' and stops, seeing tears. 'Oh, *Clare!*'

She buries her face in his coat, pummels his back with small gloved hands. 'Can't you see it, you daft man? I've bloody well fallen in love with you! And I know it's bloody stupid because you have this, this ... ' she sniffs, has to pull a hand free to wipe her nose on the back of her glove, '... stupid crush on this mythical bloody Lucy!'

'Clare!' He lets go of her. They stand apart, and now she's glaring at him.

'Don't you *Clare* me! It's true – she's in your head all the time, isn't she? Last night – early this morning – you weren't shagging me, it was her! I'm a fucking flesh 'n bloody doll with a Lucy face. Go on, deny it.'

He can't. There's far too much truth in what she says. Fallen in love with him? She's a lovely, middle of the road, decent girl with a good brain and pretty legs, or is that a pretty good brain and decent legs? His mind is whirling round, as an image of Lucy appears to be standing in front of him, just as he saw her that day in the Mason's Arms, a mysteriously wonderful figure who first caught at his mind the evening he bought the charger and remains there; she who has driven him – is driving him – insane.

'I'm sorry, Clare.'

Is that all he can say? Clare spins round and marches off downhill, almost at a run, yet she hasn't gone a hundred yards before he sprints after her, catching her up, grabbing at an arm, nearly causing her to fall over on a patch of residual ice. He holds her firmly, pushes the stray hair away from her face and kisses her. She's resistive at first, her hands down by her sides, then her arms come up and round and the two figures are seen by a passer-by as in a true lover's clinch from the movies. *'Lovely couple,'* the elderly woman thinks and goes home to embrace a surprised husband.

'Let's go back to the hotel. Then I'll try and explain, if I can, Clare, love.'

'Am I a love?'

He has to nod. 'You're a love, my love.' He draws breath. 'There's something I'm seeking, I don't know what, something I haven't yet found.' The statement made, in this of all places, is absolutely true, though never expressed so simply before, maybe not even realised before. 'Peace?'

He's kissed her. That must be something. And he's promised to explain; that could be good. 'Peace,' she agrees and they join hands to walk back to the hotel.

'Ah! Mr Jones, there's been a call for you,' the middle-aged man on reception greets them, offering Clare a beaming smile. 'I hope it's not too cold for you out there. A chilly day, not at all Christmassy. And, ah, dinner is at seven.' He hands Jones a folded piece of paper.

They walk into the lounge where, three hours earlier, Clare had first properly expressed her feelings. It is still unoccupied, but then, there aren't all that many residents presently in the hotel. Clare unbuttons her coat, unwinds her scarf and dumps them both in the same chair where she'd previously sat. Jones unfolds his paper, reads, and she watches as his expression changes.

'Don't tell me.' She reaches over and takes it from unresisting fingers, allowing him to remove his coat and place it over hers. She reads aloud. *'From Miss Lucy Salter. Thankyou. Concert incredibly successful and my interpretation felt beautiful. Whatever support you gave worked. Be in touch later. Your soul. Lucy.* Reads like a telegram. Is she your soul?' and she hands the paper back. Her voice sounds flat, almost tired.

Jones motions towards the other armchair of the group, waits for her to subside before settling down on the settee. 'It's a long story,' he begins, 'which takes us back over three years or so. A September in fact, when I was still only employed part-time and scrounged around for the rest of it. I'd been in this antiques place, you see, and found a marvellous piece of ceramic art for next to nothing. Then, when I came out, I saw her and ... '

He speaks for nearly half-an-hour. Clare, unsure at first, gradually finds her interest aroused. The idea of preternatural thought as possessing power she'd not ever considered. What happens in her own head is no-one else's business; certainly the idea her thoughts could influence any other person is mystifying.

'... I didn't believe it myself, not at first. But now ...' he tails off, unsure how to convince her.

'And you really really believe she can sense what you're thinking?'

Her answer comes with his little nod. 'I do.'

'Does she know about me, us?'

He pulls a face. 'I think,' and then grins, 'we're not tuned in to sharing friends. Just support for her music and for what she is.'

'And what *is* she, a girlfriend or what?'

'I've never thought of her that way, not really. I had Briony, you see. And Daphne. Lucy's not in that league.'

'And I am?'

'No!' The emphatic denial surprises her at the same time as it offers her hope.

'Huh!'

'It's true. Briony was, well, Briony. Daphne needed a male companion when she was at her most vulnerable but she got over it. Lucy isn't anywhere near the same.' *How could she be?* 'She doesn't need a *man*.' The implication is obvious.

'And I do?' It cost her to ask but she has to know.

'Clare, my love, you're different. Different from anyone else. You're just great company, lovely to be with,' and he has to add, truly a tinge mischievously, 'in every which way. None of the other town girls come anywhere near. And I've met a few.'

So she's recently heard. Girly gossip has an interesting habit of getting everywhere, especially from thwarted females. 'Celice?'

'I'm not going to elaborate, Clare. Not fair on her. Just as I'd never tell anyone about this jaunt of ours.'

'I suppose that's something. But my mum knows and she's got ideas.'

Another grin. 'As mothers have. Even Lucy's,' and he recalls the out-of-the-blue invite to tea that day shortly after Samuel's demise.

Clare gets up out of her chair. 'I'm going up to wash and change. You can try and raise the paramour on the thought-waves while you're alone; perhaps explain just how she got her, what was it, *beautiful interpretation?* And make up your mind. I don't fancy being two-timed by an astral vision.' She flounces out, dragging her coat and scarf behind her.

Clare: *I'm an idiot. All this guff about telepathy! Sending her mental telegrams, 'hope you do well, dear, 'cos I've got this other girl in bed with me'. And he reckons we did it so just so she can have her own public orgasm on the piano! Huh! I'll show him!*

And then her own mind plays a trick on her, reversing her idea. In his arms, whilst experiencing the oddest of feelings instinct informed her were *orgasmic*, had also come a weird expression of joy for the girl caressing the keys of a grand piano; what was it she'd said?

… I wouldn't want her hurt. I'll always remember what we achieved between us, all three of us I mean. He wouldn't have … not with me – if this concert thing hadn't occurred …

She's stripping off, preparatory to using the shower thing. Not having one at home, she'll experiment.

I'm not sure where I am now. He won't abandon her, 'cos she's special. But

183

I'm sure I mean something to him too. So, thanks, Mr Shakespeare, 'I'll frown and be perverse, and say thee nay, so thou wilt woo …'

The shower jet is unexpectedly fierce and rather hot. Somehow she manages to get it more accommodatingly pleasant and luxuriates.

Tonight. After a nice dinner, we'll see.

Jones: He watches her leave the room and it expands to a huge, cold, vacant space, the glow of her presence dimmed out. Odd.

If anyone had suggested I'd be nuts over a girl like her at college, I'd have clouted them. Only daughter of a single mum, local grammar educated, no degree, got as far as waitress in a tea shop?

He'll give her half an hour or so.

When will Lucy be back in the country? He'd not thought to ask – it would be brilliant to see her again. Perhaps she'll come back to Louth? She did say she would.

The lounge has lost its comfort. Perhaps she's finished? An hour to dinner. He gets up to go upstairs as another couple come in, clutching magazines. They exchange pleasantries, comment on the weather, mutually inquire if the day has been a good one and discuss the possibilities for Boxing Day. Another ten minutes have passed; he's sure Lucy – no, Clare, *Clare* – will have finished with the bathroom.

She's dressed. The new frock and her mum's borrowed necklace, stockings, unusually for her with all the attendant hassle of a suspender belt, a quick rub over the black semi-heeled shoes. A dash of scent – he liked it before – and an extra brushing of her hair. She feels nice. She preens in front of the mirror. *Good enough to eat,* the phrase comes into her head from somewhere. *Telepathy?*

He's standing by the door, somehow she didn't hear him enter? Oh lor!

'Good enough to eat, Clare, my love.'

'Do you think so?' She turns towards him, heart pumping, and watches, feels, his eyes run from shoes to hair. He paces towards her. Will he?

He leans in, touches her lips. 'You're lovely.'

Just that? Lovely? She sees a different look in his eyes. Has he still got Lucy on his mind or is this for her?

'Perhaps just a little something else?' He reaches into his jacket pocket and produces a small flat parcel. 'Happy Christmas, Clare. You'd have had this earlier this morning, but ...' and left the rest unsaid.

She takes it. 'We were preoccupied?'

He smiles and nods. 'Open it. It's appropriate.'

She struggles with sticky tape then tears the festive paper. It's a leatherette box in maroon with a brass clip. Oh. Oh goodness! The lid pops; it's a silver bracelet, three carefully interwoven strands and a clasp with a small shiny – and it isn't, is it? A diamond?

'With love and appreciation of all that you are, Clare. Do you like it?'

'It's lovely!' She holds it out. 'Put it on for me please.'

Carefully he eases it over her wrist and snaps the catch shut. 'There. Goes well with the necklace.'

She has to kiss him again, feels another twist within her inner girl. So mixed up inside. All she bought him was a tie, a stripy one in his college colours; she'd looked them up. The packet was in her case. 'I've a present for you too. It's in my case.' She pushes away from him, finds it and hands it over.

'Oh, Clare, clever girl! College colours! Thank you so much!' and she gets another kiss. That's three in almost as many minutes, golly gosh.

Sense boringly prevails. He goes into the bathroom to follow her example and she has to be patient, taking to the small bedroom chair and getting back into her novel. She keeps her head down as he dresses until he says 'there' and she looks up. He's wearing her tie, how nice. And his jacket is smart, the shirt a clean white one. She's proud of him.

'Time to go down.'

She stands close, adjusts his tie. Their eyes meet. He's taking a deep breath, then opens the door and they go down to Christmas dinner, hand in hand.

༄

Elizabeth Salter hears the 'phone go. 'I'll take it, dear,' she calls to her husband, ensconced in a cushioned chair in the conservatory, reading, pretending it isn't as cold as it is.

'Fine,' he calls back, knowing, guessing, that it will be Lucy's agent fellow.

Elizabeth listens carefully. She knows him of old; underneath the 'hail fellow, well met' heartiness he's seriously professional and what he says means a great deal.

' ... she wow'd them, Elizabeth,' he can call her by her Christian name for after all, he represented her for the last ten years of her career. 'Took them by storm. Such a rare talent, your daughter. She's got something, something I've never had the opportunity to listen to ever before. Incredible voice, that instrument, when she's at the keys. None of the others managed to get it to speak like she does.' He goes on and on, giving her an almost phrase by phrase if not note by note run-down.

Eventually she manages her important query. 'When can she come home?'

'Oh, I'm bringing her home with me tomorrow. Flight's booked. She's too good to leave flogging herself around the States, though I reckon Carnegie would like her back. So expect a call when we land. I'll put her on the train. That okay?'

Elizabeth returns, slowly, to the conservatory. The thrill of hearing of her daughter's success is tempered by a concern. She knows, all too well, how draining the life of a concert pianist can be, drawing on an emotional reservoir, night after night, yet alone the travelling from venue to venue. Her daughter is barely twenty-one, has been to London, to Paris, Salzburg, New York – and that is only the beginning. If, and she has really no reason to doubt Basil's word, Lucy is as good as he says, then the requests will flood in, for Berlin, Vienna, Milan, and who knows where else. The girl's life will not be her own and she remembers her personal years of comparative fame. Marriage stopped all that, not that she regretted it for one moment.

Adrian looks up. 'Do I need to ask?'

She shakes her head. 'Brilliant, apparently. Inspired. You know Basil. She's coming home tomorrow. Back with us the day after, I should think.'

'That's good news. Will she manage some time at home, or is she still ratcheting around?'

Elizabeth smiles at his choice of words; 'ratcheting' about sums it up. 'He didn't say, but probably he'll let her rest for a wee while. Perhaps we can arrange a small holiday with her. We may not get another chance.'

'Good idea. I'd like that.' He picks up his book again. 'Fancy a glass of something? We can toast her success.'

'I'll fetch the glasses.'

✧

Lucy is miffed at not managing to talk directly to Jones. His parents had given her the hotel number after overcoming their evident surprise at receiving a call from New York. The call to the hotel, answered very efficiently, told her he was 'walking out with his wife'. She'd managed to bottle up her surprise and irritation before asking them to relay a message and now she's inwardly annoyed. Nothing had prepared her for a somewhat dubious revelation told to her by a hotel minion! But then he's never, not once, mentioned he was married, so she's sure they've got it wrong.

She's had a quiet morning, a nice little lunch and rested up for a couple of hours this afternoon; now she's feeling quite relaxed, despite the disastrous telephone call.

Basil has confirmed her travel times, which was good. Only a final dinner with her sponsors, accompanied by Stephanie and then on to the airport. London tomorrow afternoon. Back with mum and dad within forty eight hours.

There's a knock at the door. 'Come in!' It's Stephanie, with yet another dress.

'Can't have you appearing in the same dress twice, honey. Try this on? I have your sizes off pat, babe.'

Lucy wrinkles her pert little nose. Honey? Babe? These Americanisms! The dress is fabulous, a strapless low cut pearly grey – her colour – with a nice minimal flare on the skirt, down to her ankles. Shoes to match! Gee! She giggles as she is zipped up. 'Can I take these home with me, Steph?'

187

'Sure thing, honey. Not my size! Now, do me a twirl. Yes, that's okay. It'll stun 'em.'

'I won't have to play anything, will I?'

Stephanie shakes her head. 'Not tonight, hun. It's a jolly.'

Jolly? Hun? She pretends to understand. 'Okay then. What time do we leave?'

''Bout an hour. The hotel's hairdresser is on her way up.'

She feels like the proverbial million dollars. In the hotel lobby she is met by a small number of photographers, flashbulbs pop, notebooks are poised for her comments.

'Did you feel stressed, lady?' How'd you remember all them notes?' 'Enjoyed your stay in the Big Apple?' 'Where're you goin' next, hunney?' 'Great playing, gal,' questions, questions, questions. She did her best, with Steph defending her. If this is fame, then it's very wearing. How do these celebrities manage to cope?

She asks Steph the question in the limo and gets a laugh. 'Honey, *you* are a celeb. Here, read this if you haven't seen it.' A copy of the New York Times, folded at a certain page, is thrust at her.

She scans the column. 'Salter's playing transcends the highest state of the *genre*. Her interpretation of the Chopin is nothing short of divine; music truly for the gods …' and so it went on and on.

'And in the Tribune, here … ' More of the same. Suddenly she feels the tears welling up. This was not only her, it was *them*. Her connexion with her virtuality, her spirit, her power. Without it, maybe she'd have been perfection, yes, but not divine, not like they say.

'Hey, hun, can't have waterfalls. You'll ruin your eyes. Here, let me …'

Somehow she gets through. More press, more photos, introductions. The dinner, when her appetite has virtually disappeared, is a nightmare, picking at this and that, lovely though it undoubtedly is. She keeps her hand over her wine glasses and drinks copious amounts of water. Speeches. Votes of thanks. Basil says his thing. Toasts. On and on. Her dress is sticking to her top, probably just as well.

Then it is over. Her first case has been packed from the hotel and is already in the limo. Stephanie helps her change in the ladies' room, into a neat little dark green costume, another gift. Flat shoes. The dinner dress is carefully folded and added to the second case.

Quietly they slip out of the discreet entrance of the Madison Square building and the big smooth car speeds away. Bye bye, New York.

Twelve hours later and it's London, Heathrow. She feels rotten, dizzy, overstretched. Basil is as solicitous as his *persona* allows, makes her drink a half pint of water and take an hour siesta in the arrivals lounge. She's grateful the English press haven't found her, though Basil tells her cheerfully they will, once the story gets across the Atlantic. They take the public transport system into London and the Underground to Kings Cross. She has to help lug her cases and briefly wishes she'd not asked to bring the dresses back, though no doubt she'll change her mind again once safe at home. Being a 'celeb' in the States didn't entitle her to the luxury of a porter here, probably because Basil would have to pay and she has discovered he doesn't like paying for anything unnecessarily.

He does at least buy her ticket and sees her into the train. 'I'll phone your folks to let them know which train you're on,' he says and pops a dry kiss on her forehead. 'Be in touch. Take good care of those fingers of yours.'

For the first time for what seems like months, she's on her own, excluding the other couple in the compartment. Her mind goes into free fall. Will Jones realise she's back in the country? She needs to find out what went on that night, who he was with. He won't be able to deny anything, for she'd had a vastly different sensation, unforgotten and hopefully repeatable; essential as a means of ensuring all her future concerts reach the same audience tenure. The train is moving. Another hour and a half and she'll be nearly home. Hope Basil gets the message through. Dad will wince at the cases. Mum will want to see her in all the dresses. Then perhaps she should go back to Barnsdale, to say 'thanks' once more. Maybe see if the lounge piano will let her play *properly.* And a visit to the Schweitzer's; they'll be thrilled for her. The precious copies of the New York papers are tucked into her suitcase top. And the College. Her tutor. Oh, it's good to be home …

Seventeen

Tradizione ... Arrangement

The New Year has arrived. The bookshop is quiet. Jones begins to worry, needlessly. The figures for last year are with the accountant and he is assured the provisional results show a healthy increase on the previous twelve months, even with an additional amount for wages. Nevertheless, he feels some cause for concern. If they do not take a certain amount each week he is subsidising Clare's wages from last year's profits. It is what the book-keeper calls 'negative cash flow' and sounds distasteful. Despite the hint from the man that he should 'consider his assistant's position', no way will he entertain the remotest idea of telling Clare she isn't wanted.

She has been very understanding and for that he owes her. Since the foray into the depths of Derbyshire, they've kept a discreet silence about matters *d'amour*. That night, the one after their endless 'discussions' as she'd called them, they'd declared a truce and enjoyed what mutual pleasures seemed appropriate. (Imagination may run riot here if required, folks) The truce lasted for the next two days and nights, by which time there was a state of what – albeit temporary – they laughingly described as amounting to unofficial married bliss.

Clare knows her face reflects a glow not achieved by cold weather, fires or excessive alcohol and deep inside there is a steely determination not to let the pleasures experienced be the last. Tact and diplomacy has to rule however, Lucy is still a force to be considered.

During a cosy pre-coital chat Jones had rambled on about his college life, how monastic he'd been in comparison with his contemporaries though he'd more than made up for it in Stamford with Briony's willing – eager – participation. He hadn't seemed at all bashful over his exploits either, something she found difficult to understand, believing men never told new conquests about former ones, until she realised this Briony was merely a relief valve for his hang-ups over Lucy. This in turn put her on her guard, for no way would she fall for that vacancy; she and Jones were having it away because he liked *her* or not at all. And like her he did, if actions spoke louder than words. She'd laughed over his tale about the college guy's trophy wall and so without uttering the scathing comment initially in mind, left a silky souvenir out for him, just for fun. She was quite sorry when the old Traveller took them back home, safe and sound. Her mother, of course, welcomed him with literal open arms, waited until he'd gone after a welcoming cup of tea and some digestives then sat her down and gave her the interrogative grilling.

Had he, did he, what was it like, was he 'prepared', how did she feel, did she reckon he'd 'pop the question' or merely keep bedding her for mutual pleasure?

'Mother,' Clare says, once the torrent has eased, 'I'm not letting on. What happened, happened, it was fun, yes, I enjoyed my time away, but that's it. Don't, just don't, presume. Else you and I may fall out. Right?' She daren't mention that the 'preparedness' referred to had never entered their heads but knowing where her moon calendar lay, wasn't overly bothered. *Que sera, sera.*

A couple of weeks later comes the precursor to a potential disturbance to their now settled lives. She and Jones have maintained a steady (now platonic) relationship based far more on aspects of the book trade than anything more personal, though it's nice not to have to worry too much over the niceties anymore. She can behave naturally, not concern herself about a slipping bra strap or similar trivia, as he in turn no longer has an issue over such small matters as locking toilet doors. They respect each other, but it is an easy respect.

'Clare!' His call comes from the upper floor and catches her just as she's balancing precariously, one foot on a chair, another on a bookshelf, in order to heave six copies of a poor-selling autobiography onto the top shelf. Once up there, someone's bound to ask for a copy; it's a natural law of cussedness.

She is summoned and climbs the stairs for the nth time that morning.

'Look,' and with no further comment he passes her a postcard that came in the morning's mail.

It's postmarked Stamford. *Dear Jones,* she reads, *I'm sorry not to have written or telephoned you before, but I've been resting. I'd very much like to come and see you both soon, before my engagements are finalised. Do please let me know when it would be convenient. Yours ever, Lucy.* She can't see any kisses. *Both!* Lucy has written 'both'! She glances up at him. He nods.

'You've noticed.'

'So what's she saying, that she knows about us and doesn't mind? She wouldn't come if she felt upset.'

'So it seems. What do you think?'

Clare shrugs. 'She's your girlfriend.'

'Not in that sense of the word. Friend, yes, very much so. Girl, indubitably. However, I don't want to muddy the waters. I like us as we is,' grins at her raised eyebrows over the odd grammar and delivers another, if somewhat stilted, view: 'You and I, dear lady, get on so well that it has become a situation I wish to maintain. Oh, *you* know what I mean!'

'Fine. I like us together too,' and seeing as the opportunity has occurred, she uses it, 'though we could be, sort of, *more* together. If you take my meaning.'

'Mmmm,' is all she gets, uselessly. 'I'll suggest a weekend to her, shall I?'

The weekend offered is accepted by phone and Jones is now in a dither, listening to her voice. Clare, he thinks, hopes, will be unaffected by the impending visit and will go steadily through the routines of checking stock, ringing special orders through and chasing recalcitrant customers who appear to forget they've asked for specific titles. She – Lucy – is coming up by train to Lincoln, would he be able to meet her? She'll stay for the two nights at the same Hotel in the town as before, and hopes they'll be able to have dinner there on at least one evening?

'Of course,' he replies, with odd vibrations chasing down his spine. This girl is the One, the Being from whom he's never been detached, ever since that fateful day, even if she'd been sitting quiet in a remote part of his mind during busy times – and those included the more rumbustious ones *dans la chambre*.

'It'll be lovely to see you again,' he's hearing, 'and your other girl.' It's as though she's talking from a colleague's viewpoint, or a sister's, or a same sex contemporary from college. What does she know or feel about Clare, he's wondering, as she goes on: 'and my mother sends her best wishes.'

'That's nice,' he almost croaks as his mouth is going dry. 'I'll see you on Friday then.'

'Yes please, Jones,' he hears. 'Till then, my love, 'bye.'

That evening he proposes to takes a walk to ease his congested mind, even though it's dark, rather more than cool, and there's a dampness in the air that could lead to rain – or worse. His mother does her best to dissuade him. 'Can't you take one of those nice young ladies to the pictures instead, Al?

His father grins at him from the corner armchair where he's doing the crossword.

'And which young lady would want to leave her nest on a night like this?'

Clare would, Jones knows, but he won't ask. He has a mission in mind and not only would Clare be a distraction, but she could ruin his idea.

The route is well known, familiar, and each crossed road and turn of path has its specific pressure of association. Two other pedestrians go past, heads down, hunched against the damp and cold, appearing and disappearing through the dim pools of sickly street lighting. Jones walks briskly, letting the sting of the evening air abrade his cheeks as if he was a penitent accepting a priest's rebuke. In crossing the meadow he has to rely on instinct to guide his footsteps, taking care to stay on the rise of the land. The exit gate meets his path by an error of a mere two yards, creaks on rusting hinges and slams shut behind, echoing into the hollow of the road's decline in front. The lodge's resident dog utters a solitary bark. Now it's a quarter mile of road, footsteps thudding on gritty tarmac.

The entrance to the Hills is on his left, barely discernable in the run of fencing, a hand's feel reaches the catch, clicks it back, the gate swings to the right and back behind him. Another thud as it closes. To his left the ripples of the small river can be heard rather than seen and care has to be taken to avoid a slide on the slippery mud-edged bank. It is another half mile to where he wishes to go and he slackens his pace, treading softly, as if unsure who else may be sufficiently idiotic to risk a confrontation on a bleak January evening. Here the river runs narrower and hence faster, the water burbling over its shallow stony bed and Tennyson comes readily to mind, *"Men may come and men may go, but I go on for ever"*. The bridge will be close – ah, yes, the path rises to meet the abutment.

The footbridge's planks have the thud of timber resonance, a familiar sound. When he was last here she was alongside him, warm and feminine, and it was summer and innocent yet full of secret promises. And before that, another momentous evening of hidden mystery when, persuaded by forces not understood, he'd had a yearning for her closeness impossible to comprehend, of necessity subjugated by the materialistic view that thought power didn't happen. Telepathy was a magician's plaything, which for sanity's sake he had to believe. Yet he had 'talked' to her and heard her reply; apparently he'd aided a decision that changed her life – and his, if truth were told. Once he'd been carefree, some would say a chancer, then fate intervened and his soul collided with another's. Lucy.

Lucy. She'd come across the miles, this girl, or at least, her virtuality had. He'd seen her, in the shadow of the trees, reflected in the waters below him, a figure floating against the backdrop of the hill. Would she again? This is what he has to discover, for his mind

194

will not rest. How many times have they linked? Here, on that Christmas evening; on the escapism jaunt to Crich Stand; fleetingly when she was close on her last trip here with her parents – she had found him by willpower that day – and latterly, lost amidst the purples, pale pinks and reds colouring his mind's recollections of the Christmas day morning's grapple with Clare. That was a fierce yet strangely beautiful link, the authority of twin soul's working in muscular, repetitive tandem, the thrust of passion adding an immensity to her need for power. Would she hear *his* soul's cry now, in the depth of their place, the only place and time when he had truly felt a physical need for her? Lucy!

A small fragment of sanity was trying to quell these thoughts. It cannot be, says a infinitesimal part of his brain, but the rush of the rest of his mind drowns out sanity. Lucy! He grasps the hand rail as he has done before, grips tight, tenses muscles, tries to raise these incomprehensible mysterious thought waves. Lucy!

∝

Elizabeth is pleased. Whereas she had found herself anxious to the point of distress over the prospect of her daughter's attitude having been irrevocably changed by her exposure to the elitism of Carnegie and all that went before, after forty eight hours of suburbian home life she had her own sweet Lucy back. More mature, infinitely more self-possessed certainly, radiating a confidence well beyond her years but still her own daughter, and how proud of her she is! It's now two weeks since her return and, apart from occasional enquiries after interviews from various aspects of the media, sanity has returned. She can hear her now, immersed in the task of adding another – and rather complicated (i.e. difficult) piece of Chopin to her repertoire. The baby grand has been replaced with the loan of an eight foot concert Steinway, and what a beautiful instrument it is too. Just as well the drawing room has the wonderful bay window facing the garden to add inspiration, let alone the space. Mind you, at this time of night there's not much to see out there. Adrian has said he'd add some external lighting, just for effect, but what would her neighbours think?

She leans back in the armchair, closes her eyes and just listens.

Such magical sounds, the phrasing is excellent and the intonation, well, sublime. The same segment, played several times, each time a little different. It's so good that her daughter has the confidence to experiment; however, it isn't *quite* right, not yet. Once more, with a tiny little hesitation after the D flat. And again. Dear girl, don't overdo it. Have a rest.

She's stopped. There's a couple of minute's silence; Elizabeth is tempted to go and stand by her, watch her fingering, though this is not a piece she herself learnt, far too demanding. Then Lucy begins again, and this time there's no hesitation, no mistake, the music rises and falls, cascades into a nerve rending thrill, the confidence, the sheer, irrepressible confidence of the girl, bringing a glorious top melody through the base notes. She can't help herself, the tears begin to flow. This is *her daughter,* her Lucy, at the peak of perfection. No repeats, not now; Lucy is confidently taking the piece through to its conclusion, the final notes glide down to a gentle falling peace. Her music is magic, sheer magic.

She cannot move, not for a moment or two; to do so would destroy the afterglow.

'Mother?' She's standing at her elbow, her approach silent, softly graceful.

Elizabeth opens her eyes. The dream hasn't vanished, only filed into memory. 'Lucy, oh Lucy, dear, that was marvellous, absolute magic.' She reaches out and grasps a hand. 'These fingers of yours, how do you manage it?'

Lucy retrieves her hand, takes another chair from the table and moves it so she can sit close. 'I need to talk, mother. And it is important.'

'Of course, dear. How important?'

'Rather a lot. Remember we had Jones for tea that day, ages ago?'

'Yes, I do. He was rather sweet, wasn't he?'

Lucy smiles. Jones and 'sweet' weren't necessarily synonymous. 'Then you took me on the trip to find him at Louth?'

What is the girl coming to? Elizabeth reminds herself it was she who arranged it, in a fit of match-making enthusiasm. Not very successfully so far, despite the lad's declaration on the day in the Regents Park Hotel.

'Have you kept in contact, Lucy?'

There's a deeper smile, a knowing smile. 'Yes, we have, and that's what I want to talk about. You'll probably tell me it's nonsense, mum, so I'd better say now, it's isn't. Definitely not.'

'Sounds intriguing.'

'More than intriguing. Do you believe in the power of thought?'

'Mmmm. Depends.'

Lucy has her hands in her lap, tightly clasped. What she is about to say may alter her status in her mother's eyes, but again, it may not. 'Jones and I are, and I use the word advisedly, engaged.'

'What!' Elizabeth sits bolt upright. *'Engaged? To be married! Since when?'*

Lucy laughs, gently and musically. 'Not the way you think, mum. And before you jump to conclusions, no. Certainly and definitely no. However, we have been, er, together.' She pauses, to let her mother take it in. 'Not physically. Mentally. Hence my question about power of thought. It's Jones who powers my playing the way I do.'

'I don't understand.' She's bewildered, completely bewildered. 'How can he? He's never near you when you play and as far as I remember, he said he doesn't play the piano either.'

'Maybe not,' says her daughter, carrying on in a very earnest fashion, 'but there's a link between us I can't understand and don't particularly need to, because whatever it is, it works and that's what's allowed me to learn to play the way I do. I asked him whether I should desert the hotel life and go to London, he said yes. I asked for his help when I played for the Count's *soirée* in Austria, and his mental support came exactly right. Then when I did the concert at the Carnegie, he was there, powering me along. And tonight. You heard me struggle with the Chopin Polonaise?'

'But you mastered it, darling. You played it through *so* beautifully.'

Lucy nods, accepting the compliment. 'Thanks, mum. But I struggled until Jones appeared and you noticed the improvement, didn't you? He's still with me, in my mind. We can't help it. It's not all the time, though. He comes and goes, as probably I do in his mind too. But the link is always there when we need it and he needed *me* tonight so he called, just when I could use his power as well.'

Elizabeth cannot grasp all that her daughter is saying. She briefly wonders whether there's a hint of insanity in all this, but immediately forces the thought away. No, not her child, never. So what brought it on? 'When did all this begin, Lucy?'

'Ages ago, but I'm sure I've hinted at it at some other time. It began when I was still at school.'

Dimly, she does recall a much earlier conversation to which she'd not given much credence at the time. 'Remind me? At school, you said?'

'The beginning of my last year. We sort of mentally collided, I felt his interest in me then. Then it happened a few more times, not actually speaking, but we knew we were aware of each other.' Lucy's sure she is repeating something of what may have been expressed earlier as her mother believes; however, she carries on. 'He was at that Barn Hill concert you made me do and I felt his concern then, his love for my music. Dad took me to see Barnsdale and he was there too, probably coincidental, or maybe fated. We knew who we were then. But you brought us together, inviting him for tea. That wasn't anything to do with me, mum, nothing at all. You invited him, I didn't. But we talked and everything fell into place. The trip to Louth? Your idea. We talked a lot more. He and I, there's a shared love between us, a lovely, deep feeling based on my ability to play; it's not a sexy thing, though I'm not saying it mightn't happen. He's just, well, *there.*'

Elizabeth is feeling quite faint and sags back into the chair. This is totally, completely out of her comfort zone. She's not been particularly sensitive to paranormal feelings, unlike some people she knows, so where Lucy's inherited this telepathic concept from, she's no idea.

'Are you going to repeat all this to your father, or shall I tell him?'

'I'll tell him, mum, when the moment's ripe.' Lucy's eyes are wide and even to her mother, mysterious. 'It's not make believe, I promise you. You'll see,' and she stands up. 'I'll play that piece once more, to prove it to you. He's still waiting for me out there, but it's cold and he needs to go home.'

⤳

She'd come. He felt the rush, the joy and the immense pleasure as the crescendo of music echoed along in his head. He even saw her at the keyboard, the way her hair swayed in time with her body's response to the essential mood of the composer's intent. How long he'd waited, the time it took her to complete the piece, he'd no idea. She'd play it again, just for him.

Half an hour later and with the chill percolated through, he was frozen to the bone. The link faded, the colour evaporated. Black depths of night became a stark contrast and though a few chords repeated in his brain, scarcely sufficient to maintain the believability of this odd action of his. Walking out into the depths of the country purely so he could seek to imagine a girl playing a piano? Get real, Jones.

The thought won't go away. He lies awake for some considerable time, tossing the whole scenario around, finding question after question. How the initial surge of identity with the girl had occurred, the relevance of the symbolism of his Rie charger, why she'd appeared when he least expected, and far more to the point, given his attachment to Clare, why the instinctive need to look for her at the weirdest of times. Was this evening's trek into the wilds of the Hills so weird? At least a purely personal decision, or was it? Had she put a marker into his mind without him realising?

She's still there, now asleep, but the imagery is so real, she could be alongside him, the gentle rise and fall of her breasts, with eyes closed, the softness of her hair waved across the pillow. Her warmth is a benefice, an encouragement to drift towards peaceful slumber. An innocent, perfect, dream girl.

He wakes early. It's still dark. As ever, he has to put mind and body back together, slowly, in order to start the day in some semblance of sense. Today is – the thought process winds slowly into gear – Thursday? Which means tomorrow is Friday. Friday is when his distant love will come and they will talk and smile and laugh and be together. He sees them reprise the walk through the Hills, possibly a visit to the Church, to share the peace and serenity of the old stone nave. A trip to his old school, for the sake of old times, to show her where his classroom was, and the quadrangle and how only prefects could use the central steps to the big hall. The big hall, where he first acquired a love of music from the evenings with the Music Club, and, when it could be arranged … where she was to play?

His first action once behind the old oak desk in the top floor office of his bookshop is to find the current secretary of the Music Club. It's a while since he put her in touch with Lucy's agent, what's-his-name Fortescue, Basil, wasn't it? He hasn't heard whether they even considered her for this winter's programme, certainly her name wasn't on the list of events on his membership card and now is as good a time as any to discover why.

'Marion? Hi, it's Jones from the Mercer Row Bookshop. Yes, thanks, and you? … Great. Yes, not bad. Weather's not brilliant though, is it, whichever way. Yes…. Now, I wonder if you'd considered Lucy Salter for a pianoforte Concert. I passed your name onto her agent, wondered if he'd been in touch …yes, but … Oh, really? Hmmm. Well, I'm sure I might be able to apply pressure … know her? Yes, I do. Quite well. She's coming up for the weekend, so I'll ask … anytime. See you at the next concert? Oh, goodness, so it is. Nearly forgot. That's good. If there's a spare seat … thanks. Thanks very much.'

He puts the handset down, fishes in the top drawer and finds the Music Club's prospectus. She's right, there is a concert on Saturday night; how did he not remember? That'd be good – something of mutual interest. And it's a pianist! Not a name he recognises, but expects Lucy will. He has a tinge of regret that it won't include Clare; she's already told him her mother's taking her out to see the Pantomime in Cleethorpes, though he surmises it's daughter holding mother's hand as an excuse. Pantos are *not* his scene, she knows that and didn't even try to persuade him to tag along, even before Lucy's visit was planned.

There's still an air of an uneasy truce between them; he suspects the days away in Buxton caused more grief than delight now time has passed and he's more and more ambivalent over their relationship. Lucy's fault or his?

The day goes on. Clare still smiles at him, still issues mini chocolate logs or digestives with his mug of tea, which is when they spend time together in the office provided there's no-one in the shop and the door bell stays silent. Today she puts her feet up on his desk in proprietorial fashion and isn't too particular how her skirt's draped. Yes, it's a girl's ploy, and no, he isn't so gentlemanly perfect that he cannot enjoy the view.

'Do I get to meet your angelic virtuoso?' she asks as she flips her skirt in an unconscious gesture.

'Don't do that. It upsets my equilibrium. And yes, I hope so. As you're hell bent on foolish pantomimes on Saturday, it'll have to be Sunday evening. She mentioned dinner at the Hotel.'

'Might not be as good as the Buxton one,' she says as she lifts and drops her skirt fabric once more in sheer devilment.

He pretends to cover his eyes. 'Hussy,' he calls her; she grins and hoinks her lovely legs off the desk and back onto the floor. There's still a latent spark of sexual interest between them, despite the pressure of The Visit.

The telephone rings; unusually for this time of day, another hour and they'd be away off home.

'M R Books, Jones, can I help you? ... oh, hello Marion. Quick return.... *you what*?'

Clare hears the rapid chatter, a bit about 'cancelled' and 'can you see if ...'

She watches his face, expressions of disbelief, something akin to anger (though she's never seen him really cross) and then a grin.

'I'll see what I can do. Bit of a turn up after all we'd said earlier ... coincidence? More than that. Jolly old fate intervening again. I'll call you back as soon as, though maybe it'll be a bit late ... okay. Bye.'

She's curious, very curious. Fate? Coincidence? Intuition, and as a young female she's plenty of that, tells her it's something to do with The Lucy. She's right.

'You'll never guess.'

Eyebrows are raised. 'You're grinning, hence it's her. Go on, tell.'

'Music Club concert, Saturday night? Their pianist guy has cancelled. Sprained wrist: tripped over something apparently and put his hand out to stop himself from falling. So, as Lucy's going to be here anyway ... '

'You think she'll stand in? Bit of a downer, a small town Music club do after playing in where did you say, the Carnegie Hall in New York! Bet she won't.'

'Bet she will.' He knows she will because it's them. Him and her. 'What d'you bet then?'

'If she does, I'll forego the panto and come and listen. And I'll try and persuade mum to come as well. How's that?'

'It'll do. You're a sport, Clare. Thanks.'

He wastes no time. Clare disappears back down stairs to check around before closing up. The number – the Salter's home number – is carefully preserved in his notebook. It is ringing, and ringing. Don't say they're out? On the point of giving up, it's answered.

'Hello?'

Zing! Lucy, praise be, vaguely hesitant, but his Lucy. 'It's Jones. How are you?' So correct, so polite.

'I'm fine, thanks. This is a nice surprise. Did you want to speak to me?'

'Who else, my love, who else. I have an impossible question to ask, a tremendous favour. It's to do with the weekend.'

'Oh?' Does he sense an immediate change into a guarded mode? 'I hope you're not saying I cannot come, because my room's booked, and I've got my … '

He interrupts her. 'Nothing like that. Quite the opposite. Lucy, dearest girl, will you consider playing for the Music Club on Saturday night? Their booked pianist's bent his wrist or something and has cried off. Which leaves them in an awful hole. I'm afraid I'm to blame, because I only checked today whether they'd talked to your Basil chap about a proper engagement, so the secretary girl chanced her arm and rang me back with the query. I said I'd ask. So I have.'

Silence.

'Lucy?'

'I'm thinking.' Another pause. 'Will you be there?'

'Of course.'

'And your other girl?'

'Clare?' He chuckles down the phone. 'She bet me you wouldn't say yes, but if you did, she'd give up going to the pantomime with her mum and come. So you see how important it is. I'd really love you to say yes.'

'Then I will. And for free, that way Mr Fortescue won't have to mind. What would you like me to play?'

'Need you ask, my love? The Chopin piece of course. And what you charmed the Carnegie lot with, so I can hear it properly.'

She laughs and he loves the sound of her happiness. Something connects in his mind and unbeknown to him another strand, another gossamer thread, is woven betwixt the twin minds of common frequency. Each is vibrating at the same pitch, and neither is aware how significant such a phenomena may yet become.

Eighteen

Carezzando ... Caressing

The Morris Traveller, emerald green paint and woodwork with its peeling varnish, is becoming an elderly lady. It's a few years now since Dad handed her on to me, and though she'd always had lots of tender loving care, even the best of us age. She's reluctant to start, which may not be an uncommon phenomena at this time of year. Even I do not like lurching out of bed these January mornings, despite still thoroughly enjoying my work, especially with the delectable Clare as companion. I always give her a – chaste – Good Morning! kiss so perhaps the Traveller is jealously sulking, feeling out of favour. True, she's not had a run for a while, but this evening she cannot, just cannot, let me down.

I involve dad, for after all, the Traveller was originally his, so surely there'll be some encouraging *rapport*. Dad does some polishing of the distributor cap and spark plug bosses, tut-tuts over the grubby appearance of the old girl's innards. (This is not my scene particularly – handy though I may be in many ways, oily metal isn't my thing).

We leave her to think about things for ten minutes. 'Over-flooded her, you have, son,' he says. 'Let 'er evaporate the excess fuel.'

These things I'll either have to learn to do, or, and I hope the old girl isn't listening … *I'll sell her off and buy a new one…*

After a cup of tea and the addition of another sweater because leaning over a bonnet of a damp winter's evening is a rather chilling activity, I get dad to do the honours. Eureka! He revs her up, gets out and grins. 'She'll be fine now. See you later, son.'

The road to Lincoln is empty. As I run down the steep hill towards the railway station, the Traveller now properly warm, I begin to whistle. The tune is familiar, since it is the theme that echoes through the magical composition she plays so beautifully. So I'm happy, very happy, because my virtuality is coming towards me and the threads that bind us are getting shorter and shorter. Very very soon, we'll be together, another marker in life's journey, a convoluted journey where I'm the one who cannot seem to find the correct way to go. I *must* find the right route. Will these next few days, hours, provide us with the definitive directions to the one that I seek?

The train is on time: I wish it could have been an evocative rush of steam with a hiss and blast of nostalgia, her figure appearing out of the mists along the platform, shades of 'Brief Encounter'; instead the dream is replaced by the prosaic efficiency of far more modern rolling stock.

'Lucy!' I call as she descends. She's so slender, in my eyes the goddess my mind has created. A waisted coat in cream, a tied belt, a high collar onto which her deep brown hair cascades. A small black feathered creation tops off the hair beautifully. I think it's called a 'fascinator', which suits. A smile, a coquettish smile.

'Hello Jones,' she says, putting her case down onto the platform. We embrace, carefully, but do not kiss. This is a public place. Then I release her and collect the case. We walk close together to the exit; receive a nod and a touch of cap from the station attendant, for that is the effect she has on those around. Twenty-one year old elegant elegance.

The Morris waits. I utter a prayer. Her case I place in the back and latch the doors. I open the passenger door, see her carefully ensconced, return to my seat, turn the key and – yippee! yes, she starts. Now I can lean across and touch Lucy's cheek with patient lips. Her eyes part close, dimples appear, nothing need be said. This is us. The One and I, together.

I drive carefully across the dark distances of the empty countryside. Headlights catch the twists and curves, the random rabbit's dash for the verge. We still maintain silence, idle chatter superfluous. Our respective minds will be exchanging each other's possession, an unconscious top-up of togetherness. She is not a Clare or any lesser being; she is the Lucy who possesses the talent to enrapture my soul. Not body, soul.

Into the erratically lit streets, a few cars pass the other way; there is one in front now and we both turn into Mercer Row. We pass the shop and she looks at me then. 'Still going well?' she asks and I nod.

'Really well,' I say, 'thankyou.'

'Clare?'

'Well, thanks. I won my bet so you'll meet her tomorrow night at the Concert.'

'Then don't I get to visit the shop?'

Ah. Silly me. Of course, she promised a revisit, when, eighteen months ago? I grin at her as we turn into the Market Place and the other car goes on.

'There's no obligation, Lucy, but of course you can.'

We're at the Hotel entrance. I stop immediately outside; get out to open her door. It's the gentlemanly thing to do and I offer a hand, which she accepts in order to extricate herself from the rather small red-leathered bucket seat, before letting go and brushing out the folds of her coat. Now I can see it's camel hair and expensive. 'Nice coat,' I say, appreciatively. I get another smile but nothing else. She stands and waits while I retrieve the case and we cross the threshold together.

She signs the register, collects a key. 'I'll get someone to take your case up,' the man offers, but she shakes her head.

'Thankyou, no, it won't be necessary. My friend will bring it up for me.'

I get a stare, as though the man is assessing the relationship and wondering about the hotel's reputation. 'I shan't be long,' I say in full knowledge of his thoughts and mine too, to be honest.

Her room is adequate, given the size of the establishment and where it is. Very obviously not her ideal as she gazes around. 'It'll do,' her comment, 'though not quite what I'm used to. But seeing as I'm paying … ' I place the case on the rest and stand awkwardly as she removes the feathered hair piece, unfastens the coat's tied belt and undoes buttons, slips it off. I catch it, conscious of its borrowed warmth, fold it and lay it across the bed. She shakes her hair, brushes a hand across to free captive curls, and there she is, my Lucy. My dear, dear Lucy. Precious, tantalising, lovely, *powerful.*

'Stay for dinner,' she says, breaking the spell. 'Then we can talk. If you've nothing else to do?'

I'd wondered about that earlier, what I should do, whether I should invite her to the only other decent eatery open in town at this time of year, the one with vaguely Italian overtones, but wasn't sure of her inclinations. Now she's pre-empted me, embarrassingly so. At least I'd warned mum I might not be in for the evening meal. (She'd nodded and said, 'of course, dear, now just you treat her proper like,' as if I'd do anything else.)

'I should be asking you.'

'Nonsense,' she replies, gaily, 'I'll claim it on expenses; after all, I am here to play, aren't I?'

The Music Club secretary, Marion, had been absolutely over the moon about her acceptance, as indeed, so she should, given Lucy had said she wouldn't be looking for a fee. I'd been a bit sneaky there, saying she'd accept the same amount as the fellow who'd crashed out, but as an honorarium, plus expenses. Lucy doesn't know this yet. The Club volunteer committee had rallied round, had posters smartly re-printed and scooted about covering up the old ones. I'd proudly put one up in the shop window, never ever having thought I'd have *her* name on my frontage. There's also probably a small poster on the hotel's notice board.

'You are, my love. Didn't you see the poster in the shop window as we passed?'

A quick shake of those lovely tresses. 'Too dark and I wasn't really looking.'

'It'll be a full house. Not everyday we get a Carnegie girl to play.'

'I'm not *that* famous. Not yet, anyway.' Her smile fades. 'I need to freshen up and change. Go and tell that reception man you're staying for dinner; I'll be down in half-an hour?'

I'm dismissed. Controlled. No chance to peek, unlike a Briony who would have relished the caress of male eyes over her more intimate assets, or even a Clare, though she doesn't specifically flaunt hers. With Clare it's a case of 'I've got what every girl's got, and you know what it looks like, don't you?' – not that it's something she'd ever say. It's me, understanding her pragmatism. Don't get me wrong. I honour Lucy, honour her, and won't debase her in any way whatsoever, and that's what so dauntingly mysterious about our relationship.

The man on the reception desk takes my request in his stride. 'Certainly sir; will the lady be dining immediately?' Not asking me, I notice.

'She said in half-an-hour.'

'Of course. If you'd like to take a seat in the lounge, I'll see that the menus are brought to you when she descends.'

Not 'comes down', 'descends'. Oh my, real Jeeves territory, this. I sink into worn soft brown leather, then have to reach forward to pick up a dog-eared copy of 'Country Life' to read whilst we – the hotel staff and I – wait on her ladyship's pleasure.

No, I'm not scathing. She *is* a lady, and a very gifted one at that, and I'm an extremely lucky guy to be so close to her. The picture of the Rie charger flicks into mind, the one now sitting on its own shelf in my bookshop den, out of harm's way. And, oh yes, seeing as you ask, the pound note is still there. Clare made a comment once about the prospect of our nice old pound notes going in favour of brass tokens. I shuddered then, and I still shudder. Devaluation is what it's called. I will *not* devalue my Lucy. She is a lady. Steps on the stair. I look up, to a vision. Never have I seen her look so beautiful, the vision is in emerald green, her hair with an absolutely right ribbon, and stunning.

'Lucy,' I croak, rising from the depths of brown leather to greet her. There is that familiar coquettish smile and, as she reaches the floor, an accomplished small curtsey. Well, more accurately, an elegant bob; much practised, I suppose.

'Jones, don't look so surprised. I can make an effort, you know, and you deserve it. Which way's dinner?'

We're seated well; the only waiter guy does his thing in helping her with her chair, something I should have done if I wasn't reeling. Menus are offered, drinks requested, jugged water arrives and the occasion rolls on. She and I, having dinner together, alone for the first time at a meal. She eats prettily (you know what I mean, elegance before appetite) and we indulge in small talk. No profound statements of deep intent or peering into each other's eyes with lustful longing, just an ever so nice companionable affair. No, not an *affaire*. In dribs and drabs she expands on what's happened to her since we last met, which was, you recall, in London when she made her debut at the Wigmore Hall. So long ago. There is a different Lucy here, one who is superbly confident, perfectly at home in an expensive dress in a far less than expensive restaurant. (They're doing their best, I assume, but it isn't brilliant. Adequate, but not memorable.) Lucy is the memorable one, my goddess in human form.

Retreating to the lounge, such as it is, we sit alongside each other on a comfortable settee with coffee on the low table in front. A reprise of London, except here it's been dinner, not lunch – the mints aren't as nice and afterwards comes the big, big difference. Last time after the meal, she went up to her room alone, to rest – I saw her at the hotel window, remember, in her petticoat. This time ...

She sits on the bed, I drop into the chair and we look at each other.

'I suppose you'd like to make love to me,' she says in a matter-of-fact voice, dropping her eyes and her hands are twisting together in her lap. 'I don't mind, provided... '

Flipping heck! Had I anticipated how this evening might progress? No, I hadn't. Another girl, another time, without any potential recriminations, yes, possibly. (Probably, you mean, Jones; don't kid yourself, remember you're no monk.)

It is an impossible situation. I do not wish to 'take advantage' of her, I do not want to despoil her; if she wishes to present a girl's ultimate gift – her virginity – merely because she believes it is what is required, expected, the sort of *de rigueur* thing, then it isn't right. If I refuse her, will she feel a) despised, or b) somehow soiled, having in effect revealed her virtual nakedness to an unappreciative pair of eyes? And does she *really* want this?

How do these things go normally? I hark back to Briony. We'd both seen a biological need; Briony being adept at matters flirtatious had steered me back to her place of an evening, offered a drink or two, a 'goodnight' cuddle and … we've seen it in all the films and now even on the telly. Tearing each other's clothes off, a matter-of-fact coupling on a dubious bed in a – sorry – crummy hotel was *not* my ideal way of consummating Lucy and I's togetherness. Neither had I seriously considered offering to marry the girl and I'm not sure why – or am I? Do I consider that she's too good, too precious, too goddess like, up on the pedestal where I've placed her? Or is it practicalities, like I cannot afford to keep her in 'the style to which she has become accustomed' (London, Paris, Salzburg, New York, etcetera). Or is it because she'll want to continue her concert pianist career that will keep us apart more often than not? (Like it is now, actually.)

'We can turn the lights out if it helps,' she says in a very small voice.

Lucy, oh my Lucy! I'm not helping you at all, am I? Nothing for it. I stand up, reach for her, she slides off the bed edge and we embrace; I feel the supple warmth of her, hard up against my body; there's desire building. We kiss, not the light loveliness of a young girl learning but the bruising needful action of potential passion. I take her head in my hands, catch the feel of her sumptuous curls, the urgency within the pressure of her breasts against me.

We draw breath, my hands slide to her waist, for this is where her dress undoes. We're still for a few seconds. Eyes meet. It's just enough. There's a glimmer of a cheeky smile in them.

'You didn't expect this, did you, Jones?'

I shake my head, slowly, side to side. 'No.'

'Do you want to? I will if you do.'

Now I hold her at arm's length. 'We have a long way to travel, you and I,' I say, surprising myself at my decision, 'and there are years ahead of us. I love you, Lucy. You and your ability to make the most wondrous music out. I don't *need* to ravish your body to prove it, lovely though it will doubtless be, do I?' I leave her a get-out clause. 'Do *you* want to? I haven't properly seduced you, have I?'

She thinks about it. 'Honest answer?

'Honest answer.'

She shakes her head, just like I did 'No. I just thought it's what you'd want.'

'Would you be disappointed if I said it wasn't?'

Another shake. 'Surprised perhaps. Maybe relieved, 'cos, er, I'm not sure what to expect.' *Despite mum's best efforts …*

'You're a very brave girl, Lucy.' How patronising was that? 'I mean, taking a risk.'

'Not with you.' She sits down again. The bed squeaks and she grins. 'Um,' she says, and we both laugh. The moment, as they say, has passed.

'So now what?'

'I leave you to get a good night's sleep; we see each other in the morning. Come to the shop when you like. Ten o'clock would be good. Snack lunch at Joan's, a stroll through the Hills in the afternoon. Concert's at half seven, as you'll know. Maureen said the hall will be open from just before six, if you want to practice. It's a hired-in Steinway.'

'I love you, and it's 'rehearse, not 'practice'' she says, so simply yet so earnestly.

I bend down and kiss her forehead. 'You're mad,' I reply, knowing full well she'll laugh.

Chuckles actually; brings up a hand to stop me moving away and offers up a sombre face. 'You will love me, properly, some time?' she asks in a manner that sounds rhetorical.

I cannot answer. That which I seek may elude me – her soul, yes, I'll always love; her body, only when the time is right, when the gods dictate. The glass wall stays in place. And in the meantime, there's Clare, like an instant comfort meal in a packet, satisfying but unmemorable.

On my way downstairs, I have difficulty in getting my head round the exchange we've just had. It says a lot for her the way she took it, my refusing her I mean, let alone offering in the first place. Probably, as she hinted, she was *very* relieved I didn't force her, for though that's something I'd never do, she wasn't to know. Our mental vibes don't normally work at such low frequencies, but, just as I went down the steps, a *zing. Love you to bits, Jones. Never leave me?*

Never.

ॐ

Clare looks at me critically. 'You haven't, have you?'

'Haven't what?' I ask, knowing full well what she means, naughty girl.

'Huh,' she replies. 'If you had, there'd be beams and smiles and Cadbury's choccy biscuits with coffee. Instead you're looking like a lost soul. Didn't she want to?'

'Clare, my girl, your mind needs a spring clean. It's not the only thing in life.'

'Maybe not, but it goes a long way towards it.'

There speaks a girl of experience, know-how gained at *my* expense. At least it proves she did enjoy the aforesaid experience, which is something, though I hope she doesn't share her thoughts with Lucy.

'You'd better watch your step, young lady. I don't want my reputation sullied.'

'Huh.' She tidies a pile of books that didn't need tidying; I can see an element of jealousy peering over her shoulder. 'I'm relegated to the second division, am I?'

Oh dear. Inevitable, I suppose, and all my fault. I should never have given in to my altruistic side, offering her an all-expenses staff Christmas break. And no, there wasn't an ulterior motive at the time; what happened between us happened. Two young people, sharing a room and both lonely? Come on, it takes place all the time. Doesn't mean they have to spend the rest of their lives glued together.

Puzzle – how to cope?

Suddenly, there are tears. And what does a caring male do when a young lady breaks down like that? Why, puts an arm round her and attempts to provide consolation. At first she clings; I feel the softness of this girl then she stiffens up and pushes me away.

'Don't,' she says and sniffs. 'I ...' More tears. Helpless now, I let her cry. I cannot say 'I love you', because though I do in my own way, I'm sure it will be misconstrued.

'Oh, go to bloody hell,' and that is a most unusual expletive coming from her. However, I'm sure she doesn't mean it; it's only a way of relieving her feelings. Understandable. She stomps off to the little room under the stairs where I do not go.

Five minutes later and there's Lucy, taking off her camel coat.

'Hello,' her greeting, as if we hadn't walked so close to the precipice last night. 'I've seen the poster. Can I have it afterwards as a souvenir?' She gazes around, as though she's never been here before. (Granted it's a long time ago, or so it seems.) 'It's got a lovely feel to it. Far nicer than Stamford. Where's Clare?'

Clare. Locked in the loo, re-doing her flood-damaged war paint. 'Clare?' I call, 'Lucy's here.'

The door opens, she emerges, dry-eyed and, forgive me Lucy, looking very pretty, snub nose and all. She scrubs up very well, does my Clare and I knew before she came to work this morning she'd be wearing what she calls her man-killer dress.

'Hello Lucy,' said in a careful voice and with an outstretched hand. 'I'm Jones's right hand girl.'

That's it girl, define your territory.

Lucy takes the proffered hand. 'I've heard a lot about you. That's a lovely dress.'

Miaow!

'I think yours is prettier. Hope he's told you the truth.'

True, Lucy's simple plain-textured cotton dress, pale blue, just above knee high, sets her off beautifully. She smiles a eye-narrowing smile. I've seen film starlets do that very effectively.

'I think he probably has, Clare, and nothing I'm sure you'd worry about. So pleased he's found someone who can keep him in order.' She eyes the stairs. 'Can I have a peek further up?'

'Sure. Clare, would you like to show Lucy how you've got the place laid out? It's your territory.' True, Clare has re-organised the genres into relevant shelves and it's working extremely well. Clare leads, Lucy follows. I get a wonderful glimpse of comparative legs under different skirt hems as they take the stairs. A side advantage of steep staircases, this. I'm normally not allowed to stare upwards; my assistant has strict rules – about gawping at customers, that is, – but she herself, well actually, I think she rather likes to provide her own private lingerie fashion show. Enough. I follow after a discreet time interval.

The two girls are on the second floor where the more serious titles live. Children's and chick-lit – horrible phrase – plus most other quick-selling fiction titles live on ready access shelves downstairs; the first floor caters for factual stuff in the main, then on this one we go into high-brow, reference, art, music and biographies for the most part. Third floor is stock room, then it's me on the fourth. Quite a hike, up and down. No wonder Clare stays the slim-line gal.

Lucy seems to be giving Clare her undivided attention. Good-oh. I do not wish for confrontation, more a modicum of mutual respect – and admiration? Clare should admire Lucy's talent and probably her effect on me; Lucy may, and it's a moot point, admire Clare's ability to lay claim to my more basic requirements, though yesterday evening's descent (or ascent?) into a potentially deeper, even passionate, relationship might alter her view. Go beyond the mores of social acceptability and we're back to the aforesaid basics. Briony country. Dodgy.

I leave them to their conversation that sounds sufficiently amicable not to cause me concern and go up to slide behind the desk. Lucy's photograph stares at me. The charger sits there with the significant pound note. Relics of former days. Should I hide them or face up to how I've kept her image in my head all this time? I must be honest and true to my Lucy, she is the One.

I hear the girl's chatter distantly, as though I'm in another time zone, lost in a reverie. How has all this come about? The move back to Louth, taking on the shop, and Clare, then Lucy's fantastic progress; how she has grown from a mere glimpse of a vague but essential preciousness to become the real lovely three dimensional woman of my dreams. I have long sought the fleshing out of my virtuality, yearned for the moment I'd feel her heart beat against my chest, experience the taste of lips on lips, hear the declaration she'll never leave my side. Is what I seek impossible?

Steps on the stairs. Twin bright smiles, Clare with the tea tray, coffee mugs, the packet – the *whole* packet – of chocolate digestives and Lucy is right behind her.

They'd never needed three chairs – except when he'd interviewed candidates for the job Clare now had, hence a minor hiatus before Clare, in a fit of believable acceptance of her status, heaves herself up onto the side table and sits there, swinging her legs, hands under her bottom. 'Lucy can be mum,' she says.

And my girl takes it all in her stride. Hands me *my* coffee mug –

you know, the Denby one from ancient Cambridge days. It's leading a charmed life. Gives Clare the other one after she's abstracted a hand, and then sits decorously in the rather old chair in which Clare would normally curl up. Her mug is carefully placed on the long shelf alongside. All very cosy.

'Biscuits?' I ask, trapped behind the desk.

'Sorry.' Lucy reaches behind her, takes the roll off the tray and passes it across. I open it, offer the packet back to her. She shakes her head.

'Clare?'

'Hand it over then.' She's not going to get off the side table. Lucy takes them back and allows Clare to reach for it. I should have grabbed mine first. Eventually it comes back, minus at least three biscuits.

'So what do you think?'

'I think you've got it rather nice. Beats the Stamford one. Very clean and tidy.'

'Thanks, Lucy. It's Clare who's responsible. Might not have been quite as impressive if I was still on my own.'

Clare's grinning. 'We make a good team,' she says, biting into her second biscuit. 'So long as he stays up here, we get on fine. Seen your photo, Lucy?'

She can't have missed it, surely? 'I'm flattered,' she replies, 'and I know where it came from. Do you want me to sign it, Jones?'

I'm sure she is having a giggle inside, certainly her eyes are sparkling. 'Normally they don't get sent out without a signature, so you must have *persuaded* Basil.'

She might have used the word 'conned', but that doesn't fit well within my angel's vocabulary. The shop doorbell pings. Amazing how you can hear it four floors up. Clare slides off the table. 'I'll leave you two lovebirds in peace,' her parting comment as she heads for the thirty-six steps. (Should have been 'thirty-nine' then we could have called them 'Buchan's)

We're alone, in my office, in my shop. Another first. She's beautiful, my Lucy, in her simple pastel blue dress, sexy knees and all. I love her, adore her. I've sought this moment, unconsciously, over the last four years. And now it's here, I cannot believe how straightforward it has been to achieve. No hesitation on her part, no deviousness, nothing.

'Last night,' she begins to say but I shake my head.

'Was one of the best evenings of my life. Lucy, love, life's ahead of us. We don't need to rush at things. Let's take it a step at a time?'

The smile, the knowing 'I'm sure you'll be mine' smile is added to the growing list of golden gems worked into the close web of gossamer strands we've woven between us, seeking to bind our twin souls together. She reaches for the photograph frame and dexterously slips the back off, lifts the photo out.

'Pen?'

Wordlessly I hand over my best one, another legacy from Cambridge. I watch her eyes momentarily close and a slight pucker of forehead as she thinks, then she's writing 'We keep close' after a professional signature. She puts the frame back together, replaces it on the shelf.

'That's a lovely piece of pottery,' she says, gets up to examine it more closely and picks up the now very creased pound note. 'Petty cash?' I can sense it warming to her touch, the ever-so-slight moisture on her skin will transfer to its surface, give it more power.

'Much more than that.' Should I say?

A puzzled look. 'Mmm,' she says, and picks up the complete charger. 'It's beautiful. So thin! Lovely glaze. Whose?'

'A woman called Lucy Rie.'

'Ah. Another Lucy. Where did you find it?'

'In a little old antique place near the Stamford Girls' School. Four years ago last September. On the same evening as I saw, felt, an incredible person. Remember?'

She cradles it to her front like a pet cat and I immediately think of Samuel's Cad. 'That evening?'

'That evening. The pound note was my change.'

'And?'

'I've never wished to part with it. Reminds me. Keeps reminding me of a girl I've been seeking to find a way to love ever since.' This, all this, said on a Monday morning in an old bookshop's top floor office. Surreal. I will not demean her, it will have to be said again, at a different time, in a different place. I watch her, her eyes watch me as she puts it carefully to her lips, a light, symbolic touch. We say nothing as she carefully replaces it on the shelf, then: 'Don't break it.'

I shake my head. 'The day that breaks, Lucy … ' but I can't say more, not now, not at this moment.

Steps are coming up the stairs, light girlish steps. Clare. The moment had come, the moment was held and is now passed, another small additional gem to the growing collection. When will the next one appear?

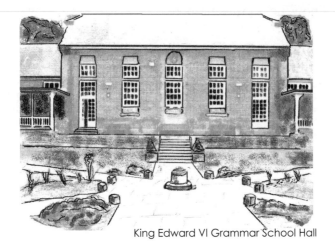

King Edward VI Grammar School Hall

ʘ\(\mathcal{N}\)*ineteen*

Andante Spianato … Flowing and Smooth

We have promised to have lunch together. Clare has been told she is to hold the fort this afternoon; Lucy and I will walk through the Hills once more, despite the weather. I wish it were midsummer.

Joan is on her mettle. Maybe she believes it is an auspicious occasion, whatever, we do not lack attention and the lunch, light and simple though it may be, is excellent and we say so. Joan simpers. Unlike her, but Lucy has that effect on people; now I'm closer to her I notice. I'm sure Joan will expect some sort of a de-brief in due course. Well, we will see.

The weather, late in this unpredictable month of January, is being moderately kind to us. Grey skies certainly, but the clouds aren't threatening and there's scarcely any breeze. Lucy's lovely coat will keep any chill at bay. We walk hand in hand at first then she slips her hand round my arm. Arm in arm. I'm proud, intensely proud. The loveliest lady in the land on my arm. The route is familiar. St

James's spire appears to stroke the clouds and we pause at the south door.

'Can we look inside?'

'Surely.'

The width of the nave and the light and airy feel grips us both. It's in a perpendicular style with a wonderful roof and massive columns to support the towering spire. I've heard the bells from the tower, all eight of them, the pride of the parish. There's a large marble font in front of us. The windows are awesome.

'I can imagine walking down this aisle.'

I look sideways at her. She isn't being facetious or devious, it is an honest statement and we are both aware of the implications of her sudden comment. I too have an image in my head, of the sheer beauty of a couture dress in white, the swish of lace against silk and the pull of the fabric's train on the amazing Victorian tiles. The gems in her tiara sparkling against the deep richness of her chestnut hair. The diamond on her finger. The mellow tonal depths of the organ playing Widor's '*Toccata*'. Is the reality of this image what we must also seek and strive towards, the two of us, or is it, like so much else within our short and immediate past together, a dream? But in my head, there comes a strengthening desire to make the image reality. Where better than within these hallowed precincts, to take the picture into my mind and promise to make firm the ideal? I swallow, grasp at the enormity and promise.

Outside, it seems darker. The afternoon has passed its zenith and soon it will be dark. 'You want to carry on?'

'Yes please, I do. Where we were before. So I can imagine you, us, on the bridge. Our bridge.' She grips my hand quite hard and I sense the hesitation before she reveals what I have most feared. 'I have to do as I'm told. I start a tour next Friday.' The squeeze is almost painful. 'Europe. Mr Fortescue's saying I'm his premiere performer. The money's good. Then I have to tour Britain apparently. He's asked about America again, but I said no to that. Do you mind?'

'You're going away?'

A small voice. 'Yes. I am. Though I shall take you with me, Jones, always in my heart, in my head. As we've been before.'

We reach the end of Westgate, cross the road; I hold the gate open for her. What can I say in reply? No, I don't want you to go? Like I did before her American trip? She isn't mine to instruct, to order. We live our own lives, to our own standards, lives that separate, swing wide apart, then converge, collide, like today.

The Park fields are barren of life, other than the magnificent trees suspended in time, stiff limbs, poised on the cusp of spring. Their leaves will spread from dormant buds, cover their skeleton forms with life and joy, havens for birds and insects, the provision of shelter for us humans, a delight on the eye. We've been here before, she and I, in just such an anticipated abundant time. Joy then. Now, a hollow in my heart, a bleakness akin to winter trees as I contemplate losing her once again, and after we've been so close.

There is silence other than the scuff of shoes on path amid the detritus of dead leaves. Not even the river murmurs.

'I shall come back, you know.'

'To me? Or to someone who's had to adapt to life as he finds it?'

She looks across the valley. 'We've adapted already. We still link.' Her gaze comes back to me and symbolically we clasp hands.

We're coming towards our bridge. It's a desolate place in this light.

'Then we'd better work to strengthen our links, Lucy. For sure, we'll have challenges ahead. You travelling and in a different world. Me, with the mundane day to day. You might meet someone else.' The thought makes me feel slightly nauseous.

She lifts our together hands up and kisses the back of mine. 'I meet many people,' she says. 'No-one like you.' No protestation, no promise, a simplistic statement with undertones of commitment so our golden threads are still in place.

Stepping onto the bridge, leaning over to stare into winter-dullened depths, my arm goes round her, once more I feel that surge of warmth from our closeness as much as from our body heat.

'Will you change? Forget me, lost in your world of books? And will Clare tempt you, more than she has already?'

Honesty. 'I don't know, Lucy. What we have isn't based on pure physicality, is it?'

Surprisingly, she chuckles. 'After last night, no. And I think I'm purer than you are, if what Clare has said is anything to believe. I'm lucky to survive her coffee.' More in sombre vein, she adds, prophetically, 'she won't last. Your Briony didn't, did she?' She rolls round, out of my clasp, leans with her back on the rail and looks further up river.

'*Should he ever be a suitor*//*unto sweeter eyes than mine* ... I've quoted Mrs Browning at you before, haven't I?' Her voice is soft, pensive.

'You've a very good memory.'

'I feel in tune with her thoughts so often. There's more. "*I will look out to his future*//*I will bless it till it shine.*" That comes first.'

'What are you saying, Lucy?'

'We're forging a pretty strong bond, you and I. I run away from you, you run after another pair of legs. Yet we're still doing this.'

I'm silent. My old philosophy professor would have an answer for the dilemma, probably Freudian and couched in dusty old tones, though no doubt it would be fairly close to the bone. What we've got going is pretty special if all that happens to us makes no difference to the way we feel about each other. And she's got a surprise coming, talking of Lizzy Browning.

'I'd better read her up, see what else is meaningful so I can quote her back at you.'

'You do that.' Her look comes round to me, she's smiling. 'Oh, Jones, we're awfully young to be so academically philosophical. P'raps it's because we're too well educated.'

'I'm not complaining. Rather that than being lost in ...' I stop. How can I say 'passion' when it might be 'lust', for we were very close to it last night; I reckon if I'd treated her to a Briony style bedding we wouldn't be here now. I'm still seeking an answer to our forbearance.

'Kiss me?'

Oh how simple a request, how easy to sweep other thoughts aside! We're standing on our bridge in the middle of a chill January, knowing our time together is slipping away, with arms wrapped tightly round and with fused lips. And, as I subsequently found when I read Elizabeth's (Browning, not Lucy's mum, though that may have been a psychological coincidence) poetry, an appropriate phrase: *Nor hands nor cheeks keep separate, when soul is joined to soul.* The embrace suits both of us and we walk back in better mood.

⋙

The Music Club's periodic Concerts are grand social occasions when all the great and the good of the locality gather to be seen. Reminds me of the Barn Hill concerts, very similar in concept. There've been some quite up-market names here too, quartets, soloists both instrumental and voice, though I much prefer pianists. Lucy leaves me at the Hotel so she can have a light meal and prepare for tonight. I reach the shop before Clare goes home. As usual when left on her own, she's done exceedingly well.

She gives me the expected 'old fashioned' look. 'Girl friend up to expectations?'

What a remark! Not one worthy of her and I say so.

She sniffs. 'And all I do for you! 'Nother girl would give you what for!'

'And you won't?'

There's a big sigh. 'When she's gone I'll still be here. Someone has to look after you.'

Ah, so it's the maternal instinct. 'And what have you said to Lucy?' Whatever she had, it would have no impact on our togetherness.

'She asked whether we'd gone out together. You've always said to be honest, so I told her, straight out. Didn't seem to upset her.'

'Obviously not, else you wouldn't have made the coffee together this morning, nor shared the biscuits.' Simple signs like that are so easy to read.

'Weird. You and her, all lovey-dovey after you've shagged *me.*'

'Clare! Don't be coarse. That wasn't … .' For the second time today I couldn't complete my ill-thought words.

'What was it then? Pretty simple to me. I'm your little fluffy bit on the side when she's not around, is that it? Do I get another dose when she's gone?'

I shake my head. When the girl's in this mood there's not a lot I can do. She'll come round, she always does. I change the subject.

'Your mum all set for tonight?'

Clare sniffs again, expressively, and I'm sure she'll be back onto the 'shagging' subject again before long. In the meantime …

'Yeah. We'll be there. Said the panto was rubbish anyway. One of her cronies went.' She collects her coat from the little toilet room, struggles into it and reaches the door. The parting shot, 'better be good, this Lucy of yours,' and she's gone.

It doesn't take me long to dash home, shower, change into best suit – this is not only a social occasion, it is for my girl – and persuade the Morris to start. Going by car is a luxury and instils a sense of one-upmanship. Okay, we know old Travellers are not top drawer, but nevertheless she oozes character. And, thinking ahead, if my Lucy needs a refuge, post performance, this will be one possibility. I'm allowed to park on the lower quad – an 'old boy's' perk.

I'm early, but that's the idea. Show moral support. As I walk across the upper quad, with its rose beds and crossed pathways like a concrete union flag, I can hear her. The run of perfect chords sets my pulse racing; she's a bloody marvellous pianist.

Up the familiar steps, part and parcel of my old school days. I mustn't distract her so I try the right hand door; it opens into the rear of the hall. Damn, it's locked – and the rattle of the Crittall handle must have echoed within, for thirty seconds later and it's unlocked from inside. Maureen, standing guard in parallel with having her own private recital, allows me access without ceremony and we stand shoulder to shoulder at the back. Lucy is oblivious, but that's the girl she is.

I can' t help it … *You are lovely* … the inner me triggers the thought waves and the sound diminishes, gently ends. She turns to look straight at me and the *zing* comes directly back like a tennis star's return volley, *'keep me close!'*

She's standing, brushing her skirt out – lovely dress – is coming down the side access stairs. No hesitation with hands towards me; I take them and once more there is the thrill of contact.

There's no reservation in her comments. 'It's a lovely instrument. And the acoustics are fine. Was I …?'

Was her interpretation up to expectations, she means. Rhetorical question.

Maureen chips in. 'Jones, if we hadn't your introduction, tonight would have been a disaster. Miss Salter,' and she smiles across me, 'Lucy, and please forgive me, – is brilliant. If our members don't reckon this is the concert of the season I'll be *very* surprised.'

Lucy drops my hands, but slides an arm around me. 'I owe my

playing to this man here. He's my absolute support. He's the brilliant one.'

I shake my head. This is only Maureen we're seeking to convince. 'Lucy's brilliant because we share our thoughts. Tonight, yes, it'll be a great evening, won't it, my love?'

She's nestling into me. We meld, she and I, and the nagging prospect of separation hurts. I must not allow this to affect tonight's state of mind. Tonight is important, very important, but time is moving on. Reluctantly I have to let her go. Maureen escorts her away, but Lucy looks back with her smile and we both know we'll stay in tune.

Now it's Clare and her mother. They will be here and inescapably I will be expected to sit with them, alongside Clare, for whom I have much affection (as you will know). What is different from the Barn Hill occasion when sandwiched between a Briony and a Daphne? I felt for Lucy then; I will feel for her tonight. Clare matters to me, Lucy is aware and has expressed no concern. The two girls do not compete for the same level of affection. Believe me, I am as mystified as anyone how thoughts and actions can work on different planes. To provide a comparison, think of Lucy as a sister – which relationship we two have adopted without discussion, without demur, then think of Clare as a – what, a comfort? A pet, a favourite teddy bear? What I have sought, I think, is to do my utmost to give all my friends the affection they seek. A résumé: – Briony, a decent (decent?) sex life and the social clout of a strapping young man as escort; Daphne, filling an aching void during the essential period of readjustment from losing a husband – a *very* sensitive relationship, that one. We've stayed friends since; she still drops me the occasional chatty letter, bless her. Better than the sporadic postcards from Briony that I've pinned up on my bedroom door. (I can't let Clare see them). Then the socialite girls from around town who've surfaced during the last year or so – I've taken them out to various functions, pictures, dances, and explored the required options with no subsequent attachments. Oh yes, and the seaside … . Clare – ah, well, our growing attachment is the product of working together, no doubt about it. Close personal proximity in the bookshop is inescapable with its attendant consequences. How does this impact on my alter

224

ego, my Lucy? Strangely, it doesn't appear to have any effect. Why not? Because, as I've said, when we're together we are on a different wavelength, that's the only explanation I can produce. And I'm still seeking the answer to the dilemma.

The audience is trickling in – and you can always tell who's into piano recitals. The knowing ones look to sit where they can see the pianist's hands dancing on the keys – so guess where I'm sitting, as I go through all this philosophical meandering. Yep, third row back, left hand side, about six seats in. Much closer than I've ever been to her during a recital, apart from that time I went to tea with her and her parents, ages ago.

There's Clare arriving – wow, in the man-killer dress and all the trimmings. Her mother's dolled up smartish as well. She's seen me. She slides alongside, leaves her mum on the outside seat.

'Hi,' she says and cosies up, presents a cheek for the welcome kiss, my guess as much for her mum's benefit as mine, a sort of 'look, see, he's mine' demo.

'Hi,' I say back and smile across at mother. Behave, Clare, I'm thinking, and she's got her mascara'd eyebrows raised. *'Don't worry,'* I'm hearing in my head. My thoughts or hers? Don't say she's going telepathic as well! Lucy, my love, listen to me – *you are lovely.*

Back comes the anticipated reply, *keep me close.* This is us, no-one else.

The hall's abuzz. Anticipation, curiosity, conjecture. One or two glances in my direction from those in the know. *It's his girl friend, you know.* I can sense the speculation. Clare begins to look uncomfortable though her mother is impassive, taking it all in her stride. Minutes pass. Then a stir as the Chairman arrives at the front of the stage.

'Ahem, er, ladies and gentlemen,' his voice lifts in volume. 'Your attention, please.' There's a diminution of chatter and a shuffling sort of silence. 'Though most of you will know by now, our planned soloist for tonight has had to cry off.' (*Really, what an expression, isn't 'is indisposed' the better one?*) He glances down at the scrap of paper in his hand. 'However, we've been extremely fortunate (*that's better*) to secure the services of Lucy Salter.'

There's a stir in the assemblage, so maybe her reputation *has* arrived before her.

'She is newly returned from a highly acclaimed performance in the Carnegie Halls in New York.' Now that *did* cause a shuffle. 'We are indebted to Mr Jones from the Mercer Row Bookshop (*good-oh, nothing like a plug*) for the introduction. And now, I'm sure we are in for a treat. Please give a warm welcome (*big hand, etcetera*) to ... Miss Lucy Salter!'

My Lucy. Gorgeous girl. Settles herself onto the stool. Her hands lie in her lap for twenty seconds, then onto the keys. *You are lovely ...* there's a vestige of a smile though she is not looking at me. First notes as my scalp tingles, the '*hair standing on end*' syndrome. When was it I last heard her, in the flesh?

We're together. I can feel the sound, her beautiful playing, in my head. Transported to an ethereal world. The end of the movement and I sneak a glimpse sideways. Clare is staring as though transfixed. She catches my glance and reaches out a hand, which I take. There's a different look in her eyes.

Lucy begins the next movement and I feel Clare's hand tightening. It stays captive for the rest of the piece and returns for the next. At the end we stand, we all stand. I look around and there are a fair few hankies out. My girl has that effect on people.

In the melee of prosaic cups of tea or coffee during the interval, served at the back of the hall by volunteers in an assortment of aprons, I was bombarded by eager questors after gossip. 'How did you come to know her? Is it true you're engaged? Where does she live? Will we hear her again? Beautiful, lovely, so emotive – the descriptive adjectives are piling out. I scarcely have a moment to slurp indifferent tea. I notice Clare pulling a face after tasting her cupful and grin back at her. The shared mental critique brings us back together. Her mother has found another ear and moved away.

'Your bet?'

She thumps me, playfully. 'Good. Very very good. I've enjoyed it so far.'

Which, from my Clare, is praise indeed. The hand bell is rung. Second half. We resume our seats. Lucy will have been officially refreshed in the Headmaster's study adjacent – I hope she didn't go for the tea. I get her back after the concert.

The last piece – her Mozart – is brilliant. The old school hall will never be the same; every time I revisit I'll hear her. The melody becomes integral to the fabric – *the spirit* – of the place. Another standing ovation; I guess she's so accustomed to adulation it's no worry, but this evening she's not walking off the stage merely with the customary bunch of flowers, she has to have the little book as well (you don't know about this, folks, it's a surprise). Yes, I know I could have given it to her privately, but this is far more meaningful – in my old school hall, after a concert, in front of my friends, acquaintances, customers, and Clare. I want to demonstrate what Lucy means to me.

Maureen does the honours. Lucy takes the bouquet and I watch carefully as the slim little parcel is also accepted. A puzzled look that clears as she looks straight at me – that telepathy again. The flowers temporarily go back to Maureen as Lucy unfastens the paper. There's an air of quiet anticipation from the audience, unaware of the significance. The paper flutters to the floor as the slim red Moroccan leather bound book of Elizabeth Barrett Browning's poems is accepted into Lucy's hands. Dearest girl. She opens the cover and sees my inscription.

"To the most precious dream I share."

Then it is her turn. Composure, it's the measure of the girl.

'Thank you so much, all of you, for the wonderful reception you've given me tonight. It has been an honour to play in such a marvellous hall and to such a receptive audience.' She pauses. 'I'd like to present my public acknowledgement to the one person to whom I owe so much, Jones. He and I go back a long way; without his support my playing means nothing. This is his gift to me – he already has mine -' the little book she lifts to her lips and the smile is there, '- my music.'

The audience claps – they really have no option. Clare lays a hand on my arm.

'Lucky old you,' she whispers with dampened eyes. There's no malice in her voice, a trace of sadness perhaps, and I lean to kiss the salty tear-stained cheek. Then I rise from my seat and edge out to the aisle and climb the steps onto the stage.

I put my arm round her – my Lucy. More clapping. This is about a public announcement of who we are as you'll ever get. I wondered, foolishly, what Briony would have made of it; then we leave the stage, arm in arm. Maureen follows with the flowers. In the H M's study doing duty as anteroom, a minute later, it's just us. The flowers have been left on a table, and Maureen's gone.

I kiss her. I've lost count. Six, seven – whatever, it's heaven. The book is still in her hand.

'Hope you like it,' I say, as we step back from each other. Her eyes are shining, so it must have been the right thing to do, for heaven knows, it cost enough, having to buy it from Stamford. (I'd remembered it from before I left, should have taken it in advance of the contract exchange but then ...)

'I'll treasure it, ever.' There's a sad smile. 'You know it's the first present you've given me?'

I nod. The inspiration had to be good; no point in letting her have something ephemeral. 'A symbol, Lucy. *Nor hands nor cheeks keep separate, when soul is joined to soul* – remember?'

The little book she places with the flowers and turns back to me. 'I think we'd better show our faces, don't you? Then it's back to the hotel?'

Ever practical, this one, so we do just that.

Burghley Park

Twenty

Appassionato ... Impassioned

It takes a few days before normality settles down. Clare, and I'm
now even more sure I chose the right person, hasn't put a foot wrong.
She's an absolute brick, that one. I could have expected tantrums or
a chilly silence, but no, she smiles, still offers a cheek for the ritual
morning greeting and has fended off all the unwelcome curiosity.
You'll realise that Lucy's performance is the talk of the erudite town
dwellers and my little ceremonial acknowledgement has even hit
the local press *'Romantic gesture at Concert'* – you know the sort of
headlines local papers love to dish out. So we've had a few in the
shop who wanted a wee bit more than a chat about the latest thriller.
Clare gave most short shift. I owe her.

Lucy – well, she's gone. On Monday morning, I collected her
from the hotel, took her back to the station; we embraced once more
on the platform before I handed her into the carriage and waved
goodbye. Neither of us know when we'll next connect. One thing
she did say, bless her, was 'look after Clare – she'll take care of you.'

You might be curious over what happened after the concert. I'm not going to say; that's precious and between Lucy and me, though the operative words are 'poetically platonic'. Suffice to say on the Sunday we went to Matins at St. James and walked the full length of the Hills in the chill afternoon, returned to the hotel, had dinner and spent the rest of the evening together – I went home around eleven.

On Friday that week, Clare finally asks. I knew she would, for since Buxton she's a different lass. So I tell her, straight out, what's in my mind.

'Oh.' Her face fell. 'So that's it then.'

I lean back in the chair and it tips back. It won't fall over, it's not that sort of chair. With hands behind my head, I offer a steady return look at this young, pretty, anxious and far too beddable a girl. 'Shall I also tell you what she said? That I'm to look after you?'

The gamut of emotions. Hope, surprise, curiosity?

'What's that mean? You already do. Far more than some employers treat their staff from what me school friends say.'

'It's 'my', not 'me', Clare.'

'Yeah, whatever.' Her eyes gleam. 'More staff holidays?'

I laugh with a sudden rush of relief. 'Yeah, why not? Fancy next weekend away?' I know I shouldn't but Lucy said and she'll be out of the country.

'Separate rooms?'

I nod. 'Separate rooms.'

'Okay then.'

And the shop was closed on Saturday for the first time ever.

Well, I had to, just had to. We went back to Stamford. Of course, Clare had never been, so new territory for her. I couldn't afford the George so it was a couple of rooms at the Garden House, just up the road. Decent, clean, nice breakfasts, chatty waitress. And yes, a few odd glances over the 'two rooms' from the Hotel staff when we were seen to be, as they say, made for each other. Been there, done that. The first night was fine and I slept like the proverbial; home was okay but I'm longing for my own place again. Clare is so attractive in a light blouse and flouncy skirt, such a pleasant thing to see over the bacon and egg in the morning.

Weather isn't good. Wrong time of year for a jaunt.

'What are we going to do?' She's lovely. A real treat.

I shrug. I'm not sure. Walk? Shop? Not a lot else. It's just that we're away from respective homes, away from shop routines, free. Or not so free. Perhaps a trip *down memory lane*. The Terrace Pad isn't too far away.

'Come on girl. Finish that toast.' I push my chair back.

'Hang on,' she says, washing the last masticated mouthful down with a slurp of tea. Tea, yugh, not at breakfast. That's one of our differences; I'm a coffee addict. Up she gets, smoothes the flounces out. I notice she's got low heels, not flats. No stockings. 'So where're we going?'

'Up the road,' I say, annoyingly. I wonder if I'll spot Cad. I bet the creature's still got a few lives left, living with someone who's pandering to its feline foibles.

The terrace pad looks totally unchanged. 'You lived here?' she says with a rising voice as if in disbelief. Surprised at the size of the place or just me living on my own? What did she expect, a four up, four down?

'Yep. Loved it, actually. My own place, did what I wanted, when I wanted,' and I knew when we got back I'd look for something similar. Home had outlived its appeal.

'Good place to start with. I'd like to have somewhere like this when I get married.'

Wistful comment or what? Or leading statement? I don't bite. Pretty obvious the place was occupied else I'd have been tempted to peer in the windows, go round the back and be nosey. 'Come on,' I say.

'Where now?'

It is beginning to rain, a fine, chilling February drizzle. The idea of a crisp frosty walk in wintry sunshine through the veteran limes of Burghley to drive away the remnant wisps of Briony's ghost cowers down and shrinks away like an evaporating puddle. So it's on to Hannah's – if she's still in business. Hot chocolate time.

She's still there. So is – I was going to say *'our'* – table. I steer Clare through the same perambulator mis-parking by an arm and sit her on the same chair or, more precisely, where Briony once sat. Clare's skirt will never behave like a Briony's, nor will her actions be as blatantly seductively obvious, will they? 'Chocolate?' I ask before the waitress comes – and yes, they are still as neat as ever. The menu cards are still pristine. The prices have risen, though – perhaps that's how Hannah's is still in business. The good ladies who lunch in this town must have had their allowances increased.

'Please,' she says and crosses her legs. Um. It's no good, the associations are too strong. I have to tell her and do.

My mug of chocolate still has its perfect crust of chocolate dust on milky foam, as Clare's is poised below her kissable lips. 'So this,' and her eyes are wide, steady, mysteriously deep, 'this table, this chair, is where she *propositioned* you?'

'Uh huh.'

I watch the remaining froth disappear before she puts the mug down with two hands.

'A year, you said?'

'Hmmm.'

'And she left you.'

'Mmmm.'

She said two words I won't repeat because this isn't that type of story. Like 'f' and 'm'.

'You're right. I did. Remember?'

'Vividly. I thought you were well practised. No wonder I ...'

'You what?'

'Oh, never mind. Why did she leave you?'

'Lucy.'

'But Lucy didn't know you then, did she?'

'We knew *about* each other. Briony called her a schoolgirl.'

'Oh dear.' Clare inspects her mug. 'More froth than drink. What would she call me?'

'Who, Briony?' I beckon the waitress over. 'Two more please, less froth – oh, and two more Danish, with apricots. Thanks.'

'Mmm. I'll get fat.'

I chuckle. 'Not in our place, Clare, not with all those stairs.' I find myself narrowing my eyes and reassessing the vision across the table. 'She'd like you, I'm sure. Don't know. Not a schoolgirl – but then she never saw Lucy, just imagined her.' As I am now. In mind's eye, the last glimpse, in a rail carriage, about to disappear out of my life once more. How can I best describe the feeling? You've just had a meal, the dessert was incredibly good, you're still hungry, you want more, it's snatched away from you. Dissatisfaction? Despair? You sneak into the kitchen/larder after hours and look for the dish – it's not there, but there's another version, equally tempting. So do you say, no, I must be faithful to the original and go hungry? We've just ordered more sweet sticky buns, apricot, not plum like the first ones. Get me?

'Lucy's not a schoolgirl.'

'No, but this was three years ago.'

The replacement mugs arrive. Not as much froth but still chocolate dusted. The pastries look equally yummy so no lunch today. Clare takes a bite. Perfect white teeth, lucky girl.

'Don't forget to brush your teeth tonight.'

She gives me an odd look. 'You care?'

'Yes, I suppose I do.'

'You care for Lucy more.'

Ah. Criticism. 'As I've said before, Clare, she's in a different league.' Whoops, wrong choice of words. 'I mean, she's er, *ethereal*. In another world, maybe.'

Clare goes back to basics. 'Not got the same ideas as me then. Work, eat, *bed*.'

I know exactly what she means. Maybe we each have our own telepathic wavelength – different girl, different frequency. Feeling somewhat overdosed on carbohydrates, I suggest a professional visit. She frowns at first but seems willing. So we go down the road towards the bridge and open the so, oh so familiar door. *Ping ping,* the bell I'd hear in my sleep. And the description of Mr Pickwick that Lucy's mum mentioned in course of conversation – ages ago, when they first came up to Louth – is exactly right. I very nearly greet him thus.

We have a polite chat. He keeps glancing at Clare – well, she's very glanceable. Business is fair. He doesn't regret buying the place, which is something. Doreen has let the upstairs accommodation to a middle-aged lady – Pickwick himself has a flat in a town house and I think of Daphne. The stock seems pretty good and I thank him for sending on the Browning I gave to Lucy.

'Glad to be of help,' he says. 'Anytime.'

We browse around and Clare seems attracted to the poetry

section. She pulls out a slim volume in dark blue and passes it over. 'We haven't one of these, have we?'

It's a Shelley. In quite good nick and not pricey – probably one I bought in a collection when I was here. A world and a lifetime away.

'Want it?' Well, I gave Lucy a poetry book 'cos we'd shared the same thoughts.

'It'd be nice, as a souvenir.'

I pass it on to Pickwick. 'Trade?'

He frowns – as maybe I would. 'Pound,' he says. It's priced at thirty shillings, so fair enough. I give him the pound without thinking; we exchange more civilities and leave. As I hand the bag over to Clare moments later, I have a vivid recall of a specific pound note taken from a ceramic dish that I put in my wallet to remind me of the One; and now I've spent it on a poetry book and it's as if I've given Clare my Lucy.

Later that day we're back in the hotel, having a pre-dinner snifter. She's on white wine, I fancied a gin and lemon. Shades of the meal I had in the George, aeons ago. We've had a fair day. We'd looked up old Chas, for old time's sake – he hadn't changed a bit – we even had a cup of tea with him. He'd liked my companion.

'Got a girl to shift about, then,' he'd greeted me when he first saw her. She'd grinned at him; her riposte was along the lines she enjoyed being shifted. Another euphemism. Oh dear.

The small volume of Shelley's poems lies on the table alongside her. I don't think it's left her hand since I bought it for her. Now she flicks it open and reads.

"Like a high-born maiden // In a palace tower // Soothing her love-laden // Soul in secret hour, With music sweet as love, which overflows her bower."

Eyes search mine. 'Is that your Lucy?'

This girl. I put my hand out for the book, keep my finger where it's open. And find another verse.

"With thy clear keen joyance //Languor cannot be: // Shadow of annoyance // Never came near thee: Thou lovest; but ne're knew love's sad satiety."

'See, he's got a verse for everything.' I hand it back to her and she reads for herself, a small frown on her face.

Hmmm, she says and puts the book down but I notice how she's slipped a piece of paper serviette in the page.

Dinner's good but not that good. There's not much going on this evening – it'd have been nice if there'd been a decent concert, but Stamford isn't London or even Cambridge. Conversation languishes after coffee in the lounge. Not even other guests to chat to. Boring. Around half nine Clare gives up. She's been thumbing through Shelley whilst I ploughed my way through the pile of Country Life magazines – mostly at least three months old. 'Good night,' she says and goes.

I examine my conscience but it's very akin to an old much used long playing record. A familiar tune, scratchy and dust laden with the same phrase repeated where it continually skips a groove. *Lucy, keep me close; Lucy, keep me close; Lucy, keep me close.* Shelley's not much help either – or is he? And do you know what, she's left the book in her chair?

Well, I had to give it back to her, didn't I? You'll remember the old Jane Austen trick, drop a pretty little handkerchief within eyeshot of your intended beau? Devious, that's my Clare. And supremely seductive. Single beds, even three foot six ones, aren't ideal, but …

In the morning, I feel terrible. I don't like myself, not at all. I'm first down to breakfast. I didn't knock on her door. Let sleeping pussy cats lie. I'm half way through my Weetabix when she waltzes in, bright as the button that is the only one fastened on her broderie anglaise blouse. She knows I love it.

'Morning love.' she says cheerily and I get a drifted kiss on a cheek as she slips into her place. 'Sleep well?'

Minx. 'Okay.' Best I can do.

'I did. Nice dreams too. What shall we do today?'

Take you on a nice long walk, disappear behind some tree or other and forget to tell you how to get home? Or trek along the river bank on a slippery path … No, I couldn't do that to her. I can't even take my eyes off the gap in her blouse. What is it about her? Oh, Lucy, Lucy, why did you have to go on that concert tour?

She's waiting on an answer, eyes on me despite the tinned grapefruit disappearing at a rate of knots; boy, has she an appetite. I know, St Martin's, where I saw off old Samuel. It's Sunday, so we'll be good. I might even seek absolution.

'If you can bear to fasten a few more buttons, girl, we'll go to church. Then lunch, then a walk round Burghley Park. How's that?'

'Fine, whatever. Don't you like the casual look?'

'Not good for my equilibrium. Do you want anything cooked?'

She shakes the curls. 'No thanks. 'Bout last night ...'

'No, Clare. There's nothing to say. *Nothing*. Okay?'

She stares at me, and I see a tear squeezing out to begin to run down a cheek. She rubs a knuckle into her eye and sniffs. More Jane Austen actions.

'But ...'

'No buts. I shouldn't have come into your room, I really shouldn't.'

'But ...'

'I know, it's as much my fault as yours, but we shouldn't have.'

'Why ever not?'

She's going to tell me what she felt and what she thinks I felt. Well, we're both aware of that (even if you, dear reader aren't sure but are guessing, probably correctly).

'Clare. Much as I love you for who you are and ...'

'I love you just as much.'

All this over toast and coffee and tea, at breakfast. Silly, silly girl. Even sillier Jones, my lad. How on earth am I going to get myself out of all this? She's not going to be rational like my Briony was, but then that one had maturity and money. Clare, bless her, has neither. But she does have a mother who, I know, desperately wants to see me cart Clare down an aisle.

Church. Matins, not matrimonial. Actually, all very calming and beautiful. Not only does my little lady have all her buttons done up but she has a nice neat jacket over the top as well. Keeps her skirt over her knees. Demure, butter not melting, sings well – lovely voice – keeps her eyes down during prayers and listens as attentively as any to the homily. Holds onto my hand as we walk out. I see the vicar's ardent appraisal too. We lunch at the George. Expensive, relatively, but my gesture of reconciliation towards this lovely creature. I'd hurt her, I guess, in trying to tell her my affection – yes, affection – wasn't anything other than exactly that. How else can it be? My heart and soul belong to another. Physicality doesn't come into it.

Afterwards we do the long walk up to Burghley; happily, the day remains dry even if damp under foot and rather grey. She stays quiet but still has my hand captured. The route I'd done before. We kick at leaves, swing hands, watch pigeons or something fly around. The House eventually appears through the trees and Clare stares.

'What a huge place!' I can tell she'd never seen an historic house that size before.

'I used to do volunteer guiding around the state rooms, three years ago. It's lovely inside. Late Tudor, but magnificent.'

'Can we go inside?'

'Not this time of year. It's only open around Easter.'

'Oh.' She's disappointed, but there's nothing I can do about it.

'Best walk back, before it gets dark. We've got to drive home, you know.'

A big sigh. 'Spose so. Back in my own little bed tonight. No one to cosy up to.'

'No, 'fraid not. Work tomorrow. Irate customers who found us shut yesterday.'

She actually chuckles, so it isn't too bad. I kiss the tip of the little button nose of hers. We seem to have got back on easy terms again, thank heavens.

᠅

Lucy: I cried, I couldn't help myself. Bitter sweet thoughts piled up from the intense intensity of our hours together twisting and turning in my head; the joy of his closeness and the dull ache of pain from this impossible barrier between us. We are so, so close, parallel minds, in each other's heads, we can laugh and recite poems at each other and hold hands and hug and even kiss; then the glass wall is there. Look but don't touch. Am I that fragile?

She fingers the small red leather bound book. It is an early edition, Roman dated nineteen oh three. Gold blocked design on the ever so slightly worn cover. Who originally owned this? Was it previously gifted in love, she wonders, like it has been gifted to her?

"To the most precious dream I share.", his inscription in flowing hand.

As she slowly and carefully turns the pages, not from the spine but from the edge as she's been taught, she can hear the words in his voice and can recall the times they've spent together and before, the times their minds sought and found each other's soul. They've met, parted, met and parted so many times, as pendulums swing, as tides ebb and flow, each time closer, closer, closer.

Should I really have suggested he made love to me? Conceivably a stupid idea because I followed my ill-thought concept of its expectation; a male considers a girl should submit after a date? But he didn't. Am I a virgin goddess to be placed on a pedestal?

Will we maintain our bond?

The pages – each poem brings a fresh vision and a new perspective ...

"What do we give to our beloved?
A little faith all undisproved ..."

When she reaches home that lunchtime her mother takes one look at her and avoids any immediate inquisition. Her daughter's eyes are puffy and reddened, there's precious little of a smile and no bounce in her step. Elizabeth's worried but daren't show it. Lucy takes her bag upstairs and her mother hears her moving about, probably hanging up her concert dress. Then silence.

Lunch is ready. Elizabeth summons her husband from his office den and quietly explains her fears.

'*In love?* Heavens, woman. I know you've been dangling young Jones in front of her but I thought she was immune!'

'So did I. Even when he told us he liked her in London that time, I mean, I know I was rather forward, poor boy. There's always been something going on between them – she has some peculiar idea he supports her playing, but I don't understand quite how. They're close, certainly, but how close ...'

'He hasn't ...?' Adrian becomes alarmed; the thought of his precious only daughter tripping over the accepted boundary lines is appalling.

Elizabeth shakes her head vigorously. 'No, I'm sure they wouldn't, but something's wrong. Treat her carefully, Adrian, please.' She goes to the bottom of the stairs and calls. 'Lunch, Lucy dear!'

No reply. She gives her a few minutes then climbs the stairs. Knocks on Lucy's bedroom door, waits, enters. Her girl is asleep, or so she thinks. In order to wake her, she places a careful hand on Lucy's forehead and the girl rolls over.

'Oh mum!' Her eyes are still wet and there is a screwed up handkerchief in her fist. She's taken off her travelling dress and lies there in merely a crumpled slip.

Elizabeth sits on the bed edge and strokes the tangled dark hair strewn across the pillows. 'Lucy, darling. Please say?'

There's still a rapport between mother and daughter despite Lucy's adulthood and unassailable position in the world of classical music. Elizabeth is aware of how privileged she is; not many mothers will have been granted this gift. 'Lucy?'

The girl turns and buries her head in the pillow; her mother hears the sob and watches shoulders heave.

'Is it Jones?'

Another sob.

'Lucy?'

A head shake. Could be yes, might be no.

'Darling, you'll feel better if you say.'

There's a minute's silence, then she rolls onto her back. Elizabeth leans over and kisses a tear stained cheek.

'He gave me a book.'

'Oh?'

Lucy reaches under her pillow to find it and hands it up to her mother.

'Browning ... ,' Elizabeth says and opens the cover. There is the inscription. 'Oh, my darling!'

'But he doesn't love *me!*' Her voice rises to a squeak.

'Only what I *do, play music for him.*' She struggles to sit up. 'He's going out with that girl Clare.'

Elizabeth ignores the comment about Clare. 'You're sure he doesn't have feelings for you? I mean, this is a very romantic gesture.'

Lucy sees him in her hotel bedroom, her offering, his denial, and yet she knows he's had other women, he's said so. How can she possibly explain without seeming cheap and silly?

'He's kissed you,' her mother guesses, accurately. 'And I'm sure he loves you.' The London statement she's never repeated; she's seen no need to – before now. 'He's said so to me, a good while back. And he wouldn't have asked you to go up to Louth unless … '

'All he wanted was for me to play for his stupid Music Club!'

'Nonsense! Didn't it work for you? Didn't he …'

'*Music! That's all it was! Not* me! Me, me, ME!'

'Lucy!' Her daughter doesn't raise her voice like this. Adrian will have heard. She stands up. 'Please come and have some lunch. Your father will want to know how you got on. Wash your face and put on a decent frock, there's a good girl. I have an idea. You'll see.' Without waiting for a reply, a rejection or a counter argument, she leaves her daughter and returns to her husband, now ensconced in an easy chair in the sitting room with the day's paper.

'Tantrums?' There's a slightly amused expression on his face.

Elizabeth takes a deep breath. 'I'm right, dear. She's hopelessly in love with the boy – young man – and has this strange idea he only loves her for her music.'

Adrian stays quiet, knowing his wife won't give up on the quest.

'We may have to take drastic action.'

'Hmmm?'

'This concert tour she's doing?'

'Yes?'

'We'll cancel it. Or pretend to. Let Jones think she's ill. See what happens.'

'Lord help us! That *is* drastic. Fortescue won't be a happy bunny.'

'I'm going to let him into the secret – I'll have to if it's going to work.'

'But Lucy, will she go along with it?'

'Maybe. If she's determined enough.'

In the early afternoon, after a subdued and rather quiet lunch, Lucy having come down in an old plain dress that reflected her mood, Elizabeth takes her into the music room where the Steinway stands.

'I want you to play your favourite piece of Chopin for me.'

'I don't want to play just now.'

'Not even for Jones?'

Lucy shakes her head. 'What's the use?'

'Do it, girl. Play! Get on that stool!'

Her mother doesn't adopt that tone of voice very often, if ever, and so Lucy obeys.She settles herself down on the stool, wriggles, places hands on the keys.

'I can't.'

'You can. Play.'

First tentative notes, the melody is quiet, hesitant. She stops.

'If you believe in your love for that young man, Lucy, you'll play. And you'll think of him. You say he responds to you. Tell him. Tell him you love him, that unless he reveals his true feelings for you, you'll give up playing, because that's what's happening inside you.'

Lucy feels tears coming again. '*I don't know!*'

'I realise it's a risk, darling. Only you can make it happen. I'll be in the garden for a while.'

Jones: When we got back to the car, there wasn't really anything else for it but start the drive home. Neither of us suggested tea – the George's lunch had done us proud – despite the long walk appetites weren't in evidence. By the time we'd reached Sleaford it was getting dark and spots of rain appeared on the windscreen. Clare hunched down into her seat, silent, not a talkative lady in the car at the best of times. So it was a subdued parting at her gate. She didn't offer an invite in, maybe she guessed I'd refuse her. We gave each other a parting quick kiss, a 'See you in the morning then,' and that was that.

I didn't feel like going straight home, so drove – unusually – out to the Hills to endeavour to restore some equilibrium to the unsettled mind. Yeah, unsettled. The weekend had been strange, neither a success nor a failure. In an odd way I'd enjoyed it, largely because

I'd laid a few ghosts – and seen old Chas again. Good that he was still hale and hearty.

Inevitably, Lucy floats back into orbit. I can't get her out of my head, despite Clare's best efforts. Okay, I did take pleasure in those best efforts in a masculine way – who wouldn't – and she was a sparky companion. But not a Lucy and I sought an answer why. Desperately.

He parks up in the muddy bit of field that serves as a car park, alone in the drab dark, the loom of the tree clad valley slopes barely distinctive against the dense cloud covered sky. Intermittent slashes of rain diminishes any incentive to walk, anyway it wouldn't be the same. No alluring lady on his arm. It's nearly six o'clock. Only this morning he and Clare were in church together. Now he's alone. He could have proposed to her during their walk in Burghley Park, like Briony proposed to him. She'd have said 'yes', he's sure of it. So why didn't he? She's sweet, sexy, and – very sincere. And he's as good as told her he loves her, and he's sure, as she certainly behaves in the appropriate fashion, she loves him. So why, why, why?

After the Briony fiasco, she did a runner, so did he. And fell over Clare. If he ran – and where to, for heaven's sake – who else would appear to divert his true affection?

True affection? True? If he did run, would he miss Clare? Had he missed Briony? No and No. Or perhaps ' maybe and no'.

The rain must have stopped.

If I try and reach her, will she respond? It's been a week since. True, I had an odd feeling all last Monday, a hollow feeling. Perhaps I should have made more of an effort, but I can't get over the same old problem. She's a pure, lovely girl on the threshold of a stunning career and I'm a dull bookseller who's messed around with other women's affections. She deserves better. I'm still seeking a way round this dilemma … ah, perhaps … if I … yes, I know …perhaps there *is* a way…

He drives home. His parents are their usual welcoming selves, but it's a stuffy atmosphere. He goes along with the usual Sunday evening boring telly, watching a grainy black and white variety show, but it stultifies his mind so he doesn't have to think. Come tomorrow morning…

Clare: I'm going to be tough with mum. No questions. Good weekend? 'Spose so. He was right though. I've properly messed up. We'd have been okay if … but then when a girl's had it, likes it, feels good afterwards, she wants it again. And again. And I still love him, weirdly. *The little book of Shelley's poems? I'll return it. It's hers.*

⤳

All Elizabeth's scheming has come to nought. Her girl has played, off and on, throughout the week with no startling results. The playing is still good, but only good, not brilliant. The light has dimmed. She talks to Basil but doesn't reveal the true cause of this fit of depression.

He's airily dismissive. 'Once she's on a platform she'll be fine. I know her; like a few other virtuosos, they can be moody, irritable, then on a high. You were once, Elizabeth. I'll look after her, or see that the venue keeps an eye. Put her on the train, I'll collect her.'

So on the Sunday evening Lucy is packed off on her three month tour with tears and a large suitcase. She allows her mother a parting gift of action on her behalf.

'Do let Jones know what I'm doing. Tell him his poetry book will be with me all the time. Please, mum?'

'Of course dear – but couldn't you 'phone him yourself, or write to him?'

She shakes her head. 'We'd only get cross with each other. Tell him …' and her eyes are prickling with incipient tears, 'just tell him to *keep me close.*'

So, before the day gets busy, Elizabeth finds the Mercer Row Bookshop's number and, albeit with some trepidation, first waits for Adrian to get started in his office out of the way before she dials. To her surprise, the phone is answered immediately.

'Jones. M R Books. How can I help?'

'Good morning, Jones. This is Elizabeth Salter. Have you got a moment?'

'Mrs Salter!' She senses his surprise. 'How nice to hear from you.

243

I hope you and Mr Salter are well? And Lucy, of course.'

'We're fine. It's Lucy I'm concerned about. She's become quite down since she visited you two weeks ago. Rather depressive, I'm afraid. So I've taken the liberty of calling you. She asked that I told you of her schedule and to say the little poetry book will be with her wherever she goes. Can I give you the list of her engagements?'

His finds his pulse is racing. Of such is her effect on him. 'Yes, do. She'll be well into her first week by now?'

'Oh no, we only put her on the train yesterday evening. She's due in Paris in two days time.'

'Yesterday? So she's been at home a fortnight?'

'That's right. And not her normal self, sadly. Her playing has gone off, not the vivacious style we're all used to. I'm worried, to be frank.'

She was at home, in Stamford, all this last weekend – and I didn't know! We could have collided but I had Clare with me. She was the block. Oh, oh, oh.

'What can I do?'

Elizabeth nearly said 'marry the girl'. Instead, she remembered Lucy's other phrase. 'She also said *to keep her close.*'

'When is she back?'

'Mid May. She links up with another of Basil Fortescue's performers for the Scandinavian weeks, then a final concert in Berlin. She'll still be in touch by 'phone. Now, can I dictate the venue list – or would you rather I posted you a copy?'

Clare would be in any time now. 'Please put a copy in the post, Mrs Salter. And when you next talk to Lucy, do please give her my very best wishes for the tour.'

'Thank you, Jones, I will.'

And that was that. *Keep her close.* He'd failed her. All this time and it was if he'd never met her. He hears Clare's key opening the shop door. He'd come in early to start the ball rolling on his next move and Elizabeth has it pushed out of his mind.

She's a wee bit reserved this morning. We exchange ritual 'good morning' pecks but there's no sparkle. No one would ever believe we'd spent an energetic few hours together in a single bed only the

244

night before last. Does it make it any easier?

'Sit down a moment, Clare?'

Her eyes widen, but she sits. 'I'm asking a favour.'

She doesn't say a word but twists her hands in her skirt. Who is the most nervous? 'I want you to run the shop on your own for a while. Do you think you could?' Of course she can, except she'll panic every now and again. Perhaps another girl in to help? 'You can have another girl in to help part time.'

'But ...'

I shake my head. Why is it people always start an argument with a 'but'? 'But nothing, Clare. You're very capable. And I ran it on my own before I took you on.'

'We're a lot busier.' She flips her skirt, as she does. 'Could I get my mum in to help?'

What a brilliant idea! 'Good idea, Clare. Of course you can.'

'When?'

'End of the week. I may be gone a while, but I'll keep in touch.'

'Lordy,' she says. Then gets up and gives me a hug. 'P'raps I'll find another boyfriend.'

I laugh. 'I was afraid that might happen. No, seriously, Clare, you don't want to be hooked up with me. There's another lady who keeps on pestering me and I don't think I can resist her.'

... I shall find some girl perhaps ... I daresay she will do ...

I get another hug. She's standing in front of me and blow me down, it's that broderie anglaise blouse again without all the buttons done up. I grin at her. 'Mind you, that bra has a strange fascination ... '

She grins back at me and fastens the buttons properly. 'Sorry, quick dressing this morning. Perhaps I'd better buy a suit if I'm going to be manageress.' Then she goes all solemn again. 'It's Lucy, isn't it? She's an awfully lucky girl. If you give her as good a time as you gave me ...,' and reaching down into her bag, she pulls out the Shelley to place it on the desk.

'Clare!'

'I know. Sorry. I still love you, Jones, for all you've done for me, for what you are. Always will in my own stupid way.' She turns her back, I can sense tears, but she goes downstairs. Shortly afterwards the first customer of the week comes in and her sales chat is the same as ever. That's my Clare. Yes, I do love her for who she is. Now, there are important things I must do, so please excuse me for a while … .

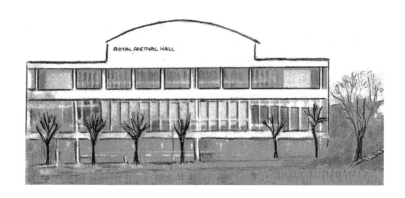

Twenty One

Amabile … Loveable

'Mrs Salter? It's Jones.'

'Jones! Did you get my copy of Lucy's schedule?'

'Thank you, yes. I'm ringing to let you know I'm about to go to Paris. Is there anything you'd like me to take? I'm passing through Stamford tomorrow.'

'Paris? Oh no, my dear! She's still in London for the week. The Paris concert has had to be postponed, last minute thing, the other soloist has gone down with 'flu and they won't stage it on a single soloist. So Basil's put her into the Festival Hall alongside …' and she mentions a name that doesn't mean anything to him. 'I'm sorry, perhaps I should have let you know, but …'

'I quite understand. You wouldn't have known I've put my assistant in charge of the bookshop for a while. Thought I'd like to give Lucy my support.'

Elizabeth takes a moment to digest the implications. 'Ah. I see. Well, I'm sure she'll be thrilled,' which in her mind may well be an understatement, or so she hopes. 'Shall I let you have her London address? She'd have come home for a day or two but all this travelling you know ... '

'Yes. Thank you. I had hoped to surprise her.'

Oh, you'll do that all right. Get it right, young man.

She passes on the address of the person Lucy's staying with, a contemporary of the R.C.M. days. Jones thanks her and puts the 'phone down. London! Well, that saves expense and a lot of hassle.

The following morning he drives to Lincoln, leaves the faithful Traveller with an acquaintance and takes the train to London. At Kings Cross he consults the bus numbers and takes the appropriate route to try and find the address. Somewhere in Kensington, all very high class stuff. And not via the Underground, far too clatterery. Will she be in? The Concert her mother referred to isn't until tomorrow night. He's glad it's not raining but it's jolly cold. His bag's not *too* heavy but still an inconvenience. He won't leave it at Left Luggage because he doesn't know what he's going to do tonight.

The bus conductor gives him the nod. 'I think it's the first road on the right, son,' he says, 'but I'm not sure.'

'Thanks. So long as I'm in the right patch.' He swings off the platform and the Routemaster lurches away. The houses in this street all have imposing steps to canopied front doors and painted iron railings guarding the basements. Very Regency. The number twenty two has a dull black front door but a polished bell push and brass letter box. It's half past three. Tea time. He pushes the bell and hears a vague tinkling somewhere in the depths. Footsteps, light footsteps. A girl's? And a *zing* ... the door opens. Lucy.

She's crying, laughing, wiping wet cheeks and blowing her nose. And in his arms, having the breath squeezed out of her. She struggles and he lets her go.

All the questions tumble out, the exclamations, as the happiness within her explodes. *Jones!* Here, in London, seeking her as she has unknowingly sought him all these years. The glass wall shatters around them and she is his. His.

'Come back to Lincolnshire with me. I've bought a house, well, sort of. At least I've made an offer. It's got a big room with a view over a garden down to the Westgate fields. For your Steinway. I want you to marry me.'

'But ...'

Jones laughs. 'The last girl who said that to me nearly got the push, Lucy.'

'But ...' and she's grinning at him. It's going to be fine, just fine. 'But what about Clare?'

'Clare? She made me see sense and gave me back to you. Where's your Browning?'

'In my bedroom.'

'Fetch it, go on.'

While she's out of the room, he fishes in his pocket for both the ring in its little dark green box and the Shelley. Where her host – hostess – is presently he doesn't know but doesn't much care. This is him and her. The One. From the depths of a Stamford twilight and five years ago to now firmly into his world, not as a virtuality but a reality.

She comes down with that precious volume in her hand.

He takes it, thumbs the pages, finds the right one and passes it back for her to read.

A brief silence as she takes it in. '*Unfit to plight with thine*.? What *are* you on about?'

'I didn't think I deserved you. Because ...'

Her finger comes up to his lips. 'I don't want to know. The rest of this – we've quoted it at each other before haven't we? *Soul joined to soul*. Ever since Stamford.'

'But ... '

She laughs and the musicality of her laugh is nectar. 'Now *you've* said 'but'.'

'Forgive me?'

She shakes her head. 'Nothing to forgive. We've always been 'us'. Others, even your strange Briony or Clare, are – were – only a small part of *you*. As I believe I am the greater and most important part. Right? Oh, and you said Clare 'gave you back to me'. Is that why I had this blank space in my head? Couldn't reach you? How did she take you from me? Is that why?'

He nods. 'I bought her a book, for a pound. The pound note that's lived in my special piece of pottery, the one I bought that very first evening. I put it in my wallet to remind me of you and accidentally spent it on Clare. That's when it all went wrong. Didn't you feel it?'

'I must have. I've been so miserable and my playing's been right off. I wasn't looking forward to tomorrow night. So did she give you the pound back?'

'No, the book I bought with it. This one.' He holds out the Shelley. 'Her return gift. I think she read a few lines.' He pointed at the opened page. 'There ... *Shall I nestle near thy side? // Wouldst thou me? And I replied, No, not thee!*'

'Oh, poor Clare!'

'Not so. She'll be fine. A strong lady, that one. She knows.'

'She still a friend?'

'Good Lord yes. Left her running the shop. So I can be with you.'

'How long for?'

'How does *'ever'* sound?'

Lucy's silent. Then sits down to stare up at him. 'You mean *'ever'*?'

Jones nods. 'Ever. Didn't you hear me ask a question?'

'Er ...'

So he gets down on his knees in front of her and says it again, formally. 'Miss Lucy Salter, please will you marry me?'

'Oh, yes,' and her eyes are moistening. 'Oh yes, Alphonse Jones, I will,' and she giggles in sheer happiness.

'But how ...'

'There you go again. Clare told me, if you want to know. P'raps she was getting her own back. But,' and she giggles again, 'you'll always be Jones to me. Even in bed,' she adds and blushes.

∾

The Festival Hall Concert was a howling success. Well, it couldn't be any other. Lucy was on top form with her lover-to-be in the audience and the little Browning volume, as a direct result of Clare's reported suggestion about a Jones photo or something of his, tucked in her pants, uncomfortably, true, but a constant pressure and reminder of who she is and who she is going to be. Afterwards, with no time to spare, they scamper back to Kings Cross and take a fast train to Peterborough where Lucy's father meets them just before midnight.

When she'd rung to arrange the pick-up she hadn't explained, therefore Adrian is surprised when *two* young people, hand in hand with bags in the spare hands, emerge from the platform.

'Don't mind do you, daddy?' she says, relinquishing both hand and baggage to give him a hug. 'Only I've brought a gift home with me.'

'And a friend?'

'Oh, no, he's the gift. Come. I want to get home. We'll explain later.'

They sit in the back of the Singer and Adrian sees hands held in his rear view mirror. Instinct and his wife's instruction from advisedly better intuition keeps him quiet; he can see it might be a while before they get to bed. Just as well they keep a guest bedroom in operable condition.

Elizabeth meets them at the door and isn't surprised in the slightest. 'Hello, you *two*. Good concert?' *How matter of fact is that?* 'Want something to eat?'

She sits them down and feeds them with hot milky drinks and digestive biscuits, the best she can do at this time of night – or rather, morning.

'Well? Glad my directions were adequate,' is her dry comment to Jones. She and her husband stand watching the pair at the table. 'I take it you're still friends?'

'Engaged, mother,' says Lucy, wiping her mouth. 'Subject to daddy's formal approval of course. We've got a house in Louth and...'

'Hey, now hang on, young lady. Did I hear you right? Engaged? To be married? What about the concert circuit, your career?'

'Oh, I can still play, daddy, that's not a problem. Until I get pregnant, that is.'

Her father subsides into the armchair, ignoring the gaffe. 'So you're happy, I take it?'

'Very. Though my Jones,' and she reaches for a hand, 'has been a bit slow, he's finally broken with his past. We've been engaged with each other for years, but only in mind. He's been seeking a way round the quandary for ages, haven't you, darling?' cheekily she asks, putting that hand to her lips. 'But then a bright young girl called Clare showed him how, so now he's all mine,' and the light in her eyes says it all as Jones, having correctly waited for parental blessing, slides the ring onto her finger. The mental promise made in the nave of St. James he has ultimately kept. Sought and won.

Encore!

Finale ... not quite,
there is always another concert...

The repetitive meet, part, and meet continues for nearly four months as Lucy fulfils her obligations to the Concert circuit and Jones works towards the rendezvous with fate – their wedding. He has to mortgage the shop to help pay for the St Mary's Lane house, the rest has come from Lucy's parents and her professional work. He wasn't too surprised, though gratified over how much she was prepared to add to the kitty.

'Darling,' she says when the topic is aired once more, the weekend immediately before their wedding, 'remember it was you who convinced me I needed to turn professional. After Barnsdale? So it's only right. Anyway, I need a music room and this one's fantastic!'

As indeed it is. A big bow window – what she'd dreamed of having in her own home since childhood – and overlooking the front garden and down towards the trees; beyond are the open fields and parkland where they'd sometime walked and begun the long journey through the years towards this moment. The ebony black Steinway glistens, reflected sunshine from the brilliant late summer day stippled onto the polished oak flooring and the bookcases on the back wall that now house her music and their precious collection of volumes, of poetry in particular; Browning, Shelley, Brooke … The Rie charger stands proud on an occasional table.

'You're a happy girl?'

'I can't hardly believe it, more to the point. Of course I'm happy.' Her fingers stroke the newly installed instrument that is her life in harmony. Since leaving school she'd dreamt of success, though not originally in music. 'You want me to christen our room?'

Her concert tour over, her reputation is assured; the next engagement – Edinburgh – isn't until well after their wedding. Until then she has time and enough to extend her repertoire; this lovely room will absorb magical sounds and Jones knows, understands, this will be far more than adequate compensation for the trials undergone during his seeking for this reward.

'Chopin?' his inevitable suggestion.

'Our signature piece? Barnhill and back to school days? Or the Fantaisie?'

He nods. Memories, happy ones.

'Grey dress with diamante trim?' Her wardrobe has just been moved from Stamford, it's all here. 'I've still got it.'

'Bet you can't get into it after all these years,' Jones says, knowing full well she will try. She runs light heartedly up to the airy and spacious room above where, in not so many days time, and with no reservations, she will properly be first wooed and won.

The dress hangs with other memorable frocks, the ones from the Carnegie days and the one from her most recent tour Jones insisted he bought for her. But for this significant afternoon, the pale grey and silky thing with short sleeves and not too low a front. The black bolero top. She struggles, the hemline is not where it should be, the zip not quite to the top but it will do.

He is seated in the new armchair. She settles onto the stool and looks across the room. He is all she ever wanted, her shadow. Sought and found.

'Fantaisie – Impromptu in C sharp minor – Opus 66,' and her smile is infectious.

She feels it, those chill shivers running up and down her spine. A presence. Jones is here. The music has her in its grasp and she can do no other but extend her spirit into her fingers, fluid, flexed and phenomenal. The notes melt into ecstasy. Chopin, at his best. Jones is crying and Lucy doesn't know, but what she does know is that she has achieved a goal. Reached a pinnacle. And within a fragment of mind's dimension the last link, no longer tenuous but a macrofilament of mental cognisance, is woven betwixt her and another soul, no, not another soul but his soul. The one with whom the tie of thought has been forged. Not of any wish of her eyes, or ears, but of her mind. And now she knows who; not a shadow, not a virtual being, but one who has sought her down the years.

Jones feels her strength. The amazing girl on the piano stool in a swirl of grey with glistening shining pearl drops of diamante who has captured his essential soul. He is drawn towards her but will not move until the last note. The girl of the evening pavement, of the shadows by the school, of the time he acquired the Rie charger and has experienced its power ever since. The girl of the quiet immensity of the promise in the church nave. His mind takes wing and flies towards her, no longer captive. The seeking is over, as the two have become One.

✒

Lucy Elizabeth Salter and Alphonse Jones were married in St.Martin's Church, Stamford, and the wedding was reported in the Louth Leader and the New York Tribune as well as in the London Times. Lucy went on to become a much sought-after pianist in her day, playing to capacity audiences including a Royal Albert Hall Promenade Concert until, after several years, she took a sabbatical to give birth to her first child, a girl. The baby was subsequently christened in St. James Parish Church in Louth and they named her 'Ria Clarony Lucy Jones'.

Clare – godmother – eventually married a local farmer. She worked for Jones in the flourishing Mercer Row bookshop for a further three years before she too followed Lucy into maternal status. Jones heard on the grapevine that Briony had eventually married an American oil magnate. He never heard from her again.

Acknowledgements

The story owes much to formative years spent in the Louth environs, so posthumous thanks to those indefatigable individuals who were then responsible for guiding a young person's activities in such a manner as to allow memories to vividly return and form the backbone of the tale. The echoes ripple down the years.

Thanks too, towards the encouragement and information given by many – and some unwittingly – during the story's development, too many to fully list but specifically:

St Marys Books and Prints, Stamford,
The Burghley House Preservation Trust
Volunteer staff at St.James Church, Louth and St. Martin's at Stamford,
Hotel staff at both Barnsdale Lodge near Rutland Water and Lee Wood Hotel at Buxton where I enjoyed wonderful hospitality during my research stays.

I'm also obliged to all the 'back-room' staff who turn electronic files into print under beautifully thought out covers (Nicky, well done!).

The back cover is derived from a bookcase photographed at the Eagle Bookshop in Bedford, another invaluable resource for the cognoscenti – like the Stamford shop mentioned and 'Scriveners' in Buxton, a warren of literary delights.

Chapter heading pen 'n ink sketches are executed and derived from photos taken by Bruce Edwards.

And thanks too, to Annabelle for her unstinting support and one of the early proof reads; and to Helen for another.

NB: Some locations still exist in the manner described, others have been subjected to literary adaptation in one way or another, but the opening sequence came from 'real life', and the Lucy Rie charger survives, though it didn't come from Stamford.

The Louth Bookshop has metamorphosed into a first-class cake shop.

And maybe there is a Clare out there . . . and a Lucy? though she and her achievements are but a beautiful dream.

Poetical quotations are taken in context and the author fully acknowledges their origins, mainly from handsome volumes owned by my mother who doubtless would have chuckled over this tale. Should there be any queries over rights these will be addressed.

JB, Treegarth, July 2011

If you have enjoyed this story and its make-believe, then look for 'Greays Hill' – an historical tale of murder, mayhem, and intrigue with spicy Northumbrian romance built in. (Spring 2012)

For a free-to-read short story or two,

visit

www.jonbeattiey.info

You'll also find fuller synopses of all the previously published titles and details of how to obtain signed copies.

The 'Manor' series ('Contour', 'Trig Point', 'Benchmark') follows Roberta and her journey through several life-changing sagas: the new man in her life, the heart-warming way a desolate young girl's life is transformed, the rebuild of a shattered dream and the achievement of an ambition.

'Twelve Girls' is an inspired collection of vignettes, linked yet individually written to produce an intriguing whole.

'Windblow' tells of the way a young couple build a new life from the disastrous and lawless fragments around them, how eventually their quandary is resolved for the greater good.